Words of Redemption
An *Accidentally on Purpose* novel
By L.D. Davis

Also by L.D. Davis:
Accidentally on Purpose
Pieces of Rhys a novella

Prologue

~Kyle~

New Year's Day. I wake up in a rehab centre in Maine. I don't remember how I got here, but I have a feeling of dread in my gut. The last thing I vividly remember is going back to the company New Year's party after Emmy sped off. I remember feeling severely uneasy, unfocused, and stressed out. I wanted to leave and go after Em, but as usual, my dad politely bullied me into staying. It was polite because we were in a room full of people. Jess tried to lay a guilt trip by using our fake engagement, but I wasn't having it. I didn't want her. The one I wanted had just driven away.

"You're not going anywhere," my dad had snapped after catching me outside asking a valet for my car.

"The hell I am," I grumbled back.

"There is business to be done in there. Hiroaki Yotamoto's flight leaves at noon. You have to go kiss his ass now. I'm sure Venner will move faster if he knows Yotamoto was in."

"Why don't you go kiss his ass, Walter?"

Dad is a big guy, over six feet of bulky muscle and some extra padding. When he throws a punch, there's nothing playful or sissy-like about it. I was caught off guard when his fist connected with my skull. I stumbled back several steps, but I wasn't surprised really. I didn't fight back, but I tried to look unaffected even though my head was splitting. I couldn't show him any weakness, but fighting him could have dire consequences for my mother.

"I'm not going to kiss his ass, you little worthless shit, because I put you in charge of this operation," he whispered roughly in my ear as he painfully gripped my shoulder. "You're going to do whatever the hell I tell you to. I raised you and cared for you, you scumbag, while your mother was going out

~ 2 ~

of her fucking mind. If you don't do what the fuck I tell you when I tell you, I'll take everything from you and I'll take her away and break her. Are we clear?"

"Crystal," I snarled, shoving his dirty hands off of me.

"Now get back inside, play the doting fiancé and get Yotamoto on board."

When my car arrived at the curb, I looked at it, weighing my decision. I could jump in the car and leave everything and lose everything; or I could do what the bastard told me to do. If I left, he would fire me from Sterling Corp, and I wasn't sure I had done enough yet to save the thousands of jobs that were in danger of disappearing. Furthermore, it would be very difficult to save my mother from his wrath, because he would convince her that I was the problem. Part of me was also hoping to just once have my dad on my good side and appreciate me not just as a business man, but as a son.

As I once again turned my back on the woman I loved and marched back inside to the party to swoon both Yotamoto and Jessyca, I felt my body vibrating with anger and angst. Walt breathing down my neck wasn't making me any less stressed. I downed several drinks to try to numb my feelings and ease my thoughts away from Emmy. It wasn't working. Reluctantly, I excused myself and locked myself into a bathroom stall to get high, even after I had promised Em I wouldn't do it again.

I remember leaving the bathroom and shaking hands with and bowing to the Japanese businessman as he made his departure. I remember getting in my car again, fighting with Jess as I dropped her off, and I remember racing to Em's.

After letting myself in, I could hear her upstairs moving around. I knew in my heart she was really going to leave and it was too much to bear. I silently moved into the kitchen, drank Tequila straight from the bottle and took another hit.

I remember hearing the small bumping sound of something falling to the floor, reminding me that she was packing to get away from me. I remember the feeling of my hands flexing and closing into fists. Flex. Fists. Flex. Fists. I

~ 3 ~

remember moving down the hall towards the stairs, and I remember nothing else until I woke up in rehab.

I look down at my hands because they hurt. I stare at the bruised and scraped knuckles as understanding begins to wash over me.

"I didn't," I say aloud to myself. "I wouldn't have."

But, did I? Was it possible? Even to her?

I leap off of the bed, ready to rush out of the room to ask someone to fill me the fuck in, but a folded piece of paper on the desk catches my attention, as it was meant to do. My name is written in large letters on the front in my dad's handwriting. With my heart beating hard in my chest and my lungs barely able to take in the air I needed, I picked up the note and opened it.

Only one sentence was written, but it is enough for me to fully understand my injured fists. It is enough to make me, a full grown man, cry like a little boy.

"You broke your toy."

I broke Emmy.

Chapter One

A year and a half ago...

~Lily~

"I don't know when I'll be back," Emmy said in a hoarse, nearly unrecognizable voice. "Honestly, it could be a very long time. You can handle *SHOTZ*, right?"

I didn't want to be the one to break it to her that I had been "handling" the bar since she hired me. I did all of the hiring and firing and ordering and organizing. I made sure everyone got paid; I made sure the business was always up to code and I fixed anything that needed fixing. Emmy was a good boss, but she was an owner in name only.

"Of course I can handle it," I said. "If I need anything –"

"If you need anything, call Mayson," she said quickly. "I'll call periodically to see how things are going and sign whatever paperwork I have to through fax and FedEx, but you can talk to Mayson for anything else."

I knew something was terribly wrong. Emmy was quiet about her ownership of the bar. Most of the employees just thought she was a regular, not their boss, but I was privy to that information. She wasn't my best friend or anything, but I had to admit my feelings were a little hurt knowing that she was basically cutting me off.

"Are you okay? Is the baby okay?" I asked.

"The baby is fine…" she said carefully. I thought she was going to give me more information, but she didn't. She reiterated a few things, wished me luck, thanked me and ended the phone call.

"This is exactly why I need to take this place off of your hands," I whispered as I hung the phone up.

~~~

A month after Emmy's disappearing act, deep into a Saturday night, Kyle Sterling walked through the door at *SHOTZ*. He always caught my attention. He was a good

~ 5 ~

looking man, and even though his relationship with Emmy was as volatile as it was scandalous, I liked him. He was my exact opposite of course – regal, rich, preppy and well put together. I always thought he looked like he just stepped off of the cover of *GQ*. I never had a problem with my short and slightly plump stature, and I didn't have any issues with having blue or green stripes in my dyed black hair or having tattoos and piercings. I was a jeans and t-shirt kind of girl and I was always comfortable with the way I looked, except when Kyle was around. I know I worked in a bar, but whenever Kyle walked in the door I felt underdressed and otherwise overdone. I found myself fidgeting with my clothes, adjusting my hair and even wiping away some of my makeup if I was able to steal away to the bathroom.

When I saw him walk in, I immediately began to feel my usual inadequacies, but then I took a good look at him and forgot about myself for a while. Kyle's hair was disheveled, like he had just woken up, and he had a beard that was at least a few days old. His shirt was hanging loosely on his slightly thinner frame, not tucked in and definitely not ironed.

When I didn't see him after Emmy left, I assumed it was because they had either gone off together, or they had a mutual break up, but looking at his pale face and sleepless eyes and thinking about how badly Emmy sounded that day, I was positive that something terrible indeed did happen. Kyle always exuded confidence, extreme amounts of confidence in fact, and I never got the impression that there was anyone or anything that could make him come undone. That is, until I saw him walk into the bar that night.

"Hey," he said when he reached me at the bar. He looked around the room with a hopeful expression. "Is Em around?"

I shook my head very slowly. "She's gone."

He threw his head back in frustration. "Why does everyone keep telling me that?" he more demanded than asked.

"Probably because it is true," I said softly.

"Do you have any idea where she went?"

"No, and I am under the impression that she does not mean

to come back for a long time. I have to talk to Mayson if I have any issues with the bar."

"Fuck," he whispered harshly. He stared down at the worn mahogany bar with his fists clenched in front of him. I watched in shock as his expression changed from anger to angst, from angst to self-loathing, and from self-loathing to torment. The torment warped into resignation, and the resignation finally returned to anger. I just wasn't sure whom he was angry at.

"Give me a double shot of Hennessey," he demanded.

"Oh, I don't think that is a good idea," I said, shaking my head. "How about a beer? We have that Blue Moon you like on tap."

Kyle's dark brown eyes honed in on me. "A double. Shot. Of Hennessey."

"Fine," I said, slamming a shot glass down on the bar. "But if you puke on my bar again, I'll throw your ass out myself."

"I'm not going to puke," he said and tossed his keys onto the bar. "You may as well take them now."

I snatched up the keys, gave Kyle one last look and went back to work. I kept an eye on him through the night as he tried to drink away his emotions. He spoke to no one but me or my other bartender Vic when he wanted another drink. After a while, he stopped asking and just held up his glass or pointed to it. Twenty minutes before closing, I put on my favorite song *Closing Time* by Semisonic, indicating the end of the night. It was a fun and polite way of telling everyone to get the hell out.

"I'll call a cab for you," I told Kyle as I cleared away his empty glasses.

"You have my keys," he said, clearly intoxicated. He swayed a little on his barstool and he looked a little green.

"I will return your keys when the cab gets here," I promised. "Please don't puke on my bar."

He snorted. "It's not your bar. It's Emmy's."

"Thank you, Captain Obvious," I said, rolling my eyes. I took the glasses to the back to be washed. When I returned, I picked up the phone to call a cab.

~ 7 ~

"You drive me home," he said, swaying again.

Vic stepped up beside me and crossed his beefy arms as he glared at Kyle. "This isn't a chauffeur service, buddy. We'll call you a cab."

Kyle didn't even look at Vic. He focused on me with those troubled brown eyes, those troubled, *sexy* brown eyes. I didn't even really like guys like Kyle, typically. I usually went for guys like me – tatted, pierced, and dyed – not straight laced guys like Kyle Sterling, but I couldn't deny my attraction to him. His gaze holding mine damn near made me breathless.

"Lily will take me home," he said with a small cocky smile.

"Listen, pal," Vic started, pointing a finger at Kyle.

"Vic!" I snapped. "Go clean something!"

"You aren't seriously considering taking this douche bag home," he said incredulously.

He had some nerve to talk about douche bags. Vic very often used his big muscled body to intimidate people. He was a good worker, but his self-inflated ego was a problem.

"Dude!" I yelled at Vic. "What do I need to control you? A cattle prod?"

"No one controls me," he said darkly. He threw Kyle one last look of disdain and disappeared into the back.

"And I'm douche *excrement*," Kyle called after him.

"So..." I said, slightly confused. "In essence you are a douche *puddle*?"

"Yes," he nodded as he swayed.

"If it's any consolation, I don't think you're a douche puddle." I turned away to wipe down the counter behind me, but Kyle's soft declaration made me turn back to face him.

"I'm much worse than that," he said. His cocky smile was gone. He still swayed, but his eyes were so damn sad, I had to look away.

"I'm sure that isn't true," I said, returning to my task.

"I hit her," he said so quietly I wasn't sure I had heard him right. I froze and looked at him in the mirror. "I don't remember it, not really. A little bit. I hear her screams in my sleep, but I really don't remember. I was high and drunk, but I should be able to remember hitting her and I don't."

"You're drunk," I said quickly. "You don't know what you're saying."

I didn't want to believe him. His admission totally fucked with my image of him. I knew he had a temper, and I also knew he wasn't exactly the friendliest person, but on the rare occasions I saw him smile or heard him laugh, I knew there had to be a decent guy beneath all of that. The way his eyes blazed with love and lust when he looked at Emmy always made my heart ache. I wasn't too sure that she quite appreciated it. Yeah, I knew the story – she had a boyfriend for a while and Kyle had a serious girlfriend, but why would she stick with him through all of that if he didn't have something great to offer? No, I didn't want to believe he had hit her like he said, but even as he started to speak again, I knew in my heart it was true.

"I *am* drunk," he admitted. "But that doesn't make me a liar."

I turned around to say something, but Kyle opened his mouth and sprayed my bar with vomit.

"I'm sorry," I said to Lily again as we raced down the highway. "I'll replace your sneakers."

"It's okay," she said tightly. "Don't worry about it."

"I just wanted to feel numb for a while," I found myself admitting.

"It didn't work, did it?" she asked softly.

"No. Everything feels a little fuzzy around the edges, but it still hurts like hell." I looked over at her. "When I was nine years old, my older brother died right in front of me. It was my fault, and that hurt a lot."

Her mouth fell open. Even in the dark car with only the dashboard lights aglow I could see her eyes wide with horror and pity.

"This hurts more than I can remember that hurting, Lily. And then I feel guilty for hurting more for Emmy than I did for my own brother. I feel so fucked up in the head right now. I want to get high so fucking badly," I said, running my hands through my hair.

"Well..." she said and cleared her throat. "I'm fresh out of...whatever it is that you...snort, smoke, or inject – or swallow."

"I just got out of rehab yesterday," I said with a dark, mirthless chuckle. "I'm such a fucking winner."

"We will just have to occupy you and keep you from going that route," Lily said.

"What are you going to do? Hold my hand all night?" I snapped.

"If I have to," she said with determination.

I looked doubtfully at her. "What difference does it make to you what I do?"

She gave me a nervous glance before smoothing it over with a pretty decent poker face.

"What difference does it make?" she asked nonchalantly.

"What will you get out of it?" In my experience, hardly anyone below *my* means did something for me for nothing.

"Who said I had to get anything out of it?" she snapped.

"Everyone has a price," I said sourly. "What's yours?"

"Just make sure I can get back to my car after I'm done holding your hand and we'll call it even."

"No money?" I snorted. "I can hardly believe that. How much do you want for babysitting me, Lily?"

"What makes you think I want or need your money, Kyle?"

"You're just a barmaid in a small bar in the suburbs, Lily. Why wouldn't you want or need my money? Maybe you need a new tattoo, or a new piercing." That was mean, even for me, but I was drunk and bitter and hurt. I took it out on the only person in the vicinity.

Lily was silent for a long time after that. She didn't look at me. She only looked at the road and the GPS, and the lady's voice on the GPS was the only sound. I realized that I just insulted the one person who was willing and able to save me from killing myself or someone else by getting behind the wheel and she was the only one who may save me from overdosing on meth. The craving was stronger than ever. I had no one to turn to that really gave a damn. My mother had her own problems, my father didn't give a shit, and whatever friends I had weren't really friends at all. Jess was the last person on the face of the Earth that I wanted to talk to. I could call the sponsor I was given by the rehab center I was in, but how much would he really care? And he wasn't physically there to stop me. Lily could have thrown me out of the bar the moment I confessed what I did to Emmy, but she didn't, and she didn't after I puked either, and she was the one that had to clean it up.

"Emmy tried to teach me to be nicer to people," I said quietly as we neared my apartment building.

"It didn't work," Lily said. "Clearly."

I couldn't argue with her, so I remained silent until I had to direct her to my assigned parking space. I didn't feel as drunk as I did before I vomited, but when I tried to get out of the car, I was hit with a wave of dizziness and damn near fell on my face. Lily reached out and caught my arm and then steadied me against the car while she closed the door and activated the alarm.

"Now take your time," she said, taking my hand. She slowly led me to the sidewalk.

I grinned down at our hands. "You really are holding my hand."

"Yeah."

"I think I'm still drunk."

"You're really good at stating the obvious," she said.

"I have to pee," I said, stopping on the sidewalk.

"Okay," she said slowly, eying me skeptically.

I released her hand and pulled down the zipper on my jeans.

"What the hell are you doing?" she cried.

"I can't wait until we get upstairs," I said and pulled my semi-hard dick out without caring that Lily was standing right next to me.

"Oh my god," she said and then averted her eyes while I pissed onto my neighbor's car. I hated that guy and his stupid yappy dog.

I felt myself swaying and a second later Lily's hands were on my back to steady me.

"The last thing we need is for you to fall into your own piss," she said with a loud sigh.

I gave myself a little shake and turned back around to say something to Lily. I turned too quickly and almost fell backward onto the car and into my own pee, but Lily reached out and grabbed my shirt. She started to look relieved until she looked down and saw that my dick was still hanging out of my pants. Rarely has any woman ever looked at my manhood with disgust, but Lily did.

"Put that thing away!"

"What's wrong? Never saw a penis without a piercing before?" I teased.

"If you don't put it away now, you'll never be able to use it again," she growled.

I put my boy back in my pants and went to take her hand again.

"Don't touch me with that hand," she said and shook her head in disgust.

"Why?"

"You have Penis Pee Hand!" she said incredulously. "I'll hold your other hand, but not your Penis Pee Hand."

We managed to get up to my apartment without me falling down or touching Lily with my PP Hand. I had not been nice to her even once all night. I fully expected her to deposit me into my apartment and take off, but instead she pushed me towards the hallway leading to the bedrooms.

"Please go take a shower and brush your vommity teeth."

"You're not going to hold my hand in the shower?" I asked her. "I may fall and crack my head."

"Maybe you need your head cracked," she said and walked off towards the kitchen.

I staggered to my master bathroom and started to strip out of my clothes. I unbuttoned my jeans and started on my shirt. Like a little kid, I got my head and arms stuck trying to pull off my shirt.

"Damn it!" I yelled as I staggered around the bathroom trying to free myself. To make matters worse, my jeans began to slip. "Fuck it!" I yelled.

I heard the bathroom door open and knew Lily was probably watching me with disbelief. I could hardly believe it myself. She grabbed a hold of my shirt and yanked. I stumbled forward, but her hands were on my bare chest, keeping me upright.

"Wow," she whispered, looking at her hands on my chest.

I looked at her with my eyebrow raised and flexed. As if my skin burned her, she quickly pulled back her hands. Her face reddened as she took a step back into the bedroom.

"You can handle the rest," she said quickly and practically ran out of the room.

My shower had a sobering effect. My head began to clear some as I stood under the steaming hot water. As the effects of the alcohol began to dissipate, my emotional pain intensified. Emmy was gone, completely. I called her every day after I woke up in rehab. I emailed her every night before I went to sleep, and I sent her letters via snail mail. She never answered any of it. Eventually, she changed her number, deleted her email address, and all of the letters came back to me unopened. I left rehab several weeks early, against professional advice, and went to find her.

What I found was a house in the process of being emptied by movers, but no Emmy. I found her best friend Donya hostile, but no Emmy. I found her cousin Mayson a little less hostile, but still no Emmy. No one in the office had seen her since the company's New Year's Eve party. I even called her mother, who was much less hostile than Donya and Mayson, and even more helpful.

"She was here, but she's gone now," Samantha Grayne had said.

"Gone where?" I asked. My heart raced when I considered the fact that she may have gone to Luke to tell him about her son – the son that I wanted to raise as my own. "Did she go to Luke?"

"That would be the smart thing, you know," she sniffed. "But no, she didn't. She's not here, Kyle, and she won't be back for a long time. I can't tell you where she is. I feel for you, I guess, but she's…broken. I think you broke her, even though she won't say so, but I think you did. I won't tell you where she is."

She hung up on me then. I was sitting in my car when I called her, and all I could do for a half hour afterward was stare at a picture of Emmy taken at the very beginning. It was a week before the gala and the night that I would first tell her I loved her. It was a picture she obviously took with her cell phone, lying in her bed and smiling broadly up at the camera. She looked so carefree, so unburdened with life – with me. I never again saw that level of happiness in her eyes.

When I was sure that I could leave the parking lot I was sitting in without driving directly to my dealer, I headed to the

Main Line to get rid of Jessyca. I felt a little bad for what I had done to her, but what she had done to me was beyond cruel. She knew about Emmy, how could she not? She knew I was in love with her, and every time she felt me drawing close to dumping her, she would make little comments regarding my dad and Sterling Corp. We both knew what she was talking about, but neither of us ever said it. I didn't want to push her and jeopardize everything I was working so hard to save, and she didn't want to push me to push her. But I didn't want Jess. I wanted Emmy, and Emmy was fucking gone. I would never be able to pretend with Jessyca again.

"If you really mean this, Kyle, I will destroy you and Sterling Corp!" she screamed as I stormed out of her parents' home.

"I'm already destroyed, Jess," I had said darkly.

I drove to *SHOTZ* out of desperation. I hoped that everyone had lied to me and that Emmy was really hiding out there. It was an irrational hope, but it was the only one I had to hold on to, and the only one keeping me from completely falling apart.

Standing under the shower, I wondered how I had made it thus far without the self-destruction that I strongly felt was necessary. Then I thought of Lily. I didn't know whether I should curse her or thank her.

~~~

When I came out of the bedroom, showered, vommity teeth brushed, and dressed in some warm clothes, I found Lily sitting at my dining room table busy with her cell phone. Across from her on a plate were two baked potatoes, a large sports drink, and two aspirin. I stared at the items with a heavy heart.

"Emmy use to give me this hang over treatment," I said in a low tone.

"Where do you think she got it from?" Lily asked and then gestured to the seat across from her. "Sit down. The sooner you start the better."

I sat down and started to un-wrap a potato. "Was I in the

shower that long?" I asked.

"You were in there for a good while," she said, peering at me over her phone. "Long enough for me to sneak out and go to Wawa and that diner down the road."

"Thank you," I murmured. "You're being very kind to someone who hasn't ever been nice to you."

She looked at me thoughtfully for a moment, but then turned her attention back to her phone. I watched her as I ate. Her slate gray eyes narrowed in concentration. She occasionally bit down on her bottom lip, and when she would release it, she would run her pink tongue over it. I was really looking at her for the first time, I guess. She wasn't the kind of girl that guys like me looked twice at. It wasn't that she wasn't pretty, because she was. In fact, she was far prettier than I ever believed before. Admittedly, I was shallow and didn't see past the ten thousand bracelets on her wrists, her sometimes colorful hair, the intricate floral tattoos on her arms and clavicle, and her pierced eyebrow and tongue. Being a typical guy, I let my eyes drift down to her chest and almost nodded in appreciation. How did I not notice her ample breasts before?

"Texting your boyfriend?" I asked after eating a whole potato and drinking half of the drink.

Her eyes widened as she looked at me. "Oh, no. I don't have a boyfriend," she said, shaking her head and waving that thought off. "I'm playing a word game."

"Are you...a lesbian?" I asked carefully.

She looked at me as if to say "What the hell is wrong with you" and said "No. Why would you even ask me that?"

"You looked a little disgusted at the idea of having a boyfriend."

"Well, I'm not a lesbian," she said. "But that part of my life is just as complicated as yours, but we don't need to go there."

"I told you some very personal things tonight," I said, staring at her. "Do you understand how difficult it is for me to open up to anyone, let alone someone I barely know?"

She sighed and looked at me with some compassion.

"Kyle, I know how hard it was."

"Do you really?" I asked darkly and set my fork down.

"Yes, I do. I know it seems like I don't know you, but…" she bit her lip and shook her head. "Never mind. I get it though. So that's all that really matters." She sat back in her seat and pretended to focus on her game again.

"But what?" I pressed. "Finish your thought."

She looked at me carefully for a few seconds. To my surprise, she began to blush, and when she spoke again, she didn't meet my eyes. "I know it seems like I don't know you, but I know you more than you know me. I've been watching you since that very first night you came in."

I watched as she shifted uncomfortably in her chair, and then her words really hit me. I couldn't stop the words from tumbling out of my mouth.

"You like me," I said. "I mean…you have a thing for me?"

"A *thing*?" She rolled her eyes, but still didn't look at me.

"Oh," I said stupidly. "You never said anything."

"And why would I say something?" she asked and finally met my eyes. She gave me a look that told me I should have known better than to say what I said. "You had two serious girlfriends and one of those girlfriends happened to be my boss and *she* had a boyfriend. You're right. I should have *totally* spoken up."

She put her phone down and got up from the table. As she walked towards the powder room by the door, she turned and walked backwards and with a smirk said "And because guys like you *totally* dig girls like me." Before she went into the bathroom I saw her smirk turn into a frown.

I sat there staring at the rest of my potato in a stunned silence. Lily wasn't the first woman to be attracted to me, obviously, but at the moment she seemed the most significant. I was sure that I was rarely on my best behavior when I was inside *SHOTZ*. My relationship with Emmy was as volatile as it was passionate. How many times had she witnessed me being a possessive and controlling dick to Emmy? How many times had she witnessed me say distasteful things to Mayson?

Probably more times than not. The fact that she *liked* me – or whatever it was – after witnessing me at some of my worst moments was indeed significant, but I didn't know what to do with the information. I was very much in pain over losing Emmy and as cliché as it may be, I couldn't imagine ever loving someone else again.

Then there was the obvious, what Lily herself had pointed out. Guys like me don't typically 'dig' girls like Lily. I was very well aware of my tolerances, good and bad, and I wasn't sure if I would be the guy that could look past her appearance.

The bathroom door opened and Lily walked out yawning.

"Are you done?" she asked as she reached in front of me to take my plate.

"Yes. Thank you."

"You're welcome. Take your aspirin and finish your drink," she said and carried the plate into the kitchen.

"Thanks, Mom," I said.

"Oh. Was that a joke?" she called.

I swallowed the aspirin with the rest of my drink as she had commanded. I got up and carried the empty bottle to the kitchen where Lily was washing the plate and fork I had used.

"I *am* capable of humor," I said.

"I don't think vomiting on my sneakers and showing me your dick is humorous," she said dryly. Her eyes grew large as did the smile on her face. "Actually, the second part was humorous."

"Is that some kind of jab at my manhood?" I asked.

She gave a noncommittal shrug as she dried her hands on a dishtowel.

"Wow," I said as I followed her back into the dining room. "I thought *I* was the asshole."

"I never claimed I *wasn't* an asshole," she said as she plucked her phone off of the table.

I followed her into the living room and said "I don't think you're capable of being an asshole."

Her smile faded almost completely. "I guess it's a good thing you really don't know me," she said quietly. Before I could comment, she spoke again. "How are you feeling?"

I raked my fingers through my still damp hair. "Physically or emotionally?"

"Well…both really. Emotional pain can be physically painful," she said and for a few seconds her eyes were focused on some point in her past. "How are your hangover symptoms?"

"I think once I lay down I'll be fine."

"Your drug craving?"

She didn't even blink while asking. It didn't seem to faze her, which made it easier for me to discuss.

"Not as strong as it was an hour ago," I said with a sigh. "But it's still there."

"It will always be there," she said softly. "You'll just have to find ways of pretending it's not. I'm not even going to ask about the emotional stuff. It's going to hurt for a very long time."

"Was that supposed to make me feel better?" I frowned.

"No, but I'm not going to bullshit you about it. I'm not going to tell you that you will feel better after you get some sleep, or that in weeks from now it won't still be your first thought when you wake or the last thought before you fall asleep." She looked at the floor between us. I saw her swallow hard before speaking again. "It can be…two years later and you think you're fine, but you can wake up one morning and boom…there it is again. Feeling just as fresh as it did the day everything fell to shit."

I'll never forget that moment. It was the very moment that I really did see through Lily's appearance and saw the hurting human woman. I never argued that I was a dick, but I wasn't heartless. I couldn't overlook Lily's pain when we were the only two people in the room having a very candid conversation. Seeing her pain, however magnified my own, and my anger flashed.

"So, you've been heartbroken," I snapped. "Though you won't say so. But I'm sure that you didn't beat a helpless pregnant woman while you were fucked up on meth and alcohol. I'm sure that you didn't break that same woman's wrist while in a rage because she tried to purge you from her system by trying to fuck another guy. I'm sure you didn't force that woman into a dysfunctional relationship with you out of selfishness, stretching her thin, wearing her down, and fucking her up piece by piece. You're only brokenhearted, Lily. My heart is *shattered* and on top of that I have to carry the fucking enormous burden of my own guilt and self-hatred!"

She stared up at me with her eyes wide in shock and her mouth hanging open.

"I don't even know if her baby is okay," I pushed on, though I shamefully felt my voice trembling. "I could have *killed* him – both of them!"

I was the one who just yelled, but Lily was breathless when she spoke. "Did…were you on drugs when you broke her wrist?"

"Yes, but that doesn't excuse it, Lily," I growled.

"No," she agreed in a whisper while shaking her head. "It doesn't excuse it." She turned away from me, but not before I saw two tears slip down her cheek.

"Where are my keys?" I demanded.

She turned back to look at me with a startled expression. "Why?"

"Because they are my damn keys and I want them." I held my hand out. She looked at it like it was diseased.

"I'm not giving you your keys." She looked at me dubiously.

"This is the last time I'm saying it, Lily. Give me. My fucking. Keys."

She narrowed her teary eyes. "No."

I closed the distance between us with two strides. I stood so close to her, I could feel her hurried breathing as her chest rose and fell against mine. She boldly met my eyes and stood stock still as I ran my hands over her generous hips and over the front pockets of her jeans. To be thorough, I pushed my hands into her pockets in search of my keys. Her breath hitched, but she didn't look away from me. I pulled out what felt like a small wad of cash, probably her tips for the night. I let it fall to the floor and reached back in and pulled out what must have been her license and maybe a credit or debit card. Her other pocket was empty. I slowly moved my hands back over her hips to her ass. As I ran my hands over her back pockets, I boldly squeezed her ass with both hands. She inhaled sharply and I heard her swallow hard, but she still didn't look away from me. I slid my hands back up her ass and into her pockets, but only produced a pack of gum from one pocket and several small pieces of paper and a few business cards from the other.

I broke eye contact first. I felt her blow out warm air onto my chest in relief, but it was short lived when I held up the papers and business cards.

"Someone is busy collecting numbers during her nights at work," I said mockingly.

"I'm 'brokenhearted'. Not celibate," she bit back.

"Oh, so you're not looking for romance with any of these men. None of them are me," I smiled without humor when she winced slightly. "How about a compromise, Lily. You give me my keys and I'll fuck you."

Her mouth fell open and she started to pull away, but I snaked my arm around her waist and pulled back to me.

"That's why you have the numbers isn't it?" I asked. "Isn't that what you want? Just sex? Give me my keys, and I'll prove to you that what you saw earlier wasn't my best."

I can't say that I was very surprised when her hand cracked across my face in an open slap, but I *was* very surprised when she shoved me away just far enough to throw a punch *and* hit her mark. I put my fingers up to my mouth as I glared at her. I was again shocked when I saw that she had drawn blood. A lot of blood. This little Lily did *not* hit like a girl.

She stood a few feet away from me, breathing fire. If I weren't already full of so many conflicting emotions and desires, I would have thought she looked mighty hot right then.

"So, is that a no?" I asked before pulling off my shirt. I

~ 21 ~

held it to my bleeding, split lip.

"Would you like me to repeat myself?" she asked as her fists clenched at her sides.

"I only wanted my damn keys!" I yelled, taking a step towards her.

"You only wanted your damn drugs!" she yelled back.

"You would have gotten something out of it," I said bitterly.

"Here's a newsflash, Kyle," she said putting her hands on her hips. "Just because I admitted that I kind of liked you doesn't mean that I'm ready to jump into bed with you and your half-mast dick."

Half-mast!

"I wasn't aroused!" I yelled.

"Yeah, I get that!" she yelled. "Because I'm not Emmy or Jessyca, or any other woman you're attracted to. You don't have to continue to remind me that you find me completely unattractive."

I stared at her like she had just grown a third tit on her forehead. "I never said you weren't attractive!"

She used her fingers to make air quotes and said "*You're just a barmaid in a small bar in the suburbs, Lily. Maybe you need a new tattoo or a new piercing, Lily. You've never seen a dick that wasn't pierced, Lily. You're incapable of finding a guy who will want to fuck you, Lily.*"

"Hey, I didn't say that last part," I pointed a finger at her. "And you completely took everything else out of context."

"How can I take 'you're just a barmaid' out of context, Kyle?" She growled in frustration and pulled on her hair. "You've made it pretty clear you find my tattoos and piercings and probably my hair unattractive."

"I *never* said that, Lily," I said, already getting tired of the argument.

"No, but you implied it. Thank goodness you didn't actually *say* it; because that would have hurt a little bit more I'm guessing."

She kicked off her sneakers, muttering about 'stupid

vommity sneakers' and started to walk away.

"Where are you going?" I asked, unsure if I should follow her or not. I didn't want to get punched again.

"To find a warm bed!"

"Where are my keys, Lily?" I asked, with much less urgency than I did earlier. The long ass day seeking Emmy, the drinking, the emotional turmoil, the argument and punch in the kisser suddenly weighed down on me. I didn't want meth as much as I wanted to just also find a warm bed, but if she gave in and produced my keys, I would probably wake up pretty fast.

"You can't have them!" she screamed from what sounded like my bedroom.

I sighed heavily before going through the apartment turning off lights. Out of curiosity, I opened the closet next to the bathroom. Lily's jacket hung there, welcoming me to dig through her pockets.

"They're not in there!" she called from the bedroom.

Out of spite, I went through her pockets. I found her keys and more numbers.

"How many fucking numbers did you get?" I yelled.

"*Some* men *do* find me attractive!"

I slammed the closet door and turned off the rest of the lights.

"I never said you weren't attractive," I said again as I moved down the hallway.

The bedroom was illuminated by the light from the master bath. Lily was in my bed, under the blankets with her back to me.

"You know I could call my dealer to me," I said, standing beside the bed.

"You could if you had your phone," she said.

Shit.

"Where's my phone, Lily?"

"In the car. I saw it there and forgot to bring it in."

I threw my head back in frustration. "And why do you get my bed?"

~ 23 ~

"The bed in the guest room is a full size bed. I think I've earned the right to sleep in a Californian king."

"I was in rehab for a month," I pointed out. "I think I deserve to sleep in my own bed."

"So sleep," she snapped.

I threw my bloody shirt into the bathroom trashcan and turned off the light before using the light of the digital clock on the table next to my bed to find my way back to the bed. I threw back the covers and got into my bed. As my head sunk into the pillows, I sighed. I wasn't exactly content for obvious reasons, but it was nice to be in my own bed, even if I was sharing it with Little Slugger.

"You split my lip open," I said to her after a few quiet minutes.

"You deserved it," she said as she yawned. "Besides, you took your shirt off. It was a win win."

I chuckled, an honest to goodness real bit of laughter. Lily looked over her shoulder at me.

"What I was trying to say before you had your temper tantrum is that even though those painful emotions may follow you for a long time, you will eventually be able to live with them. You will eventually be able to smile or…laugh. Life only seems to stop, but it only stops for you, and it's only as long as you want it. The rest of the world will continue on without you, but you don't want to miss too much, because then you'll have regrets on top of your regrets. It can become a vicious cycle. You just have to try to live through it, Kyle. You have to try."

"But…"

"No buts. Yes, you did awful things, but no one is going to punish you more than you are going to punish yourself, but you can also redeem yourself. If there was no redemption for anyone, then every criminal should just be executed because the time they'll spend in prison would be pointless. I do believe you can be redeemed, despite your stupid big mouth."

I felt like there was an elephant sitting on my chest and a large lump had formed in my throat. I had not cried since I was a kid, but I felt myself on the verge of tears. I started taking very deep breaths to help fight it off. Lily rolled over and crawled across the bed until she was close enough to rest her hand on my bare chest. She didn't say anything, but I appreciated the gesture. I usually didn't like to be touched by anyone who wasn't my mom or Emmy, but Lily's hand was comforting at a time when I thought being comforted was impossible. Maybe because I didn't think anyone wanted to comfort me.

After a while, the weight on my chest wasn't so heavy and the lump in my throat began to dissolve. Lily's eyes were closed, but I wasn't sure if she was actually sleeping or not.

"Lil?" I whispered.

"Hmm?"

"I never said you were unattractive."

She groaned. "Instead of apologizing for groping my ass and yelling at me, you're going back to *that*?"

I sighed, slightly frustrated. "I am sorry, but I'm...I'm like that. I have asshole tendencies. I've been trying to work on it since Emmy laid into me about it, but I don't think it's ever going to go away."

"Probably not," she murmured. "But then again, that's a big part that makes you so appealing and attractive to women. Some of us like aggression in our men."

I was once again reminded that she *liked* me, and now I had some idea why, but I didn't focus on that. Not quite.

"I'm not sorry for grabbing your ass," I said firmly.

"If I could open my eyes, I'd be rolling them right now."

"But back to what I was saying earlier," I said, ignoring her eye rolling comment. "I never said you were unattractive."

"Oh yeah? What color are my eyes then, hotshot?"

"Slate gray," I promptly answered. "I've never seen eyes such a deep color of gray."

She appeared to freeze for a moment, but then she relaxed somewhat. "Very good. You get a gold star for remembering my eye color."

"You bite your bottom lip when you're concentrating." The words fell off of my tongue, bewildering even me. Lily froze again. I think she even stopped breathing. "When you release your lip, you lick it a couple of times with the tip of your tongue. Just the tip because you seem uncomfortable when your tongue ring comes in contact with your lips or teeth."

"I hate seeing people play with their tongue rings," she whispered. "It's gross."

"I agree, but I think I like yours. You don't do that."

"Thanks?" she said uneasily.

I chuckled again and patted her hand on my chest. Without much thought, I laced my fingers with hers.

"You have a smattering of freckles across the bridge of your nose and cheekbones. It's cute, but hot at the same time."

"You noticed all of this in one night?" she asked, slightly breathless.

"I did. And I'm not even finished."

"Oh," she said in a small voice.

"Honestly, I always went for girls with bodies like Emmy or Jess – Jess is tall and slim, with some mild curves. Emmy, as you know is thin but pretty curvy."

"Are you going somewhere with these descriptions of the exes?" she asked dryly.

"Yes. I like your body, Lily. I think you're very attractive, especially when you're angry and just punched a guy. So, don't ever think that I don't think you're attractive."

"Thank you, Kyle," she said softly before clearing her throat. "But let's face it. You can't get past all of the other stuff. My tattoos are never going away. I thought long and hard before each one and I have no reason to laser them off. I like my pierced eyebrow, my pierced tongue, my pierced ears and my pierced ni - " She stopped mid word, but it was obvious what she was about to say.

"Your nipples are pierced?" I asked in awe.

"Yes," she said in exasperation.

"Is your clit pierced?" I asked.

"No!"

"Lily, you're right," I said with my own exasperated sigh.

"I'm not used to all of that, and I don't know if I ever will be, but I can't even think like that at this point in my life."

"Then the conversation is over," she said softly. "I appreciate what you said, but I'm okay with letting it drop now."

She started to pull her hand out of mine and roll away, but I grasped her hand and wrapped my arm around her and pulled her closer.

"Please," I whispered the one word.

"Okay," she whispered back.

As usual, while I was drifting off to sleep my head was filled with images and sounds of Emmy. Her smile, her frown, her angry face, and her sad face. Sometimes I would get flashes of me hitting her, though I could never really put all of the little pieces together to get a full picture.

Sometimes I heard her laughter or her cries of ecstasy, but sometimes I heard her cry of fear and pain, but I couldn't place in my mind what the scene was when she made those awful sounds that tend to haunt me into my sleep. I tried to focus on better things, like kissing her. I loved her lips and her mouth.

As Lily shifted slightly in my arms, I wondered what it would be like to kiss her. I had never kissed a woman anything like her, especially one with a tongue ring. Now I was the one shifting slightly. The thought of her studded tongue flickering over mine sent a jolt right to my earlier insulted manhood. My brain gave me an image of Lily on her knees with my erection in her hands and on the tip of her tongue while her piercing gleamed. I had heard rumors that oral sex was that much better when the giver had a pierced tongue. I couldn't shake the image from either of my heads, and before long I was thinking about her nipples.

The good news was that I didn't think too much about Emmy for the rest of the night. The bad news was that I couldn't stop thinking about Lily.

Chapter Two

~Lily~

My body was ready to wake up from its slumber, but I wanted to chase after the fading dream I had. I tried to force myself to sleep again, but my toes betrayed me by flexing and pointing to the foot of the bed, and my arms stretched over my head until my fingers grazed over the headboard.

Damn stretching limbs.

Defeated, my eyes fluttered open and stared at the windows I was facing. The mid-afternoon sun pressed against the glass, but the room darkening blinds let only the smallest traces of sunlight through. I rolled my head and shrieked. Kyle was lying next to me, on his side with his head propped on one arm as he gazed at me. His hair was damp from a recent shower, I assumed, and his beard was gone.

"I went to sleep thinking about what it would be like to kiss you," he said in a velvety voice that nearly made my panties burst into flames and melt off of my body. "I woke up with the same thought, but I thought I wasn't thinking straight because I'm really fucked up in the head and heart right now. I went out for a long run and forced myself to focus on the task at hand. I took a shower, shaved, and went about trying to get on with my life post Emmy as a recovering addict. No matter what I did today, the desire to kiss you didn't go away. Maybe it's because you are right here...in my bed..." He ran a finger over my jawline that left me trembling. "Tangible..." His thumb dragged across my bottom lip and shamefully, I gasped.

"So, I've been laying here for the past half hour watching you sleep, trying to decide if I should wake you with a kiss or wait until you wake up; or if I should be an asshole and send you away so that I wouldn't be tempted."

"You should probably send me away," I struggled to breathe out.

"I probably should," he agreed. "That would be wise, but I

don't always behave wisely." His fingers traced over the stars tattooed on my neck.

"Well, here's your chance to prove you're not a complete boob."

Hell, I really wanted him to kiss me. I had been thinking about it since the first time I had ever seen him, but I really didn't want him to kiss me. If it weren't for his broken heart, we wouldn't even be discussing it, because I wouldn't have been there. I didn't want to be the rebound girl; especially since the woman who was making him rebound was my boss. I never actually believed any of my fantasies about Kyle would ever come to fruition. It really wouldn't be healthy for either of us to be anything other than friends.

Then again, it was only a kiss, and he would probably hate it or it would make him think of Emmy and he wouldn't want to take it any further. Then again, stranger things have happened.

While I was at war with myself, Kyle had apparently made up his own mind.

"I hate 'what if' scenarios," he said, as his thumb dragged across my lip again.

"Well, *what if* I don't want you to kiss me?" I asked in a growing panic. "*What if* I don't kiss you back?"

A small, but dangerous smile appeared on his face. "You *do* and you *will*."

His hand firmly – possessively – cupped my face and he brought his lips to mine. I stopped breathing and my heart stopped when his tongue smoothed across my lips seeking entrance. Stubbornly, I didn't let him in. His tongue swept over my bottom lip and suddenly I felt his teeth on me. He didn't bite me hard enough to bleed, but I parted my lips in a surprised reflex and his tongue dove into my mouth. I couldn't stop the moan that escaped my throat when his tongue found the tip of mine. When I flicked my piercing over his tongue, Kyle moaned loudly into my mouth. I reached up and grabbed the back of his head to kiss him deeper. Our tongues met again and again in an erotic tango, both of us moaning and groaning.

Kyle shifted so that his body was over mine without ever taking his lips from mine. He had one hand at the back of my head, gripping my hair and his other hand smoothed back and forth over my waist and hip. There was a blanket between us, but there was no mistaking his erection pressed against my thigh. Whatever misgivings I had earlier were burned away by my own lust. I was at his mercy and I loved every second of it. I loved his hard body pressed against mine as his tongue battled with mine and his teeth nipped at my lips. I ran my tongue gingerly over his injured lip as an apology. He accepted it with a light moan.

Kyle pulled away and ripped the blanket off of me. He grabbed the hem of my t-shirt and pushed it up, but stopped just under my breasts. I watched with fascination as he bent over and planted kisses across my belly. His hands released the hem of my shirt and caressed my skin. He looked at me with heated eyes and pulled off his own shirt. He finished what he started and pulled my shirt off, revealing a black, nearly transparent bra.

"Oh my god," he whispered as his hands smoothed down my chest towards my breasts. The palms of his hands just covered my hard buds when I saw movement from the doorway.

I screamed when I saw a man standing there glaring at us. Kyle scrambled to cover me as he cursed.

"What the hell are you doing here!" he demanded of the man as he got off of the bed.

"Get rid of your whore and meet me in the living room," the asshole said coldly and walked out.

"Who's the asshole!" I demanded as I pulled my shirt back on.

Kyle pulled his own shirt on and looked at me somberly.

"That asshole is my dad."

~~~

I stood just inside the bedroom door listening to the escalating argument in the living room. It had been ten minutes since father and son began yelling at one another. I thought

Kyle had a bad temperament, but his father reminded me of a fire breathing dragon.

"I don't *want* her and I'm fucking done pretending that I do!" Kyle yelled.

"This isn't just about you! Martin Venner has every intention of handing that business to Jess – your marriage would have ensured - "

"My life is not a fucking business transaction, Walter!" Kyle roared. "This isn't just about you getting their business. You think that I don't know the shit you've done!"

There was a moment of silence and then Walter asked "It was you? You're the one screwing with my accounts?"

"Yes it was me," Kyle said and then roared once again. "What the hell is wrong with you? Do you realize how much shit this company is in because of your greedy actions!"

"You told Emmy," Walter yelled. "That bitch would love to destroy me!"

"The only thing she knows is that you're a cheating, dishonest, asshole, *Dad*. I didn't tell her any of the details."

"You're lying! She specifically said that she knew I was doing bad business! Where would she have heard that, Kyle?"

"You paid her a bribe, Walter! It doesn't take a genius to understand that isn't the first shitty thing you've done!"

A bribe? Why would Emmy take a bribe? She had plenty of her own money.

"Who else knows?"

"It doesn't matter! I didn't throw you under the fucking bus if that's what you want to know. I've been cleaning up your fucking mess as quietly as possible, risking my own neck."

"I guess I should thank you," Walter said very reluctantly.

"I'm not doing it for you," Kyle spat. "I don't care about you."

"Fine. You don't give a shit about me and I don't give a shit about you, but you better go fix this thing with Jessyca."

"Jess can go to hell," Kyle said through a clenched jaw.

"Obviously you learned what you did from Jess. So you

know she can make this entire thing blow up in our faces."

"I'm done caring! I lost everything trying to fix this and I'm done!"

"You haven't begun to lose, you ungrateful bastard," Walter said in a threatening growl. "I should have never claimed you as my son. No son of mine would be such a fuck up. I should have let your mother run off with the fucking loser that fathered you."

Oh shit!

"I'll keep that in mind when the FBI comes knocking."

I heard some shuffling and grunting and the unmistakable sound of fists hitting flesh. I ran from the room and nearly froze when I found Walter pushing Kyle around and throwing punches at him. What gave me pause was that Kyle was not fighting back. He blocked what he could but he was allowing himself to get his ass kicked.

What the hell!

"Stop!" I yelled, running into the room. I ran full force into Walter, shoving him so hard he fell back onto the dining room table. "Get out of here!" I yelled even though it wasn't my home.

Kyle grabbed me around the waist and pulled me away from his faux father. Walter stood upright. He was glaring at me, but he spoke to Kyle.

"Nice guard dog," he said. He walked past us to the door. "You're fired for illegal drug usage and fucking your assistant," he said to Kyle. "You're banned from the estate and I will find a way to cut your ass off."

"I don't doubt that you will," Kyle said dryly. "Now get out and leave your key."

Walter reached into his pocket and then threw a key on the floor before slamming the door.

Kyle released me and I spun around to look at him. His mouth was bleeding again and there were bruises forming on his cheek. His right eye was already turning colors and starting to swell. This time I pulled off my own shirt to hold to his lip.

"Why didn't you fight back?" I asked as I led him to a

chair. I made him sit down and hurried into the kitchen to make him an icepack. I almost felt let down that he didn't fight back. I never believed Kyle Sterling to be someone's little bitch to beat up on. Not even close.

"I wanted him to get it out of his system," he said when I returned with the icepack. I carefully put it over his eye and held it there.

"What do you mean?" I asked.

"He won't go home and beat the shit out of my mother instead," he said darkly as he stared straight ahead.

I felt like he had just punched me in the chest. While this was new to me, it most likely was not a new development in the Sterling family. Most likely Kyle had been witnessing such behavior since he was a child and probably experienced a good deal of beatings himself.

"Even if I knew that beforehand, I'm not sure if I would have been able to just stand there and watch him do that to you," I admitted reluctantly. I felt sick knowing that it was a possibility Walter Sterling had not finished getting "it out of his system" and he would finish with his wife.

In well under twenty-four hours, I had learned that Kyle had beaten Emmy, but he couldn't remember it because he was high and drunk. He was an addict, still struggling to stay clean. He had a brother that died as a child and Kyle believed he was responsible. His father was defrauding some people. Kyle couldn't dump Jess and commit to the woman he really loved because he was trying to fix the mess and keep Jess from bringing it to light. Walter Sterling was an abusive husband and *clearly* an abusive parent, but apparently he was only Kyle's parent in name only because Kyle was fathered by someone else.

It was a lot to learn about a man who seemed to live a fairly private life. I was never meant to know any of it, but now that I did, I didn't know what to do with it. It should have been a clear indication that he had too much going on in his life, and now with his faux father out to destroy him, things weren't going to get any easier anytime soon. I had my own problems and demons to fight and skeletons in my closet. I wasn't sure if I could be helpful, if he even wanted my help. We had made out, but it didn't mean he wanted anything more from me.

Kyle slid a hand over my hip and down to my front pocket. He slipped his hand into the pocket and pulled out my cell phone.

"What's your password?" he asked in a dead voice.

"Um. Anna." When he looked up at me with discerning eyes, I looked away.

"Who's Anna?"

I gave a small shake of my head. I didn't want to talk about it, at least not right then. I wasn't sure if I wanted to discuss anything as serious as Anna with him. I was sure he was going to be done with me soon enough. I didn't want to waste the pain it would cost me to tell that tale for someone who was probably already losing interest in me, and someone who had enough of his own problems at the moment.

Kyle sighed and then unlocked my phone. He quickly dialed a number. I heard a woman answer on the third ring.

"Eliza, it's Kyle," he said and then stood up, disregarding the icepack. He tossed my t-shirt onto the chair he had just vacated. "Remember what we spoke about before I went on leave?" he asked her as he walked away from me.

Kyle went into business mode, talking to this Eliza person. He went into the guest room where his office was set up. The desk was covered in files that he was rooting through as I walked by to go find a shirt that didn't have blood all over it.

I felt disgusting still wearing the same clothes I put on twenty-four hours before. I stepped into Kyle's walk-in closet and was surprised by how organized it was. On one side his suits were arranged by color, as were his dress shirts. The other side held more casual clothes, also color coordinated. His shoes were arranged by type – dress, casual, and athletic. I took a more casual button down, blue shirt and then took a pair of boxers from a bureau in the bedroom. Judging by the snippets of conversation I was hearing from the other room, he was going to be awhile. I went into the master bath and stripped out of my day old clothes and started the shower.

I honestly didn't know how Kyle was going to feel about me rooting through his closet and drawers and subsequently borrowing his clothes, but when our little moment of time together ended, and I knew it would, I at least wanted to be wearing clean underwear. Even if they weren't mine.

As I washed my hair with his shampoo, I tried to think of my week ahead and all of the things I had to do at *SHOTZ* and *not* about my morning in bed with Kyle or all of the things I learned about him. I tried to think about the alcohol I had to order, the upcoming inspection with the fire marshal, and the major scrub down the place needed, and *not* about Kyle's tongue in my mouth and his hands cupping my breasts. I tried to focus on the event I was having at the bar on Valentine's Day that would benefit local cancer patients, and not the fact that all of the things I had learned about Kyle not only didn't truly repel me, but made me feel a little deeper for him. He reminded me of a lost little boy who had been very ill behaved and now he was just trying to redeem himself but no one noticed or cared.

But it didn't matter what I thought or what I felt. Even though he wanted to kiss me so badly, I knew it wasn't really about *me*. As he said himself, he was fucked up in the head, and I didn't disagree. After his faux father's visit, there was no disputing that. He was fucked up in the head pre-Emmy, but I believe he went over the edge when he beat her and he was still in the pit he had fallen into. I was just another warm body who happened to be occupying the same space with him. I was replaceable and forgettable.

I didn't want to have to have that uncomfortable conversation, about how he was sorry he made a mistake, etc. I already knew it was a mistake, but I didn't need it said to my face. After I got out of the shower, I quickly dressed in Kyle's clothes and pulled my own jeans back on. I found a small plastic bag under the sink and stuffed my bloody shirt and day old underwear inside and tied it tight. I opened the bathroom door half expecting to find Kyle sitting on the bed, but he wasn't there. Standing in the doorway of the bedroom, I listened for him. I didn't hear his voice, but I heard the clicking of a keyboard in the guest room. I was half tempted to leave my phone behind, but I needed it.

Kyle sat in the guestroom with his back to me, typing madly on the keyboard. My phone was a few inches from the laptop. I left the bag with my clothes outside the door and walked in.

"Are you finished with this?" I asked him as I picked up the phone.

He nodded without even giving me a glance or pausing in his typing.

"Your keys are in the freezer," I said as I crossed the room.

He didn't answer or give any indication that he had heard me, but I knew he did. I left the room, grabbing my bag along the way. I went into the kitchen and took his keys out of the freezer. I put them on the end table next to the couch. I thought about leaving a note, but what could I possibly say? There was nothing to say. I was sorry for his problems, especially his family problems, but there was nothing I could do. He let me in briefly, but he was already shutting me out. I didn't want to be *that* girl, trying to save someone who didn't want me to save him. I wasn't trying to test Kyle, but if he really wanted me or my friendship, he knew where to find me.

I took my jacket out of the closet and slipped quietly out of Kyle's life.

Chapter Three

A year and a half later...

~Kyle~

"I wish you never found me in the bar."

Emmy stood with her back to me, looking out of the large window at the far off Philadelphia skyline. I knew she was trying to put some distance between us, but I didn't care as I approached her from behind. I inhaled the scent of her hair. It reminded me of vanilla and cherries, a sweet smell that invaded my senses and made me want to tangle my hands in her hair and pull her to me and let her feel the affect that she had on me.

"If it wasn't there, it would have been somewhere else," I said in her ear as my hands slipped down her sides and rested on her hips.

I felt her tense under my hands. I knew if I ran my thumb across her nipple or slipped my hand into her jeans, she would yield to me. If I wrapped my arms around her and kissed her slender neck, her stubborn will would break and she would be mine forever. I wanted her to want me without me seducing her into it, but being so close to her was almost too much to take after such a long absence. I was just about to pull her up against me, but she suddenly moved away.

"I should go," she said and speed walked to her enormous pocketbook.

"Emmy," I said, closely following her. I caught a hold of her wrist just as she reached the door. It was the same wrist I broke two years ago. The thought made me sick to my stomach, but I quickly pushed it out of my mind. I had to remind her of what we had, how much she used to want me and how much I still wanted her.

"I can't deal with losing you again," I said to her. "What do you want me to do?" I would have done anything for her to keep her. I would have given up anything.

She looked up at me, her mouth slightly parted and a

confused and pained look in her eyes.

"I don't think…" she shook her head as she stared at me with her beautiful brown and green blended eyes.

"Nothing I can do?" I asked. "We just had a really nice night. I know you don't really mean that. You had a good time."

"I did, but…" she blinked hard, trying hard to look away from me. "It's not enough," she whispered.

I knew she was still struggling with her feelings for me. I could feel it in my soul. If I had to seduce her to make her break through those walls, then so be it.

"Kiss me," I said, leaning in close to her.

"No," she said, but it wasn't as firmly as she probably meant it to be.

She tried to move away, but I grabbed her shoulders. Yeah, I was out of line, but I had been out of line since the first time I kissed her.

"Kiss me, and then if you still want to walk out of the door, I will let you," I said.

"I can't," she whispered, but made no effort to get away from me.

"Because you know how it will make you feel," I said. I used my own body to press hers up against the door. I pressed my erection against her thigh, not far from her heated core. "You want to kiss me, though. Don't you?" I whispered.

I moved in slowly, preparing to taste her lips and sweet mouth again. It's something I ached for every day for nearly two years. As a last ditch effort, Emmy closed her mouth tight. I flicked my tongue across her bottom lip and almost groaned.

"Open," I demanded and tried to part her lips with my tongue. I growled low in my throat, growing frustrated and harder with her refusal to give me what we both needed. "Open your fucking mouth. You want to kiss me," I said. "Open."

When she still didn't open her precious lips, I decided on a different route. Moving quickly, I put my hand up her skirt and was immediately rewarded with her damp pussy and engorged clit. She gasped and I stole the opportunity to finally get my tongue into that luscious mouth. I heard a low groan escape from her throat, and knew that I had her - until with strength I never knew her to have, she shoved my hand away from her and turned her head, releasing herself from our kiss.

"You want me," I whispered in her ear. Again, I thought she was folding, but again I was wrong.

"I didn't come here for this!" she screamed as she shoved me away from her.

A sudden burst of anger boiled up to the surface of my own lips. Why the fuck did she come here if she didn't want what I wanted? Did she come here just to tease me?

"Then what did you come here for?" I yelled at her. "Did you think that we could just pretend that nothing ever happened between us?" I closed the distance between us, trying to calm down. "I know you love me, Emmy," I said.

I reached out to touch her, and she almost let me, but with a pained expression on her face, she shoved me away again.

"You hurt me!" she screamed. "You put your hands on me and you hurt me."

"I was fucked up on drugs, Emmy. I'm sorry. I don't even remember it," I said, as if not remembering it was a viable excuse for my actions.

"It's not just the drugs and the abuse, Kyle. You weren't strong enough to stand up to your dad and to Jessyca."

"But I eventually did!" Even in my ears, I knew I sounded like a little boy saying that.

"Eventually was not soon enough, Kyle," she said bitterly. She reached into her house-sized bag and produced the bracelet I had given her after she had her cast removed. She thrust it at me, but I stepped back from her, as if the thing was poisonous.

"That was a gift. I don't want it back." Somehow, it felt like taking back the bracelet would sever us forever. Sever everything, all of our feelings, all of our memories, all of *us*.

"You need to take it back," she demanded. "This is why I'm here. I've been holding onto it, in essence holding on to you. I have to let you go."

I could tell that it pained her to say that. She didn't really want to let me go...did she?

"You don't have to," I said, feeling hopeful that she would agree.

"What do you expect me to do, Kyle? Tear my son away from his father and move into your shiny new apartment with you? Tear him away from his family and everything he knows? Is that what you want? It probably is, Kyle, because you don't give two shits about the aftermath when you get what you want. You smooth talk your way into getting things your way and then when it gets too fucking hard you duck out or shove some meth up your nose. You beat me and you could have killed me and Lucas. That broke me. I will never be with you again."

She shook the bracelet in my face. I was too sickened by her words to move.

"Take the fucking bracelet!" Emmy shrieked.

Stunned, sick, and feeling like the biggest fuck up of all time, I took the bracelet from her. It may as well have weighed ten thousand pounds; it felt so heavy in my hand.

"Thank you," she said, straightening her shoulders. She opened the door and stepped out.

"I am very sorry," I said to her back.

Without a second glance, she walked away. I kicked the door shut before I went after her again. I stared at the closed door for a good five minutes before I finally stumbled back to the living room.

That was it. She was gone. I knew she was gone forever. There was no hope left, nothing left for me to hold onto but the stupid ass bracelet.

With a roar filled with pain and anger, I threw the bracelet across the room, barely hearing it clink to the floor over the sound of my own grief.

Chapter Four

~Lily~

The last thing I wanted to do was put on my corporate high heels and work behind a desk in paper pushing servitude, but the quickest way to my goal was to humble myself, cover my tattoos and walk into Sterling Corporation like I belonged there.

Okay, so it helped to have a friend on the inside.

Mayson tucked a pencil behind her ear and spun in a full circle in her chair, looking for a misplaced file. Her desk was overflowing with them. So was her floor.

"Ummm…" Mayson bit her bottom lip and tapped a file with her fingers.

"What are you looking for?" I asked, reaching for a chocolate in a mug perched on the corner of her desk.

Her eyes narrowed at the chocolate as I un-wrapped it.

"Only because you're unemployed and homeless will I allow that act of treachery, Lillian Whitman," she said.

"Yeah, but I'm not unemployed anymore, right?" I asked before popping the chocolate goodness into my mouth.

She broke out into a smile. "No, you are not. I'm just not sure where to put you. There have been a lot of changes, people coming and going – mostly going…" She frowned. "Anyway, I don't want to throw you to the wolves, you know?"

"I can handle anything you throw at me," I said and sat up a little straighter. "I've been tending bar since I was seventeen. I've handled plenty of wolves, and pigs, dogs, and jackasses."

"Seventeen? Is that even legal?" she asked warily.

"Define legal."

"Never mind," she said, shaking her head. "Lily, you've never been in the corporate world. There aren't just wolves and jackasses, there are *sharks*."

"Listen, we're wasting time," I said, stealing another chocolate. "I can handle anything and anyone. I'll learn anything I need to learn quickly. You know I'll work my ass off."

Mayson sat back in her chair and eyed me carefully. "There is a position that I'm having a hard time filling. I wanted to hire from within the company, but not many seem to want it."

"What is it? Cleaning toilets?" I smirked.

"You remember Kyle, don't you?" she asked carefully.

I didn't blink, raise an eyebrow, or shift in my seat. I had memories of Kyle that most likely no one else but he and I were aware of.

"Yes, I remember Kyle," I said. "What about him?"

"He's heading a new department. The assistant that replaced Emmy has been promoted, so she was unable to follow him. As I said, the department is brand new. He needs an assistant and office manager. Besides the fact that he is extremely demanding and can be a real dick, it's just going to be a lot of work getting everything rolling correctly. The pay is spectacular, and you'll get benefits after sixty days."

"Well..." I sighed. "You know I'm not looking to stay with the company forever, right? This is just a means for me to get where I need to get. How long do you think it will take to get this department up and running?"

"A year, maybe less. Depends on your team," she said with a shrug. "I figured you'd be here a year to eighteen months."

"That's about right."

"Usually, I wouldn't hire someone for a position like that if they weren't planning on staying for a long time," she said. She looked like she was having second thoughts.

"Listen, Mayson," I said, leaning forward. "I like a challenge. If you have any other positions that are equally challenging and have a spectacular pay, I'll take any of them. If not, let me be the dick's assistant. I promise I can do it, and I promise I will not leave before the department is up and running. Who knows? Maybe I'll find out that I like the corporate world and never leave."

Mayson snickered. "I highly doubt you'll change your dreams after working for Kyle Sterling for a year. You'll be running for the exit at the end, trust me."

"So, you'll give me the position?"

"Yes," she said with resignation. "You'll have to go through some basic training and orientation for a week or so, and then you'll be able to join Kyle."

"Thank you," I breathed. "I owe you for this."

"I look forward to endless free food and drinks when you finally open your establishment." She stamped a yellow sheet of paper and handed it to me. "Come back tomorrow morning at eight-thirty and go see Harriet down the hall. She'll get you started."

"I'll be here," I said getting to my feet.

"Good luck," she said, already distracted. She spun around in her chair again. "Now, where's my pencil?"

I stepped into the corridor and headed towards the elevators, wondering if I had finally climbed aboard the train to Crazy by taking a job working directly for Kyle Sterling, but I didn't have much of a choice. I really needed that paycheck. As Mayson had pointed out, I was already homeless – I was homeless before the bar burned down. I spent my nights on a friend's couch in North Camden, and even that was beginning to look unreliable. If I didn't get a decent income soon, I was going to end up sleeping on the streets of Philadelphia.

The elevator arrived as I tried to shake that thought. I was putting the paper Mayson gave me into my bag as I stepped on, only glancing at the one pair of shoes in the cab to make sure that I wouldn't run into anyone. While I was in my bag, I thought I'd have a piece of gum. The smell of spearmint in the bag was strong, but the gum eluded me. With a sigh, I gave up and finally dared to steal a glance at my one elevator companion.

Kyle Sterling pinned me against the wall with his cold eyes.

Well, at least we're getting the awkward part done with...

I didn't get a "hello" or a "hey" or a "what's up" or anything decent from Kyle when he finally spoke.

"What are you doing here?" he asked. His eyes flittered over me with something that looked like disgust.

"Same as you," I answered. With great effort, I didn't roll my eyes at my new boss. "I'm taking the elevator down to the lobby."

"This elevator is going to the twenty-first floor," he said coolly.

I looked at the one lit up button. Maybe if I had been paying attention and not thinking about being homeless, I would have noticed the up arrow lit up above the doors. I punched the L button with a little more force than necessary.

"You haven't answered my question," he said, stepping up beside me.

"Applying for a position," I said, watching the numbers tick up to twenty-one. It felt as if the elevator was moving painfully slow, delaying Kyle's departure from the cab that suddenly felt much smaller.

I saw him nod once out of the corner of my eye. "Of course. Mayson helped you out then?"

"Mmm hmm," I nodded.

How much slower can this thing go!

"Where did she put you? Mail room? Data processing?"

I finally looked at him, one of my newly waxed, ring-free eyebrows raised in a challenge.

"What makes you think she's put me in the mail room or data processing?" I asked.

"Up until a few weeks ago you were merely a barmaid for several years," he said from his high horse. "Where else would she put you?"

"So, because I was 'merely a barmaid' I must not have any redeeming corporate abilities?"

He only stared at me with his cool gaze. His silence was a loud and clear response to my question. I turned my attention back to the dials and was relieved to see the number twenty-one light up, quickly followed by the dinging sound I never thought I'd enjoy more. Kyle took his time stepping off of the elevator, but then he stood in the entranceway, holding the door open, staring at me again.

"Why do you need to know where I will be working?" I asked, not hiding my irritation.

"I could use a file clerk in my department," he said.

"A file clerk?" I laughed. "Well, as your assistant and office manager, if I find that I can't control my urge to staple you to a wall, I'll ask you for a demotion – to file clerk."

I gave him a gentle shove and grinned with satisfaction at his surprised face as the elevator doors closed.

~Kyle~

I stood at the elevator, punching the down arrow repeatedly, but the cab continued on its descent to the Lobby. Another elevator arrived, but I knew by the time I got to the first floor, Lily would be gone. I took the elevator to the tenth floor instead and stormed into Mayson's office without knocking.

She looked surprised by my arrival, but her expression was quickly replaced by one of annoyance.

"My Grace," she started in a phony English accent. "What brings you to these lower parts of the kingdom?"

"Did you hire Emmy's old barmaid as my assistant and office manager?" I demanded to know.

She narrowed her eyes. "I only did that not even ten minutes ago. How do you know about that already?" She frowned and her shoulders slumped some. "I wanted it to be a surprise."

"Oh, I *am* surprised," I said, trying to rein in my anger. "I ran into her on the elevator. You do realize that I need more than a barmaid to help me run my department, Mayson. If this is some effort to make me look foolish…"

"Why would I do that?" she snorted. "You need to simmer down, get your panties out of a twist, Sterling. Lily ran Emmy's bar for years. Em was basically owner just in name, because Lily did everything, and she would have done much more if the place didn't burn to the ground."

"Running a little bar in suburbia isn't the same as running a whole department in a company like Sterling Corporation."

"It's not that different," Mayson said, waving a hand in dismissal. "She's not just a dumb bartender, Kyle. Did you know she has a business degree?"

"Did she do it by mail order like she did her bartending certificate?" I snarled.

"No, you dick. She got her bartending skills all on her own, but she got her degree from University of Penn. Is that good enough for you?"

University of Penn wasn't what I considered an *elite* school, but it was a very good one. I wasn't very impressed, however. Lily squandered her degree on mixing drinks and getting groped for bad tips in a small bar for years.

"She has no experience in the corporate world," I argued. "She will only slow me down."

"I think she will surpass even Emmy's abilities," Mayson said, rooting through a stack of files.

I glared at her. Emmy was probably the best administrative assistant that ever walked through the doors of Sterling Corporation, and I wasn't just saying that because she was mine. I had to steal her away from my father and then fight him and my other superiors to keep her. I felt that Mayson was only saying that to get under my skin, not because Lily could possibly actually compare to Emmy.

"Put her somewhere else," I said through a clenched jaw.

"I'm not putting her somewhere else. You're going to have to trust me on this one."

"Why should I trust you?" I glared at her. "You hate me, you said so yourself, and I don't doubt that you know a few other things about me that can do nothing but intensify your hatred for me. How do I know you're not setting me up to fail?"

She stopped rooting through her files and stared at me.

"I don't like you, Kyle," she said in a matter of fact tone. "And yes, I do know a few more things about you that I didn't know before, but there are a few things you need to keep in mind. Lily is here by my recommendation. I'm not going to let her make me look bad. As for the other things, I'm not holding any of it against you."

"Why not?" I asked, taken aback by her words.

"That's my business. I happen to like my job, Kyle, and I kind of want this company to succeed. So, if that means having to make sure that the biggest dick in the building gets a winning team, then so be it. Now get out of my office. Some of us actually work around here."

I left her office not because she commanded me to, but because there was nothing left to say. Mayson was delusional if she thought that a woman who was mixing drinks for a living not even a full month ago was going to excel in the demanding position she was just hired for, but Mayson was so adamant about her decision, I chose to let it go.

When – not if, but when Lily crashes and burns, Mayson can crash and burn with her.

I immediately felt bad for wishing bad things upon Lily. She saved my life nearly two years ago and I owed her more than a job for that, especially after the way I shrugged her off. However, my personal feelings for her did not change her competency for the position, and once she realized that, I would gladly give her another position she was qualified for.

~~~

She opened the door wearing nothing but a shirt and a pair of SpongeBob panties. I grew hard at the site, thankful that my coat was long enough to cover the fact that she just turned me on.

As my hand closed over my wallet in my pocket, I claimed that I couldn't find it anywhere. It was the only excuse I had for showing up at her door, the only believable one. I was desperate to see her again outside of work.

I stayed with her all weekend, through an enormous snow storm. I felt more alive in her presence than I had ever felt. I saw a side of her she didn't allow me to see at work. She was brutally honest, yet tender; and she was funny, witty, and sweet. She loved to laugh and had a smile that lit up everything around her. I loved holding her in my arms, smelling her hair, kissing her lips, and sliding inside of her. Everything about Emmy was heavenly, and I was solely responsible for her becoming a fallen, broken angel...

Darkness falls across my vision and I can't see anything, but I can hear myself beating her and I can feel my fists making contact with her soft body. Her terrified screams fill the air. I try to make myself stop, but I can't, and the beating and screaming and crying and the sound of glass

I bolted upright in bed, Emmy's screams still echoing in my head. I fumbled for the light next to my bed, illuminating my bedroom and pulling myself out of the darkness of my nightmare. Though I was fully awake, the dream clung to me, and I knew that the dream was most likely a memory and not something my mind made up.

Shaken and too afraid to close my eyes again, I rolled out of bed and changed into sweats. I pulled on a pair of socks and sneakers, grabbed my keys and left for an early morning run to clear my head.

The nightmares came off and on since I woke up in rehab that long ago New Year's Day. I knew that I had physically harmed Emmy, but I didn't know to what extent. My dad refused to tell me only because I wanted to know so badly. Had I told him it would pain me to know, he would have told me every solitary, gruesome detail. Mayson all but confirmed she knew what happened, but if she wanted to tell me, she would have done so already, rubbing my face in my shame with a jovial laugh.

I was hoping that Emmy would enlighten me during her visit, but she was adamant that she didn't want to talk about it, but as she was leaving she had said that I put my hands on her and I broke her. It reminded me of her mother's words from so long ago: "She's broken and I think you broke her." It killed me inside to know that I had done that to her, and I knew it wasn't just about the physical abuse. I dragged Em through the mud for so long, taking advantage of her love for me. Whether she knew all of the reasons behind my behavior or not did not excuse my actions.

I even felt some guilt towards Jess. In the beginning I believe she really did love me, and at one time I really loved her, too, but after a couple of years, I knew she wasn't for me. I would never be truly happy with her and I wasn't the man she wanted me to be. Pressure from my dad and her dad kept us together, and before I really could stop myself, I was obsessed with Emmy and making foolish mistakes. Even though Jess seems cold and heartless from the outside, I know for a fact that I broke her heart too.

I'm an asshole of epic proportions, and a pussy. I devoured Emmy's light with my darkness, made Jessyca into a bad person, failed to protect my mom, failed to save my brother, and folded under any pressure exerted by my dad. I deserved nothing less than to run into traffic and get run over by a SEPTA bus, but I didn't even have the guts to do that. Instead, I ran back home as dawn was breaking and got ready for work.

~Lily~

The morning commute from South Jersey to Philadelphia is a nightmare. The roads are crowded, the buses are crowded, the trains are overstuffed tin cans and the sidewalks are overflowing with cranky commuters. Stopping in any kind of shop that sells coffee is dangerous, and you risk losing a limb for an overpriced cup of Joe.

When I walked through the doors of Sterling Corp, I felt like I had slid into home base, but my reprieve was short, as the building also was starting to fill up. Coming from a night crawling lifestyle, adapting to this morning rush to work was going to take some patience, strong doses of caffeine, and possibly some chocolate. It was still early, and I had not even begun my work day yet, but I was already salivating thinking of a chocolate milkshake topped with whipped cream and cherries at the end of my day.

Focus on the milkshake, and everything will be okay. You can do this!

I found Mayson waiting with a dozen other people at the three elevators in the lobby. She smiled and waved me over.

"Good morning," she said too brightly.

"Hi," I said, making myself smile.

"I heard you had a run in with Kyle yesterday," she said in an apologetic tone. "I'm sorry."

I shrugged. "No big deal. I can handle him."

"Are you sure? Because I can put you in another department."

"No way," I said as we slowly moved forward towards an open cab. "That will only reinforce his pretentious idea that I'm incapable of doing this job."

She nodded but looked doubtful.

"You don't think I can do it either," I said in a matter of fact tone.

"I think you can do it, but I also think you don't know what you're getting yourself into. Kyle is -" She didn't finish her sentence, because the man in question stepped onto the crowded elevator.

He glanced at me when he got on next to me, scowled at Mayson, and then turned his attention to his phone. On the way to the tenth floor, the elevator stopped at every floor, mostly to let people off, but sometimes someone would get on to head upstairs. When it stopped on our floor, I started to follow Mayson out of the cab when a strong hand wrapped around my forearm. I stood on the threshold, staring back at Kyle in shock. I had almost decked him (again), my natural defense after being around sleazy men in bars for my entire adult life.

He blocked the elevator doors from closing with his foot as he glared at me.

"Where are you going?" he demanded.

Mayson grabbed a hold of my other arm, forcing my briefcase to slide down my shoulder and hang at my elbow.

"What are you doing, Sterling?" Mayson demanded. "She has to go to orientation and training this week. You know the routine."

"No, that will not work," he said, tugging me towards him. "I need her to start now. We're already far behind."

Mayson tugged me towards her. "If you're already so far behind, then what's another week or so?"

Kyle pulled. "You've already taken too long to fill the position. A week or 'so' is detrimental."

In the elevator, the other employees and one FedEx guy watched Kyle and Mayson as if they were watching a tennis match and I was the ball. Only one person seemed irritated by the hold up, but she remained silent.

"Dude, are you crazy?" Mayson snorted, pulling harder on me. "Just yesterday you were crying about her lack of experience, but you won't let her go to training? It's as if you're *setting her up to fail*." She said the last part scathingly.

His eyes narrowed as he pulled much harder than Mayson. I was sure that my arms were stretching and by the end of this, my knuckles would be dragging on the ground when I walked.

"You were so confident about her abilities," Kyle snarled. "You assured me that she knew what she was doing. If she is so capable of doing this position, then why does she need to spend a week and a half training?"

Mayson's mouth popped open and her eyes widened. She yanked me, hard, and started to speak in a high pitched tone, but I interrupted.

"I am going to ask you both nicely to release me or this is going to get very ugly," I said in a calm and steady voice.

Mayson looked guilty and immediately released my arm with a quick apology. Kyle, however, continued to hold on to me and glare. I looked down at his hand on my arm and back to his face.

"Let's not repeat history," I said in a low voice. "Don't make me embarrass you in your own building."

Any other guy would have released me, but Kyle was too proud to back down from a woman more than a foot smaller than him in front of eight other people. Ignoring the need to bring him down a peg, I spoke in a firm, but polite tone.

"I am going to spend the morning getting oriented with a few things," I said to him. "I still need an ID badge, an email set up, and to sign a few things. When I am finished, I will join you on the twenty-first floor."

"She can't even go to the bathroom without an ID badge," Mayson pointed out. The magnetic strips on all of the badges are what allowed the employees to move about the building without someone buzzing them in.

Kyle looked from her to me. For a moment, I thought he was going to suggest I pee myself or pee in a bucket in a corner, but he let out a sigh that I just barely noticed and released my arm.

"You have until eleven," he said, backing into the elevator. "And you better come prepared."

His cold brown eyes bored into me until the door closed, breaking the contact.

~ 53 ~

"I told you," Mayson said as we walked down the corridor. "You don't know what you're getting yourself into."

You'd be surprised what I know…

~~~

At ten minutes to eleven, I stepped back onto the elevator, toting a company issued laptop, a new ID badge with a hideous picture of me blinking, a stack of papers and booklets outlining company policies, procedures, perks and benefits and Kyle's brunch that he ordered from the café around the corner and insisted that I deliver to him.

When I walked into the first room full of cubicles, I was surprised to find how understaffed it was. Did everyone go to lunch early? Was there a Sterling Corp cut day that I was yet unaware of? There were twenty cubicles in the room and only half as many people. Everyone looked busy and frazzled and barely looked at me as I passed by towards what I assumed was Kyle's office. I tapped lightly on the door and was rewarded with Kyle barking for me to come in. I pushed open the door and found him seated behind his desk staring intently at his computer screen.

I took a quick look around his spacious office. The entire wall behind him was made of glass, giving him a perfect view of the city and City Hall that he probably didn't appreciate. There was the usual guest seating in front of his desk, but there was also a couch and big comfortable looking chair in a corner. There was also a small bar and mini fridge, and a small closet. There was another door that I assumed was a bathroom or maybe it led to a dungeon or a BDSM room. It could have led to Oz for all I knew.

"Please tell me that half of the cubicles in there are empty because half of your staff caught an early flu or they're on vacation or out to lunch," I said, placing his lunch on his desk. Without being asked, I put my armful of crap down on a chair in front of his desk and began unpacking the contents of his lunch bag.

"No, Miss Whitman," he said, not looking up at me. "We are extremely understaffed, which is why I really could not afford to not have you here for the first few hours of the morning."

"God forbid you would have had to go get your lunch yourself," I remarked, folding the empty bag.

He glared at me. "Serving my needs is part of your position."

An unbidden image of me *serving his needs* and my own burst into my head.

You've read way too many erotic romance novels, Lil, I thought to myself as I gathered my crap out of the chair.

"Just point me to my cubicle so that I may begin serving your needs, my Liege," I sighed.

He growled. Like really *growled*. "Your office is next to mine, on the right."

"I have my own office?" I asked, cheering up a little bit. Maybe working for Kyle wouldn't be *so* terrible.

"I did just say 'your office' didn't I?" he asked with a cold stare.

I pulled open his office door and stood on the threshold. There was a closed door to my left and a closed door to my right.

"When you said on the right, did you mean my right or your right?" I asked.

I had never seen someone look as irritated as Kyle looked right then. He got up from his desk, marched across the room and firmly gripped my shoulders. He steered me to *my* right, threw open the door and steered me inside.

"Do you need assistance finding your desk also?" he asked blandly from behind me.

I rolled my eyes, knowing he couldn't see me. "I'm assuming it's the giant block of wood over there."

"You have ten minutes to get yourself situated," he said and then left me alone in my small, but fashionable and functional office.

I wasn't into the whole corporate thing, but even I was excited about having my own office, with a smaller but no less spectacular view of the city. I didn't have a bathroom and a

~ 55 ~

couch in my office like Kyle did, but I had seating for visitors, a place to hang my coat, a small fridge and a big comfy chair at my desk. I had more amenities here than I did in my current living situation. I took one good look out of my window, completely appreciating the view and then quickly got myself "situated" before heading back to Kyle's office with a pen and notebook in hand.

His lunch was barely touched and he was back on the damn computer. I eyed the soup and salad, thinking about my own lunch. I assumed that I'd be able to go soon, but then again, I was just a servant and probably had to eat the scraps of Kyle's lunch out of the trashcan instead of enjoying a real lunch.

"There is something we need to quickly discuss and get out of the way," he finally said after a few minutes. I looked away from his lunch and found him leaning back in his chair, watching me.

"The five hundred pound gorilla in the room?" I asked, meeting his gaze straight on.

"Yes," he nodded slowly. "The five hundred pound gorilla in the room."

I took a long deep breath and stared at a pen lying on Kyle's desk as I spoke. "Listen, I'd rather not discuss it if you don't mind. Honestly, it hurt a little more than it should have and I've had so much pain over the past two years. I'm really just trying to move on with my life, which means I have to focus on the present and the future and not the past. I promise I won't let my feelings for you interfere with my work here."

His brow creased in confusion. "You still have feelings for me? After all of this time and the way I allowed you to leave?"

"I didn't say they were good feelings," I said quickly. "Regardless of my feelings about you personally, I'm here to work."

Kyle leaned back in his chair with a loud sigh as his eyes studied me. "It wasn't my intention to hurt you, especially considering what you did for me."

I looked at him in surprise. Was that something like an apology?

"I didn't do anything for you that you didn't deserve," I breathed. "Please, can we just get to work?"

After a moment of hesitation, he nodded. He seemed to recover from his moment of sensitivity and said "I'm still not convinced that this is the right position for you."

"Well, why don't you put me to the challenge? When I prove you wrong, I expect a bonus."

"What if I'm right?" he challenged. "What do I get if *you* are wrong?"

"A file clerk," I said dryly.

My stomach chose that moment to rumble in the quiet room. I didn't give any indication that my stomach had just made that crazy noise. I looked at him, pen poised to write while he stared blankly at me. After a half a minute of this, Kyle raised an eyebrow and a few seconds later pushed his salad across the table.

Chapter Five

~𝒦𝓎𝓁𝑒~

I almost instantly regretted forcing Lily to begin her position without the orientation Mayson fought me so hard about. She asked question after question, often interrupting me while I was speaking or bursting into my office while I was working, or phoning me after I told her to stay out of my office. When she wasn't asking me questions, she was asking the staff, which kept them from getting their work done.

I started to tell her this was why she wasn't right for the job, that maybe she should reconsider taking the file clerk job or perhaps working in the café around the corner, but she halted me mid-word by putting up her hand and pointing at me.

"Don't you *dare* say it," she hissed. "Don't even consider it. This is your own doing. It was your decision to throw me into this position head first without any training. You can't deny me the opportunity to ask someone else questions and then get mad when you have to answer them yourself."

There was nothing for me to say. She was correct. I left her in her office and went back to my own. I sat in my chair, staring out at the busy city as the day winded down and the fall sky grew dim, signaling the darker winter days ahead.

Admittedly, Lily did ask good questions. She asked very specific questions regarding the operation of our department and our clientele and I never had to repeat myself. She asked about my routines, how they could improve and what I needed from her. The following morning she beat me to work as Emmy used to do, except along with my morning coffee she also brought me a muffin and a banana, because "breakfast is the most important meal of the day and you'll find yourself more focused when you're not hungry."

She asked the staff about their needs and concerns and took care of some of it immediately. Within days, she had them eating out of one hand while she cracked the whip with the other. I was impressed, but too proud to admit it. Instead, I increased her work load and added extra pressure. I was still unsure if she was cut out for the job. We were already very busy and work was becoming stressful for everyone, and I wasn't sure when HR was going to finish filling the necessary positions in my department.

"Kyle?" Lily walked into my office without knocking.

I scowled at her. "Do you believe in knocking?"

She looked up from the file in her hand. "You're right. I'll knock next time."

"What do you need now, Lily?" I asked tiredly. It had been a long day and a long week. Though I would still be working from home over the weekend, I was anxious to get the hell out of the building for a couple of days.

Lily pushed her glasses up on her nose, forgoing her contacts today. Her hair was pulled up in a messy bun, held together by a couple of pencils. She wore a white shirt with a little black scrap of lace peeking through the opening near her ample cleavage, and a red and navy plaid skirt that fit her like a layer of skin and stopped just above her knees. She wore a pair of navy heels, giving her five-three body an extra four inches of height. The glasses, the outfit, and the hair created the illusion of a naughty school teacher.

Admittedly, working near her was distracting. I thought she was pretty before, but since she let her hair revert back to its natural colors in shades of reds and browns, took out her eyebrow ring, and eased back on the eyeliner her face glowed with a gentle beauty I didn't quite see before. She still wore too many bracelets on her wrists, even when she was wearing a long sleeve shirt, and I was sure she was still very much inked under her clothes. The three tiny stars tattooed just behind her ear were still visible when she pulled her hair back, and every once in a while I would catch a glimpse of her tongue ring. Memories of that studded tongue flicking over mine often had me adjusting myself during the work day. It didn't help matters when she dressed like a school teacher in need of a spanking.

I just need to get laid; I thought as she rounded my desk

and stood beside me. I inhaled the light floral scent that followed her throughout the office and was thankful I was sitting down and my growing erection could be well hidden. I didn't know what was wrong with me, why I was unable to look at her without thinking dirty thoughts. The woman drove me crazy, infuriated and frustrated the hell out of me. I often had the desire to throttle her, yet my body had a different reaction.

"I was looking at the report for the Hillsdale file," she said, laying the file out on my desk in front of me. "There's a huge discrepancy in here, a very expensive discrepancy."

I followed her finger down the report as she read. Her breath feathered over my face. It was scented with chocolate and coffee. I was just beginning to wonder how that would taste when I saw the "expensive discrepancy."

"Shit," I hissed, snatching the paper up. "Who put this together?"

"Samantha Greski," she said, absent mindedly scratching her head. "I checked the computer log to see who did it."

"We can't afford mistakes like this, and this isn't her first."

"Or second or third," Lily said. "I checked on a few of her other files. She's been very careless."

"Fire her," I commanded, slamming the file shut. "And then fix this."

"How about we just move her to another department?" Lily asked, taking the file from me.

Scowling, I leaned back in my chair and looked up at her. "I'm assuming you have a problem firing a person, which is a problem in of itself."

She rolled her pretty gray eyes. "I'm not too soft to fire anyone, Kyle. I just don't think this is the right position for her. She took it because you told her to and she didn't feel like she had much of a choice if she wanted to keep a job."

"You've been in the company for six weeks," I said, and sarcastically added "I'm eager to hear your suggestions."

Entirely too comfortable in her boss's office, Lily turned

and sat her round ass on the edge of my desk.

"I think she should take a supervisor position in customer service," she said.

"Oh, I knew this would be good," I sighed and shook my head.

"You said yourself in her employee reviews that she is dedicated, kind, and eager to please," Lily argued.

"Those reviews are confidential," I growled.

"Yeah, but technically, I'm her boss. That doesn't apply to me. I think she would do really well in a customer service capacity, and if you think about it, you'll probably agree."

I was annoyed that she was sitting on my desk throwing me suggestions about how to take care of an employee after only being with the company for less than two months. I was further perturbed by my own inability to come up with a decent plan to keep Samantha employed instead of hurrying to fire her when in the past I had nothing but good things to say about her.

"You have a week to move her to another position," I said grudgingly.

"Thank you," she beamed. "I'll go tell her."

"When you're finished, have her give you all of her accounts." I smirked and said "You get to spend the weekend fixing all of her mistakes."

Her mouth fell open but only very briefly before she recovered herself.

"Is that a problem?" I asked. "Weekend work will often be a part of your position, even when we are in our slower periods."

"It's fine," she said with a sigh.

"You'll have to save your partying for another time, Miss Whitman," I said, turning my eyes back to my computer screen.

"I suggest you stop making assumptions about me, *Mr. Sterling*," she said. I looked up just in time to watch the door close behind her.

~~~

Monday morning as I walked into my office, Lily followed close behind me carrying my breakfast and coffee and my appointment book. The glasses were gone and her hair was down, but her skirt was shorter than what could be deemed work-appropriate, and the buttons on her light purple shirt looked as if they were about to pop off due to the pressure exerted by her breasts. It took great effort for me to tear my eyes away from those buttons and to look into her tired eyes.

Her eyebrow was raised and I realized that she had caught me staring.

"Would it be more convenient for you if I took my shirt off and worked in my bra?" she asked, setting my breakfast down on the desk.

It would have been just as wise for me to ignore her question as it would have been for her not to ask it in the first place, but I didn't always behave wisely.

"Only if you're wearing the black bra you had on last Friday," I said, without cracking a smile or giving any indication that I was being funny.

"You're in luck," she said, also not giving any indication of being humored. "I just happen to be wearing that very bra."

I almost looked at her chest again. I wondered if her nipples were still pierced and remembered the brief moment my hands had closed over her jeweled breasts, clad in probably the same bra we were speaking of.

I shook myself of my thoughts and quickly sat down before she noticed my erection.

"You look terrible," I said. She looked like she hadn't slept all weekend. "I hope you got more work done than partying."

Lily rolled her eyes and set my appointment book down on my desk with more force than necessary.

"The work is complete, *boss*. You have a nine-thirty telephone conference with Nuland & Smith and a luncheon with Mangini at twelve-thirty. The company car will be ready for you at ten after."

"I'll need you to accompany me on the Mangini luncheon,

but you better drink plenty of coffee between now and then. I don't want you looking as exhausted as you do now."

"Good idea," she said, taking my coffee. She put the mug to her pretty mouth and took a long sip. She licked her plump lips, licking away the tiny drops of coffee that had been left there. It was an innocent action, but I had to quickly sit down to hide how it made me feel. She put my mug back on my desk and without a word walked out of my office.

Holy shit.

I picked up the mug and looked at the light coating of red lipstick that was left on one side. I took a sip where she had taken a sip, and it did nothing to help my erection. I quickly put the mug down and threw myself into my work in an attempt to shake Lily from my mind.

At five minutes after noon, Lily met me in front of my office. She no longer looked exhausted. She appeared alert and full of energy.

"You look better," I told her as we headed to the elevators.

"I took a nap," she shrugged.

I narrowed my eyes at her. "You took a nap on company time?"

"It was necessary. It's not like I shagged my boss in his office on company time. *That* would be *unnecessary.*" She gave me a knowing look, forcing me to abandon the topic.

In the elevator, Lily stepped close to me. Her breasts lightly brushed against me as she straightened my tie and smoothed my shirt. I inhaled her scent as she brushed off my jacket before she nodded approvingly and stepped away.

"Do I meet your approval?" I asked dryly.

"I hate your tie," she said easily. "It looks like something my grandpa would wear, and he's dead. It looks like an old dead man's tie."

I looked down at my red and blue striped tie. Jessyca had given it to me more than five years ago. She was usually very good about fashion, but I had to agree with Lily. It looked like something I swiped out of a thrift store. I was used to wearing it and put it on out of habit. I owned very nice clothes, but I didn't like to spend a lot of time matching shirts with pants or ties with suits. Pretty much anything I threw together without thought matched, even if it was hideous like my tie.

On the way to the lobby, Pete from IT got on the elevator. Pete had been with the company for ten plus years, but I rarely spoke to him. I didn't even know his last name or anything about him, but Lily seemed to quickly have made friends with the man.

"Hey, Pete," she chirped.

Pete beamed down at Lily. I almost made a disgusted sound but stopped short.

"Hi, Lily," he said. His eyes flitted over her body. "You look great."

"Pete, I need something from you," she said, exuding confidence.

Pete's eyes widened, along with his grin. "Anything, sweetheart."

"I need your tie."

"My what?" he asked. The poor sucker probably thought she was going to ask him out on a date. I almost snorted at the idea of gorgeous Lily going out with balding, pudgy Pete.

"Your tie, babe," she said, her fingers already loosening the knot around his neck.

Both Pete and I were dumbstruck at Lily's nerve. Not many women were able to trap a man in an elevator and force him to take off his tie without any promise of kinky play with the accessory.

"Thank you, Pete. I'll return it in a couple of hours," she said as the elevator doors slid open.

"Maybe I can buy you a beer after work and you can return it then," Pete said with too much hope in his tone.

"Sure," she said, but I knew it wasn't just an answer to shut him up as most women would do. I knew she would really have a beer with him in lieu of the borrowed tie. It was both impressive and disgusting.

"You don't have to have a drink with him," I told her as I climbed in the car behind her. "I'll pay him for the use of his tie."

She balanced herself on her knees, practically in my lap as her fingers hurriedly untied my tie.

"I don't mind," she said, her warm sweet breath washing over my face. "Pete's a nice guy."

"Pete thinks you're going to be his girlfriend," I snorted.

"Pete is just lonely. His wife died a couple of years ago and his son just went away to college."

"I didn't know he was ever married," I said, feeling a little guilty for not knowing anything about the man.

"You can learn a lot when you talk to other people about non-work related topics," she said, meeting my eyes.

Emmy had helped me to be more personable at one time, but the stresses of life at that time forced me to become introverted again. I wasn't insensitive to the needs and problems of others. I have helped Sterling employees at my own expense and I often donated to charities, but I never struck up a conversation with the random Pete's, discovering their trials and tribulations.

I watched Lily's face as she wrapped Pete's tie around my neck and tied it. What were her trials and tribulations? She had spoken about having pain on her first day. Was it physical? Was it emotional, and if so, from whom? I wondered how much I could learn from her if I just asked. How much would she be willing to reveal? How much could I *convince* her to reveal if I reached my hand up her short skirt?

The car stopped suddenly to avoid an accident. Reflexively, I grabbed Lily's hip to keep her from slamming into the front seat. Even after the car continued on smoothly, I didn't release her. I had not felt curves like hers since the last time I had the privilege of holding her. Her eyes locked with mine for a second before she put all of her focus into my tie.

"Much better," she murmured, smoothing my tie down my chest. I didn't miss the fact that her hands paused over my pectorals and abs.

I was forced to release her when she sat down on the other side of the car. Her skirt rode up her thighs, revealing creamy, smooth skin. She tugged nervously on the hem, trying to cover herself. We were silent for the rest of the short trip. Lily stared out of her window and I stared at her, fantasizing about her thick thighs wrapped around my waist and her bare breasts pressed up against my bare chest.

When we arrived at our destination, I got out ahead of her and offered her my hand to assist her out of the car. She hesitated, looking at my hand with her mouth slightly open. I urged her on with a quick, firm wave of my hand and she finally put her soft hand into mine. As she climbed out, her skirt rode impossibly further up her legs and I was rewarded with a glimpse of black, lacey panties before she stood up and adjusted her skirt. The October wind whipped her loose tendrils about her face, making her appear wild and uninhibited.

I possessively put my hand on the small of her back and guided her inside the restaurant, hoping no one would notice how aroused this red headed beauty just made me.

Chapter Six

~𝓛𝓲𝓵𝔂~

"Marco, it's nice to see you again." Kyle was shaking hands with a man that must have been chiseled out of stone in the image of the gods.

Mangini was around the six foot mark, with jet black hair, steel blue eyes, and a smile that made me stumble. Fortunately, no one noticed that I grabbed onto the back of a chair to keep myself from falling on my face in front of Mr. Wonderful.

"Had I known you were going to bring a date, I would have brought my own," Marco said, as his eyes fell on me.

Kyle cleared his throat and his business smile faltered for a second. "This is my assistant Lily," he said quietly.

Marco's eyebrows shot up as he looked at Kyle in amusement. "Oh, is our lunch going to be as serious as that, Kyle? You may have warned a friend that we were going to have a *serious* business meeting." He looked away from Kyle and met my gaze. "Ciao, Bella," he said in a smooth tone.

I extended my hand for a handshake, but he engulfed my hand in one of his and brought it to his lips, never looking away from my eyes. Little shockwaves of energy shot up my arm. I'm not a girly girl by any means, but I couldn't stop myself from smiling like a fool.

"Ciao. Come stai?"

His eyes widened in surprise. Out of the corner of my eye, I saw Kyle look at me with bewilderment at first, but then irritation.

"Ora sono molto meglio," Marco grinned.

Yes, I'm much better now, too.

"Why don't we sit down?" Kyle suggested and then his mouth set in a firm line. He forced Marco to drop my hand by forcing his way between us. He pulled out my chair for me and gave me a glare that indicated that I was to sit down immediately. I took my seat and Kyle took the seat beside me.

"How are things at Sterling Corp, Kyle?" Marco asked after we ordered our drinks.

"Improving more each day," Kyle answered with confidence. "We didn't let a few bad apples spoil the whole bunch."

"One of those bad apples is your own father," Marco challenged. "How are you handling that?"

"I'm handling it," Kyle answered tightly.

"How are *you* doing at the company? At one point you were thought to be in on the whole conspiracy."

"You know that I wasn't, Marco. You know what I did."

Marco thought about it for a moment as he tapped the table with his finger. I felt a little uneasy. Things had quickly gone from easy to intense in less than three minutes, and I really had no idea what they were talking about. I knew about Kyle's 'dad' stealing money from the company and investors, and I had heard rumors that Kyle was somehow involved, but it never made since to me. Kyle had a place in the company while Walter Sterling not only lost his place in the company, but had done a little time for his deeds.

"You saved thousands of jobs," Marco acknowledged with a nod. I tried to hide my own surprise at that. I never heard that, not exactly. Now Kyle's words from that long ago morning made some sense.

"And I saved people like you a lot of money," Kyle added.

Marco nodded again. "Yes, you did. So, what do you want from me now?"

"Some of that money I helped you to save," Kyle grinned. I grinned because he grinned. It was one of the rarest sights I had ever seen.

"I should have known when you showed up with the pretty assistant that you were going to reach into my pockets," Marco laughed. "You have plenty of your own money, Sterling. Why do you need mine?"

"I have a project you may be interested in," Kyle said and leaned forward. "I want to develop affordable housing for working middle to lower income families."

I looked at him with bewilderment. I didn't know that Kyle Sterling cared about where the people below his class lived.

"What would I want with housing for the poor?" Marco spit out. "You'll build them nice homes and they'll wreck them. That's what they do. It will become nothing but a hassle and a cesspool for drugs, crime, stupidity, teenage pregnancies and breeding more lower income children that will grow up to be like their disgusting parents."

The image of the man chiseled by the gods was obliterated as I glared at him.

"I resent that," I said sharply.

"Lily!" Kyle snapped.

"No, you're not going to hush me," I snapped back at him before turning back to Marco. "I resent your words."

"Have I insulted you, Lily?" Marco asked casually.

"I grew up in low income housing. There have been more drugs and crimes in your high class society than there ever were in our development. My mother worked her ass off to care for me and my sister, and both of us are college educated and drug free."

"Then you and your sister are an exception," Marco shrugged.

"Why not make us the norm?" I challenged.

"Lily, that's enough," Kyle whispered harshly in my ear.

"Allow her to speak," Marco said casually. "What do you mean make you the norm?"

I took a deep breath before speaking to try and quell my anger and gather my words. I didn't expect to have to do much talking at this meeting. I was there to look pretty, take notes, make appointments, and look pretty.

"Look," I started slowly. "I understand where you are coming from, I really do, but we were very fortunate. The proprietors of our development set very high standards for the tenants and held us accountable for our actions. Sure there were some problems, but nothing too crazy. The development was mostly occupied by working families who wanted more out of life, but the fact of the matter is not everyone can have 'more.' But they always worked for it. Maybe you can have the same type of community. There has to be standards and accountability and you cannot lower the standards or ease back on accountability. You can give people who are willing to work for 'more' that opportunity, and even if they never reach a higher place in life, they will definitely have laid the way for their children as my mother did for my sister and I."

Kyle stopped trying to get me to shut up and was now looking at me with interest. Marco gazed at me from across the table while his fingers continued to tap on the table. The waiter appeared to bring our drinks and take our orders, but none of us had looked at a menu yet. Marco sent him away without taking his eyes off of me.

"Did you have a good childhood, Lily?" he asked.

"Yes, despite living in a 'cesspool of stupidity," I answered sourly.

"You've mentioned a sister and a mother, did you have a father?" Marco asked.

Kyle shifted in his seat, but he didn't stop this line of questioning.

"What does that have to do with anything?" I asked quietly.

"I am trying to get an idea of what kind of people live in these developments," he shrugged.

"My father left us when my sister was only six months old. I was almost two. I don't have any memory of him."

"I'm sorry to hear that," Marco said sincerely.

I glanced at Kyle who was now staring at his glass of iced tea with a distracted expression.

"At least you have your mother and sister," Marco said with a soft smile.

"I only have myself," I responded quietly and picked up my menu.

Kyle was staring at me. I could feel his eyes boring into the side of my face, but he remained quiet.

"In the end, I guess that is all we have," Marco solemnly

said.

I nodded my agreement just as the waiter reappeared to take our orders.

"What do I get out of making an investment into something like this?" Marco asked me and not Kyle after the waiter had gone. "If everyone is middle class to low income, how do I profit from such a thing?"

"I'm not sure what Kyle had in mind," I said. "This is his project not mine."

Kyle took his cue and jumped in. I relaxed into my seat and for the next two hours I sat back to enjoy the ride that was Kyle Sterling while he was talking business. He was animated, bright eyed, and enthusiastic about his proposal. Occasionally, the men would refer to me for my opinion. I didn't see how my opinion mattered, but I gave it anyway. When I wasn't talking, I was eating and drinking Malibu Sunrises. The bartender made them really well –not as well as me, but well enough.

"I have to get back," Marco said later after glancing at his watch. "I have another meeting. I would like to meet tonight for some drinks if you're available. I love the Philadelphia night life. It's unlike any other city in the world."

The two shared a knowing look before they each broke out in a grin.

"Those were good times," Marco said.

"Yes, they were," Kyle agreed.

"We used to party pretty hard," Marco explained to me. "Kyle always got more women than me, thanks to his ultimate dance moves."

My eyebrows shot up as I looked over at my typically moody boss. "*You* have dance moves?" I asked.

He waved a hand. "That was a long time ago," he said dismissively.

"I'll bet he still has them," Marco grinned. "We will persuade him to dance for you tonight, Lily."

"Oh, I'm invited out for the night of debauchery?" I teased.

"Of course," he said, getting to his feet. "I'll call you with the details in a couple of hours."

Kyle stood up and shook his hand. Marco rounded the table as I got to my feet. He embraced me briefly and kissed each cheek.

"Ciao, Bella. Ci vediamo più tardi stasera."

"Yes, see you tonight," I smiled and watched him walk away. "I like him," I announced.

Kyle scowled and then gestured for me to walk ahead of him. He put his hand on the small of my back and guided me along.

~~~

"Do you know anything about your father?" Kyle asked in the car ride back to the office.

I looked over at him a little startled. It was the first he spoke since we left the restaurant nearly twenty minutes before. We were stuck in traffic. I suppose he needed something to entertain him.

"That's a personal question," I remarked.

"Unfortunately, we already have a very personal relationship," he said grimly.

I couldn't stop my sardonic smile. "Yes, I suppose that is true," I said. After a moment I said "My father lives twenty miles from the town I grew up in, where my mother and sister live now," I said quietly as I watched the traffic outside of my window.

I haven't spoken of my father in years, since I was with Gavin, and even then we rarely had reason to bring him up. I was a little uncomfortable speaking to Kyle of all people about something so personal, but he had his own daddy problems. Maybe he understood a little.

"When I was in high school, I went on a quest to find him. I found that he had a wife and four children – two boys and two girls." I finally looked at Kyle. He was watching me with interest. "The oldest is a girl only a few weeks older than my sister. I met her once, completely by coincidence. I went to a party in another town and she was there. Even before I asked her name, I knew who she was. Nina Whitman looked *just like me*. She looked more like me than my real sister Lydia. I lied to her, gave her a fake last name and then I left the party. I walked home five miles in the rain, in the dark so no one would see me cry. I was so *angry* and *hurt*. How could he look at *her* every day and not think of *me*? How could he not think of the baby he left behind?"

The memory was more painful than I anticipated. I felt as if someone had closed a tight fist over my chest. I put my hand there and rubbed softly to alleviate some of the pressure. Kyle looked at me somberly.

"I never went looking for him again. I changed after that. I became a different person. I did everything I could not to look like Nina. I started dressing differently, dying my hair, getting pierced and inked. I wasn't satisfied until I could no longer see her face when I looked in the mirror."

"You've never thought about contacting your father directly?" Kyle asked.

"What for?" I shrugged. "I wouldn't have been able to handle that kind of rejection. He could have found me just as easily as I found him and he didn't. Anyway, he was the one that left."

We were quiet for the rest of the trip back to the office. When the car pulled over, Kyle threw open the door but didn't immediately step out.

"Lily, I'm sorry your father is a jackass," he said sincerely.

I gave him a small smile. "I'm sorry your fake father is a jackass."

He actually smiled at me before stepping out of the car. When he offered his hand to help me out, I didn't hesitate in putting my hand in his. Like in the restaurant, Kyle put his strong hand on the small of my back and led me through the lobby to the elevator. We were alone in the cab, but he stood so close behind me I could feel the heat of his body. I turned around, bumping into him in the process. Kyle was like a rock and unmovable, but I almost fell on my ass. He grabbed me around the waist, saving me from injury for the second time that day.

"You need to be more careful," he murmured, looking down at me.

I nodded gently in agreement and tore my eyes away from his. I started to untie Pete's tie from his neck. "I better get this back to Pete before I forget," I said, trying to ignore the fact that my body was pressed to his.

"You're going to make me put on the hideous tie?" Kyle questioned. His arms circled around me a little tighter.

"You can go without one for the rest of the day. Just leave your shirt unbuttoned some. You'll look like the hip boss," I teased.

The elevator dinged before our floor, indicating that someone else was about to get on. Kyle immediately released me and took a few steps back. Feeling as if I had just done something wicked; I turned back around and faced the doors just as they opened.

~Kyle~

I wanted to pick Lily up from home that night, but she insisted on taking the train into the city early so she could have her promised beer with Pete. I convinced her to at least allow me to pick her up from the bar they were at. When I saw her walking towards the car, I cursed to myself. Her hair was piled on top of her head, revealing those stars on her neck. Her eyeliner and mascara was laid on kind of heavy, but it made her look dangerously sexy. She had on a pair of jeans that she must have painted on, showing off her beautiful ass. It was a warm night for October, so her jacket was thrown over her arm. She wore a tight *Guns N' Roses* t-shirt, perfectly outlining her ample breasts, and she wore a pair of knee high boots that had to be four inches in height.

"Hey," she smiled at me as she climbed into the passenger's seat. "Thanks for picking me up."

I gave her one more head to toe look before pulling into traffic.

"No problem," I said.

"You smell really good," she said, sniffing the air near me.

I scowled slightly. "Do I usually smell badly?" I asked.

"No. You always smell good, but you smell *really* good tonight."

"Thanks," I said flatly.

We were silent for the rest of the trip to the club where we were to meet Marco. We went to the front of the line and I gave my name. The bouncer immediately let us in. I took Lily's hand as I pulled her behind me in search of Marco. I found him a couple of minutes later on the second floor in the VIP section.

I greeted him with a handshake, but he pulled Lily into an embrace, lifting her off of the floor as if *they* were old friends. I tried not to scowl at them as I took my seat. Lily stood by the railing for a minute, looking down at the dance floor as she moved to the music. I had not realized I was staring at her until Marco said something.

"She's really cute. Are you sure you're not hitting that?"

~ 75 ~

Now I scowled as I looked at my friend. "No, I am not hitting that," I said stiffly.

"Not even once?" Marco questioned.

Almost, but no, I thought. "No, not even once, Marco," I said tiredly.

A waitress in a very short skirt appeared to take our drink orders. Lily came back to our sitting area and sat down on the arm of the chair Marco was sitting in instead of the open space right beside me on the couch. I felt like physically moving her over, but I refrained.

"I want to dance," Lily said, wriggling her ass. "Which one of you gentlemen is going to dance with me?"

Boldly, she took Marco's drink from his hand and sipped it. Marco's eyebrows shot up and he winked at me before looking up at Lily's face, but not before he checked out her ass.

"I'll dance with you, Bella," he said. "Unless your boss would like to dance with you first." He looked pointedly at me. Lily looked at me, also, but her expression was doubtful.

"Go dance," I shrugged and flicked my hand indicating that they could run along.

No time was wasted as the pair walked off hand in hand. The waitress brought our drinks and put them on the table. I took my drink and got up to look at the dance floor. *Green Light* by John Legend just started as Lily and Marco moved to the center of the dance floor. They danced with some distance between them at first. Marco was singing the song to her; I could see his lips moving in time with the song. Lily bounced around a little more as she sung Andre 3000's part of the song to Marco. At the end of the song Marco picked her up with one arm and spun her around. Clearly, they were enjoying themselves.

I frowned and ordered another drink.

By the third song, there was no more distance between Marco and Lily. He grinded on her ass as she danced and when she turned around to face him, her arms looped around his neck and his hands slid down to her ass. They were practically screwing on the floor and it was pissing me off. I couldn't explain why it made me so angry, especially since she had the tendency to anger me more often than not. Why should I care who she's grinding on? But I did.

After another few songs, the pair came up stairs, breathless and thirsty. Lily ordered another drink since hers was now watered down. Even as she sat down on the arm of Marco's chair, chatting with him, she didn't stop moving her ass. When her drink came, she drank it quickly, anxious to hit the dance floor again.

"I'll go with you," I heard myself saying as I got to my feet.

She looked at me with surprise, but then shrugged. "Show me your dance moves, boss."

I took her hand and led her down to the dance floor. I don't think I would have been able to watch her dancing with Marco anymore.

Lily was a little slower warming up to me than she was Marco. This pissed me off even further. When she turned her back to me to dance, I put my hand on her waist and roughly pulled her to me. I felt her gasp, but she didn't stop dancing. I let the music flow through us and soon we were moving as one, her body flush with mine as we moved. Surrounded by other moving bodies and under the roving lights, it was hot on the floor. Beads of sweat formed on Lily's neck. I couldn't stop myself from putting my lips on her neck, right on those damn stars and licked away the little beads that had formed there. She froze for a moment and then turned around, but kept dancing. She didn't meet my eyes, but she didn't move away from me when I grabbed her waist again.

When Sean Paul started singing *Temperature*, Lily loosened up again, dropping her ass to the floor with her dance moves, trailing her hands down my chest and thighs. When she turned around again, I was surprised that she bent over, pointing that beautiful ass in my direction. Surprised, but not immobile, I ran my hands up her back and moved them down as she stood upright again. My hands stopped on her ass. Completely out of line, I squeezed her ass before moving my hands back around to her tummy, holding her to me while we danced.

After a couple more songs of completely inappropriate behavior on my part, she stood on her toes and put her hand on my neck so that she could whisper in my ear.

"I need a break," she said.

I nodded and took her hand and led her back upstairs. Marco was talking to a couple of women as we approached, but then he sent them away with a simple wave of his hand.

Lily and I ordered another drink, before she excused herself to use the lady's room.

"I saw you dancing," Marco remarked with a grin.

"So?" I said, narrowing my eyes.

"So, are you sure you're not hitting that?"

I scowled at him.

"Positive," I said through a clenched jaw.

"But you want to," he said.

"We were only dancing," I snapped.

Marco laughed again. "Keep telling yourself that, Kyle."

~~~

I made several mistakes during the night. The first was allowing myself to be bothered by Lily dancing with Marco. The second mistake was taking Lily to the dance floor myself and dancing with her the way I did. The third mistake was licking her neck, and the last mistake was enjoying every moment of it.

Lily was very quiet during the quick car ride to the train station.

"Thanks for the ride," she said quietly with her hand on the door.

"I expect you at work bright and early as usual," I said coldly as I stared straight ahead. "Don't use this night out as a reason to show up late."

I felt her eyes on me, but I didn't look at her.

"Trust me," she said tightly. "I wouldn't want to use my boss's grinding on my ass and licking my neck as an excuse to show up late to work tomorrow."

She threw the door open and had one foot out the door when I said "It was just dancing, Lily. Don't make it into something it wasn't."

She paused for only a moment before getting out of the car and slamming the door. I powered the window down and called to her just as she reached the stairs for the train.

"Try to wear a more work appropriate skirt tomorrow," I said.

Her face grew cold and stony before she turned away and disappeared down the stairs.

Lily was already at work when I arrived early the next morning. She put my breakfast and coffee on my desk without a word and without even looking at me before walking out again. She stayed in her office for most of the morning until she had to bring me a stack of files.

"All of these need to be looked over and signed," she said quietly as she placed the stack on an empty chair. "The priority files are marked with an orange dot."

Again she didn't look at me before walking out of my office. I picked up my phone, poised to call her back in, to make her look at me with those gray eyes, but I put the phone back down. She was my employee and I was her employer and nothing more.

I went back to work and tried to forget about the nagging little voice in my head that was calling me an asshole.

Chapter Seven

~ℒily~

Donna Summer was the friend in my head, because she got it, she really did. I did work hard for my money, and he never did treat me right. The he in question isn't a person for me, though. The he in question is the universe and its infinite desire to consistently screw me over. First tragedy struck in the early summer. Then the bar burned down, quickly followed by my sudden homelessness. My employment under Kyle Sterling was hot and cold, because Kyle was hot and cold. One moment he was cold and telling me how much I suck as a human and the next he was grinding on my ass on the dance floor. The most recent proof of the universe's hatred towards me was the loss of a part time, under the table bar job.

The bar was in a scuzzy neighborhood and the owner was a pig. I warned him several times not to touch me. Giving me a lousy paycheck at the end of the week didn't mean he could grab my breasts. My knuckles were still bleeding from missing his jaw on my second punch and the palms of my hands were scraped from landing on my hands and knees after he literally threw me out. My foot, however, did not hurt after I kicked him in the balls.

Desperate to save money, I hiked through the city instead of taking any form of public transportation until I hit a PATCO station. The night wasn't too cold; it was comfortable enough for a walk, even a million block walk. I was almost to the train station when some douche rag bum rushed me, shoving me into a brick wall and demanding my messenger bag. He had a nice utility knife that I'm sure he could also use to open bottles, cans of beans, and maybe clip his toe nails, but he chose to wave it in my face. I wasn't sure which was worse, the damn knife or his foul breath.

"You're not taking my bag, asshole!" I yelled in his concealed face.

"Give me the bag or I'll cut your ass up," he said in a low

voice.

I struggled against him, kicking him in the shin and punching at his back and arms. He shoved me hard against the wall and tried to rip the bag from me.

"Give me the fucking bag!"

"Go get your own bag, dirt bag!" I shoved at him and he stumbled backward.

"Hey!" A masculine voice shouted not too far away. "Hey, what are you doing to her?"

The rest happened very quickly. The douche rag, determined to get his prize, jabbed his knife at me, slicing my palm as I tried to defend myself. While I gripped at my bleeding hand, he yanked on the strap of my bag, knocking me to the ground in the process. He jerked the bag off of me and took off. I got to my feet just as the stranger who had called out to us reached me.

Angry, furious, adrenaline rushing, I tried to go after the robber, but strong arms encircled my waist.

"What are you doing?" a familiar voice asked. "He just tried to kill you!"

"He took my bag!" I yelled, trying to thrash out of his arms.

"Is that bag worth your life? Hey! Calm the fuck down!"

Frustrated, but resigned to the fact that the perp was probably long gone, I settled down. Reluctantly, the man released me.

"Are you *crazy*?" Kyle yelled.

"I'm not the one who just stabbed me," I snapped, holding up my bleeding hand. "So, no. I'm not the crazy one."

"No, you're the idiot who just tried to chase the guy with the knife that just stabbed you," he said, yanking his tie off. "Give me your hand."

I took a couple of steps back, holding my hand behind my back. "Why should I?" I challenged.

"Do you want to bleed to death on the sidewalk?" He asked, scowling deeply.

"Look, I didn't ask for your help." I pointed with my

uninjured hand. "And I'm not going to bleed to death, you ass."

"Fine," he said. He looked at me like I was street carcass and said "You're on your own."

I gave a small shrug and said "Fine."

He walked by me without another word. I moved into the light of the nearest lamppost to inspect my hand, praying it wasn't as bad as it felt. I couldn't afford a hospital visit.

I was relieved to see it didn't look too deep, but the cut ran from one side of my palm to the other. The bleeding wasn't slowing down and thanks to the dickless wonder that stole my bag, I had nothing to staunch the flow of blood. Maybe Kyle was right. I was going to bleed to death on the sidewalk. Thieves would pick my pockets and steal my clothes, leaving my body naked and at risk of being eaten by stray cats.

"I don't want to be eaten by stray cats," I murmured to myself.

I looked away from my hand when I heard footsteps. It wasn't safe for me to be standing alone on the street at this time of night. It wasn't even safe for me to be walking, clearly exemplified by the jerk who robbed me, but now I was a sitting duck – a sitting Lily.

"I'm not leaving you bleeding in the street," Kyle said, stepping out of the shadows. "Give me your hand. *Now.*" He waited patiently with his hand extended.

"You're not wearing gloves," I said, feeling a little worn down by his evil stare.

"I'll wrap it up until I can get you to a hospital," he said, his tone flat and uncaring.

"I don't need a hospital," I said. "I just need it cleaned and bandaged."

"Maybe the police can convince you to go to the hospital," he growled and I heard him mutter something about being stubborn.

"I'm not going to the police either," I flared. "What's the point? They'll keep me there for hours looking through photos for a guy whose face I couldn't see. It's a waste of my time and theirs."

He sighed louder than necessary. "Fine," he snapped. "Give me your hand."

Reluctantly, I extended my injured hand. I bit my lip as he expertly tied another hideous tie around it.

"I really should go through your tie collection," I said. "This is ridiculous."

He eyed me with indifference before walking away. After a few steps, he turned around and glared at me. "Are you just going to stand there?"

Before I could object, he took my uninjured hand into his in a firm grip and began to lead me down the street. My heart pounded in his presence and under his touch and I could feel it in my injured hand as it throbbed in cadence with my heart. At the next intersection, we swung a right and walked a half a block closer to a group of bars before Kyle hailed a cab. He gave the driver an address in the city, not the New Jersey address I had left him at before.

"I just moved," he said when I gave him a questioning look. "It's not far."

A few minutes later we were deposited in front of a high rise building on the riverfront. A doorman let us into the lobby where Kyle was greeted by name by a smiling concierge. Two guys in security uniforms sitting behind a tall desk nodded at us. Kyle barely acknowledged all three men before ushering me into an elevator and pressing the top button.

Of course he has to live in the Penthouse suite.

In the elevator, I tried to reclaim my hand, but Kyle held fast to it.

"Dude," I said and looked from him to our hands and back to him.

Reluctantly, he released me and pushed his hands into his pockets.

"My place is messy," he said. "I haven't really unpacked yet. It may take me a few minutes to find what I need for your hand."

I shrugged a reply and watched the numbers above the doors light up and tried to ignore the pain in my hand and the moody man beside me staring down at me.

The elevator came to a soft stop on the twenty-fifth floor and the door slid open. I followed Kyle out of the elevator and to one of two doors in the hallway. He unlocked the door and let me in ahead of him.

"Oh my god," I whispered.

I had never been in a penthouse before, but even my imagination couldn't come up with the greatness I saw in Kyle's new home. There were boxes all over the cherry hardwood floors, but that didn't take away from the beauty of the penthouse. The living room, dining room, and the kitchen all flowed together in a great open space. There were no walls to separate guests from their host and the floor to ceiling windows gave a breath taking view of the lit up Ben Franklin Bridge and the city beyond that. There was a bar on one wall, complete with all of the liquor I could imagine, glasses, and stools. It made my heart ache and I was itchy to go play with it.

As I moved in a little further, I saw that there was a secondary living room area with a fire place and more comfortable looking furniture and a television. That room was partially closed off by one wall, but no doors. I quickly realized we were only on the first floor. There was a set of stairs near the second living room that I assumed led to the bedrooms.

"There is also a library and guest space at the end of that hall," he said, pointing past the stairs. "The bedrooms are upstairs."

"This is a lot of space for one person," I murmured, turning in a slow circle as I looked around.

"I had chosen something smaller originally," he said, moving in a little closer to me. "But this one became available. I really like the space."

"I really like it, too," I admitted before meeting his eyes. "But it's pretentious."

His eyes narrowed slightly, but then he looked down at my hand. His tie was soaked through with my blood.

"This way, please," he said quietly.

I followed him down another hallway on the other side of

the stairs to a bathroom that could easily have doubled as a bedroom. He put the lid down on the toilet and gestured for me to sit. He peeled the blood soaked tie off and dropped it in the trashcan.

"I would apologize for the tie, but the world is a better place without it," I said and flinched when he put my hand under lukewarm running water.

"This could have been really bad, Lily," he said with a big frown. His fingers traced over my scraped palms and then my bruising knuckles. "This isn't from the mugger."

"No. That's from a wall," I said pointing at my knuckles. I pointed at my palms and said "That's from getting thrown onto a sidewalk. And that," I said, pointing to the hole in the knee of my jeans.

Kyle's eyes darkened before he kneeled to check out my knee. "Your knee is bleeding, too. Did that asshole at *Earl's* do this?"

I narrowed my eyes at him. "How do you know about *Earl's*?"

"I know a great deal more than you think I do," he said with anger. "When were you going to tell me you have *two* more jobs and that you were sleeping on someone's couch in a slum house in Camden?"

I watched him with my mouth hanging open in shock as he worked on my hand. Every few seconds his intense eyes would bore into mine. I had to wonder what exactly he did know about me, how he found out, and how long he had known. I wasn't a super private person, but there were many things I chose not to share with others. Some things were too painful to share with others – did he know about those things, too?

"Well?" he said, after I didn't respond.

"I didn't think it was any of your concern."

"Anything you do that can affect your work with *me* is a concern of mine, Lily."

"My work is not affected," I argued.

"The hell it isn't," he growled. "When you come to work exhausted, you're unfocused and do shoddy work."

"I don't do shoddy work!" I exclaimed and stomped my foot like a little girl. "I've been working my ass off for you!"

"You can be better if you leave your bartending jobs," he said, slamming a vanity door closed. "You and Mayson insisted that you were more than just a barmaid. You're doing a hell of a job *not* proving your case."

Incensed, I snatched my hand away from him and got to my feet. "Screw you, Kyle."

"Yeah, I'm sure you would love that," he said dryly as he easily pushed me back down into a sitting position.

"Don't make me punch you in the mouth again," I warned.

"I know you're a badass, Lily," he said, as he began bandaging my hand. "But I'm a bigger badass. Remember that."

"Yeah, I know all about it," I said, rolling my eyes. "How did you find out all of that stuff about me?"

"I have my sources."

"Stalker," I murmured. Then something occurred to me. "Did you just *happen* to be behind me when that asshole took my bag, or were you following me?"

"I didn't start following you until several blocks before you got robbed," he said casually.

"You *followed* me?" I yelled and stood up again.

Kyle pushed me back down. "You shouldn't walk alone in the city at the hours that you do."

I put my free hand to my forehead. "Oh my god. You're crazy. You're so damn crazy. The next thing I know you will lead me to some locked up room of pain and chain me to some kind of sex table."

He looked at me with a thoughtful expression. "I don't have a room like that, but I can make it happen."

I narrowed my eyes at him, but said nothing. I should have laughed a little, since it was his attempt at a joke, but I was a little freaked out by his stalking.

"Make sure you keep it clean and dry," he said as he finished with my hand.

"I know how to take care of it," I said and stood up again.

"Take off your jeans."

"What?" I stared at him incredulously.

"Your knee needs to be looked at," he said in a boring tone.

"My knee is fine. It hardly hurts at all."

"Are you always so stubborn?" he questioned with a scowl.

"Do you not think I should be stubborn when a man asks me to pull off my pants?" I challenged.

His scowl deepened. He leaned in so close to me, I could feel his warm breath on my face. "I'm really the only man that matters right now." His eyes flickered down to my jeans and then back to my eyes. "Take off your jeans."

If I were any other girl, I probably would have melted out of my jeans - and my panties. He was so *hot* standing over me, glowering, demanding that I take off my bottoms, and I couldn't deny the sizzle of sexual tension zapping between us. But I wasn't any other girl.

I pushed past Kyle and walked away, lest I lose my pants.

~Kyle~

I leisurely followed Lily to the front door. She was limping slightly, but she was so damn headstrong, she would never acknowledge it. I caught up to her just as she pulled the door open, but I easily pushed it close again and blocked her in with my hands on either side of her on the door.

"Where are you going?" I asked her as I inhaled that floral scent wafting off of her skin.

"*Home*," she snapped. "What the hell are you doing?" She pushed back on me, but I pressed back until my body was pressing hers against the door. I heard her sharp intake of breath and watched her jugular vibrate as her heart pounded in her chest.

"It's really late, and it isn't safe for you to be out alone. Stay here for the night." I didn't give her an option, because it wasn't an option. I wasn't going to let her back out after what had happened to her earlier in the night.

"I'll be fine," she stubbornly said.

I pulled away and spun her around by her shoulders. She looked up at me with large eyes as I again pinned her to the door.

"If I didn't show up when I did, you could be waking up in a morgue right now. So, no. I don't believe you will be *fine*."

She licked her lips and swallowed hard. "He wasn't going to kill me."

"Oh, but he tried," I said. "Your hand got in the way."

She looked away from me and thought about this for a moment. Her body relaxed a little under me.

"Okay," she said. "Maybe you're right. Then call a cab for me or drive me home."

"No," I said simply.

She pushed against me, but I didn't budge. She only succeeded in making me aroused as her curvy body pressed against mine. I knew she could feel it, but she pretended not to.

"You're a bully," she said with a cute little frown.

"You already knew that," I murmured as I traced the tiny

stars tattooed below her ear.

"I have taken down bigger guys than you," she said as her eyes closed on their own accord.

"I don't doubt it," I said and dipped my head to kiss the stars. "But I'm not any of those other guys."

"This is sexual harassment," she whispered even as her hands explored my chest.

I knew I should stop. I knew this could only end badly. I should have known from past experience that sleeping with my employees had terrible consequences, but I had been fighting my growing attraction to Lily since the day she stepped onto the elevator. Honestly, she wasn't easy to forget after that hot morning so many months ago.

She was the complete opposite of the type of woman I would typically be attracted to, rough around the edges inside and out, but it was the rough part I liked the best. I knew she was still inked and pierced, but I wanted that part of her, too. Kissing the stars on her neck drove me fucking crazy. I wanted to discover every aspect of her body - the ink, the piercings, and the curves. I wanted to experience that incredible mouth again and again, with my own mouth, with my cock...

"We should stop," she sighed as I lightly bit her earlobe. "Kyle..." Her hands pressed against my chest. "Kyle..."

I cupped her breasts in my hands and was rewarded with a deep, long groan from Lily's lovely lips. I felt her nipples harden in my palms and I received another reward: feeling the studs that pierced through the sensitive nubs. This time I groaned just before I took her mouth.

I *dreamed* of feeling her studded tongue on mine again. I flicked my tongue over the piercing, making us both moan. I pressed my erection against her as I made her tongue submit to mine. I dragged my thumbs over her nipples, making her cry out into my mouth. I had to get her out of this shirt and see and taste the jeweled buds for myself. I released her from the kiss and *tore* her shirt open. Buttons bounced on the hardwood floor as Lily looked at me with heated eyes.

"You don't really want me to stop," I said haughtily. I

kneaded her lace covered breasts in my hands.

"No, I don't," she panted.

Suddenly, Lily shoved me away. Hard.

I stared at her with my mouth ajar. Like me, she was out of breath. Her lips were slightly swollen and her hair had begun to fall out of the ponytail she had it in. Her shirt hung open, revealing her sexy bra and her soft, padded belly. She looked sexier than ever. I stepped forward to claim her, but she shoved me away again.

"I don't want you to stop, but we *need* to stop," she said, and then pulled her shirt together. "This isn't about me. This is about Emmy."

I cringed at the sound of her name while I had a hardon for Lily. "She doesn't have anything to do with us."

"Oh, but she does," she said pointedly. "You are trying to forget about her and you want to use me to do it. Maybe I seem easy to you, but I'm not."

"Did it occur to you that I find you attractive?" I growled.

"Yes," she nodded. "And you probably do, but I stand by what I said. You are using me to forget her, and I don't want to be *used*."

Was I over Emmy? Absolutely not. I saw her face every day. I missed her, and I wished I could have convinced her to stay. I felt like shit for what I had done to her, and I didn't think I could ever forget that, but I *knew* she was better off where she was. It hurt like hell. It was a sometimes blinding pain that nearly unmanned me. It was extremely difficult to see her happy somewhere else.

I had occupied my time as of late literally chasing Lily. I knew where she was almost all of the time, and when I could I watched her from afar. I don't know what I was looking for with her, but it had become a bit of an obsession since that night out with Marco, a couple of months ago. Stalking after Lily *did* make me forget about Emmy sometimes, but I didn't think I was using her. I was sure that I really wanted her, but then what about afterward? I wasn't ready for a relationship, but I wanted something more than a working relationship with her. There were so many things about her I really liked, and the fact that she had literally saved me the night she drove me home from the bar made me feel a connection to her I couldn't just sever, but I knew if I took her now, I'd just hurt her.

"This isn't about Emmy," I said quietly. "But I would be using you in a matter of speaking, and I don't want you to feel used."

She hugged her shirt to herself. "Thank you. I think."

I put my hands up in surrender. "But please stay here for the night."

After a moment of hesitation, she nodded.

I gestured for her to follow me and I led her to the spare bedroom next to mine.

"You have a bed and a bathroom," I said, flipping the light switch. "There isn't much else in here yet."

"I don't need anything else," she said quietly as she surveyed the room. "Anything is a step up from a couch in someone else's living room."

I pursed my lips, wondering if I should tell her what I knew. She looked at me with trepidation.

"I guess you have some kind of uppity remark about barmaids sleeping on couches in the hood," she said.

"No."

"Then what is it?"

"The boyfriend of the woman you live with is elbow deep in some serious illegal drug action."

Her eyebrows shot up as her eyes widened. "Nate? Seriously?"

"Yes."

"How do you *know* this shit?" she asked, shaking her head in disbelief.

"I know a lot of 'shit'," I answered.

"You're creepy."

"It's not safe for you to be there."

"It's not safe for her children to be there either," she said and bit her bottom lip as she stared at the floor in thought.

"I can't do anything about that, but I can take care of you."

~ 91 ~

She looked up at me with her mouth open. "Take care of me? I can take care of myself."

"You're not doing a very good job at it," I snarled.

"You're such a snob," she snapped. "You would never lower yourself to sleeping on someone's couch."

"Lily, it's not *safe*," I said firmly. "Move in here. I won't charge you rent. You can help me unpack, do my laundry or something and quit those bartending jobs."

"Holy shit, you're insane!" she yelled, throwing her hands up. Her shirt fell open, but she didn't seem to care. "I know my being a lowly barmaid disgusts you, but - "

"It doesn't disgust me," I said, cutting her off. "Your work load at Sterling is getting heavier by the day. You're already working weekends just to keep up. You can't do *all* of it. If your work suffers any more, it will affect me and everyone else that will have to pick up the slack. You have to make a choice." I didn't have to tell her it had to be a reasonable choice, because I believed she was a reasonable person.

"But..." she said, and then bit her lip. She waited a few seconds and tried again. "But I like tending bar. I'm *good* at it."

"You are," I agreed. "And I know about your plans to open your own establishment and I know that you wanted to buy *SHOTZ* from Emmy before it burned down, but working in those sleazy bars isn't going to get you anywhere, Lily."

She let out an exasperated groan and spun in a slow circle.

"Why do you care so much?" she asked. "You haven't given a shit for two years, and you didn't really seem to give a shit when I walked through the doors at Sterling."

"I did give a shit," I said quietly.

"You sure have a way of expressing it," she said dryly.

"I'm trying to prove that I give a shit *now*," I snapped.

"You abandoned me bleeding on a dark city street not even an hour ago!"

"I didn't abandon you. Believe it or not, I went to the next block to see if I would see the creep that cut you."

She looked at me skeptically before looking away at

nothing in particular. She rubbed her forehead with the back of her hand. I couldn't help but to look at her voluptuous body since she didn't close up her shirt.

"So, you want me to quit my bar jobs – or *job* now – and move into your deluxe apartment in the sky," she said. She pulled her shirt together when she caught me staring.

"I will pay you to take care of my home and for whatever else I need that doesn't fall under your current job title."

"Because you *care*," she added sarcastically.

"Yes," I answered. "And I owe you."

She looked at me warily and then said "You still owe me sneakers."

"I will take you shoe shopping tomorrow," I promised.

"And now you owe me a shirt."

"I will replace your shirt," I said, eying the little bit of flesh that wasn't covered.

"You will give me the shirt off of your own back," she said haughtily. "*Now*."

I didn't take my eyes off of her as I undid the cuffs on my shirt and started to unbutton it.

"What if I wake up later and say I don't want to move in or quit my other job?" she asked as her eyes fell on my chest.

"You don't have a choice. Do as I say or I will fire you."

Her eyes widened and her mouth opened so widely I saw her tongue ring glistening in the light.

"That's the deal, Lily," I said as I pulled off my shirt. "Take it or leave it."

I handed her the shirt. She folded it over her arm and looked at me warily.

"You're mean," she whispered.

"But you love me that way," I said. I turned away from her and left her alone in the room.

Chapter Eight

~Lily~

It was nearly noon when I woke up from the best sleep I have had in months. It was going to be really hard to give up the ultra-comfy bed and return to the lumpy couch at Anita's. I didn't really believe that Kyle would fire me if I didn't do as he wanted. It was a bluff and I was calling it.

I reluctantly rolled out of bed as I considered what I was going to do about my current clothing situation. My jeans were probably salvageable, and I could put on one of Kyle's shirts, but it would have been nice to have some clean underwear.

As I rounded the bed, I halted when I saw a neatly folded stack of clothes at the foot of the bed. There was a black shirt, a dark pair of jeans, and a matching bra and panty set. I blushed at the royal blue sheer undergarments and wondered if Kyle had personally selected the items.

I checked the sizes of each thing, and sure enough he had the sizes right. I glanced back at the chair I had thrown my clothes on before going to bed. It was empty. He must have checked my sizes when he took the clothes, but I was still wearing my underwear and bra. I doubted that he had checked those sizes without me knowing. Either he had two lucky guesses or he was a really good stalker.

I left the clothes on the bed and went to use the bathroom. Before I went to bed, there was only toilet paper and hand soap in the bathroom. Now there were big, fluffy towels, wash cloths, an unopened state of the art electric toothbrush, toothpaste, a comb, a brush, ponytail holders, a few hair clips, deodorant, body wash, shampoo and conditioner, a fluffy robe and warm looking slippers.

"Wow," I said as looked at all of the items spread out on the long vanity. "Someone had a productive morning."

It's a shame he wasted his money for the one day I'm here.

I meant to only take a quick shower, but the water was so

perfect under the two shower heads, I couldn't make myself get out until I was all wrinkled. I wasn't going to let that perfect shower, the warm robe, and walk-on-air slippers stop me from confronting Kyle about his bluff. The fact that I actually looked attractive in the bra and panties wasn't going to stop me either.

I marched out of the guest room (after admiring myself in the mirror for ten minutes) in search of Kyle. I found him a couple of minutes later on the first floor in the second living room, typing away on his laptop with ESPN on the large flat screen. This room seemed to be the only room set up completely.

"Hey," I said as I stopped just over the threshold.

"Hi," he said as his eyes roved over me. "How are the clothes?"

"They fit me perfectly. Thank you. Did you go out yourself or did you pay someone?"

He raised an amused eyebrow. "I did it myself. Do you like my selection?"

I knew my face must have turned a shade of pink. "Yes," I said and quickly pressed on. "Listen, I appreciate you stalking me, probably digging up all of my secrets, and looking after me, but I'm not staying here, and for now I will keep my bar tending job."

"Fine. Keep the job - for now - but stay here. You will have a bed, not a couch, privacy, and it's an easier commute to work."

I considered this for a moment while biting my bottom lip. Living with Kyle could have many unpleasant consequences. Working with the man who could simultaneously make me feel blinding anger and fill me with knee-weakening desire was hard enough. Living with him would either lead me to kill him or fall stupidly in love with him.

"Lily," he said as he stood up. He walked over to me and traced a finger over the stars under my ear. "You're trying so hard to take care of yourself and to take care of your family. Let me help you."

"So you know about that," I said quietly.

~ 95 ~

"All of it," he said, and his other hand gingerly touched the bracelets on my wrist.

I pulled my hand away as if he had burned me and took a few steps back. "That is private!" I snapped. "You have no right to know that! What is *wrong* with you?"

I stormed away from him, but he was right behind me.

"*Lily*," he said my name with exasperation. I had one foot on the stairs when he grabbed my arm, but I snatched it away and jogged up the stairs.

"I didn't dig into your life to learn the things I've learned about you," I said angrily, knowing he was right behind me. "It was all dumped on me in one night, but I would never do what you've done!"

"You work for me, I had to know who you are," he argued. He stood in the doorway of the guestroom, watching me as I pulled on my sneakers.

"All you needed to know was that I didn't have a criminal background."

"Which you do," he said pointedly.

"I punched a guy for stealing from me."

"You punched him with a baseball bat," he said in bewildered amusement.

"You should consider that and hope you're not next!"

I shoved him out of the way and started back down the stairs.

"Lily, you're overreacting," Kyle said once again on my heels.

"I'm not reacting nearly as much as I should," I snarled.

When I got to the front door, I started to open it, but Kyle closed it from behind me like he had last night.

"You need to calm down," he said in my ear.

"Kyle, I will *hurt* your balls and leave you on the floor without a second thought. Are you understanding me?"

He pulled my damp hair away from my ear. "I told you last night, Lily. I'm the bigger badass. You don't scare me. Now listen to me."

I struggled to push him off of me, but Kyle was much

stronger than me. He grabbed my arms and pinned them behind my back and pressed me against the door.

"*Listen to me*," he growled in my ear. "Do you know how hard it is for me to do this? To reach out to you and *want* you to be here? Do you realize how hard it is for me to care about you? I wish I didn't. I wish I didn't give a shit what happens to you, but I do. So, do me a favor, Lily, and stop making this harder than it needs to be."

I almost couldn't catch my breath. My injured hand throbbed painfully and my arms began to ache. My chest was twisting with anxiety, but my head was muddled. Kyle once again managed to leave me flaming mad and wanting to hold him at the same time. I needed to get away from him before I either broke his balls or kissed him.

"Let me go," I whispered. "Please."

Reluctantly, he released me. Wisely, he took a few steps back when I turned around.

"I need some space," I said as I tried to get my breathing under control. I reached behind me and pulled open the door. I didn't have my jacket and I forgot my phone on the bed, but I didn't care. Kyle stood stoically still as I slipped out the door.

He didn't follow me.

~~~

When I got off of the elevator, the concierge approached me.

"Miss Whitman?" he asked pleasantly.

"Yes?" I responded and looked at him warily. Did Kyle send him to carry me back upstairs?

"Mr. Sterling has requested that you wait for a car to pick you up to drive you wherever you may need to go."

I had no money on me since it was stolen with my bag. I glanced out of the revolving door. The sky was darkening with swollen rain clouds and the flags at the top of the flagpoles whipped back and forth in the wind. Hugging myself, I looked at the concierge and nodded my approval.

I sat down on a wing backed chair, waiting for the car to arrive. I wasn't sure where I was going to go. I didn't have anywhere to go really. My oldest friend lived in Ohio, and any friends I had made since moving to Philadelphia years ago mostly disappeared after my life fell to shit several years ago. The few that remained were good for hanging out for a dinner or a few drinks from time to time, but I couldn't go to them with my deeply personal problems. I was pretty much alone almost all of the time and I had become accustom to that. Having Kyle of all people diving that deep into my life threw me off.

"Ma'am," the concierge said minutes later and gestured to the black Escalade with tinted windows outside at the curb. By the time we got outside, the driver was standing at the open back passenger door.

"Ma'am," he said as I slid in the backseat.

He rushed around to the front and climbed inside.

"Miss Whitman, my name is Corsey. Where would you like to go?"

"Umm," I sighed. "I'm not really sure. Can we just drive? Are you able to do that?"

"I can drive wherever you want to, Miss Whitman. Would you like to stay local or would you like me to go over the bridge?"

"Over the bridge is fine," I said, settling back into my seat.

"Is there any particular music you're interested in for the ride?" Corsey asked as we pulled onto the main road.

"Whatever you put on will be fine."

I looked down at my hands. The half dozen bracelets I wore on each arm drew my attention to scars hidden by the jewelry. I didn't know how Kyle found out about them or how long he had known. It was a very, very personal part of my life that I liked to not only keep hidden from others, but from myself. When the bracelets did come off my wrists, I never looked at the scar tissue there. It was a reminder of all of my failures, my darkest moments, and my most grievous losses…

Gavin and I were high school sweethearts when we moved to Philadelphia to attend college together. I took a job at a seedy bar in South Philly and Gavin took a part time position

~ 98 ~

waiting tables. We had many ramen noodle dinners, freezing winter nights under threadbare blankets, and there were many roach and mice massacres in our tiny apartment, but we were happy.

Though we were pretty careful, we weren't careful enough and I became pregnant towards the end of our third year together. I cried about it for days, until Gavin finally convinced me that giving birth to his spawn wasn't the worse thing in the world. My trepidation was replaced acceptance and my acceptance leaped into excitement. There were going to be many sacrifices, especially on my part. I was going to graduate late because the baby was due half way through my last year. Life was going to be rough for a little while, but Gavin was in the top twenty of our class and I had absolute confidence that he would find a good position in a firm soon after graduation. Even if he didn't, we knew we loved each other and our baby so much that we would do whatever was necessary to be a safe and happy family.

When I was only six months pregnant, I went into labor. By the time I understood what was happening and got to the hospital it was too late. I gave birth to a baby girl. We named her Anna. Two days after Anna came into this world, she died. I was beyond devastated. There are not enough words in any dictionary in the universe to describe the level of pain and suffering parents feel after they lose a child. We never even had the chance to get to know her.

Gavin pressed on, focusing on school in order to bury his pain, but I didn't press on. I stayed in bed for months, living under a heavy black cloud that was slowly crushing me. I felt like I had lost part of my soul. Only Gavin's love and care kept me from disappearing into that darkness forever.

As graduation for Gavin neared, I realized that I needed to be there for him. I wanted him to know I was happy and proud of him, especially since he landed a job a month before graduation. I tried very hard to just live through my pain and make the best of our time together. The new position was back in Ohio and I still had to complete my last semester. I wasn't thrilled about heading back to Ohio, but at least we would be in Cleveland and still enjoy city life.

Gradually I came back to life and Gavin moved back to Ohio. We talked a few times a day and alternated visits between Philly and Cleveland once or twice a month. My younger sister Lydia was also in Cleveland at that time, going to college there. Sometimes Gavin brought her with him when he visited, and I was glad to know that they had each other's friendship there in Ohio in my absence.

As the anniversary of Anna's death drew near, I felt myself sliding back into that dark haze. I wasn't sure if I'd be able to pull out of it on my own, so I decided to fly to Cleveland for a few days. Gavin would make me feel better. Gavin would keep the darkness from swallowing me entirely. I didn't tell him I was coming home. I decided it quickly and was on the next available flight out. I figured I'd surprise him and the pleasant surprise would be good for both of us. The surprise wasn't just in my arrival, however. It was also in what I found waiting for me in the apartment that was supposed to be ours.

It was around six-thirty when the cab dropped me off in front of the apartment building. As I climbed the steps to the second floor unit, I heard Lydia's and Gavin's voices from inside. I couldn't hear what they were saying and I didn't even find it suspicious. I was glad she was there with him so close to the anniversary of our daughter's death. I got to the top of the stairs. The pair was in the kitchen, and from the smells wafting out of the apartment, they were cooking together. Interesting, but not suspicious. I had just put my hand on the door to open it when Lydia wrapped her arms around Gavin's neck and the two kissed, deeply, and passionately. It didn't seem like it was the first time.

I inhaled sharply. Lydia must have heard me because she pulled away and looked right at me. Her mouth fell open in surprise, forcing Gavin to look, too. The rest of the details are gritty. I had screamed and cried and shouted hateful things at both of them. Gavin tried to hold me and comfort me, but there was no comfort to be had. I was completely shattered inside. My pain was just as deep as it was the day Anna had died, except now there was no one to save me.

I tried to take my life in that same hour that I discovered them. I had locked myself in the bathroom with a large kitchen knife. The pain was excruciating, but it didn't compare to my emotional pain. Gavin eventually broke the door down to get to me. I died twice that day, and though I physically recovered, a large part of me was still dead.

The last time I saw Gavin was the day before my release from the psych facility I ended up in for forty-five days. I had requested a very strict visitor's list, only allowing my mother to visit me, blocking out Lydia and Gavin. I allowed Gavin to come in on the last day, though. He sobbed through his apologies. He and Lydia were going to tell me. They didn't mean to hurt me. They both loved me very much. He was so scared to find me bleeding on the bathroom floor. I cried while listening to him, but I didn't speak until his visiting hour was almost over.

"I hope that whenever you die, it's slow and painful. Then you will know how I feel."

Gavin married Lydia six months later, two months before their first child was born. They had two more children over the course of six years. He and Lydia sent me holiday cards every now and then, which I promptly threw away, but I didn't speak to either one of them again after I left Ohio seven years ago. On their seventh wedding anniversary, on their way home from dinner, Gavin and Lydia were in a terrible car accident. Gavin died a week later. Lydia's injuries were so extreme, she will never be able live a pain-free life or walk without assistance again.

I was devastated by Gavin's death, even though I had not spoken to him since that last day in the hospital. I felt like his week of suffering was a direct result of the last words I had ever said to him. The guilt weighed me down, threatened to pull me back into the abyss, but it was what he left behind that made me pull myself together.

My mother, who had moved to Philly to watch over me after my suicide attempt, gave up what little she owned and moved back to Ohio to help my sister with her children. I refused to go to Gavin's funeral, and I still refused to talk to my sister, but my mother was struggling trying to care for Lydia and the kids. I never met any of the kids, knowing that I would be reminded of Anna, but they were Gavin's children, and Gavin was once my only reason for breathing. So, I gave up almost all of what I had, too, to make sure that his children would be clothed, fed, and have anything children should have. I send them nearly half of what I earn every month. Lydia tried calling me several times to thank me and to try to make amends, but I didn't want to talk to her, because what I was doing wasn't for her. It was for Gavin's kids.

When *SHOTZ* burned down, my dwindling financial security went with it. I had hoped that Emmy and I would work something out so that I could take ownership of the bar. It would provide me with more income to take care of the kids, but also give me some collateral to work with so that I could get the money needed to make the bar into the establishment I wanted it to be. I was half way through college when I knew I wanted to open my own, but with *SHOTZ* gone and nothing to work with, it was going to take a while longer to realize my dream, but my first priority was Gavin's kids.

Kyle made valid points, I realized. My friend's house in Camden wasn't necessarily safe. Who would help the kids if something happened to me as a result of being there? I could get hurt or killed anywhere, obviously, but why put myself in harm's way? Not to mention that living at Kyle's would save me the money I use for traveling to and from work, and if I worked for him by taking care of his home I would probably make more money than I did basically working for tips tending bar.

There were other things to consider if I was going to live with Kyle. He was sometimes an epic asshole, and his latest stalking bit was unsettling. I felt that he was hot and cold at times, one minute he wanted to be my friend/lover and the next he was pushing me away, trying to convey to me how worthless I was. I didn't think he was going to change his mind after a week and throw me out on my ass, but I could easily see him withdrawing from me and treating me like crap. I believed he was a very troubled man, that he craved to be loved and cared for, but he didn't think he was worthy. I knew his failures with Emmy was part of it, and of course his idiot faux father, but there had to be more, but unlike Kyle, I wasn't going to use enormous resources to dig up his past and use it in my favor.

I also had to sort out my feelings for Kyle if I was going to live with him. Sometimes I really wanted to break his big mouth on his gorgeous face and shut him up for a while, but then that would prevent any possibility of feeling that obnoxious mouth on my own. My feelings for Kyle had grown exponentially since I started working for him. While I was able to see past his hard outside exterior, I *liked* that hard outside exterior. It was part of the package that made him so desirable to me, but even though it had been two years since he was in a relationship with Emmy, he was still reeling from it. He was still hurting and still self-loathing for what he had done to her, and if she showed up at his door on any given day asking for another chance he would most likely give it to her. Where would that leave me? I had avoided any kind of serious relationship since Gavin, because I wasn't over what he and Lydia did to me. Even when I thought I was at least past it enough to date, I tended to date men I wasn't really attracted to so that there was no chance in my getting hurt. Getting involved with Kyle would be a whole other story. I was extremely attracted to him and I knew he probably would definitely hurt me, even if unintentional.

I peeked up front at the dashboard. We had been driving around for almost two hours. Corsey was really quiet and hadn't spoken once during the ride. I occasionally heard him humming along with a song, but he allowed me the quiet that I needed to think things through.

"Corsey, can you drive me to Camden?" I asked.

"Sure thing, Miss Whitman," he said with a nod and a

smile.

I started to settle in my seat again when a thought occurred to me.

"Do you work for Mr. Sterling directly? You got to the building very fast."

It would have actually surprised me to know that Kyle had a car service. He was often pretentious, but the only time I had ever seen him being driven around was when it was work related.

Corsey looked in the mirror at me for a few seconds. I found this suspicious.

"I do work for Mr. Sterling directly," he said evasively.

"But I'm his personal assistant," I said. "I've never seen you before today. You're not listed in any of the contacts I have for Kyle."

"Miss Whitman, you will have to have this discussion with Mr. Sterling," he said with finality.

I looked at him with suspicion. What the hell was the big secret? Did he only drive Kyle to super-secret Sterling Corp meetings? Was he an accomplice in some kind of sex ring? What the hell?

Then it dawned on me.

"When Kyle can't personally follow me around, you do it," I said and watched for his reaction.

His eyes glanced at me in the mirror, but he said nothing.

"Well, then," I said, feeling a little perturbed. "I guess I don't have to tell you the address, do I?"

"No, ma'am."

Yep. I was definitely going to hurt Kyle's balls.

~Kyle~

I stood with my hand on the door, resisting the urge to go after Lily. I had never meant to *feel* anything for her, and I sure as hell didn't expect to *feel* regret for my actions that so obviously hurt her. My intentions at first were professionally motivated. I wanted to be sure she had a clean background before entrusting her with the more sensitive aspects of Sterling Corp and my personal life. I was surprised to find that she was sleeping on someone's couch in the ghetto, so I dug a little deeper to make sure there wasn't a drug, alcohol, or gambling problem. Soon I was peeling off layer after layer of Lily's life until I was completely obsessed with this seemingly selfless woman. I wasn't worthy of her or her friendship, but she had given up so much I wanted to give her something in return. But like I often do, I fucked that up, too.

I should have never touched her. I should have never lost control like that. I had to stop acting on my impulses. Kissing Lily was an unmet experience. Hearing Lily's moans of pleasure and feeling her hands on my body are experiences that I can compare to nothing or no one else, including Emmy. It wasn't just that she was being physically stimulated, but I could almost taste her feelings for me in her kiss, feel her heart beating for me in her fingers. Her eyes hid nothing, and I took advantage of that. I had to keep my hands and lips to myself, but her body practically screamed my name every time I was near her and it was extremely difficult for me to ignore. I tried to be an even bigger ass to deter her, but she managed to break through those walls with very little effort.

Several times in the office, I had wanted to bend her over my desk and let her feel what she did to me, but what was worse was there were even more times that I wanted to just wrap my arms around her and hold her. I wasn't sure which one was more dangerous, but either way, I had to learn to keep my hands to myself. I would give her a safe and secure place to live until she was able to take better care of herself, but I had to try to be as neutral as possible, or I would only end up breaking her as I did Emmy. That was my forte. I broke things, and Lily would be no different.

I moved away from the door and pulled my phone out of my pocket. I called the concierge and then called Corsey. I waited patiently by the large windows in my living room until the concierge called me back to tell me Lily got into the Escalade. After the sensitive memories I forcefully unveiled for her, I didn't want her wandering around the city alone. At least this way I would know where she was and that she was in safe company.

~~~

I was dreaming about Emmy again. She was wearing the blue dress she wore the night of the gala. I was running my hands over her smooth, soft bare back as I danced with her on the dance floor. I held her close and sung Wonderwall *with the band softly in her ear. It felt so real. I could feel the curves of her breasts pressing against my chest. I could smell her skin and her hair and I could feel her breath on my neck.*

"I love you," she whispered. "You're all I want. Just you."

"You have me, Em," I said.

"But I really don't, do I?"

Her tears dampened my shirt. I could feel them on my skin and they seeped into my chest, through bone and tissue and into my heart.

"I'll give you anything you want," I promised her.

"Except yourself."

The one and only love of my life untangled herself from my arms and turned her back on me. I didn't even get a glimpse of her face before she walked away. I was helpless to go after her. My feet were glued to the floor and my arms were pinned at my sides. I couldn't even reach out for her. My voice was immediately absorbed into the dead space around me as I called to her uselessly. I could do nothing but watch as the crowd parted for her and then swallowed her whole.

When I was finally able to move, everything around me grew dark. The crowd, full of familiar faces, looked at me with menacing eyes as they advanced. I knew if I didn't get away from them, and get back into Emmy's light, I would die. Maybe I deserved to die, but I didn't want to die, but as their hands began to close over me, I knew I didn't have a choice in the matter...

Breathless, I jolted upright in my bed, searching the dark for Emmy in her blue dress. I clawed at my chest in an attempt to get air moving through my lungs again. My heart pounded so loudly, it almost drowned out the sound of my panicked gasps. Movement in the doorway caught my attention, but it was so dark. It just looked as if the darkness was moving towards me. In my half-sleep state, my panic grew. A soft hand landed on my chest and gripped at my hand and half a second later the room was bathed in light.

Lily stood before me with her wide gray eyes.

"Hey," she said, touching my face. "It's okay. You were dreaming."

"Fuck!" I managed to gasp out.

"I'll go get you some water," Lily said softly. "Better yet, a shot of whiskey."

She started to pull away, but I held fast to her hand. I've had so many nightmares in my life, and not once has anyone been there to help me return to reality. I wasn't going to just let her walk away. Chances were that she wouldn't return.

Without any hesitation, Lily sat down on the bed and gently pushed me back so that I was lying down once again.

"Close your eyes," she gently commanded.

"I can't," I answered even as my breaths began to regulate.

"You're not even really awake, Kyle," she said. "Close your eyes."

"Stay here." I squeezed her hand in warning.

"I will stay here as long as you want me to. Now sleep."

Her other hand was in my hair, caressing and comforting. My eyes grew heavy, but I didn't want them to close. I didn't know what I would see. I didn't know if I'd see Emmy bruised and battered. I didn't know if I'd see my brother's dead body. I didn't know if I'd see my mother on the bathroom floor, bleeding and at the brink of death. I didn't know if I'd see the depths of hell, waiting for me.

As I struggled to keep my eyes open, I looked up at Lily. She offered me a small smile when I didn't deserve it after what I did to her. She could have left me drowning in my nightmare in the dark, but she didn't. I should have pushed her away, because I didn't deserve her, but I didn't have the energy to do it. Just before sleep took me completely again, I realized that Lily, like Emmy, had her own light.

~~

Sunlight poured through the skylight, bathing my room in a bright light. I blinked up at it for a moment, trying to figure out what time it was. I looked over at the clock on the bedside table. It was after ten in the morning, the latest I could remember sleeping in a very long time. I felt the need to stretch, but I didn't want to disturb the sleeping form curled around my body.

My memory of the night was slightly muddled, but I remembered the nightmare and I remember Lily appearing out of the darkness like some kind of Dream Super Hero. I felt like a pussy for my behavior and the things I said. I wondered if I peeked into my boxers if I would discover I had grown my very own vagina, but the obvious growing monster stretching the fabric debunked my whole vagina theory.

I needed to get up and get away from Lily, despite how fantastic it felt for her leg to be draped over mine, her arm across my body and her head cradled in the crook of my arm. I was surprised that she had even come back the night before. I knew I'd have to keep my hands to myself and I didn't want to make her change her mind by trying to slide between her gorgeous thighs.

Just as I started to untangle myself from Lily, her eyes fluttered for a few seconds and then opened. She blinked up at me with those damn gray eyes and my resolve to get away from her left me. I made a slight adjustment and bent my head to gently touch my lips to hers. I gave her a single, lingering chaste kiss and pulled back to gauge her reaction. Her brow

~ 108 ~

was furrowed in concentration. Her eyes were stormy, but heated. I used two fingers to tip her chin. She didn't stop me when I moved in to kiss her again. I slid my tongue along her bottom lip, getting a preview of her gorgeous mouth. I nipped at her lip, eliciting a light groan from her. I laced my fingers in her hair and sought out Lily's ornamented tongue with my own. Her hands gripped the back of my head and we both moaned as the kiss deepened.

I put my hands on her hips and pulled her on top of me. Her hair formed a sweet scented veil around us as our tongues performed a perfectly orchestrated dance. Her mouth was warm, sweet, and addicting. Unfortunately for me, Lily as a whole was becoming rather addicting. I pulled away from her mouth and immediately missed it. I put my hands in her hair, pulling it off of her face so I could look at her. She sat up straight, straddling me. We groaned together when her cloth covered pussy connected with my erection. I cupped one side of her face and dragged my thumb across her plump lips. She leaned into my touch and reached up to press my hand with both of hers. That was when I saw her bare wrists, lacking in the bracelets she was never without.

"When did you take the bracelets off?" I asked her, though it probably wasn't the best time to ask.

She seemed to remember she was no longer wearing them. Redness seeped into her cheeks as she put her hands down and pressed them to her sides. "Last night," she said and then bit her lip.

"I'm sorry I brought up painful memories," I said, running a hand through her hair.

"Thank you for apologizing," she said and then smiled wryly. "Now I don't have to hurt your balls."

I narrowed my eyes at her and then I made her screech when I flipped her over onto her back. I leaned down and took her mouth again with a groan. I sat up far enough to pull her shirt off, getting another shriek out of her. I groaned again when I discovered she wasn't wearing a bra, revealing a very well-endowed set of breasts. They were perfect in shape and size, each one more than a handful even for my hands, and her studded nipples only made them more enticing. There was nothing between my mouth and her jeweled breasts.

"Fucking beautiful," I groaned before I leaned down to run my tongue over one of her hard nipples.

Lily moaned loudly as my tongue flicked over her piercing. I covered the bud with my mouth and slowly sucked it in, making Lily curse under her breath before moaning again. I reached up with my other hand and pushed my thumb between her lips. She eagerly sucked on my thumb. I couldn't wait until I could feel those lips wrapped around my cock. I pulled the thumb out of her mouth after a moment and swiped it across her other nipple.

"Oh my god," she groaned as I dragged my damp thumb repeatedly across her hard nipple.

I switched sides, paying equal attention to her other breast. Lily moaned and writhed under me as her fingers wove through my hair. Feeling Lily's adorned nipples against my tongue came second only to feeling Lily's adorned tongue against my mouth. So, I didn't forget what that felt like, when I was done with her rigid nipple, I kissed her again as I grinded my cock against her.

Soon I was moving down her body, leaving a trail of kisses between her breasts, down her belly and over her pierced belly button. Slowly, as if I were pulling the wrapper off of a delectable treat, I pulled on her shorts. Immediately I saw what looked like tattooed vines licking at her sides, following her curves and ending just above her pubic bone. They were part of a much bigger tattoo on her back that I had yet to see, but I thought they were sexy and I made a point to follow each one with my tongue before I finished pulling her shorts off.

After Lily's shorts and panties lay in a heap on the floor, she suddenly got up on her knees and started to pull my t-shirt off. She threw the shirt across the room before wrapping her arms around my waist to hold me close while she kissed and nipped at my chest. I grabbed a handful of her hair and yanked her head back and attacked her mouth with my own.

Her fingers pulled on the elastic waistband of my boxers and seconds later her hand was on my cock.

"Lay down," I commanded.

She gave my chest one last bite, before doing as she was told while I quickly removed my boxers. I smoothed my hands over her thighs and gently parted her legs. I dragged a finger through her folds and pressed it inside her moist heat. She watched me with hooded eyes, biting on her bottom lip. I pulled out my finger and held it up so she could see how wet she was. I reached up and rubbed her moistness on one of her nipples. Lily moaned and licked her luscious lips as her gray eyes bore into mine.

Holding her gaze, I slowly pushed three fingers inside of her. Her wet canal was tight around my fingers and seemed to get tighter the further I pushed them in. When my fingers were as deeply inside of her as they would go, I pulled them almost all of the way out and then slammed them back in. Lily shrieked and mindlessly pushed back against my hand. I pulled my fingers out again, loving how wet they looked and slammed them back again. With my other hand, I pressed my thumb over her clit. Lily's hips shot up off of the bed as she cried out. I took the opportunity to slam my fingers back inside of her again. I started to fuck her with my fingers, fast and hard while pressing on her swollen clit.

"Come for me, baby," I growled and held my fingers deep inside of her, flicking my fingers against her sensitive spot and pressing hard on her clit.

Lily's hips bucked against my hand as she came, calling out my name like a mantra. Her vaginal walls became impossibly tighter as they squeezed my fingers almost to the point of pain. I pulled my fingers out of her slowly as she came down from her orgasm. I slipped all three into my mouth and groaned. I moved over her body and leaned down to kiss her. She wrapped one leg around my waist and my cock nestled between her wet folds. I gently rocked my hips, rubbing the length of my manhood along her slit.

I gazed down at her. Her gray eyes were full of desire

and affection. I knew if we continued, Lily's feelings for me would intensify. Hell, I knew my own feelings would intensify, but I wasn't able to give her what she needed. After all she had been through with losing Anna, Gavin, her sister, and in a way her mother, Lily needed someone to commit to her, to take care of her, make her feel safe and make her happy. She needed an unselfish man to cherish her, put her on a pedestal and love her unconditionally without any real risk of ever hurting her. She was broken, and since I, too was broken, I wasn't the one to fix her.

I was finally thinking with my head and maybe my heart, but I was so close to sinking inside of her. My body was at war with my sensibility, just as it was with Emmy the night of the gala. I had her trapped in the kitchen, and I wanted nothing more than to melt into her – body and soul – but my life was complicated and hers wasn't, and I didn't want to complicate her life. She brought some light to my dark life and I didn't want to extinguish it. Even after she gave me permission via her tender touch, I almost didn't continue. Sometimes I wish I hadn't. I wouldn't have become a nightmare for her. I didn't want to become yet another nightmare for Lily.

I needed to keep Lily in my home to keep her safe, but I needed to make sure that she didn't love me. If I hurt her now, it could save her a great deal more amount of pain later.

Without warning, I rammed my cock inside of her beautiful cunt. Lily screamed and clawed at my back as my erection filled her and stretched her. I moved inside of her slowly at first. I knew I'd have to be an ass, but I didn't need to add insult to injury and hurt her physically.

It was hard to control my rhythm with Lily. I loved how her curvy, naked body felt under my own, and I couldn't get enough of feeling her hard, studded nipples rubbing against my chest. Her sex was tight, wet, and warm. I had never felt anything so fucking glorious in my life. It felt as if Lily's whole body was made for my own. It was nearly impossible to believe that I once questioned her attractiveness.

"You're so beautiful," I moaned before kissing her deeply. "So, fucking hot," I groaned a moment later.

"Can I make this ride go any faster?" she teased with my nipple between her teeth.

I looked at her with amusement. "This ride can go faster *and* harder," I said and then rammed my cock inside of her.

"Before I fall asleep of absolute boredom, I suggest you find a way to make me come," she panted.

"Are you insulting my sexual prowess?" I growled as I leaned down to pull one her nipples between my teeth.

Lily groaned and pushed her hips up to meet my thrusts. "You have sexual prowess?"

I bit down a little harder on her nipple, making her yelp in surprise.

"Enough talking, baby," I said as I pulled her legs up to my shoulders. I pulled out until just the tip of my cock was at her entrance.

"Yes, enough talking," she said. "Show me – *holy shit!*" she screamed as I slammed into her balls deep.

"Oh, *fuck*," I growled as I slammed into her again.

Lily cried out in pain or pleasure, or maybe both, but she didn't ask me to stop. She held onto me as I fucked her hard and fast, as per her request.

"I want to hear you come," I commanded as I rolled a nipple between my fingers.

"Don't tell me what to do!" she yelled even as her pussy clenched onto my cock. Seconds later she was falling apart beneath me, screaming, near sobbing, and groaning out my name as her body seemed to pulsate with her orgasm.

Before she had time to recover, I rolled over, pulling her on top of me and impaling her on my cock. Lily threw her head back as she came again. Her hips involuntarily grinded against me until her orgasm began to subside. I held onto her waist and started to pump my hips, drilling my cock inside of her.

"You look so fucking hot when you come," I panted as

I reached up with one hand to touch her gorgeous face. Her hair was wild around her face. Her eyes were stormy and her cheeks were red. Her lips were swollen from all of the kissing and I wanted to kiss her some more. I shifted our bodies until I was in a sitting position with her legs wrapped around me. I grabbed a handful of her hair and pressed her head to mine. Lily moaned into my mouth as I continued to push my cock inside of her.

Lily's fingers lovingly caressed my face, my head, my neck, and my back. It wasn't just the heat of the moment coursing through her fingertips and the palms of her hands. I didn't believe I was overanalyzing or being arrogant. It was the same way I used to touch Emmy, trying to show my love through touch. Lily loved me. I had to fix that.

My orgasm was imminent. I kissed her harder as I bored into her harder. She wrapped her arms around my neck and her cries of ecstasy were lost on my tongue. With a deep growl, I began to come. As I shot stream after stream of cream inside of her magnificent body, I realized I loved her. It was on the tip of my tongue to tell her, but I stopped myself just in time. Loving her would only bring her enormous pain later. So, I ended what could be before it could even begin the only way I knew how.

As my cock spurted out the last bit of semen inside of Lily, I groaned out the one word to end it all.

"Emmy."

I stared down at Kyle in disbelief. He looked up at me, confused at my expression at first, but then realization crossed over his face and he looked just as horrified as I felt.

"I'm sorry," he blurted out.

I slapped him hard across the face with my injured hand and scrambled off of him.

"I *knew* it!" I screamed as I gathered my clothes off of the bed and floor. "I *knew* it was about her! You bastard!"

"Lily, I'm sorry," he said, and it sounded as if he meant it, but it didn't matter.

"For a little while, I actually believed it was about me," I laughed cynically. "How could I be so stupid?"

Kyle had pulled his boxers on. He was standing in the middle of the room watching me with a blank expression on his face, as if he was viewing the weather report for a region that had nothing to do with him. I didn't even bother getting dressed before I raced out of his room. I went into the room that was now temporarily mine and tried to slam the door behind me, but when I turned around Kyle was in the doorway, holding the door open. His eyes drifted to what was left of my life that I retrieved from the house in Camden, a few boxes and a couple of suitcases stacked close to the door.

It was his home. I would not tell him where he could and could not go in his own home, but I didn't have to acknowledge him. With an ache in my chest that made me want to vomit, I dropped my clothes on the floor by my bed and went into the bathroom. Kyle followed as far as that doorway, where he leaned against the doorjamb with his muscular arms crossed over his chest. Continuing to ignore him, I stepped into the walk-in shower and closed the door, giving myself very little privacy through the glass. I turned it on and adjusted the temperature until it was just what I needed. I tried to pretend that Kyle's distorted form wasn't on the other side of the glass as I closed my eyes and willed myself not to cry.

After Corsey took me to pick up my things in Camden

the night before, I went to work at *Steve's*, the bar I was working at on weekends and some weekdays with Vic. I told Steve I'd work the weekend, but after that I was finished. I was already thinking about the work that I needed to do for Sterling and how it was going to start to take up a significant portion of my time. At first Vic was cool with my decision, but when I told him I was going to be living at Kyle's, he became hostile and angry. After the emotional rollercoaster Kyle had put me on earlier in the day, the last thing I had needed was to hear any of Vic's bullshit. I fought with him for the rest of the night. He had even followed me out to the Escalade, still bitching, but when Corsey got out of the vehicle and stood in front of me, Vic backed off and promised we'd finish the conversation later.

"He's a dangerous man," Corsey said after a few quiet moments in the truck. I had convinced him to allow me to sit in the front seat like a big girl.

"He's an asshole," I agreed, staring out of the tinted window.

"I mean he is *dangerous*," Corsey stressed. He looked over at me and I stared back at him, waiting for him to elaborate. "Please, Miss Whitman, don't ever find yourself alone with that man. Trust me."

I didn't feel like trying to pull answers out of him. I just nodded my compliance and went back to looking out of the window.

"Does Kyle know I'm coming?" I asked a few minutes later.

"I'm not sure. I called him about an hour ago but the call went to voicemail. He hasn't called me back. He probably fell asleep."

"Does stalking make one sleepy?" I asked dryly.

"If stalking you was the only thing he had to worry about, I'm sure he would have plenty of energy, Miss Whitman," Corsey said carefully in defense of his boss. "He is a hardworking man with multiple problems. One day you will appreciate that he is looking out for you."

This shut me up. I didn't want to come off as

unappreciative, but the whole thing was a little creepy. It was the kind of thing I only read about in books or saw on television. I didn't know men like Kyle actually existed.

Corsey helped me get my things inside the penthouse and up into my room and then left for the night. I wanted to take a quick shower and change into clothes that didn't smell like beer and fried ass, but after I turned the shower on, I looked down at my decorated wrists.

I wasn't a pussy. I rarely backed down from a fight and I almost always stood up for myself, yet I never let anyone see the person that was under all of the bracelets. I tucked her away as if she didn't exist, but Kyle had proven that if anyone cared enough to find her, they would. That girl was my past, but she was still part of me. She still helped to make me who I was, and though I had some very rocky roads in my life, I wasn't ashamed of whom I had become. I needed to take the bracelets off so that I could daily be reminded of where I had once been and where I never wanted to be again. I never wanted to feel that broken again. Maybe Kyle needed to also know that people mend in time, maybe then he wouldn't feel so hopeless if he knew that Emmy had probably mended, too.

Wrapped in only a towel, I went downstairs into the kitchen and found a pair of scissors in a drawer. I held one arm over the trashcan and cut the bracelets that could be cut. I unhooked the gold and silver ones and laid them on the counter. I repeated this with the other arm until both arms were bare. I looked at my scarred arms and shuddered. It was going to take some getting used to, looking at them all of the time, but I was brave. I could face down the demons that I would carry with me forever.

I went back upstairs and took my shower, re-bandaged my hand and then I went to find Kyle. It was almost four in the morning. I wasn't surprised to find him in his bed, but the lights were still on, his laptop was open on the bed beside him and a few papers were lying on his chest. There was a small stack of files on the floor by the bed. He had fallen asleep while working.

Without much thought, I collected the papers off of him. Recognizing the names on the paper, I stuck them in the appropriate folder. I took the laptop out of sleep mode, saved his work and shut it down. Before switching the light off next to his bed, I gazed down at him for a moment. He looked so peaceful and *normal* lying there. I admired his dark hair, his strong jawline and kissable lips. I touched my own lips as I remembered how it felt to kiss him. One strong arm was draped over his chest and the other one was above his head. I wondered what it would be like to fall asleep in those arms, but the only person he truly wanted was Emmy, and I would be a terrible substitute.

I put the laptop on his bureau and turned off the lights. I was just about the close the door when Kyle groaned in his sleep. I almost dismissed it before he started pleading his mother not to use the belt.

What the fuck?

The pleas suddenly stopped and I heard the rustling when he sat up. I could hear his ragged breaths and incoherent, frantic whispers. I moved across the dark room to the bed and put a hand on his hand to try to calm him while I turned the light on with my other hand. He looked so terrified that it actually scared me. I got him to calm down, but then he wouldn't let me go. After a while, he finally fell asleep, but when I tried to get up, Kyle gripped me in his sleep. With some hesitation, I climbed into bed beside him.

I woke up hours later molded to his body. I suddenly felt as if I weren't close enough to him. I wanted to melt into him and become a part of him. My emotions were strung high so soon after waking up, and my body was acutely sensitive. What I needed to do was drag myself away from Kyle before he unknowingly took advantage of my heightened emotions and senses. I looked up to see if he was sleeping, only to find him peering down at me. Whatever resolve I had to leave was washed away with that first, sweet kiss.

Standing under the water, I wanted to wash away the taste of Kyle's skin. I wanted to see my desire for him slip down the drain. I needed the water to cool the heat that still lingered between my legs and I wanted to scrub away the memory of his body pressed against mine. More than anything, I wanted to be rid of how I felt when he touched me. He had touched me so affectionately, not at all like a man who was just using me to forget his ex-lover. His gaze made me feel…loved.

Maybe Kyle did love me, in his own twisted way, but I couldn't ignore that Emmy was still very much the center of his universe. I was careless to sleep with him. It felt right at the time, but that didn't mean that it was. Someone should have slapped me across the face just as hard as I slapped Kyle, because I was just as much to blame.

I stepped out of the shower and found Kyle still standing in the doorway, but he was holding a towel. He stretched out his arm to hand me the towel even as his eyes grazed over my naked body. I took the towel from him and wrapped it around my torso.

"You don't have to stand there," I said to him. "I'm not going to reopen my suicidal wrist wounds."

"I need to know that our working relationship will not be affected by what happened between us," he said in a tone that was almost cold, definitely withdrawn. At first it stung, but I wasn't entirely stupid. I knew he felt something for me, even if it would never match what he felt for Emmy and it would never get us anywhere.

"Our working relationship has been affected from day one," I pointed out. "And you spent more than half of the weekend trying to convince me that you give a shit about me, and trying to get me to move in with you while simultaneously trying to get me into your bed." I offered a cynical smile in his direction as I applied toothpaste to my toothbrush "Congratulations. You've succeeded in convincing me of two of the three."

Kyle appeared unaffected by my words. With a straight face, he said "Regardless of what has happened here or of our cohabitating arrangements, we will need to keep a high level of professionalism in the office."

"You want a high level of professionalism in the office?" I asked around the toothbrush that was scrubbing furiously in my mouth. "You got it. I will professional your ass off. Now if you don't mind, can you please get out? I have to get ready for my last shift at *Steve's*."

"So, you've decided to quit after all." He gave one approving nod.

"Yes," I said and then spit in the sink. "We didn't really have an opportunity for pre-sex conversation so I could tell you."

"You're going to carry on with our agreement then?" he asked, slightly surprised.

I rinsed the toothpaste out of my mouth and spit again. "Regrettably, living here on a temporary basis makes sense. At least I can stop lying to my mom about my living situation," I murmured more to myself.

"Your mother still thinks you're living in your own apartment?"

"Yeah," I nodded. "She has enough to worry about. I don't need her worrying about me, too."

"Don't take that for granted," Kyle said quietly as he turned to leave. "Not everyone has a mother that cares enough to worry."

He left me alone to wonder what the fuck that was just about.

~~~

I slammed the beer down on the bar, making it splash out onto the bar and onto my customer.

"Who pissed you off?" he said in frustration as he looked down at his beer splashed pants.

"I'm sorry," I muttered, tossing him a towel.

The Eagles game blared on all of the televisions in the bar. *Steve's* was packed with football fans, cheering on good plays and booing like only a Philadelphia sports fan can when something didn't go right. I usually got into it with them, kept them engaged and happy, but I wasn't in the mood to care on my last day.

"I really need to talk to you," Vic said in my ear while I made a couple of drinks.

"So talk."

"Not now. It's impossible to talk now. Later, after hours. Let me drive you home."

"I already have a ride home," I said impatiently. I walked the drinks over to two waiting customers and snatched the money off of the bar that they threw down.

"It's our last night working together," Vic complained. "At least give me that."

I thought about Corsey's words about Vic. Was it possible that it was propaganda spun up by Kyle? Thinking about it only served to make me more confused and frustrated about his insane personality changes.

"Fine," I said as I made change for the customers. "You can drive me back to the penthouse afterward, but you have to take me straight there. No horseshit. I'm not in the mood. You got it?"

"Yeah, I got it," he said with a smug smile. "What's eating at your panties anyway?"

"What do you want? To sit down and discuss my problems over a cup of tea?" I snapped and left him alone to wait on more customers.

Later that night when I explained to Corsey that Vic would be driving me home, he tried very hard to talk me out of it.

"I told you he was a dangerous man," Corsey said as he glowered across the parking lot at Vic who was standing by his car looking smug.

"Vic has never hurt me," I argued.

Unlike your boss who may as well had dropped an anvil on my chest.

"Not *yet*," Corsey said. "I can lose my job if I let you go with him."

"You can lose your job *and* go to prison if you force me to get into that Escalade," I snapped. "I don't understand why I need a babysitter in the first place."

"I'm not babysitting," Corsey grumbled. "I'm...escorting."

"And spying and stalking," I added. I put my hand to my forehead, frustrated. "Kyle doesn't even *like* me. It shouldn't matter to him what I do and with whom."

Corsey narrowed his eyes at me. I was suddenly aware of his tall, bulky stature. He had big ass hands that could have made Andre the Giant nervous and his muscles looked like they were about to tear through his nice cotton shirt.

"I wouldn't be here if Kyle Sterling didn't 'like' you, Miss Whitman," he said in a low tone.

"Okay!" I yelled, waving my hands. "I'm done with this conversation. I appreciate you trying to do your job, but I don't need you, and you can't make me go."

I turned away from him and started across the parking lot to Vic's truck.

"He's not going to like this at all," Corsey called after me.

I ignored him and climbed inside the truck. Vic closed the door and walked around to the driver's side to get in. Corsey was already on his phone as he climbed back into the Escalade, no doubt reporting to Kyle. As confirmation, my cell phone started ringing before we even pulled out of the parking lot. I sent the call to voicemail, silenced the phone, and pushed it into my jacket pocket.

"What the fuck is going on with you guys?" Vic asked, looking over at me. "Sounds like some kind of Fifty Shades shit. Is that what's going on?"

"No. What did you want to talk to me about?" I asked in a rush to get away from talking about Kyle.

"That douche bag is following me," he growled as he looked in the rearview mirror. I checked the side mirror and instantly recognized the Escalade a couple of cars back.

"It's okay," I said, unaffected by what had become my bizarre life. "What did you want to talk about?"

He resigned to being followed by Corsey with a sigh and glanced at me a couple of times before talking.

"We've known each other for almost three years now," he said carefully. "I've always tried to help you out and be good to you, right?"

I couldn't deny this. Though I knew he was an arrogant, hot headed, steroid infested meathead, he always went out of his way to appease me and offered his assistance when I needed it. It was Vic that got me the job at *Steve's*. He had offered me money, use of his car and the spare room in his house, but I had declined. Some of it was a sense of pride, but mostly I was worried about what he would want in return. Corsey wasn't entirely wrong – Vic could be a little…creepy at times. Not Kyle creepy, but the kind of creepy that made me feel uneasy. He had a habit of showing up at the same places as me and pretending it was a coincidence. Sometimes I had the feeling he was staring at me and undressing me with his eyes, but every time I looked up, he would look away with a creepy smile. Also, I had seen how he treated other women, like they were pieces of meat.

Regardless of all of that, the fact was that he was right. He had always tried to help and he had never mistreated me personally. So I nodded at him, acknowledging and agreeing with what he said, though I wasn't sure where this was going.

"I've asked you out a few times, and you always said no because you didn't think two people who work together should *be* together," he continued.

I nodded again, though that rule only really applied to him.

"And after your ex died, I thought you needed a little bit of time."

"How considerate," I muttered.

"I know you're moving in with that asshat, but if there really isn't anything happening between the two of you than you won't have any objections to us going out."

He reached across the cab and put his hand on mine. I almost recoiled in revulsion, but I managed not to.

"Umm," I started. "You're kind of putting me on the spot here, Vic," I said.

"I love you, Lily," Vic said, squeezing my hand. "I think you love me, too, and that's why you wouldn't move in with me or take my money."

My eyes grew so big they threatened to explode in my skull. "I don't understand how not moving in with you or taking your money equates love."

"You needed to keep everything neutral while we were working together," he said as if it should have been obvious to me. "You didn't want to mix business..." he pulled my hand to his lips. "With pleasure," he continued.

"Or..." I said and pulled my hand from his grasp. "I just wasn't interested."

Vic laughed and then squeezed my knee. He left his hand there as he grinned over at me.

"I like that you play hard to get, Lily. It's a real turn on."

"I'm not playing," I said, picking his hand off of my knee. "I'm really not interested, Vic. I don't know why you have everything so twisted."

"I forgive you for whatever you're doing with that asshat," he said, running the back of his hand over my jawline. I flinched away. "I'll give you a little bit of time to get your shit together. I mean, I'm not completely innocent. I bagged a girl last night in the office after the bar closed. I hope you don't hold that against me."

Oh, my god! How could I have not seen how fucking crazy you are?

I pushed myself as close to the door as possible. I felt foolish for not paying heed to Corsey's words. In stalking me, he and Kyle no doubt also saw Vic stalking me as well, and they probably dug deep on him, too. There were probably terrifying things about the man that I was unaware of, which pissed me off. They should have told me instead of behaving mysteriously.

"Do you?" Vic asked. He caressed my thigh and groaned.

"Do I what?" I asked, trying to sound irate.

"Hold what I did against me? I mean, it wasn't just her. There have been others while I waited for you, but they didn't mean anything to me, Lily. You're all I've really wanted for these past couple of years."

Maybe I needed to give him the impression that what he did was unforgivable and therefore our 'relationship' was un-repairable.

"You want me to forgive you for banging other women?"

He looked at me with a worried expression. "Yes."

"I can't forgive you for that," I snapped.

His fingers slipped down to my inner thigh, too damn close to my crotch. I cried out when he suddenly squeezed my thigh in his meaty hand.

"Now, Lily," he said disapprovingly. "We both know that you have fucked other guys. If I saw any of them on the street, I'd fucking kill them. Don't push all of this shit on to me."

Tears pricked at my eyes as his fingers dug into my flesh. Even though I knew Vic was creepy, I had not expected this. I would have never expected this in a million years. How could I have worked next to him for nearly three years and not know how deeply disturbed he was? I had told Kyle I could take care of myself, and I had cursed having a babysitter in Corsey, and now I was choking on the foot in my mouth.

"You're hurting me," I said as evenly as possible and blinked back my tears. I had a feeling he wanted to see me cry and beg, but I wasn't going to give him any of that. "I'm giving you three seconds to release me."

In the cover of dark and with my body pressed against the door, he didn't see my right hand fumbling in my jacket pocket for my pepper spray. Spraying him in the face could make him run off the road or crash into something, but it was a risk I was willing to take as my anger began to swell inside of me.

Fortunately, he released me. I looked out of the window and breathed a sigh of relief when I saw that we were close to

Kyle's building. I checked the side mirror and saw that Corsey was riding Vic's bumper. I felt a small sense of relief knowing he was there.

"I'm sorry, Lil," Vic sighed. "It's just that I've been waiting for this for a long time. I've done a lot of shit to make this happen. Don't give up on me."

I didn't know what kind of shit he was talking about. I was focusing on the fact that we were very close to Kyle's building. I was almost surprised to see Kyle standing outside of the lobby, illuminated by a couple of lamps. Almost surprised, but not quite, because it wasn't even the most bizarre part of my weekend.

"I'll be in touch," Vic said as we pulled into the circular driveway in front of the building.

I was jumping out of the truck before he could even come to a complete stop. Kyle stormed past me towards the truck, but Vic gave him a look of disdain and sped off.

"You're fired!" Kyle yelled at Corsey who was standing outside of his Escalade.

"Don't you dare fire him!" I yelled.

Kyle glared at me. "You have no idea what could have happened to you!"

"Yes, I rather do have an idea what could have happened to me," I snapped with a quavering voice that made both men pause.

"What happened?" Kyle demanded, taking a step towards me.

"Nothing," I said quickly and took a step back away from him. I wasn't a prideful person, but I didn't want Kyle and Corsey to be right. I was so angry that they had most likely kept vital details from me about Vic, and I was angry with myself for not knowing Vic even half as well as I thought I did.

"If something happened, I need to know it," Kyle said patiently as he took another step toward me. Corsey was now behind Kyle, watching me with concerned eyes.

"Nothing happened," I said and stepped into a circle of light.

Kyle's eyes widened and then grew hard. Corsey ran his hands through his hair.

"What?" I snapped.

"If nothing happened, why is your makeup smeared like you've been crying?" Kyle asked through gritted teeth.

I wiped at the tears I didn't even know had fallen. Thinking quickly, I cradled the hand I got stabbed in against my body. "I hurt my hand in the truck. I didn't cry," I said.

Kyle looked at me skeptically. My emotions were really messed up. The anger I felt towards Vic was suddenly directed at Kyle.

"I don't see where it matters! I don't understand why you have Corsey babysitting me and why you are acting so concerned about my well-being when you're obviously not!"

"What I did this morning does not change what I said to you before, Lily," Kyle growled, stepping forward again. "I still care about you."

"But you wish you didn't."

"I really fucking wish I didn't," he agreed.

"Then stop," I said.

"If I knew how, I would," he said darkly.

I turned away from him and started into the building, but I stopped just inside the doorway.

"And do *not* fire Corsey," I snarled.

I left the men outside and took the elevator to the penthouse. I let myself in with the key Corsey had given to me the night before. I went straight to the bar and grabbed the bottle of bourbon. I had taken two big swigs of the stuff by the time I got to my room and locked the door behind me. I put the bourbon down on my chest of drawers after another sip and started to strip out of my clothes. I always showered after working in the bar, but I felt extra dirty this time. My skin was crawling and I had the sensation that there was a sticky film on my body.

I turned the water on as hot as I could stand it and washed and scrubbed my body head to toe until my hand started to bleed. It had been healing fine, but I had been so into getting clean that I had not immediately noticed the damage I was doing to my hand. I got out and wrapped a towel around myself. I absently applied an antibiotic cream to my hand and bandaged it. I then turned the focus on brushing the knots out of my hair, pulling harder than necessary at the brush.

I brushed and flossed my teeth and then made my way into the bedroom. It wasn't until then that I noticed the flat screen television mounted on the wall across from my bed. Below it on a mounted shelf, there was a slim cable box and a blue ray player. There were speakers mounted on either side of the television. Below the television equipment on a media cabinet I had also missed, was an expensive looking stereo with a remote, a vinyl player, a cd player, and a docking station for my iPod. I looked around the room to see if there was anything else I had missed, and found that there were more speakers in all of the corners of the room. My bed was made with a new black comforter and the sheets under it were red, my favorite color combination. Fresh Lilies sat in a vase on the table next to the bed, and somehow that seemed to be the most significant thing for me.

I sat down on the bed and leaned over to smell the flowers. I took another look around the room and sighed. Either this really was 'some kind of Fifty Shades shit' or Kyle was really good at making his guests feel wanted. Another thought hedged into my mind, but I pushed it away. I didn't want to think about love shit.

I got up and took another hit from the bourbon bottle. I turned on the stereo and took a couple of minutes to figure it out. Soon *Blue Monday* by Orgy was blasting from all corners of the room. I turned in search of my pile of luggage and other belongings that I had left by the door before going to work, but there was nothing there now. I walked over to the closet door and flipped on the light. My mouth fell open when I saw how big it was. My suitcases were on the top shelf and my business clothes and nicer clothes were hanging on velvet covered hangers, and my shoes were lined up on a shoe rack. My eyes grew big when I saw the pair of sneakers that Kyle owed me from two years ago. How the hell he remembered exactly what they looked like was beyond me. There were also a few newer items hanging in the closet. I ran my hands over the designer dress suits and checked the sizes.

"Damn, he's good," I whispered to myself, almost angrily.

I shut off the light and left the closet. I pulled open drawers and found my clothes neatly folded and everything separated. Pants were with pants, shirts with shirts, socks with socks, and then there was a whole drawer just for my undergarments – and some of them were also new, I sourly noted. I pulled out something to wear to bed and slammed the drawers shut.

The beginning chords of *Snuff* by Slipknot drifted through the room just as I let the towel drop to the floor. My leg felt sore. I looked down at it and gasped. There was a bruise forming in the shape of Vic's hand on my thigh. I rushed over to the mirror and looked at it head on. When I saw just how close the bruise was to the junction between my thighs, I lost it. Even though the music was playing loud enough to drown out any noise I may make, I bit my lip to keep from crying out loud. Tears raced down my cheeks as I gingerly touched the bruise. I felt violated, stupid, and weak. I was very capable of defending myself and knocking the shit out of full grown men, but I stupidly put myself in a bad situation and allowed Vic to turn me into a victim.

After a couple of minutes, I pulled on a pair of panties and a t-shirt and climbed into bed without turning out the lights. I thought I heard knocking on my door, but I didn't care. I had not felt so badly since I found out about Gavin's death over the summer, but at least then I was crying for him. This time I was selfishly crying for myself after my own idiotic mistakes.

The knocks got louder, but I rolled over, putting my back to the door and tried to make the world go away for the night.

Chapter Nine

~Kyle~

Lily came down the stairs dressed in the gray suit I had bought for her while she worked yesterday. Her beautiful curls were gone and replaced with shiny, straight hair hanging loosely over her shoulders. When Lily was on the clock for Sterling Corp, she always toned down her makeup, but now it was lighter than usual. It somehow made her slate gray eyes more noticeable, which was why I took note to how blank they looked. It was like looking at the eyes of a corpse.

"I like the suit on you," I said when she reached the last step.

"Thank you," she said in a voice just as blank as her eyes. "Thank you for buying it and all of the other things."

I knew her gratitude was sincere or she wouldn't have said it, but her voice was completely void of emotion. I realize I had put her through a rough weekend, and I was probably a good part to blame, but I had a nagging feeling that Vic came into the equation somewhere. Corsey told me that he couldn't really tell what was going on in the truck, but whenever he caught a glimpse of Vic's eyes in the rearview mirror, it gave him a bad feeling. The way Lily leaped out of the truck was also an indicator, and her teary eyes all but screamed at some kind of violation. I had to try awfully damn hard not fly off at the handle when I saw her tear streaked face. For a half a second I saw bewilderment in her eyes, but then Lily's pride set in and she did incredibly fast masonry work by building a wall around herself without any entries for me.

Later, after I verbally ripped Corsey a new one (but didn't fire him), I had a couple of drinks to calm down before going upstairs to check on Lily. Her door was locked and the stereo was blasting at a high decibel, but I could have sworn I heard faint crying. The alcohol did nothing to calm me as I banged on the door again. When she still didn't respond, I was tempted to get the key from downstairs and let myself in. I had images of her bleeding on the bathroom floor, but deep down I knew that wasn't the case, that she would never go to those extremes again, regardless of how horrible her weekend had been. I figured she just needed to be left the hell alone, so that's what I did, but it didn't stop me from tossing and turning all night worrying about her.

The ride into work was quiet. Any attempts I made for conversation was batted down with short, cold responses. The only lengthy conversation I got was work related and very a-matter-of-fact. I wanted to question her about Vic again, but for once I kept my big mouth shut.

The rest of the day was much of the same. Lily was pretty quiet unless she had to speak. She managed small smiles for the staff where necessary, but otherwise, her face was a blank slate. She knocked on my office door instead of barging in like she usually did, she didn't sit her cute, round ass on my desk, and she didn't argue with me and put me in my place when needed. She was demure, a complete opposite of her usual open, casual self. The worst thing was looking into her eyes and seeing nothing.

One of my favorite things about Lily was being able to gauge what she was feeling or thinking by looking at her eyes, but now I was shut out completely – not that I deserved to really be in the loop in the first place. After calling out Emmy's name, I was surprised she didn't wrap her hands around my neck and squeeze.

I had followed her into her room after I purposely called out the wrong name while we were having amazing sex, and finally got to see the tattoo that covered her back and wrapped around her hips. Lilies climbed and twisted up her back, reaching to heights just below her neck and shoulders. One word was scripted at an angle across the tallest and prettiest of the other flowers: Anna.

After seeing the back piece that was tribute to her lost daughter, I was reminded of all the things she had been through. Being the ass that I am, I just had to put her through one more fucked up situation. I wanted to apologize to her and tell her that I had done it on purpose, but I remembered why I did it in the first place – to push her away. By the time she got out of the shower, I had resolved to continue being a dick to make sure she wouldn't quickly or easily forgive me, and so far it was working.

I hated it, especially since I knew there was something else wrong. When we got back to the penthouse later that night, Lily raced upstairs to her room without a word. It had only been a day and I already fucking missed her – missed her laughter, missed her hassling me, and missed her tell-all beautiful eyes.

As difficult as it was, I kept my distance for the rest of the week. I let her go her own way when we got home. We ate separately and whenever we had to pass by one another, we gave each other a wide birth. At work, Lily was sociable with the staff, but that part of her turned off in my presence. Over the weekend we were both busy with work, but while I worked at the dining room table, Lily chose to work in her room.

This was what I wanted, right? I didn't want her pining over me and I didn't want to destroy her like I had destroyed Emmy, but I felt like I had snuffed out a part of her, and I was having a hard time dealing with it. I didn't want to care about her, but I did. If I was going to be honest with myself, I had started falling for her almost immediately after she walked through the doors at Sterling Corp. If I was going to be honest, I'd have to say that the more I found out about her personal life and the more I watched her, the more I really wanted her deep down. Something inside of this woman pulled me toward her no matter how hard I tried to fight it.

After a week of silence, I couldn't take it anymore. Even if I had hurt her, Lily was a very verbal person and had no qualms telling me what she really thought of me. At this point, I was ready to hear her verbally bash me than to go through another week of this oppressive silence. After another night of work, Lily ran upstairs and closed herself in her room. I stopped at the foot of the stairs, trying to talk myself out of going after her. I wasn't worthy of her, but I needed to know

~ 132 ~

she was okay.

I jogged up the stairs and rapped twice on her door. Lily opened the door a moment later. She was in the middle of changing. She had on yoga pants now, but no shirt. She stepped aside, giving me access into the room.

"You've been very quiet lately," I said as I watched her pull on a shirt.

"Yes," she agreed without emotion. "You wanted a professional relationship, so that's what I gave you." She sat down on the bed with her hands in her lap.

"It's more than that." I sat down beside her. "I need to know that you're okay," I sighed. I hated admitting how much I cared about her out loud.

"You need to know that I'm okay," she rolled the words around in her mouth before looking up at me.

Well, at least her eyes weren't blank anymore.

"You need to know I'm okay so you can knock me down again? You need to know I'm okay so you can tell me how much you wish you didn't care that I was okay? Do you need to know that I am okay so you can continue stalking me and then use what you discover to hurt me? Do you need know I'm okay so you can fuck me in your bed and then call out another name? Or do you need know I'm okay so you can then put up a stone cold wall to repel me? Why exactly do you need to know that I am okay! You're one big fucked up contradiction! But if you must really know, Kyle, if you really *have* to know if I'm okay, the answer is no! I'm *not* okay!"

"What do I have to do to make it okay?" I yelled back at her in frustration. She was right, of course, but I didn't want her to pack up her shit and leave. The thought of her leaving, even after the messed up week and a half I made her have, made my chest ache. Emmy was always there with me, tucked away in a corner of my mind on some days and at the forefront on other days, but that didn't change how I felt around Lily. She infuriated me. Sometimes I wanted to throttle her, and sometimes I wanted to tape her mouth shut, but she also made me smile. I craved her touch, even if she was just straightening one of my hideous ties, and I felt comfortable in her presence. I didn't deserve her, but I wasn't ready to let her go.

"Stop being a pussy!" she yelled and got to her feet. She stormed across the room to the bathroom and swung the door behind her, but it only closed half way.

I followed her across the room but stopped just outside the door when I heard the tell-tale sound of her peeing. "I'm not being a pussy by not wanting to hurt you," I argued through the door.

"Newsflash, Kyle, you're already hurting me."

"But I don't want to *break* you!" I yelled.

The toilet flushed and then Lily came into view when she stood over the sink to wash her hands. She kept glancing up at me, her mouth set in a thin line. She dried her hands before stepping out. She stood on her tip toes grabbed my jaw in one, slightly damp hand.

"You're not going to break me, Kyle. You're just going to really piss me off."

She wasn't pissed off already?

"My god, you're making me crazy. I feel like I have some kind of personality disorder around you. I'm up and I'm down. I'm angry and I'm...Well, let's just say you drive me nuts," she sighed. She caressed my jaw. "We have to start over."

"From where?" I frowned and rested my hand on her hip.

"I don't know, from right here I guess. Let's not spend the night lost in emotionally charged conversations. We have to find some sense of normalcy, Kyle. My life has been topsy turvy for months and I really need something near normal."

"What's 'normal' to you?" I asked, still frowning. I was even more pissed at myself, because again she was right. Her life flipped upside down when Gavin died and instead of giving her the support she very well needed, I only added to her stress.

Lily released my jaw and rested her hand on my chest. "Tonight we can be two friends – not boss and employee, not...whatever the hell else we have been in the past. We'll order some dinner and chill in my room and watch a movie on my new television with my awesome new surround sound system."

The corners of her mouth had quirked up a little to form a small, playful smile. As I looked down into her gray eyes, I was awed by how quickly she had went from ranting at me, ready to kick my ass, to forgiving and smiling. At least I think she was being forgiving.

"A new TV with surround sound? How did you get so lucky?" I asked, focusing on her beautiful mouth.

"I have a sugar daddy," she said with a shrug and eased away from me.

What the hell? How did she get me smiling, too? I could feel it on my face as I watched her walk back to the bed. I rubbed my jaw where her hand had been.

"I can't believe you touched me with your PP hand," I called to her. I ducked just in time before a pillow sailed past my head.

~~~

We were supposed to be watching reruns of *The Big Bang Theory* but I had not looked at the screen in a long time. Lily lay stretched out beside me, looking at me with sleepy, but content eyes. I was on my side, my head propped up on one arm while my other hand explored the contours of her body.

I had started with her hands, running my fingers over each of hers before rubbing my thumb over her now visible scars on her wrists. I brought each scarred wrist to my lips and kissed them. When she smiled, I smoothed my fingertips over her plump lips before, stroking the soft skin on her cheekbones, and then down to her delicate neck. I ran my fingertips over each shoulder, across her smooth chest, and down the sides of each breast. My hand had made slow, lazy circles on her stomach before slipping down to her waist, leisurely across the top of her pelvic bone to the other side of her waist. Lily had a few extra pounds, more than I was used to, but I loved it.

"I'm pretty sure this isn't what I meant by 'normal'," she murmured as my thumb stroked over her hip bone.

"It could become our normal," I said after a moment. I could imagine lying there with her like that day after day and never getting sick of it.

"You say that now," she sighed. "But later you will be at conflict with yourself again."

I couldn't agree with her, but I couldn't disagree either.

"Okay, then we won't think about later. We will just worry about here and now." I leaned over and lightly pressed my lips against hers.

Lily pulled away from my lips and pinned me with her worried gray eyes. "I can't," she whispered.

"Why not?" I frowned down at her as my fingers moved over the elastic waistline of her yoga pants.

She frowned back at me. She looked like she was going to tell me why we couldn't kiss, but then she stopped. Then she said "We agreed not to have any emotionally charged conversations tonight."

"You agreed," I pointed out. "I didn't agree to anything."

Before she could answer, I slipped my hand into her pants and under her panties. I had her groaning a half second later as my middle finger dragged over her clit.

"That's so not fair," she breathed.

"Haven't you realized by now, Lily?" I asked as I stroked her clit over and over, making her squirm and groan. "I don't always play fair."

I took her mouth with mine, seeking out her tongue with my own. Her studded tongue stroked over mine and it was my turn to groan. As I kissed her delicious mouth, I pushed one finger inside of her. Her hips involuntarily rose up to take in more. Despite her words, she was moist and ready for me.

I pulled my hand out of her pants and gripped the waistband to pull them off of her, but her hands covered mine in an effort to stop me.

"You're going to be mad," she said and her mouth set in a grim line.

I looked at her in confusion. Why the hell would I be

mad after I got her pants off of her? Did she grow a dick overnight or something equally disturbing? To answer my silent question, Lily released my hands and with a sigh, she nodded for me to continue. I pulled her pants and panties down mid-thigh before I understood what she was talking about. 'Mad' could not adequately describe the blood boiling feeling I had when I saw the large hand shaped bruise on her thigh.

Where his fingertips must have been, the marking was darker in shade, indicating that he squeezed her pretty damn hard. The bruise was extremely close to the junction between her thighs. He would have only had to extend his hand to touch her there.

"You told me nothing happened," I said, gingerly touching the contusion.

"I was angry and humiliated," she said, staring up at the ceiling. "I didn't want to discuss it."

"You should have told me," I said, climbing off of the bed. "You should have said something the moment your feet hit the ground when you got out of his truck."

I grabbed my phone off of the table next to the bed and had Corsey on the phone before I could even get out of the bedroom.

"That bastard hurt her that night," I growled at Corsey.

"In the truck?"

"That's the only time she was left alone with him, Corsey! On your watch!"

"Is she okay?" he asked, genuinely concerned.

"She has a hand shaped bruise on her thigh! He was so close to…" I stopped myself before I said it out loud, because whatever little reserve I had left would have gone out the window.

"It's my fault," Corsey said, disgusted with his self.

"You're damn right it's your fault," I growled, as I started to change out of my lounge pants into a pair of jeans. Lily was standing in the doorway, watching and listening with clear apprehension.

"How do you want me to handle this?" Corsey asked.

"I'm going over there and I'm breaking his fucking head."

"I don't think that is a wise decision, Kyle," he said.

"It wasn't a wise decision for you to allow her to get into that truck with a known psychopath either!"

"Stop yelling at him," Lily hissed, stepping into the room. "It's my fault, not his and you're not breaking anyone's head."

"Let me call a few guys," Corsey said. "We'll go have a talk with him."

"I'll handle it myself," I snapped and ended the call.

"You can't go over there, Kyle," Lily said, standing over me as I tied my shoes. "You're going to get hurt or in trouble with the law, and that's the last thing you need right now."

"Those are necessary risks I'm willing to take," I grumbled. "Not that long ago, you were calling me a pussy. Now you're trying to talk me out of this."

"Yeah, because this is *stupid*!"

"I'm going to kick his fucking ass for touching you like that," I growled, getting to my feet.

"You're not going over there," she said, crossing her arms and sidestepping to block me from leaving.

"You're not going to stop me," I said, scowling.

"You're really angry and you can't see or think straight, but you can't go. I won't let you. Besides, you have vagina fingers. You can't go fight someone with vagina fingers."

"Perfect," I said, glaring at her. "He'll smell what he will never have."

"That's…you're disturbing sometimes," she said and sidestepped again to block me.

"You're not going to stop me," I repeated and started to go around her.

Suddenly my arm was wrenched and pulled and twisted behind my back. My elbow and my shoulder erupted in pain. Something cracked against the back of my knee and I went down onto both knees. Lily's arm circled my neck and

~ 138 ~

squeezed.

"Oh, you were easy," she purred in my ear. "Pussy."

With my one free hand, I reached up and around her as far as I could and threw her over me, freeing my neck and my arm. She lay on the floor, looking up at me with a stunned expression on her face, but it only lasted a couple of seconds before she used the palm of her hand to jab me in the chest. As I struggled to catch the breath she had knocked out of me, Lily sat up on her knees and taunted me.

"You throw like a girl," she grinned.

I narrowed my eyes at her and launched myself at her. She landed on her back again, but this time I was on top of her, pinning her hands above her head and trapping her under my body. I stared down at her parted lips as I felt her breathing hard beneath me. She tried to squirm away, but she only succeeded in rubbing her cloth covered crotch against my denim covered cock. I took in her flushed face and wild eyes. Her hair had come loose from its bun and some of it swept across one side of her face. She looked so fucking beautiful, lying there out of breath and excited. I closed the few inches between our lips and savagely crushed her mouth with my own as I rocked against her.

Lily moaned into my mouth as I kissed her and pulled her tongue between my teeth. I sucked on her bottom lip before pushing my tongue back inside of her mouth. I grinded against her, loving how rough the material felt between us. I released one of her hands and tangled my fingers in her hair. I pulled away from her lips and kissed a trail down her jaw and to the little stars on her neck and continued grinding against her. She gasped as I tasted her skin. She tasted like soap, sweat, and something sweet and floral.

Suddenly Lily's body tensed beneath me, and her moans deepened. She pushed her hips up off of the floor to grind her clit hard against me. As she started to cry out from her orgasm, I absorbed it with my mouth on hers. Before her climax could die down, I was up and quickly pulling off her pants and panties. I tossed them to the side and started to undo the button and zipper on my jeans. When my eyes fell where Vic marked her, my anger intensified again. Seeing my expression forced Lily to distract me. She sat up and yanked my jeans and boxers down just below my ass, setting my erection free. Her hand wrapped around my shaft and gave it a few good strokes. I groaned at her touch, but as good as it felt, I needed to be inside of her. I needed to release the rage I was feeling and I only wanted to do that while buried balls deep inside of Lily.

I didn't bother pulling my jeans off before I pressed her back down to the floor and without warning, I slammed into her. Lily screamed, but she wrapped her legs around my waist, inviting me to go deeper inside of her hot, moist, sex. I pulled her arms back above her head as I slammed into her again. Unable to keep my mouth off of hers, I swallowed her screams as my cock assaulted her again and again.

When I relinquished her mouth to kiss and nibble at her neck, Lily cursed and prayed and called out my name as her next orgasm hit her. Her body rocked up to meet my thrusts as she came. As her pussy squeezed at my cock, I felt my own orgasm approaching. I looked into her eyes and held back the words that hung on my tongue and groaned deeply as I began to spill inside of her. Lily's legs tightened around my waist, holding me inside of her as I shot stream after stream deep inside her.

When I had emptied myself inside of her, I released her arms and kissed her tenderly as I stroked the side of her face. After a minute, I rolled off of her onto my side and wrapped an arm around her waist.

"Did I hurt you?" I asked, looking down at the bright mark on her thigh.

"I hardly noticed," she murmured, snuggling closer to me and resting her head in the crook of my arm.

I kissed her once more before pulling away to gaze down at her. "You're fucking beautiful," I whispered to her.

Her eyes had closed, but she smiled sleepily. "I guess you got used to the tattoos and piercings after all."

"I wouldn't want you any other way."

She seemed content with that. Soon her breathing slowed and her body relaxed. Once I was sure she was asleep, I got up to go take care of Vic.

Chapter Ten

~£ily~**

I opened my eyes in a panic. I could tell by the light filtering through the blinds in Kyle's room that it was much later than my usual waking time of five-thirty. It's still dark at five-thirty in the morning. Before looking at the clock behind me, I guessed it was probably about eight or later.

"Eight-thirty!" I groaned, pushing myself up in the bed.

I didn't remember getting into his bed. I remember falling asleep on the floor, but Kyle must have moved me during the night. I was impressed. I wasn't obese, but I wasn't a light weight either. The fact that he could lift me was kinda hot, and he was kind enough to pull a pair of his boxers on me so my bare ass wasn't hanging out.

"Hey," said the hot guy as he exited his bathroom, buttoning the sleeves of his dress shirt. He looked sexy with his tie just hanging around his neck waiting to be tied, his muscles pressing against the fabric of his shirt, and his hair still damp from a shower.

"You let me oversleep," I said groggily, swinging my legs out of the bed.

"I'm giving you the next two days off," he said as he stood in front of his mirror.

"That's not funny," I snapped and rushed for the bedroom door. "There's a lot going on today. You should have woken me up."

"I'm serious, Lily," he said in a firm tone just as my feet crossed the threshold.

I turned around and looked at him. He was tying his tie now. It wasn't the best looking tie.

"What are you talking about?" I asked, rubbing my tired eyes. "You wouldn't even let me have the afternoon off last week for a doctor's appointment. Why are you making me miss work?"

"When was the last time you had a day off?" he asked, watching me from the reflection in the mirror.

"I don't know," I shrugged. "It's been a few weeks."

"It's been six weeks. Six weeks without a day off is too long, even by my standards."

I was about to ask him how he knew when I was last off since it was on a Sunday, but I forgot for a moment that he had stalked me for a long time.

"I can't take any time off now. You just told me not that long ago how busy we are, and your schedule is insane this week. I'm going to go take a shower. I'll catch a cab or something. You don't have time to wait for me. You have a nine-thirty appointment."

I started to move down the hallway, but Kyle's stern voice made me pause.

"You're staying home today," he said. "Beth can follow your itinerary and step in as needed."

I poked my head back into his room. "You're serious, aren't you?"

"Extremely serious," he said.

"Okay," I said slowly. "Thank you."

I didn't know what else to say. The rushing and panicking had filled in any possible awkwardness, and a day of hard work was sure to do the same, but now there was nothing to stop things from being awkward. I wasn't sure what kind of mood Kyle was in, even after his generosity of giving me a couple of days off. Was he angry at himself again? Was he angry at me? Was he going to treat me with indifference? Or was he going to treat me like a burdensome piece of property?

I went into my room and slipped on a sweatshirt. The house was pretty warm most of the time, but I was a little chilly. I pushed my feet into a pair of slippers I rarely got to wear and went downstairs. Kyle was already in the kitchen, eating a cold leftover slice of pizza. I prayed that there was coffee somewhere in the kitchen. I opened a cabinet and discovered K-cups on the top shelf, way out of my reach. Before I could formulate a plan to reach them, Kyle's body pressed against mine. He slipped an arm around my waist and reached over me to grab the coffee. He dropped the box on the counter, tilted my head, and swept my hair off of my neck. His lips and tongue on my neck sent tingly warm sensations across my neck and radiated down my spine.

"Something about you in my boxers is extremely hot," he murmured against my neck.

"Why do you think I'm still wearing them?" I teased and then sighed when his tongue flicked over my earlobe.

"No working today," he warned.

"I can log in and work on a few things," I suggested.

"No, you cannot," Kyle said. "Take a break. Watch a movie. Do a jigsaw puzzle. I don't care what you do, as long as it does not constitute as work. If you need to go anywhere, call and wait for Corsey. Don't go off by yourself. I mean it."

"I don't like having a babysitter, Kyle," I said, getting a little aggravated.

"I know, Lil, but it won't be forever." He kissed the top of my head and released me. When I turned around, he was already walking across the living room towards the door. He gave me one last wave and left me alone in the huge penthouse.

I started my cup of coffee and looked around. I had not had an actual day off in more than I can remember. When I wasn't working for Sterling I was working in the bar. When I wasn't working in a bar I was working for Sterling. It had become one hectic, tiring circle, but as reluctant as I was to quit my job at *Steve's*, I had to admit that it was the best thing for me before I ran myself into the ground.

With a cup of coffee in hand, I went upstairs to shower. I smelled like sex, which made me grin like an idiot, but I'd rather smell like soap. When all the sex was washed off of my body, I carried all of my dirty laundry downstairs to the laundry room. I figured since I was doing laundry, I may as well do Kyle's.

"How domestic of you, Lillian," I said out loud and rolled my eyes after I put in my first load.

I went back upstairs to get Kyle's dirty laundry. I found

an overflowing hamper in his bathroom. With a sigh, I started to pick up the items that had fallen to the floor. I was muttering about Kyle having pockets deeper than Scrooge McDuck and as much class as the Royals, but still unable to keep up with his laundry when I picked up a blue shirt with bloodstains on it. It was very similar to the shirt Kyle had on the night before. In fact, I was positive that it was, but when I last saw him in it, it was blood-free.

I sat down on the edge of the tub, trying to process what I was seeing. The shirt not only had blood on it in several places, it was torn at the collar, as if someone had grabbed it in a struggle.

"Damn it, Kyle," I said as understanding set in.

After I was asleep and dead to the world, Kyle must have gone to try and kick Vic's ass.

It's not that I didn't think that Vic needed an ass whooping, because he did. I just didn't want Kyle to be the one to administer it. Vic was obviously off kilter, and years of steroid abuse was setting him up for a murderous rage. While Kyle's body muscle was impressive to say the least, Vic was almost twice his size. I am clear proof that size isn't everything, but me taking down a few drunken guys or even handsy assholes wasn't the same as Kyle trying to take down a roid-enraged crazy man. The opportunity for him to get hurt or even killed was high. If he made it out alive and unscathed – which he most likely did since I didn't really see any indication on him that he had been in a fight – there was still a legal issue.

I'm not a saint. I seriously don't abide by all laws, and I've been in enough fights of my own in my lifetime, but the last thing Kyle needed was trouble with the law. His superiors within the company still didn't fully trust him, and I often heard murmuring about what part he had played when business at Sterling went to hell in a hand basket. Many believed that he was just as much a criminal as Walter. He didn't need to give people anymore reason to question him.

While I was very much aware and forgiving of Kyle's violent past with Emmy, I was having a hard time with parts of past Kyle sifting into present Kyle. He was drunk and high when he hurt Emmy, but last night he was clean, sober, and angry. And if he really did go after Vic, especially after what we did on his bedroom floor, it told me that Kyle had the ability to be cold and calculating. *That* scared me.

I shoved the shirt into the hamper and dragged it down to the laundry room. I was so tempted to call Kyle and yell at him or to go down to the office and confront him, but I needed to get my thoughts and feelings together. Instead, I picked a random box for the kitchen and began the process of unpacking Kyle's home.

~~~

Kyle's fridge only contained the necessities in a healthy bachelor's life – a few eggs, cream for the coffee, carrots, lettuce, and bottled water. I wasn't a rabbit and I didn't eat like one. When I texted him and told him I was going to have Corsey drive me to the grocery store, he insisted on taking me himself. His last meeting of the day was canceled, so he was going to skip out of work a couple of hours early.

Since it was my day off, I had dressed in some skinny jeans, a t-shirt, one of Kyle's hoodies that I found in his closet and the DC sneakers he had replaced more than two years after his vomit destroyed the identical pair. My hair was back to its normal wild and curly state, but I skipped the makeup. After months of applying only light makeup for the corporate world, I had learned that I really liked my natural, speckled skin. I still went heavy on the eye makeup when I was working at the bar, but since I was only going to the grocery store, I didn't see the point in bothering with it.

I was waiting on the couch watching the early edition of the news when Kyle came in. I waited a couple of minutes for him to change his clothes before he took my hand and led me out the door. In the elevator, he pulled me into an embrace and gave me a quick and gentle kiss on the lips. It was a small sentiment, but it made me smile despite the uneasiness I was feeling inside. I had not mentioned to him in any of the text messages or phone calls of the day what I had discovered in his hamper. He would figure out that I figured it out eventually.

"How was your first full day off?" Kyle asked as we cruised down the cereal aisle.

"Fine." I shrugged and stopped to grab a box of Capn' Crunch. "I got a lot done around the house. The kitchen and dining room are completely unpacked, and the living room is more than half way finished."

"I said no working," he said sternly, but then leaned over and gave me another peck on the lips. "But thank you."

This Kyle was awfully affectionate. I should have been giddy about it, but it made me even more uneasy. What if he was affectionate because he released all of his anger on Vic's face?

"We have to get laundry detergent," I said more to myself and wrote it on the list I had made earlier. "I almost forgot."

"Right," he agreed, a little distracted by the array of disgusting healthy cereals. "I was almost out last time I did laundry."

Which must have been a century ago.

"Well, now you're out completely. I did my wash and yours."

His head swiveled in my direction. "You washed my clothes?"

"I thought I may as well since I was washing my own," I said casually. I pretended to be very interested in oatmeal. "I had to throw away your shirt. The ad for the laundry detergent lied. It does not wash out blood."

I rounded the corner before him and moved into the next aisle. Top forty music played from the speakers above us. An older man further down the aisle had a cart with a squeaky wheel, and in the main aisle behind us a mother wrestled with her three small crying children. There was noise and activity all around us, but between Kyle and me was a big silent bubble.

I put a bottle of olive oil in the cart. A minute later Kyle put a small box of natural sugar next to the cereal. We finished the baking aisle in silence and moved on to coffee, tea, hot cocoa and soups and gravies. I grabbed a bottle of Hershey syrup and Kyle grabbed coffee. We continued on in silence for another aisle. In the dairy department, we stood side by side looking at the vast array of coffee creamers. At the same time, we both chose a different flavor and put them in the cart.

"I had to do it," Kyle said when I had started to move on to the cheeses.

"You know, I actually kind of give a damn what happens to you," I said, as I inspected a package of cheddar. "He could have seriously hurt you or even killed you. Not to mention the legality of the whole situation – you could have screwed up your entire life because you wanted to be a vigilante. And what scares me is…" I trailed off. I had not planned on telling him what scared me.

"What scares you?" he asked after a thoughtful moment.

"Never mind," I said, shaking my head.

"Lily," he said, enclosing my wrist in his big hand. He pulled me away from the cheeses and off to the side so that we weren't in anyone's way. "Tell me what scares you."

A woman a few years older than me was pretending to look at the yogurt, but every few seconds her eyes would turn back to us. A college kid was restocking a display of Snack Packs, but he didn't seem to be paying us any mind.

"Your mind wasn't compromised by drugs and alcohol this time," I whispered to him. "What you did was carefully calculated. I don't condone what you did to Emmy, not by a longshot, but I know you didn't mean it. This time you were very aware of what you were doing. It scares me that you can willfully and knowingly become violent like that."

He got very close to me, almost nose to nose. "If someone had come after me and kicked my ass up and down the eastern seaboard after what I did to Emmy, I would have not only deserved it, I would have *welcomed* it," he whispered harshly. "In fact, I'm still waiting for it. If it takes ten years for someone to knock the shit out of me for what I did, I'll deserve it no less. I wish someone *had*. It actually pisses me off that no one has. It makes me think they don't love her enough to do it.

"Vic hurt you, Lily," he said and his jaw clenched. "He is *dangerous* and he was prepared to do *much* worse than bruise your damn thigh. Trust me on that. I had to make sure he understood that hurting someone I love is not acceptable."

I was stunned. I looked everywhere else but at his face, because I didn't know what to say. I didn't know whether or not to address the fact that he wishes someone would kick his ass for what he did to Emmy, or if I should address the fact that he knew so much more about Vic than I realized. Hell, I didn't even want to touch the love thing with a ten foot pole.

I noticed that the woman at the yogurt was paying way more attention to us than the yogurt, not even having the shame to look away when I caught her staring.

"What the fuck is your problem?" I snapped at her. That made her pay attention to her fermented milk.

"Come on," Kyle sighed, ushering me along with one hand on my back to keep me from willfully and knowingly kicking the yogurt lady's ass.

We moved on a little ways. I stood by the cart with my arms crossed over my chest while Kyle grabbed eggs. We left the dairy and moved into meat and seafood. We discussed what cuts of meat to buy for a quick meal after work, what to eat over the weekend, and had a small, hostile argument about what brand of chicken to buy, but neither of us brought up the previous conversation in the dairy department.

At the front registers while we waited in line, Kyle pulled me into his arms and without any hesitation, he bent his head to meet my lips for a full on tongue to tongue public display of affection. Whatever iciness that had lingered from his earlier speech was instantly melted away by his sexy mouth. After a moment, the kiss ended, but his lips were still lightly pressed to mine. I could feel the smile on his mouth.

"That's a first," Kyle said.

"What's that?"

"Kissing my girl in public."

My heart did a stupid flopping thing at his words. "I

understand why you couldn't make out with Emmy in public," I said. "But what about Jessyca?"

"Jess was an ice queen," he said with finality. "I don't want to talk about Jess or…or Em…" His brow pulled together as he struggled to say her name.

"Okay," I conceded. Reluctantly, I turned away from him to start loading up the conveyer belt.

When we got back to the penthouse, we had to make a second trip back to the car to get the rest of the groceries. As soon as we got through the door, Kyle dropped his bags on the floor, put his hands on my face and kissed me again. I dropped the bags I was holding, knowing damn well one of them was holding the eggs. I slid my hands into his jacket, over his hard chest and up his bulging arms and started to take it off of him. He released my face and allowed me to strip him of the jacket. He hurried me out of the hoodie, only breaking the kiss long enough to pull the hoodie and t-shirt over my head. I in turn pulled on the hem of his t-shirt and pulled away quickly to rip it off of his head and toss it aside.

Kyle's hands worked quickly to unhook my bra and pull it down my arms. He pushed me against the door as his tongue continued to assault my own. When he pulled away, I was about to protest, but he ducked his head and inhaled a breast into his mouth. His tongue swirled around my nipple before giving it a hard flick. We both groaned when my nipple grew harder on his tongue. I cried out when his teeth nipped at me, but he instantly relieved the pain with his tongue.

Not wanting to ignore the other breast, he pushed them together and tried to get both of my nipples into his mouth at the same time.

"I love your gorgeous tits," he growled before sucking a nipple into his mouth.

He released my nipple with a wet sound and started to kiss down my belly. A moment later he was on his knees slipping my jeans down over my thighs. I kicked my sneakers off and stepped out of my jeans and panties. Kyle gently caressed the bruise Vic had left on my leg and then kissed it with care. His hand traveled over my thigh and then hooked under my knee. He raised my leg and put it over his shoulder. He gazed up into my eyes as he leaned forward and licked my sex from my entrance to my clit.

I let out a long, low cry of pleasure when his lips closed over my clit. I put my hands in his dark hair and pressed his head closer. He growled as his suckling on my clit grew harder. When he slipped two fingers inside of me, my orgasm was instantaneous. I rocked my hips against his face as I screamed out his name.

He pulled away slightly to watch his fingers sliding in and out of me.

"You're so wet, Lily," he said in awe. "This is all mine," he groaned when my orgasm became evident on his slick fingers.

He rammed his fingers deep inside of me and rubbed at the sensitive area that only Kyle has been able to discover with ease. He leaned forward and started flicking my clit with his glorious tongue. The building sensations inside of me were almost too much to bear.

"It's too much," I panted to Kyle, trying to pull his face away from my sex. "It's too much!" I screamed as the nerve endings in my body went into overdrive.

My body rocked and jerked violently as I had the most powerful orgasm of my life. Kyle groaned constantly as he licked away my orgasmic nectar. When I was sure my legs were going to give out, Kyle pulled his fingers out of me and stood up. I wrapped my arms around his neck and he held me around the waist as he dipped his head to kiss me. Tasting myself on his lips made me feel drunk with excitement.

I heard his pants drop to the floor. For a moment I was amazed that he had so expertly removed them with one hand without me knowing it, but my mind was forced away from that when I felt myself being lifted off of the floor.

"Wrap your legs around me, baby," he commanded.

My ankles were barely locked around him when he drove his impressive cock into my core.

"Lily," he groaned my name into my neck. "Oh, *fuck*," he growled as he moved his hips in a circular motion.

He pulled back until just the tip was sitting at my entrance. "Beg for it," he whispered.

"You're not going to reduce me to begging," I growled and nipped at his lips.

"I'm not going to give it to you until you beg for it," he said with a smile, but it was a serious smile.

"Then I guess we're going to have a standoff."

"I'll win," he said confidently before crushing his mouth to mine. Kyle kissed me with a sweet viciousness, nipping at my tongue and my lips, completely owning my poor mouth.

I tightened my legs around him in an effort to pull him inside of me, but he was like an unmovable rock.

"Beg for it and you can have it," he said, before clamping his mouth over the sensitive skin on my neck where my tats are.

"No," I moaned as he sucked hard on my neck. "Are you a fucking vampire?" I growled, digging my nails into his back. He responded with sucking harder.

He pulled back and readjusted his cock so that it was standing straight up between us. I was about to object when he started to rub his cock on my clit. Now I was starting to get frustrated. I really wanted to feel him inside of me, but I didn't want to beg. I tried to reach between us to guide his cock inside of me, but without relinquishing my neck, Kyle held me up with one arm while forcing my hand away from him.

I groaned in frustration. He chuckled against my skin. The pain in my neck from his suctioning was beginning to become unbearable, but the pain combined with the pleasure he was giving my clit was pushing me towards another orgasm, but not fast enough. It was time to humble myself.

"I need you inside of me," I panted. "Please!"

He chuckled again and didn't comply.

"Please, Kyle!" I cried out. "I need you. Please, please, please, plea – ungh!" My pleas were cut off by Kyle ramming his manhood inside of me. He released my neck just as I started to come again. He didn't give me an opportunity to come down from my orgasm. His hands slid under my upper thighs and he started pounding into me so hard my head slammed back against the door with every pump.

Kyle kept his eyes on mine as he fucked me hard. I relished the feeling of his skin moving against mine. His movements made my breasts bounce, causing the sensitive pierced nipples to brush across his hard chest.

"I'm so close," he gasped and then groaned as his orgasm neared.

"Give it to me," I groaned. "Give it all to me!"

"Oh, shit, Lily," he said through gritted teeth.

I didn't think he could pound into me any harder, but he was slamming my body against the door with each thrust.

"I lo-....shit," he groaned.

I knew what he was going to say. I didn't think it was a term I wanted to hear in the grocery store – it had made me cranky, but now as Kyle's cock slammed into me and his chocolate brown eyes focused so intently on mine, *I* wanted to say it. It wasn't a heat of the moment thing, because I meant it.

"I love you," I breathed on his lips.

Kyle's orgasm hit both of us hard. As I felt the first stream of semen shoot inside of me, Kyle growled out my name. His ability to speak correctly was torn away from him by this powerful orgasm. "Love..." he growled out, never losing eye contact. Suddenly he shouted as I felt his cock spasm and jerk inside of me, filling me with his hot load. My last orgasm had me near sobbing as I rocked my hips against my lover. My sex squeezed every last deserving drop from Kyle as our orgasms began to dissipate.

As our breathing began to slow, I carefully unraveled myself from him. His cock slipped out with a slick sound. He held onto me until my feet were firmly on the floor. One hand cupped my cheek before he gave me a slow, but passionate kiss. Even after all we had just done, his kiss still made my toes curl.

"You begged," he teased after kissing me.

"I demanded," I argued.

"Whatever, baby, you caved."

"In your dreams," I said. I wrapped my arms around his waist and pressed my cheek to his bare skin.

"Maybe I'll stay home tomorrow, too," Kyle murmured into my hair as he held me.

I pulled away and planted my hands on his chest. "Okay. Who the hell are you and what the hell happened to Kyle Sterling?"

"Ma'am, if you'll follow me to the bedroom, I'll explain everything," he said taking my hand.

"You're going to kill me with sex," I whined, reluctantly allowing him to lead me to the stairs. "We have ice-cream to put away," I objected.

Kyle paused and looked back at me. "I wonder how you would taste with ice-cream."

Oh, wow. This is *some kind of Fifty Shades shit.*

~Kyle~

I walked up behind Lily and slipped my hands under her skirt and groaned when I felt the stockings and garters on her thighs.

"Did you wear these for me?" I asked, snapping a garter.

"Yes, but not for right now," she said, smacking my hand away.

"Why not?" I asked as I hiked her skirt up over her ass.

"Because we have to go to work," she laughed, pushing me away.

I wasn't deterred as I again pushed her skirt up and grinded against her ass. "We have a few minutes," I murmured against her neck.

She moaned as I pushed her thong aside to push my finger inside of her.

"You're all ready for me," I said and nipped at the stars below her ear.

"You're going to make us late," she breathed as I kneaded one breast with one hand and freed my cock with my other hand.

"Better late than never," I said.

"My boss would disagree," she smiled.

"Fuck him."

"About to," she said.

"Hold on to the counter," I commanded.

Seconds later, I was sliding into her wet heat and groaning her name.

"Kyle," she whimpered as she pressed back to meet my thrusts.

I put my fingers to her mouth and she instinctively sucked on them. I pushed them in and out of her mouth in time with my thrusts. My other hand pressed against her clit as I gently bit down on her neck.

"Gonna come," she cried out around my fingers.

I gave her one hard and deep thrust that sent her over the edge. I held her around the waist to keep her from

~ 155 ~

collapsing as her orgasm weakened her knees. I pulled out of her and growled as I shot my load on her ass.

After a moment of trying to catch my breath and just enjoying the aftershocks of the quickie, I grabbed a paper towel and wiped the cream off of her round ass.

"Thank you for not getting me all messy," Lily said and turned around to give me a quick kiss. "Now move your ass. We're going to be late!"

I let Lily drive us into work. A client called me on our way out the door, starting my work day. I was still on the phone when we walked through the lobby towards the elevators.

"Lawrence, I'll call you back in a little while. I'm about to get on the elevator and I'll lose the call." I ended the phone call just as Lily was stepping onto the elevator ahead of me. I positioned myself behind her as several more people entered.

Without a thought, I put my hand on her waist and kissed the top of her head. I felt her stiffen under my hand and then she looked up at me with a shocked expression before her eyes met a few other pairs of eyes that were looking on just as shocked. She not-so discretely knocked my hand away from her waist. I narrowed my eyes at the back of her head.

"Is there a problem?" I whispered in her ear.

"Not now," she whispered back fiercely.

A couple of people pushed past us to get off of the elevator.

I again put my hand on her hip, because she was mine and I was going to touch her if I fucking wanted to.

"Stop it," she snapped in a loud whisper that may as well have been a shotgun blast in the small cab.

"No," I snapped back.

The cab stopped again and a few more people exited, but not before giving us a long look. Lily didn't try to push me away again before we made it to our floor, but she was very stiff and rigid and purposely looking straight ahead and trying to pretend I wasn't there.

When we got off of the elevator, a couple of the women

~ 156 ~

in our department looked at us with wide eyes until I glared at them, making them scurry away. I stopped Lily in the now empty hallway.

"What the fuck?" I scowled. "I can't touch you now?"

"Are you out of your mind?" she cried. "Are you trying to get us both fired? We are strictly prohibited from having a relationship. Didn't you read the damn handbook?"

"I don't give a shit what that handbook says," I growled. "I'm not hiding our relationship. I did that shit before and I'm not going to do it again, so you better get used to me fucking touching you and kissing you or pulling you into my office for a damn quickie."

I stormed away from her, but I didn't miss her loud whisper.

"Asshole!"

I walked into our department and walked to the center of the big room.

"I have an announcement," I said, catching everyone's attention. "I am living with and screwing my assistant. Does anyone have a problem with that?"

Several heads shook at once and a few people snickered. I could hear Lily's quick footstep as her heels hit the carpet in an angry cadence. I turned around just as her hand flew towards my face. The resounding crack sent her employees scurrying.

"Fucker," she growled and went into her office and slammed the door.

~~~

Just before lunch, I was called upstairs. I knew it was about Lily, but I didn't care. I stepped out of my office just as she stepped out of hers. She gave me a hateful glare before walking past me. I walked after her in silence with several pairs of eyes on us.

"I'm probably going to lose my job," she grumbled with her arms crossed as we waited for the elevator.

"I'm not hiding our relationship," I said in warning.

"You're a trust fund baby, Kyle," she said, stepping

onto the cab. "You don't have to keep this job. I don't have a trust fund. I have responsibilities to take care of."

"Lily," I started.

"No, don't *Lily* me!" she yelled and stomped her foot. "You're not going to get fired. I'm just a lowly assistant – it's my job on the line! How dare you make that decision for me!"

"It's not just about *you*, Lily," I snapped and then walked off of the elevator ahead of her.

The secretary didn't make us wait before leading us into the board room. Inside sat Ned Sterling, Warrick Sterling, and Nadia Hurley, the three top leaders of Sterling Corp. Walter used to be in Nadia's position before he got canned.

"Have a seat," Ned said.

I waited for Lily to sit first and then sat down beside her.

"We're waiting for one more," Warrick said, watching us carefully.

"Who?" I asked and then "Why?"

"Sorry, I'm late," Mayson said, rushing into the room. She took one look at me and Lily and her steps faltered. Quietly, with wide accusing eyes, she sat down on the other side of me.

"Why did you call us here?" I asked without hiding my irritation.

Though the three sitting across from us gave me my job back after they realized I wasn't in league with Walter, they had since watched over me like a hawk. They questioned every major decision I made, picked through my files and breathed down my neck constantly. They didn't trust me; even after all I had given up and lost to take care of the company and the people that relied on Sterling Corp to live.

"First thing is first," Warrick started, pushing a few files to the center of the table in my direction. "These accounts had several major mistakes that could have cost us money."

Lily reached for the files before me. "I know these accounts. I'm the one that found the mistakes. I spent a whole weekend fixing them."

"Who made the 'mistakes'?" Nadia asked Lily.

Lily narrowed her eyes at the woman across the table. "A worker who is no longer in our department. The position wasn't the right one for her, so I had her moved into one that is working out perfectly for her and the company."

"You approved this?" Warrick asked Mayson.

"Yes, I approved it," she said in a soft voice. "As Lily pointed out, the woman is doing fine in her new department."

"Are you sure that she made the mistakes?" Nadia asked Mayson.

"How would I know? That isn't my department. I don't even know how to read one of those reports."

"Look, if you're going to accuse me of something, get it done and over with," I snapped. "The employee messed up. I wanted to fire her but Lily convinced me to just move her, so we did. Lily spent a whole weekend fixing the mistakes as she pointed out and I checked over them myself later that week. No one lost any money and no one gained any money that they shouldn't have. All is well in the world. What the hell do you want?"

Three sets of eyes stared at me for a moment. Finally, Ned spoke up.

"We wanted to be sure that they weren't your mistakes and that Miss Whitman wasn't covering for you."

"Why the hell would she do that?" I growled.

"It has come to our attention that you are...involved," Ned said slowly.

"Oh. My. God." Mayson said, staring up at the ceiling.

"You didn't know?" Nadia asked her.

"No, I didn't know," she said in a controlled voice and then looked at me. "Is it true?"

"Yes," I said unapologetically. I turned to my superiors. "Yes, it's true. We became an official couple over the past few days."

I heard Lily sigh next to me.

"You do realize that there are rules and regulations against such relationships, especially since your last…relationship with an employee?" Nadia questioned.

"Of course I realize that," I said. "But I really don't care."

"Kyle," Lily sighed again.

"No, Lily," I said roughly. "I refuse to hide our relationship."

I refocused on the two men and one woman across the table from me.

"I gave up a lot to keep this company from going under," I said coolly. "I lost friends, I lost my family, and I lost someone I really cared deeply about. I put in longer hours than anyone I know and bring more profit to this company than anyone I know, but I get nothing in return but a pat on the back under your watchful and distrustful eyes. If you can't accept the fact that I have a relationship with this incredible woman, than you can fire me. I really don't care anymore."

They looked at each other and back to me.

"We don't want to fire you," Ned explained. "But we may have to let Miss Whitman go or move her to another area. We can't have this outright disregard for rules."

"Actually," Mayson surprised me by speaking up. "Mr. Sterling's department is doing much better than any other department in the building right now. It runs like a well-oiled machine and even with a less than full staff, they are running at 97% efficiency. That's not perfect, but that's pretty damn close to perfect. If you move or fire Lily I guarantee that number will drop. I don't condone their disregard for the rules, but I also agree with Kyle. You all know that he went through a lot of sh…stuff…and let's be honest. You put him through more headaches than necessary and he still keeps everything rolling smoothly. I think you're going to have to overlook this one."

Again the three of them looked at one another.

"I think we need to have a private chat," Nadia said, getting to her feet. She walked out of the door, followed closely by Ned and Warrick.

The door had barely closed before both women were on me.

"You asshole!" Mayson yelled. "Can you stop fucking your assistants!"

"I told you they would want to fire me!" Lily yelled and punched me in the arm.

"Dick!" Mayson spat and shoved me.

"Asshat!" Lily yelled.

I sighed loudly and ran a hand over my face. This was bullshit. I was getting the shit beat out of me by these women while they stood outside deciding my fucking fate. I stood up, pushing my chair back so hard that it crashed into the wall behind me. I started around the table, but the three superiors re-entered the board room. They didn't sit down, but stood near the door.

"You can keep your position, Miss Whitman," Nadia said, though she didn't seem happy about it. "You are allowed your... relationship ...but we ask that you not make it so damn obvious to the rest of the company until we can make some adjustments on the regulations. Public displays of affection are unwelcome and unnecessary. Furthermore, when you are with a client, you are to be one hundred percent professional. The clients do not need to be aware of your relationship."

"This is only temporary," Warrick warned.

They left without another word.

"Well, that was fun," Mayson said dryly as she got up to leave.

"I'm sorry," I said to her. "I didn't expect you to be dragged into this."

"I don't even want to talk to you or you right now," she said waving her arms. "Once again I have to picture your tongue flopping around in a friend's mouth and...I just can't stomach it." She put a hand to her stomach and quickly left the room.

Lily stormed past me and out of the room. I followed behind her as she bypassed the elevators where Mayson was waiting and took the stairs.

"Lily," I called after her as she moved down the stairs.

At the next landing, she spun around suddenly and

shoved me against the wall. She stood on her toes to reach my mouth and kissed me hard. I put my hands under her ass and lifted her. She wrapped her legs around me and I turned around so that I could hold her up against the wall. Her skirt had risen up her thighs. I pushed it up further and tore her lacey white panties off of her. Quickly I unzipped my pants and pushed my hard cock inside of her. She panted as I fucked her hard against the wall and kissed her neck.

When she started to cry out, I covered her mouth with mine, swallowing her orgasmic cries. A moment later I pulled out of her again and came on the floor between us with a soft grunt. I was barely recovered from my orgasm when a door above us opened and footsteps sounded on the stairs. I quickly and quietly set Lily down and stuffed her panties into my pocket as she fixed her skirt. I zipped up my pants as we hurried down the rest of the stairs and to our floor.

We walked back into our department as if we hadn't just fucked on the stairs five minutes before. Just before entering our respective offices, Lily kept her stern face but gave me a wink that made me grin.

I sat down at my desk and tried to get back to work, but my mind kept drifting back to Lily's words from earlier. She could have lost her job. I would have taken care of her, gladly, but Lily was the type of girl that didn't like handouts. She liked to earn her share. I closed the window I was working in and went to my bookmarks. I stared at the screen for a long time before I made a decision.

I picked up the phone and dialed.

"Kessler and Keane, attorneys at law," a young woman answered.

"Luke Kessler, please," I said. "Tell him it is Kyle Sterling."

Chapter Eleven

~Kyle~

"Are you sure this is a good time to meet your mom?" Lily asked from the passenger's seat. She fidgeted with the one bracelet on her wrist. It was the one bracelet with Anna's name etched into it, the only one she had not thrown away several weeks ago when our relationship changed.

I sighed and said "Baby, there is no 'good time' to meet my mother."

"If that was meant to comfort me, you failed," she said sourly.

Apologizing to her was only going to make it worse, so I didn't say anything. I could understand why she was nervous. This wasn't going to be a formal meet the parents kind of thing. While Lily and I were having brunch, my mother called and summoned me via text to the estate. I had not visited with her in weeks, so I felt obligated to go. Lily suggested I drop her off at home, but I would have had to backtrack through the city to drop her off and we were already closer to my mother's than home.

"You should have at least let me change into something more appropriate," Lily grumbled.

"There isn't anything wrong with what you have on, Lil," I insisted. Under her leather jacket, she had on an old Warrant t-shirt over a long sleeved tight, white shirt, and super tight jeans that made her ass look edible, and the sneakers I replaced for her. Her hair was loose and wild the way I loved it and she wore only a touch of eye makeup – enough to accentuate her gorgeous eyes.

"I feel so…low class," she said.

"There isn't anything low about you, Lily – except when you're on your knees with my cock between your lips."

She gave me a death stare, but I grinned until she couldn't help but to smile a little.

"You didn't think too highly of me at first," Lily reminded me.

"I didn't think lowly of you either," I said, grimacing at the memories of the things I had said to her. "Besides, what she thinks isn't going to have an impact on us."

"There was a time when what your parents thought truly mattered, more than anything else," she said, looking at me with worried eyes.

"It hasn't been that way in a long time now," I said, trying to convince both of us, but I'm not sure she was convinced.

I changed the topic, trying to take Lily's mind off meeting my manic mother, though I was worried myself. Mom may be over enthusiastic and ridiculously happy or she may be all doom and gloom, and mean – or she could be all of those things, shifting from mood to mood without warning.

I was five years old when I realized my mother was different from other moms. Impulsive trips to Disney World were cool, even though mom would get a little too excited and lose me and my brother inside the parks, sometimes for hours at a time. Countless nights of sleep were disrupted to go on adventures to Narnia or to try an array of new recipes. Those times were fun, but it was the other times that stand out in my memory the most.

Like the time she swept me and Walt Jr. away to Hollywood to try to get onto the set of our favorite show, but instead she curled up in her hotel bed and refused to interact with her children for days until someone alerted the authorities. That was one of many times Walter or some relative or employee had to come and get us.

Then there were the times that mom was on a rampage, screaming, crying, and *beating.*

The suicide attempts were probably there all along, explaining her long stays in the hospital, but after Walt died at age thirteen and I was nine, the attempts increased for a while. I was only eleven when I found her bleeding from her wrists on the kitchen floor. I was thirteen when I found her comatose after swallowing pills. It wasn't until just before I left for college that she began to have longer periods of something resembling normalcy. She stayed on track with her meds and made every therapy appointment. But there's no cure for bipolar disorder and the meds sometimes need to be changed, and then the therapy appointments stop and there's that in between period when things can turn to shit.

We cleared the security gate and started down the driveway to the house. Lily and I were having a discussion about the landscaping on the property when the sight of Walter's Mercedes parked in front of the house made me halt mid-word. The next word I spat out had nothing to do with the landscaping. Lily looked at me with surprise.

"What's wrong?" she asked.

"Walter is here," I growled.

Her head snapped back to the Mercedes. "I thought they were divorced. I thought he wasn't supposed to be here."

"He's not."

I put the car in park behind Walter's car. I started to get out of the car, but I grabbed Lily's arm as she also started to get out. She looked at me wearily.

"I don't want you to come in," I said.

"You want me to stay in the car?" she asked incredulously.

"I'm not sure why he's here or what kind of trouble he is causing. I don't want you caught in the middle of it."

"You're not leaving me in the car, Kyle."

"Bringing you to see my mother was already a questionable decision. Bringing you in the middle of what is bound to be a hostile environment is a very bad decision that I will not make."

"Fine," Lily shrugged and then with maddening stubbornness said "I will make the decision myself. I'm going in."

I scowled at her. She scowled back, snatched her arm out of my grasp and then punched me in the arm. I didn't flinch, but I sometimes forgot how hard my little bully can punch.

"The last time I saw you with your faux father, he was beating the hell out of you and about to go home to beat the hell out of your mom," she said with fiery eyes. "If you think I'm going to just sit here in the damn car while a free for all is going on inside, you're out of your pretentious mind."

"What have I done lately that has been pretentious?" I threw my hands up in frustration.

"Your very existence is pretentious! Your pretentious penthouse, your pretentious car..." She gestured wildly at the house and surrounding property. "Your pretentious upbringing!"

I dragged my hands over my face as I tried not to lose my fucking mind. Lily had the ability to drive me crazy like no one else I've ever known. I didn't want her getting hurt if things were to get crazy inside, nor did I want her to see some other things...

"You're staying in the car," I snapped at her. "That's the end of the discussion."

"You are right about one thing," she said. "That *is* the end of the discussion." She punched me one last time and then got out of the car.

I growled as I followed her lead and jumped out. I slammed the door and stalked around the car. Lily was already standing at the door waiting for me. Her hair whipped around in the winter wind. If I wasn't so pissed at her, I would have pressed her up against the wall and kissed her while her hair veiled us from the cold.

"You're a pain in the ass," I growled at her instead.

"I'll remember that later when you want to snuggle," she said, rolling her eyes.

"I don't snuggle!"

I used my key to unlock the door and ushered Lily in ahead of me. I turned to the security pad next to the door and entered a code to keep the alarms from going off. My anger intensified knowing that the only way Walter was able to get in was through my mother. When he moved out, I arranged for all of the locks to be changed and had a new security system installed. This was the fifth time my mother had given him the security code, and she always regretted it later. It gave me some indication of what her current state of mind.

Not sure where they were, and hoping to God they weren't in bed, I started towards the kitchen at the back of the house with Lily close behind me. As we got closer, I heard Walter's gruff voice and my mother's soft tone.

"We can go away as soon as my affairs are settled," I heard him saying.

"Where will we go?" Mom asked in a small voice that I recognized as severely depressed.

"Where ever you like, Felicia. Whatever will make you happy."

I stepped in the room at the end of his sentence. Four eyes turned to me, drifted down to Lily beside me, and then back to me. Walter's eyes flared with anger. Mom sat at the island looking miserable, yet a little hopeful. Her golden brown eyes were muddy looking, and the skin around her eyes was sagging with weariness. Her dark brown hair was heavy with gray streaks, and it looked just as limp as her body. Her shoulders were slumped in defeat and her pale fingers nervously pulled at the sleeves of her long sweater. I hated seeing my mother like this. When she was doing well, she was beautiful and confident. When she was manic, she became someone else. Likewise, when she was in a depressed state, she became someone else.

"You are not supposed to be here," I said to Walter.

He shrugged. "Your mother and I just reconciled," he said, haughtily. "I belong here. You don't."

This wasn't the first time this has happened. Walter was always trying to get back into the big house and into my mother's pocketbook. He was an heir with a sensible trust fund, but he made most of his money when he was VP at Sterling. When he was ousted for his fraudulent behavior, his shares of the company were forfeited and his annual trust fund was reduced from six figures to a mere sixty grand a year. He lost nearly everything he had and almost cost my mother the house that has been in her family for over a century. For a man who was used to living the high life his entire life, he was unable to accept his current financial situation. More than a few times my mother had been duped into giving him money. Sadly, so had I. But I was done with his shit, and I couldn't let my mother get caught in his web again.

"Mom, he is not going to change," I said. "He is not good for you."

Walter looked at Lily with an amused, but disturbing smile. "You remember those words, young lady. He will damage you eventually, and when he asks for forgiveness, remember what he has just said."

I felt Lily stiffen behind me. "Do *not* speak to her," I warned with clear intent in my voice. "Get out of this house."

"No," my mother's small voice said forcefully. She looked at me like a mother looks at the child she is disciplining. "It's different this time. I want him to stay."

"You're not thinking with a clear head right now, Mom," I said patiently.

Walter shook his head as he walked around the island to stand beside her. It only intensified my boiling anger.

"Felicia, he always treats you as if you are stupid when you have these episodes," he said, rubbing my mother's back.

With great effort, I ignored him. "I know everything feels hopeless right now, but -"

"You *don't* know!" Mom snapped. "You have no idea how it feels. I'm in this big house by myself day after day after day. I don't have anyone."

"You have me," I said, placing a hand on my chest. "You don't need him."

"It's not the same thing," she said bitterly. "And I don't want you."

I felt Lily's hand close on my upper arm.

"I'm the only one that has stuck around and taken care of you," I reminded her. "Miranda left and never looked back. Walter only cares about his own needs, and -"

"And you killed Walt Jr.," she said scathingly. "Everything was fine before your stupid actions snuffed out his life. It was your actions that destroyed all of us."

Though it was not the first time she has made similar comments, the pain in my chest never dulled. It never hurt any less than it did the previous time. I could have lashed out at her and told her it was her inability to get a grasp on her disease that fucked us all up, that and her abusive husband, but I didn't. I sucked in a deep breath as I felt Lily's other hand on my back. I didn't want her to see this shit.

"Regardless of what you think of me," I started patiently. "This is not a good decision for you. I can't keep coming over here and fixing the damage he does."

"I don't *need* you!" she shouted.

"You are fighting a losing battle," Walter said with a smirk. "Your mother has made up her mind."

"If you don't shut your mouth, I will put my fist in it," I growled at him.

"Don't speak to your father like that!" Mom snapped.

"He's not my father!" I shouted.

"That's right," Walter said, nodding. "You are just a bastard mistake. You never really appreciated everything I gave to you. Everything you have is because of me. Hell, you have more privileges in *my* family and *my* family business than I do. You should be a little more considerate, especially since you are the one responsible for taking it all away."

My fist was going into his mouth. I had enough of him. I had held back from beating his head in for years, but there was no reason not to now. I moved to go after him, but a blur of red hair rushed past me. I just barely caught up to Lily before she could put *her* fist into Walter's mouth. I wrapped my arms around her waist and lifted her off of the floor.

"You sonofabitch!" she yelled. "Someday the universe is going to repay you for all of the pain and trouble you have caused! And *you*!" she pointed to my mother, even as I carried her struggling body away. "When this blows up in your face again, you better hope that I don't convince your son to leave you to rot!"

"Take your little, low class, punk whore and get out," Walter snarled.

I released Lily so quickly, she fell on her ass. Before she could get up, I was already throwing my first punch, making Walter eat my fist. My mother screamed for me to stop as I threw two more punches. The second punch opened his bottom lip and blood started streaming from it. Walter wasn't a pussy, he wasn't going to just sit there and take a beating. He threw a punch that connected with my jaw, but that didn't slow me down. I punched him twice more before he lunged at me and threw me against a couple of stools. The stools crashed to the floor as my back rammed into the island. He tried to throw another punch, but I blocked it and then planted my fist right between his eyes. He fell to the ground hard. His head bounced off of the floor, but I had only knocked him down, not out.

My mother shoved me, slapped me in the face and shoved me again. "I hate you! You ruin everything!" she screamed before racing over to Walter.

"Time to go," Lily said, pulling me away from the scene on the floor. "Come on, baby, let's go."

I allowed her to pull me out of the kitchen, through the house and out the door. Once we were outside, she reached into my jacket pocket for the keys and unlocked the car. She opened the passenger's side door.

"Get in," she commanded.

Without argument, I got into the car. She quickly buckled me in before closing the door and rushing around to get in behind the wheel. She turned the car on, buckled her seatbelt and took off like a bat out of hell down the driveway.

We didn't speak for the ride home, nor did we speak when we first got into the penthouse. Lily held my hand and I allowed her to lead me upstairs into my bedroom and into the bathroom. She kicked off her sneakers and quickly stripped out of her clothes before stepping into the large stall to turn the shower on. Once she had that going, she returned and started to strip me out of my clothes. I helped her by kicking off my sneakers, but I let her do most of the work and then pull me into the shower.

Under the water, Lily wrapped her arms around me and rested her head on my chest. I held her close and rested my cheek on the top of her head. We stood there silently like that for a long time, but we weren't close enough. I tilted her head back and looked into her sad eyes, reflecting what she saw in my own eyes no doubt. I brought my mouth to hers and kissed her tenderly at first, slowly stroking her tongue and lips with my own. The kiss soon turned feral as I pushed Lily up against the wall and took total possession of her mouth. I kept my tongue tied with hers as I put my hands under her ass and lifted. She locked her hands around my neck and wrapped her legs around my waist. I grunted and she cried out into my mouth as I drove my cock inside of her with one hard thrust.

Reluctantly, I stopped kissing her so I could look into her eyes as I thrust inside of her again.

"Don't hold back," Lily whispered, before softly kissing my lips. "Give me your pain."

I looked at her with doubt as I moved slowly inside of her.

"Give me your pain," she whispered again, before squeezing her legs tighter around me.

I stopped thinking about the consequences and slammed into her as hard as I possibly could. She cried out and her face pinched, but she panted "Don't stop. Don't hold back."

I lost my fucking mind as I pounded into her harder than I could remember ever pounding into anyone. My anger. My frustration. My pain. I gave it all to her as I literally nailed her against the shower wall. I slammed into her so hard, that it hurt my pelvic bone every time it hit her body. Years of turmoil went into every thrust. Everything I had ever suffered or lost went into every thrust. I realized I was probably hurting her, but she again begged me not to stop. Even with the water spraying on us, I could see the tears filling and then spilling out of her eyes.

~ 171 ~

My climax hit me suddenly. Without warning, I was growling and groaning as my seed spilled into Lily's womb. She clung to me, sobbing into my shoulder as her own orgasm coursed through her body. When I had given her every drop, I didn't release her. I let my emotions flow through my body into hers. I held her as she did the one thing I wouldn't allow myself to do. I held her tightly and let her cry for me.

~~~

"Who is Miranda?" Lily asked later in bed.

My head rested on her belly as I held her and her fingers leisurely ran through my hair.

"My sister."

"I thought so. When I was unpacking some of your things last month, I came across some pictures. She's pretty."

"Yes, she's very pretty," I agreed.

"Where is she? What happened to her?"

I hesitated before answering. I never had to answer to anyone about Miranda. Jess knew I had a sister, but she didn't really care enough to discuss her. Em knew I had a sister, but sensing the sensitivity of the topic, she veered away from discussing her and I didn't have the desire to talk about her either. Lily was different. She knew it was a sensitive topic, but she wanted to know me inside and out, even if it meant that she had to experience some of the madness that was my life and make me talk about something that hurt to talk about.

"Miranda is ten years older than me," I started. "By the time I was born, she had enough sense to not only go to boarding school, but to stay there through the summers and most holidays. She only came home two or three times a year, and never for very long.

"When I was eight and she was eighteen, she finished school and decided to come home for a while before venturing out on her own. There were some legal things she had to handle – like getting her college fund switched primarily into her name so she could pay her tuition, and take care of any paperwork she needed for her trust fund. She didn't spend much time with our parents, but she hung out with Walt and I at the pool, played games with us, drove us to amusement parks and arcades, and the beach."

I paused at the memory of Miranda's smiling face in the sunshine at the beach. She really was pretty with her long dark hair and sparkling brown eyes, so much like our mother's, and she was fun, and kind despite who her parents were.

"That was the best summer of my life," I murmured. "After all of her affairs were settled, she still stayed for some time. I think she was just trying to make sure that my brother and I were going to be okay. One day, all hell broke loose. I don't remember what sparked it, but she started fighting with Walter. I had seen my mom beat her before when she was little – my mom beat all of us when her emotions were out of control. But I never saw Walter hit Miranda, not until that day. He not only hit her, he *beat* her."

I heard Lily's sharp intake of breath and her fingers stilled in my hair.

"I followed Randi to her room and watched her pack up the few things she had brought with her from school. I begged her to take me with her, but she said she was just a kid herself and she couldn't take care of me. She made me promise to take care of my mother, gave me the biggest hug I've ever had in my life and then she left. I never saw her again. She called me after my brother died, and sent letters and postcards from time to time, but by the time I was eighteen, it ended."

"Baby I'm sorry," she said and rubbed my back. "But I can't believe that you didn't stalk her once you learned how to. You've stalked less important people."

I managed a small smile. "You're not less important, and yes, I did 'stalk' her, but this was a different situation. I didn't want to be rejected by her. I don't think I would have handled it well. You can understand that, because of your father."

She nodded solemnly. "I can understand that. What did you find out?"

"She's an obstetrician. She shares a practice with two other doctors. She lives in North Carolina with her husband

Chad, a decorated police officer, and her three children, two boys and one girl. The oldest is almost thirteen now, and the twins are ten."

"Are you still afraid of being rejected?" she asked quietly.

I was silent for a moment as I considered it. When Emmy rejected me, it hurt pretty damn badly. I don't know how I managed to push myself to go to work and function, because I felt like I was unhinged. How the hell I managed to fall in love with Lily while I was still reeling from Emmy, I don't know, but the pain was still there, under everything. I wasn't sure if I'd ever get over Emmy. With that said, if Miranda were to reject me, it would hurt ten times worse than it did with Emmy. I was sure it would alter me significantly, and not for the best.

"Yes," I finally said to Lily.

She remained quiet, but her breathing changed. Her breaths were faster now, as if she was climbing towards panic. I sat up to look at her, but the moment I released her, she jumped off of the bed.

"I have to pee," she said and dashed into the bathroom.

I looked at the bathroom door for a moment before getting up. I stood outside of the door for a few seconds, listening to her cry softly. I pushed open the door and found her sitting on the edge of the tub with a towel up to her face as she cried.

"Hey, look," I said, kneeling in front of her. I pulled her hands away from her face. "I'm not crying for myself. You don't need to cry for me either."

"I'm not usually a crier," she sobbed. "But...I've been so fucking lucky in my life and I've taken it all for granted. I didn't have the money that you had growing up, and I used to think that money would have made things better for us, but it didn't make it any better for you or your brother and sister. My mother spanked my ass when I was little, slapped me in the face once when I came home drunk, but I was never *abused*. I never lost a sibling in death, and even the shit with my dad and

Nina doesn't seem as bad as all of the shit you went through with that jackass faux father," she spit out the last part as if it burned her tongue.

"And my sister..." she sobbed harder. "She screwed me over, it's true, but she never rejected me. I rejected her, and I have been rejecting her despite the hard time she's already having. I'm such a douche puddle! If she feels even half as badly as you must feel, maybe someone should kick *my* ass. Oh, my god, I just made this about me," she said, holding on to my hands. "I'm sorry, I didn't mean to. I'm really crying for you, Kyle, because despite everything, I still have what you've never had, and it just makes me so damn sad."

I sat down on the floor with my back against the tub and pulled her down into my lap. I used the towel to wipe her face.

"Don't cry for me, Lily," I said and kissed her forehead. "You have to stop crying or I won't snuggle with you."

A laugh escaped through her tears. "I thought you don't snuggle," she said.

"You are repeatedly making me love the things I don't want to," I said as I grinned down at her. "I didn't want to love your tattoos and piercings and style. I didn't want to love your skills at work. I didn't want to love the way you drive me fucking crazy with that obnoxious mouth of yours. I didn't want to love *you* and I do. Now I love snuggling, but if you repeat that to anyone, you'll never get snuggles again."

She laughed again, even though her body still shook with her crying. "Okay. I won't repeat it."

We sat there silently until Lily was able to stop crying. Her body still shuddered from the sobbing, but the tears had ended.

"What are you going to do when Walter screws your mom over again?"

I sighed. I know she wanted me to say that I would write her off, but I couldn't do that. "I will help her pick herself up again, hopefully avoid any suicide attempts, and help her carry on until the next time."

"She was so mean to you," Lily frowned.

"It's the bipolar talking," I sighed. "When she's on her meds and the meds are working well for her, she is a different person."

"Will she apologize to you for all of the things she said?"

"Not directly. She'll take me out to lunch or dinner and we will talk about everything else except for what happened. That will be her apology."

"That's not an apology. That's a lack of admission of guilt."

"It is the only way she knows how to say sorry," I said. "I'll take what I can get. Now," I said, patting her leg. "Let's put the events of the day and the past behind us. Let's go get some dinner. My appetite is back. Are you hungry, my little bully?"

She looked up at me with mischief in her eyes. "I'm hungry," she said with a funny smile. She crawled out of my lap and onto her knees. "Pull your pants down and sit down on the tub," she commanded.

"Whoa," I said, holding up my hands. "I'm a virtuous person. I will not be taken advantage of by some...some..."

"Low class, punk whore?" she asked, with her eyebrows raised.

I frowned. "Don't go there."

"It's okay. I wasn't nearly as insulted as you were." She patted the tub behind me. "Now get your ass up there. I'm hungry, damn it."

"You're a little bully," I said, getting to my feet.

"Yeah, yeah. Stop crying, pussy."

I pulled off my lounge pants and my erection sprung free. I sat down on the edge of the high tub as the bully commanded. I watched as she smiled up at me before taking my cock in her soft hand. Painfully, slowly, her tongue swirled around the engorged head. I groaned deeply as I felt her tongue ring slide over the slit at the top of my cock. I'm a guy, I like blowjobs, but Lily's blowjobs hit all others out of the park. It wasn't just her magical tongue ring that did it for me; she was highly skilled in the art of fellatio. The pressure, the rhythm and the depth…Lily understood all of it.

Slowly, her mouth began to slide down my cock as she looked me in the eyes. I groaned again but resisted the urge to thrust. Where other women would have halted, Lily continued until my whole length was in her mouth, pressing down into her hot throat. I growled as she held it there for a moment. She was enjoying watching me squirm.

"If you don't stop I'm going to fuck your mouth," I warned, nearly breathless.

Her eyes narrowed on mine and somehow, unbelievably, she took me even deeper.

"Don't say I didn't warn you," I said and put both of my hands in her hair. I quickly got to my feet, forcing her to back up some, but she didn't try to escape what was coming.

I pulled my cock out until only the tip was on the tip of her tongue. Without warning, I shoved my cock into her mouth until my balls slapped against her chin. Lily gagged around my cock, but her hands planted on my ass and held me tightly against her face. I pulled out to let her catch a few breaths before I drove forth again.

"Oh, shit," I groaned. "You have the…" I growled as I thrust into her mouth again. "Most perfect fucking mouth."

I pumped in and out of her mouth, always keeping my eyes locked with hers. My cock was covered in her saliva, and some of it dripped from the corners of her cock-fucked mouth. It was hot and dirty, like the little bully I was thrusting into.

The downside of Lily's mouth was that I didn't last very long. I felt myself getting very close very fast. I pulled out until only the head of my cock was in her mouth.

"Suck me," I commanded in a harsh whisper.

Lily immediately complied. She sucked on the head of my cock like it was a giant lollypop with a creamy center she was trying to get to. Soon my cock was jerking as I groaned. My cream shot to the back of her throat and all corners of her beautiful mouth. A few white lines dribbled out of her mouth, but everything else she swallowed with her own little moans of satisfaction. She didn't release me until she was sure she sucked me dry.

"Okay, now I can go for some real food," she sighed happily and got to her feet.

"Well, now *I'm* hungry," I said and kissed her lips.

She took a step back from me. "Seriously. I need food now."

I nodded. "I understand," I said. Before she could figure it out, I swept her up into my arms and made her squeal. I carried her into the bedroom and tossed her onto the bed. In a few seconds, I had her shorts and panties off and thrown onto the floor. I settled between her luscious thighs to sate my appetite.

Chapter Twelve

~Lily~

"Don't come in yet!" I yelled to Kyle after he rapped on my door. "I have to put on my shoes and put on my earrings."

"Umm...okay," he said hesitantly from the other side. "You know I've seen you in less than that, right?"

I rolled my eyes at the door as I slipped into one of my heels. "I want you to see the complete ensemble. This is a big deal for me. I've never been dressed up like this before – well except for Prom," I said. "But even that can't begin to compare."

I heard him sigh on the other side of the door. "You're killing me here, Lil. The party starts in a half hour."

"There isn't anything wrong with being fashionably late," I argued as I put in my first earring. "It's...fashionable."

"Very astute of you, babe. Now hurry up."

"Quit your whining!" I snapped.

The party was at the Art Museum, only a few minutes away, but I understood why Kyle wanted to make a good impression. The host, Ted Grant, was an associate of Marco's. Marco had come on board of Kyle's building venture, but because the higher ups at Sterling Corp weren't interested in the project, the men had to find another backer. Marco introduced Kyle to Ted Grant, who already had several profitable and well run properties similar to what Kyle wanted to produce. Since this wasn't a Sterling Corp related function, I was free to go as Kyle's girlfriend.

I checked myself out in the mirror one last time as Kyle again knocked on the door. I threw the door open and took a step back so that he could get a good look. His eyes widened and his mouth dropped open. Taking that as a good sign, I slowly turned in a circle so that he could see how I looked from behind, too.

The white halter cocktail dress was shorter than what I would normally wear, with the hem stopping a little less than mid-thigh. The bottom half of the dress was tight and hugged my hips and ass, but the top half was a little loose except where the neckline plunged down to just below my breasts. The dress was backless, revealing the art inked on my back. My pumps were a light metallic bronze and gave me four and a half more inches of height. My hair was flat ironed and pulled back to my left side and held in place with a white, sequined barrette, leaving the stars under my right ear visible. My makeup was light, but made my gray eyes pop, and my nails were manicured and painted in a clear polish. The only jewelry I wore was a pair of diamond earrings Kyle surprised me with after our ousting at Sterling Corp.

"So, what do you think?" I asked Kyle with a big smile as his eyes traveled up and down my body.

"Baby, where is the rest of your dress?" he frowned.

My smile fell as a hand went to my hip. "You don't like it?"

"I love it, but..." he rubbed his chin between his forefinger and thumb.

"But what?" I demanded. I was beginning to feel a little irritated. I half expected him to try tearing the dress off of me when he saw me, not to look so disapproving.

"Damn," he whispered when his eyes grazed over my hips. "Your curves look fucking fantastic, but if I can't keep my eyes off of you, other men won't be able to keep their eyes off of you either."

I rolled my eyes. I didn't think I was unattractive, but I was sure there were going to be more attractive, *slim* women at the party for other guys to gawk at.

Kyle reached out and tried to pull the fabric of my dress over the uncovered curves of my breasts. I smacked his hands away.

"Stop it! It's supposed to be like that!"

He groaned as he reached out and cupped a breast. "I can see the outline of your nipple rings, Lily!"

"So what?" I smacked his hand away from me.

"So, it's fucking erotic and I don't want anyone else having erotic thoughts about you!"

"You're ruining my night!" I yelled and smacked him with my white and gold clutch bag.

"I think you should change into something less...revealing," he said, moving past me towards my closet.

"I don't have anything else to change into, Kyle," I crossed my arms. "I like what I have on."

"What about that gray suit I bought you for work?" he asked, already inside my closet.

I ignored him and walked out of the room. I went downstairs even as he was calling out more suggestions to me. I sat down on the arm of the couch as I waited for Kyle to come to his senses. A minute later, he came trotting down the stairs carrying the gray suit and a black dress I sometimes wore to work. The hem on that dress was just below my knees and the only bare skin it showed were my arms. How boring.

I looked at Kyle with disinterest as he held up the two boring outfits.

"Choose one of these," he commanded. "Hurry up. We're already going to be late."

"You're being a pussy," I said in a boring tone as I looked at my nails. I sighed and got to my feet and looked at his scowling face. "Are you ready to go yet?"

I turned my back on him and bent over to pick his car keys up off of the coffee table.

"Shit," I heard him hiss just before the suit and dress were thrown onto the couch.

Before I could turn back around, Kyle's hands were on my hips, guiding me to the arm of the couch. He put his hand on my lower back and slowly slid it up between my shoulder blades. He pressed firmly, making me bend over the arm of the couch. I braced myself the best I could, planting my hands flat on the cushion in front of me as Kyle grabbed my ass in both hands with a low groan.

"Your ass looks amazing in this dress," he said, his

voice full of heat.

His hands slid down to my thighs and then under my dress. Slowly, he pushed the dress up over my thighs and over my ass.

"Oh my god," he growled, slipping his finger under my thong.

I moaned when I felt his knuckle roll over my clit.

"Do you like the way you look, baby?" he asked, as he rubbed my clit harder.

"Mmm hmm," I moaned.

"I can tell. You're very wet." He groaned as he moved his knuckle faster over my swollen nub. Seconds later, I was bucking my hips with my orgasm as I cried out.

"Good girl," he murmured, and ran a hand over my back.

He took his hand out of my panties, but before I could stand up, he had pressed me back down and pushed two fingers inside of me. I groaned and pushed against his hand.

"Keep still," he whispered and held me down with his hand on the small of my back.

Kyle's fingers plunged deep inside of me and then moved in a slow circular motion that drove me crazy.

"You're so fucking sexy," Kyle growled and started to fuck me hard with his fingers. "So wet…"

I moaned loudly as his fingers slid in and out of me. I could never get enough of his fingers, his mouth, and his cock. Kyle slipped his other hand in front of me and started massaging my clit again, this time with his index and middle fingers.

"Put your hand in your dress and squeeze your nipples," he demanded in a raspy voice.

I did as I was told, balancing myself on one hand while Kyle's hands continuously manipulated me towards an orgasm.

"Oh shit!" I cried out when I squeezed my own nipple. I rolled it between my fingers and tugged on the jewelry.

"Come, Lily," Kyle commanded as his fingers increased speed. "Come, baby."

My body exploded – my senses exploded – it felt like everything around me and inside of me exploded as my body was hit with a wave of intense orgasms. I gained no control of my shuddering, over sensitive body before Kyle had dropped his pants, pulled up his tux shirt, *tore* away my thong and drove his stiff rod inside of me. He grunted with each thrust as one hand held onto my hip and the other hand was flat against my back.

"Pinch your nipples," he demanded again, and again I complied, rolling the hard nipple between my fingers and tugging on the barbell. "You're so fucking hot in this dress," Kyle growled as he slammed into me.

He slid his hand up my back, over my neck and across my cheek and pressed his middle two fingers into my mouth. I sucked on his fingers as if they were a cock and continued pinching, tugging and squeezing on my nipples as Kyle thrusts increased in pace. Soon I was falling off the cliff again, screaming his name and thrashing beneath him.

"Oh, Lily," he groaned a really long groan before suddenly pulling out of me. "Turn around," he urged.

I pushed myself up and turned around. Kyle stood there with his sizeable cock in his hand, squeezing the head between his two fingers. I crouched down before him in my high as hell heels and opened my mouth. He put the head of his cock on my outstretched tongue and released it. A sudden burst of semen hit the back of my throat. Kyle yelled expletives as he came in my mouth. He pressed his dick all the way in and I closed my lips around it and sucked him until there was nothing left.

"Help me stand up," I giggled, reaching for his hand. "I don't know how hookers do this shit."

~Kyle~

We arrived at the party "fashionably late" after all. I was significantly less tense about Lily's dress than I was before, but I would have to control my urge to break the jaw of any guy that looked at her too long.

Lily was absolutely glowing when she removed her coat before we entered the party. It was her multiple orgasms, I know it. She always glowed after sex. Her eyes lit up, she smiled a lot, and her whole demeanor was relaxed, but confident.

She put her hand in mine and we followed another couple into the dinner party. The attention my little red headed bully got as I began introducing her to people I knew was immediate. Women like Lily didn't usually socialize in this type of crowd, white collar business mixed with over privileged high society. It seems extremely crude to say it like that, but it doesn't make it any less true. Every now and then we will get a couple of celebrities at these functions. Their tattoos and crazy hairstyles are accepted and praised, but middle class normal citizens like Lily are chastised by the women and the men that aren't also chastising them, want to bed her because she is different.

My earlier nervousness about bring her here had a lot to do with how catty some of the women were bound to be, but I was more concerned with the assholes that were going to be all over her, and there were many already sizing her up, including Marco. Lily seemed unconcerned about that, however, when she wrapped her arms around his neck for an embrace. He wriggled his eyes at me as his hands smoothed over her back. Because he was my old friend, he deserved to be punched harder than the other guys.

"Your man let you out of the house dressed like this?" Marco teased her.

"Just barely," she smiled up at him as he checked out the neckline on her dress.

"Stop eye fucking my girlfriend," I said in a low voice to him and pulled Lily to my side.

He grinned and held his hands up in defeat. Lily shook her head at me.

"I'm going to the lady's room," she said and started to walk away.

"I'll take you," I said, squeezing her hand.

"You are not taking me to the bathroom," she said firmly and shook her hand free of mine. "Don't cause a scene," she whispered in my ear before turning her back on me to leave.

"You're already causing one," I said to her back. She glared at me over her shoulder.

"I'm glad she walked away," Marco said seriously.

"Why?" I asked, my alarms going off in my head.

"Because I can watch her luscious ass as she does," he said, watching her disappear out the door.

"Do you have a death wish?" I scowled at him. "She's not even your type."

"She's not yours either, my friend, but here you are," he said, gesturing widely. His face grew serious again though, and I knew he was going to address something serious.

"What is it? Is it Grant?" I asked. I had not seen the man since I walked in. It was his party, but he didn't seem to be present.

"No, not really," Marco said.

"Where is he?"

"He's here. He had to step out to make an important phone call. Listen, Kyle, Jessyca is coming."

Automatically, I looked back the way Lily had left. The last thing I wanted was to have Lily and Jess in the same room. Jess would try to verbally annihilate her just because she was with me, and Lily wouldn't think twice about taking off her spiky heel and embedding it in Jess's face.

"Why the hell is she coming?" I asked Marco. The first few times I ran into Jess after our break up were not pretty memories. I wasn't afraid of her, but I started steering clear of her where ever I could. I rarely did anything socially anymore, but the few times I did I had to be sure she wouldn't be there.

She was still bitter about all that happened between us, and I didn't blame her, but I didn't see the need to have it out in public – especially in front of any business associates – every time we met.

"Grant invited her. Apparently they've been doing some business. I think she might be trying to get in on this project, Kyle."

"Hell no!" I growled.

"She might be able to do it on Grant's shirt tails. She won't be in our group on paper, but he may outsource Venner Associates and she'll still be somewhat involved."

"I will back the hell out if she comes on board in any capacity," I said, watching the door for Lily.

"It's your project, Kyle," Marco tried to say reassuringly. "Don't let her push you out like that."

"She probably only wants to come on so she can find a way to ruin me," I said bitterly.

Lily re-entered the room, immediately drawing the attention of all of the men standing in that vicinity. The women, of course, looked at her with disdain, but most of the men openly and not so openly ogled her. She didn't get more than a few feet before an older man stopped her. She was polite, shook his hand and introduced herself. He stood too damn close and I knew from experience he was telling her about his yacht and leading up to asking her to join him for dinner on it one day. I turned away from Marco to go fetch Lily. I had only taken a few steps when Jess walked into the room behind Lily. Her quick eyes accessed Lily in a matter of seconds as she passed by her, and I knew already by the look on her face that she would be nasty to Lily, but the nastiness would reach an all-time high once she realized who Lily was here with.

I reached Lily just as the asshole was telling her about his yacht. Without acknowledging him, I took Lily's hand and led her away.

"Well, that was rude," she said.

"He was going to tell you about his yacht and ask you

for dinner. The yacht is in the Mediterranean, but he wouldn't have told you that until you were boarding his private plane."

"I love the Mediterranean," Lily said with a shrug. "I think I would have taken him up on his offer."

I gave her a look that implied that her joke was not funny. She giggled and said "Oh, come on. Even after being with you I'm not *that* desperate."

"Hilarious," I said dryly, glancing at Jess across the room. Grant had returned from his phone call and she was talking to him by the bar. Fortunately she had not seemed to notice us yet.

"Why are you so serious?" Lily sighed. "If you're going to be this serious all night, I'm going to go hang out with Marco."

I narrowed my eyes at her, but she ignored it and grabbed a glass of champagne off of a passing tray.

"You're not going to kill my glow, yo," she said.

"Jess is here," I said.

Lily had just taken a sip of champagne. She gave me the "are you serious" look until she swallowed her drink.

"Why is she here?" she asked.

"Grant invited her. Marco thinks she might try to somehow get in on the project."

"Where is she?" Lily asked, but the question was answered by Jessyca herself when she stepped up beside us with Grant at her side.

I slid my arm around Lily's waist and pulled her close as I shook Grant's hand.

"Glad you could make it, Kyle. Sorry I didn't catch you when I came in. There was an immediate problem I had to take care of." He turned his attention to Lily. He at least met her eyes before letting his eyes greedily drop to the bare swells of her breasts. "Ted Grant," he said, offering his hand.

"Lily Whitman," she smiled as she placed her hand in his.

"Do you work for Kyle?" he asked.

Now I understood how I must have appeared to Lily

when I made similar comments. I felt my own irritation when he automatically assumed that she must be working for me and not with me. Though the former was true, Grant shouldn't have assumed by her appearance that she wasn't capable of more.

"Lily is my girlfriend," I said, pulling her a little closer.

Grant's eyes widened a little, but before he could say anything, Jessyca had to remind us she was standing there.

"Jessyca Venner," she said tersely, slicing the air between Grant and me to offer her hand to Lily.

Lily's smile faded slightly, but she didn't hesitate to shake Jess's hand. She must have given her a tight squeeze, because the skin around Jess's eyes tensed a little, a sign of pain, and when she pulled back her hand, she surreptitiously rubbed it. I almost laughed at her.

"Hello, Kyle," she said in a tone that I knew she thought was a little sexy and flirtatious, but it only grinded my nerves.

"Jessyca," I said curtly. "Ted, thank you for having us," I said turning my attention away from her. She pouted a little.

"You and the lovely Lily are always welcome," he said. He looked at his watch. "Maybe we can pull Marco away from Mrs. Stein and get a drink before dinner is served," he suggested. In other words, he wanted to talk a little business without the girls.

I was reluctant to leave Lily alone with Jess, or with just about anyone in the room, but I didn't go to the dinner just for the food and drinks.

"Sure," I nodded. "I'll see you in a little bit," I said to Lily, and just to make it clear to Jess, Grant and to everyone in the room what Lily was to me, I put my hand on her neck and pulled her in for a very brief, but tender kiss.

She smiled up at me, her eyes still aglow from our earlier activities. "Don't worry," she whispered. "That bitch isn't going to kill my glow."

~Lily~

The moment Kyle walked away, Jessyca Venner wanted to pretend as if we were old friends, but I could smell her insincerity from the other side of the globe.

"I love your dress," she said, looking me up and down. "Who made it?"

I shrugged. "I don't know. I don't pay attention to things like that."

She nodded as if she understood, but then leaned over conspiringly and said "If you're going to be attending a lot of these functions, people are going to ask. I like fashion, that is why I ask, but some of these other women will tear you apart if the designer isn't up to par."

"I'll keep that in mind," I said and took another sip of champagne.

Kyle looked at me from the bar across the room while Grant and Marco talked. I gave him a small nod and a smile to let him know I was okay. When Grant started speaking to him, he reluctantly turned away.

"How long have you two been together?" Jess asked, following my line of sight.

"A while," I said. I didn't really want her to know details of our personal life together.

"Have you met Marco?"

What the hell was this? Ask Lily Random Questions Day?

"Yes, I have."

"He doesn't like me," she laughed lightly. "I don't think he likes many people. He and Kyle were made for each other."

"I get along very well with Marco," I said. "He is actually very friendly once you get to know him."

"Well, I guess it was just me he didn't like," she said with that fake laugh again.

"That is probably true," I said without laughter.

I was getting bored with her idea of conversation, but I didn't really know anyone else to speak to. Most of the other women in the room eyed me with distaste, which was to be expected, but most of the men eyed me like they wanted to eat me for dinner. Even though that was the case, when a good looking guy approached me while Jess was in mid gossip about a couple across the room, I gladly shook the guy's hand as he introduced himself as Trevor.

"Lily," I said, and then tried to extract my hand, but he held it firmly in his.

"I have been admiring the beautiful artwork on your back," he said with a smooth voice.

He really was cute, for a rich preppy boy. Light hair, light eyes, and pretty teeth.

"Thank you," I said. I glanced over his shoulder and saw Kyle watching with narrowed eyes. I again tried to pull my hand away, but Trevor wasn't having it.

"I am curious though," he said, leaning in a little closer. "Who is Anna?"

"My daughter," I said quietly. I was used to answering that question – it was bound to become a popular question when I got her name printed on my back, but I didn't want to discuss it in front of Jess.

"I see," Trevor said. He didn't seem to care that I had a daughter. Thankfully he didn't linger on that. "I've never seen you at any of Grant's functions before."

"I have never been to any of Grant's functions before."

"Are you here with someone?" he asked, stepping in a little closer.

"Trevor, you pig," Jessyca smacked his arm. "She's here with Kyle."

His hand immediately released mine, and not a moment too soon. Kyle suddenly appeared behind him. Though the men were roughly the same height, Kyle made Trevor cower and appear to be much smaller. Without another word or glance in my direction, Trevor retreated.

"They're about to serve dinner," Kyle said, taking my hand into his. "I knew you shouldn't have worn this damn dress."

"Are you suggesting that I am less attractive without the dress?" I asked him as we followed the crowd towards the dining area.

"Don't do that," he warned. "You know what I mean. Every physical asset you have is put on display in this dress."

"I know, right?" I beamed. I gave his hand a little squeeze. "Baby, you're not killing my glow."

His frown deepened, but he brought my hand to his lips and kissed it.

Being ridiculously over protective, Kyle made Marco sit on the other side of me, but warned him to keep his hands to himself.

"What if she touches me first?" Marco teased.

Kyle scowled so deeply, I thought his face was going to break off of his head and fall into his soup bowl. I rubbed his arm and promised him I wouldn't touch Marco – much. Marco and I laughed at his expression.

Jess sat down across from Kyle. Grant was between them at the head of the table. He seemed to have kept the space open just for her. They smiled at each other, but not like a friend smiles at a friend. There seemed to be something a little deeper there, which bothered me. It made me believe she was going to use her position as Grant's...whatever she was...to push her way into Kyle's project. By the look exchanged between Marco and Kyle, I knew they thought the same thing.

Through the soup and salad courses, all was calm from across the table. Jess only spoke about current events and her last vacation in Brazil. Kyle and Marco talked about soccer, which irked me because I was an American football kind of girl. When Marco was later distracted by the beautiful blonde on the other side of him, Kyle started whispering dirty things in my ear. I especially loved this playful side of Kyle. Some of the shit he was saying was ridiculous and had me giggling. It was probably a little rude at a table of fifty people, but no one seemed to care. I was glad that he was smiling and content, probably feeding off of my glow.

When the soup bowls were removed, Jessyca thought it

was a good opportunity to spark up some trouble.

"So, tell us, Lily," Jess said with her fake smile. "What do you do for a living?"

Everyone within fifteen seats heard her ask the question. Though some carried on with their own conversations, many looked at me curiously.

"I work at Sterling," I said casually. My relationship with Kyle wasn't a big secret anymore, but I knew that many people who knew Kyle had heard whispers about his secret affair with his personal assistant while he was with Jessyca. Kyle had warned me that it may come up, but most people wouldn't dare broach the topic.

"So, you do work for Kyle," Grant said, with a confused expression.

"Whether she works for me or not is insignificant," Kyle said as politely as he could, which wasn't easy.

"Gosh, Kyle," Jess laughed. "Maybe I should have worked for you. Perhaps our relationship would have fared better."

I heard a couple of small chuckles from further down the table.

"I don't think a miracle, wishes from a magic genie, prayers, or otherwise would have made our relationship fare any better." Kyle said, taking my hand into his under the table.

"I suppose not all things are meant to be," she gave a small shrug. She tilted her glass of wine in our direction. "Here's hoping Lily will never have to be in my shoes."

Our half of the table fell silent as they waited for a response from either me or Kyle. Well...they wanted a show...

"Some of Emmy's actions aren't...preferable," I spoke crisply, confidently. This bitch was *not* killing my glow. "But she is generous, kind, compassionate, and is not afraid to get her hands dirty. If I ever find myself in your shoes, Jessyca, it will be because I do not exude any of those fine qualities."

"I'll drink to that," Marco held up his glass and I clinked mine with his.

Kyle's face was still very serious, but his eyes burned

with raw love and lust. If he could have gotten away with taking me on the table in front of everyone, he probably would have. I smiled at him as I saw Jess sulking out of the corner of my eye. I thought I had finally shut her up, but she found another button to push...

"So, Lily," she started again later after the third course came out.

"Yes, Jessyca?" I responded as I cut my fork through my perfectly flaky piece of fish.

"You have a daughter," she said, with interest. "I overheard you say so to Trevor. Anna is the name...inked...on your back. How old is she?"

Don't' shut down, don't shut down, don't shut down, I repeated in my head. *Don't show them where you are weak.*

"My daughter was born prematurely many years ago and died as a result," I said, meeting her eyes.

The woman across from me who had been eying me with dissatisfaction throughout the meal thus far softened.

"That's a terrible experience for anyone to go through," she said, shaking her head.

"It is," I agreed.

Even the snotty socialites that had been eyeballing me pretty hard seemed to know that this wasn't a topic for dinner conversation. Smaller, different conversations seemed to grow out of the centerpieces. Marco immediately started a conversation with Grant about the building project. Kyle reluctantly joined in after I smiled at him to let him know I was still okay. Jess didn't go away so easily though. She sat quietly for a little while, occasionally looking over in my direction. I thought she was actually sorry for being a bitch this time, but I was wrong.

Her voice sliced through everyone's conversations with her next question.

"Is that why you slit your wrists open?" she asked. "Because...Anna died?"

Hearing Anna's name fall off the lips of that devil made me want to jump across the table and embed my heel in her face.

"Even for you that is low," Kyle snapped at her.

"I was just making an observation," she said casually. "Hard to miss the ugly scars on her arms. Since she isn't hiding them, I figured she is okay with talking about it."

"Jessyca," Grant looked at her with aggravation and maybe disgust.

"It's okay," I said, smiling softly at Grant. "If you must know, Jessyca, my suicide attempt involved a multitude of circumstances. Is there any other deeply personal aspect of my life that you are interested in? Perhaps I can write it all down for you on a napkin and you can take it home and analyze it."

It drove her crazy that I not only managed to remain calm, but that people actually smiled in my direction afterward. She looked back to her meal, but before she could dig in again, Grant stood up, startling her as he took her by the elbow to make her stand, too.

"Excuse us," he said and ushered her out of the room.

Kyle took my hand into both of his and leaned over to whisper in my ear.

"When we get home, I'm going to take you out of that dress and make you glow enough to light the whole damn city."

I giggled and turned my head to meet his lips for a kiss that was very impolite for a high class society dinner.

Later when we were getting ready to leave, I made a quick stop in the lady's room. I was still on my glow, and I knew I'd be on fire by the end of the night. Just thinking about Kyle's hands on my body made me grin to myself in the stall. I stepped out to wash my hands. I knew someone else was in the bathroom with me because I heard them come in. The door a few stalls down from mine opened and Jessyca stepped out.

She walked directly to the sink two down from mine and began the process of washing her hands.

"Dinner was delicious, don't you think?" she asked.

My god, does she ever shut the hell up? Well, she did when Grant returned with her later. She was silent for the rest of the meal, only speaking when spoken to, which wasn't often.

"It was good," I agreed.

"I guess you aren't used to such elegant meals," she said, taking a lipstick out of her bag.

I didn't bother answering her as I let my hair out of my clip and raked my fingers through it.

"You know," she said after touching up her lips. Now she was messing with her hair. "He will do one of two things to you, Lily. One, he will get bored with you and cheat on you; or two, he will become extremely obsessed with you and try to kill you when you want to end things." She looked at me in the mirror with a sad, but smug expression. "Don't think that your tattoos and piercings, and lower class status is going to make things any different for you."

I put my clip back into my bag. I put my bag down on the sink, careful to not put it in any sitting water. I closed the distance between us. She barely had time to cry out before I wrapped my hand around her neck and slammed her into the bathroom wall. She didn't fight back, but her hands were on my hand as she stared at me with wide, startled eyes.

"I am in a really good mood this evening," I said calmly to her. "I look damn good in this dress, and Kyle thinks so, too. That's why he bent me over his couch and fucked me until I was nearly delirious, and I've been glowing since that first orgasm hit me. You have been trying to kill my glow since you stuck your ugly hand in my face for a handshake. You're not going to kill my glow tonight, but I will tell you this. Next time you speak my daughter's name, speak poorly about Emmy, or share your opinion on my relationship with Kyle, I will light your little socialite ass up, and you'll be glowing, too, but it won't be like this," I said, gesturing to myself with my free hand.

I released her and then wiped my hand on her plain, green dress. "Nice dress," I said, picking up my purse off of the sink. "Who made it?"

I walked out of the bathroom before she could answer.

Chapter Thirteen

~Kyle~

Mayson's door was open. She looked up at me standing in the doorway and rolled her eyes.

"If you've come to drag me into another piece of your drama, I'm not doing it this time," she said.

"No, there is no drama," I said. "I wanted to talk to you about something else."

"Like what?" she asked skeptically, with one eyebrow perched.

"Emmy."

She groaned and said "I should be telling you no and kicking your ass out that door, but I'm very curious about what it is that you want to discuss."

"May I come in?"

She cringed. "Now you're being polite. I'm really frightened." She gestured for the chair in front of her desk.

I closed the door behind me to block out any eavesdropping employees and took the seat in front of her cluttered desk.

"I need you to be straight with me, Mayson," I said.

"Aren't I always?" she asked.

"Not when it comes to her."

She was quiet for a moment as she assessed me.

"You haven't asked me about Emmy in almost two years. I half expected you to bug me about her after she left this last time, but you didn't. What has changed?"

This wasn't an easy thing for me to do, to talk to someone who so plainly hated me – and to talk to her about someone that she loved like a sister, someone I had hurt physically and emotionally.

"I need to know what I did to her, Mayson," I said.

"Why do you need to know that?" she asked softly.

"I feel like I need to know to move forward."

"With, Lily," she said.

"Yes."

She tapped a pencil on the desk. "I don't see how that will help, but I only know what you know. Sam said Em looked like she got the shit kicked out of her, but I'm sure that does not adequately describe how she must have looked. You really don't remember any of it?"

I hesitated. I was about to get very personal. Only Lily was aware of my nightmares, but I felt like I had to tell Mayson. "I have nightmares of me hitting her, punching her and more. I hear her screams – they always sound the same. There are little snippets in my head of glass breaking, furniture crashing to the floor, but I never see her face...or her belly."

She blew out a long breath and sat back in her seat. She watched me as she gently rocked her chair back and forth.

"Have you asked your dad?"

"He enjoys holding back that information. I even offered to pay him for the information, but he is so evil, even money does not sway him. I even tried using...resources to find hospital or doctor's records, but I can't find anything about that night or the following days."

Her eyes widened. "You have people that can hack into hospital records?"

I ran my hand through my hair, feeling slight discomfort talking so openly about this.

"I do."

"Wow," she blinked. "Makes me wonder what other interesting things you know..."

"You really don't want to know."

"Probably not," she agreed grimly. "Well, anyway, she didn't go to a hospital."

"Then how did she know if she and the baby were alright?" I questioned.

"Your dad sent her to some doctor...umm," she tapped a pencil to her head as she tried to recall a name.

"Walter sent her to a doctor?" I asked, confused.

"Yeah. Not in an office or anything, well not an official office. He's like some kind of underground doctor, which is damn scary. He fixed her up without questions or documentation. Umm…Doctor Larson? No…Laken…"

"Larkin," I said darkly.

"Yes!" she snapped her fingers. "That's it. You know him then?"

"Yes," I said, rubbing my eyes. "You have no idea how much you have just helped me."

"I'm not sure if I actually helped you, Kyle," she said doubtfully. "You should have moved on – Em has. Well…" she paused.

"Well, what?" I asked, narrowing my eyes.

"Well…no one has told her about Lily working here for you, or you and Lily as a couple, but I'm sure you knew that. Lily talks to her sometimes."

My scowl made her eyebrows rise in surprise. "You didn't know that Lily speaks to Emmy? They talk like once or twice a month. Oh my god, I should just shut up now."

"Too late for that now," I growled. "What do you mean that no one tells Emmy about me and Lily?"

"Look, Lily and I agreed when she first started working here not to tell Emmy. Em had just left here. She didn't say it to anyone, but it was obvious her last meeting with you was difficult. It hurt her to cut you off, but she did what was best for her and Lucas, and she really loves Luke. She requested that I not mention you, unless you die."

"How comforting," I said dryly.

"Take it as a sign of how strongly she felt about you," Mayson said, in a somewhat comforting tone. "We all thought it was best that since she didn't want to know what was going on with you that we don't let you know what's going on with her, but I have a feeling that you know at *some* things. Though it boggles my mind that you're such a sneaky son of a bitch and didn't know your own live-in girlfriend is talking to your ex-girlfriend."

"I trust Lily. I don't feel I need to check up on her like that. I keep tabs on her whereabouts for her own safety, but I don't check her phone or phone records."

"Don't start," Mayson said, pointing at me with a pencil.

"I won't."

"And don't bug her about Emmy, please? You know what? We can pretend this little meeting never happened."

"I planned on asking you to do the same," I sighed and got to my feet.

"Cool. Look at that, Sterling. We're on the same page."

I had my hand on the doorknob, but I turned back around to look at Mayson.

"This is the most civil conversation we have ever had," I said.

"It was almost normal," she agreed. "Except with your little stalking things…that's creepy."

"Why are you being so…amicable?"

She sighed, and even though her features were relaxed, they softened even further. "When I was a teenager, I had a serious eating disorder and a serious drug and alcohol problem. I beat up my mom *and* I pushed my father into an early grave. In a way, I've been in your shoes. I redeemed myself, and I think you have, too. We aren't always going to get along, and it isn't my place to forgive you, but I personally don't want to keep punishing you for what you did to Emmy."

"Thank you," I said after a moment of shocked silence. "Does this mean we can be friends now?"

"Hell no. Get out of my office. Some of us do real work around here." She pointed to the door with her pencil and waved me out.

I left Mayson's office armed with new knowledge that was either going to benefit me or throw everything to shit.

~~~

"What do you mean he's 'just gone'?" I almost shouted.

"I mean he's *gone*," Corsey said, throwing his hands up in defeat. "Either he has found a way to avoid us or he has left the area. I can't find any trace of him anywhere."

"You *lost* him?"

"Yeah, I guess we did," Corsey admitted. "He hasn't been to his house in days and he quit his job. His credit card and banking activity has ceased, too."

"Is he dead somewhere?"

Corsey looked doubtful. "I don't think so, Kyle. I don't think so."

I rubbed my forehead as I tried not to tear his head off. Corsey and a few of his guys had been keeping track of Vic and keeping him away from Lily. After the night I made him pay for what he did to her, he had stopped calling her and seemed to stop following her. By all appearances, he seemed to have given up on her, but I didn't really trust that he was completely finished with Lily just because I kicked his ass. In his apartment, we found hundreds of pictures of her. In some instances he had cut her face out of pictures and glued it to pictures of women in BDSM positions, tied, gagged, and helpless. He had everything he could need to take her without her consent and hold her for a long period of time. He had handcuffs, rope, chains, gags, blindfolds, and the scariest things we found were chloroform and the date rape drug Rohypnol.

One of my go-to guys is a detective in the city. Vic would have done very little jail time for what he did to Lily's leg. She could get a restraining order, but we all knew a piece of paper would not stop him from contacting her or hurting her again. The bottom line was that unless he *seriously* hurt her, there wasn't going to be much to do to stop him. Even all of the kidnapping paraphernalia in his home wasn't enough. The restraining instruments could reflect a lifestyle he was free to have, and the drug charges wouldn't have been enough to keep him locked up long enough to matter, especially if Vic had a good lawyer, which he did. It is why the three sexual assault charges that were brought against him over the past three years were dismissed.

I didn't tell Lily everything I knew. I didn't want her to live her life in fear, looking over her shoulder. She still didn't consider Vic to be that dangerous, more of a nuisance than anything. After several arguments, I started letting her go out on her own without me or Corsey, but I always had my eye on her though she didn't know it. I couldn't keep her locked up like a prisoner and I couldn't keep assigning her a bodyguard every time she wanted to go to the grocery store or visit a friend. She wouldn't have been happy. The most important thing after Lily's safety was her happiness.

"Keep an eye out for him," I said to Corsey. "There's not much else you can do. I suppose he's smarter than he looks."

"I suppose so," Corsey said.

"Did you find Larkin?" I asked.

"Yes. He's moved into a house out in the sticks in Jersey. He's been working out of there." He handed me a file full of information on the roving doctor.

"Thank you," I said absently as I flipped through the file.

"If there isn't anything else, I'm going to take off. I haven't spent much time with the wife and baby."

"Oh. Right. I forgot you're someone's father now," I shook his hand. "I'll see you next week."

Corsey nodded and walked out of my home office.

"Hi, Corsey," I heard Lily say to him in the hallway.

"Hey, there, Rocky," Corsey said with genuine adoration. He had given her the nickname one day after he insisted she couldn't knock him on his ass. I know for a fact that he allowed her to do it. Corsey was a beast of a fighter.

"Aww. Corse, are you still mad about that?"

"I'm not mad. You punch like a girl."

I heard the sound of my little bully's fist hitting Corsey's chest and the subsequent "Oooff!" I shook my head, trying not to smile. She really had to stop beating people up.

"This isn't even fair. I have to stand here and take it," Corsey whined.

"You can hit me. I can take it." I knew from her tone that she was probably bouncing on her toes, excited to fight.

"No, thank you. Your boyfriend - *my boss* - will kill

me."

"It's okay. I can take him," she said confidently.

"But I won't. Listen, enjoy your trip. Stay safe."

"You, too, big guy. Send me pictures of the baby."

They bid their goodbyes. I could tell by her squeals that he had lifted her off of the floor in a bear hug. If I didn't know Corsey was madly in love with his wife, I would have been unhappy about his arms wrapped around her.

"Hey, there, my sexy boyfriend," Lily grinned as she came into the office moments later.

"You're in a really good mood," I said.

"You're about to whisk me away from the ugly city to blue seas, white sands, and hunky cabana boys serving me drinks with umbrellas in them. Of course I'm in a good mood!"

She rounded the desk, sat her hot ass in my lap and wrapped her arms around my neck.

"Hunky cabana boys, huh?" I asked, narrowing my eyes at her.

"Like you won't be checking out all of the beautiful women on the beach," she said, rolling her eyes.

"You're the only beautiful woman I care about," I said, slowly caressing her leg.

She leaned in and gave me a slow, passionate kiss that had me growing hard.

"I really appreciate this trip," she said softly.

I laced my fingers in her hair. "You deserve it. You worked your ass off in the office and you were working hard before that."

She kissed me again, but I took control of it and kissed her hard, holding her head in place as I ravished her mouth. I couldn't get enough her – everything about her – her mouth, her body, her smart ass remarks, and her love. Every time I kissed her, held her hand, made love to her, or just sat and had a normal conversation with her, I never knew if it was going to be the last. Lily meant everything to me, but I wasn't sure if I could give her everything that she needed. One of the biggest reasons I was sweeping her away to Bora Bora was so that I could suck in as much time with her as I could before everything came crashing down.

"Why don't you go finish packing," I suggested after I had made her lips swollen with my mouth. "I have to go check out a piece of property in Jersey."

"I can go with you," she said, frowning.

"No, it's okay. It will be boring for you. I'll go while you wrap things up here. By the time I get back it will be time to leave for our flight."

"Okay," she sighed and got to her feet. "See you in a little bit," she said as she walked towards the door.

I got up and adjusted my erection, which Lily looked at with a cocked eyebrow. Ignoring her so that I didn't take her right there on the floor, I said "I'll be back soon."

She gave me a sexy smile and disappeared down the hall. I shut my laptop down, grabbed the Larkin folder and left the office. Lily was already upstairs, blasting some hard rock band from her stereo. I hurried out to go take care of business.

~~~

The house sat back off of the road, partially hidden by clusters of trees. It looked like any other farmhouse in Vineland, but I knew what was behind the walls of this house.

I got out of my car, walked up the front stairs onto the porch and hit the button for the doorbell. I heard it echo throughout the house, but after a half a minute of waiting, no one came. I hit it twice again, refusing to be sent away by silence, and waited in the cool May morning air. A moment later I heard footsteps hurrying from the back of the house. The door opened and Ben Larkin stared at me from the other side.

"You must be really desperate for something if you've come out of your way looking for me," he said as a greeting. He stood back and waved me inside.

I stepped inside and took in the space around me. The place was well furnished, but the furniture was cheap – at least by Larkin's standards – easily replaced pieces. When you practice medicine below the radar of the law, you can't worry about leaving behind items that have an emotional connection.

He probably took on the furniture of the last owner or got almost all of it, including phony family photos, from yard sales and thrift shops. Ben Larkin didn't work for nothing, though. He had properties in Mexico, Costa Rica, France, and other countries where he would go for rest and relaxation – or retreat if the government was on his ass.

"You have something I need," I said, finally looking at him.

His dark hair was sprinkled with gray hairs and he had a few fine lines around his brown eyes, but he was otherwise still youthful in appearance. He was twenty-five years older than me, but he could have passed as my older brother.

"Don't tell me this is about money," he said with a humorless laugh.

"I will never have any use for any of your money," I scowled.

"Well, don't leave me in suspense," he said sarcastically. "I have a client waiting downstairs."

"They can wait a while longer," I said. "Three years ago Walter sent a woman to you."

He nodded as if he understood what I was talking about. "Yeah, I saw you that day, too. You were fucked out of your mind."

My brow lowered in confusion. "I don't remember that."

"No, I just said you were fucked out of your mind," he said, shaking his head.

"What…what was the treatment?"

"You were at the estate," he said as he walked towards the kitchen. He gestured for me to follow. He immediately found a bottle of bourbon and poured a glass. He wordlessly offered me one, but I declined with a shake of my head.

"Go on with your story," I commanded.

"You were at the estate, like I said," he said unaffected by my demeanor. "You were out of your mind – yelling and speaking incoherently. Walter wanted you sedated for the ride to rehab. I also took care of some minor injuries you had on your hands."

"You drugged me?" I asked in astonishment as I looked at my knuckles. I remembered the broken skin and bruises clearly.

"It was for your own good, but before you I saw the woman."

I looked up at him. "How bad was she?" I asked, just above a whisper.

He looked at me with questioning eyes, tilted his head. "Did you do that to her?"

"How bad was it?" I repeated through clenched teeth.

He looked at me as if he was thinking about whether or not he should tell me. He swallowed his bourbon and poured another glass.

"She was bruised, head to toe. She had glass in her hair – lodged in her scalp. Her face was terribly bruised, looked like someone had kicked her right in her cheek," he touched his own cheek. "Her back was bruised pretty damn bad. I'm guessing she curled into a ball to block your blows from hitting the baby."

"I didn't say it was me," I said, shamefully hearing my voice crack as I spoke.

"You didn't have to. You wouldn't be here if it wasn't you. Did I give you what you needed?"

I swallowed hard. I felt as if all of the wind had been knocked out of me and I knew that I had not really experienced the worst of it. It took every bit of strength I had not to let my legs give out under me.

"What about her…her belly?" I asked.

Ben poured bourbon into a second glass and again offered it to me.

"Take it," he commanded when I again declined.

I took the glass and swallowed the amber liquid, feeling the burn all the way into my gut.

"What about her belly?" I asked again after the drink.

He sighed before answering. "She was bruised *all* over, Kyle, but when I did an ultra sound the baby was fine."

Imagining Emmy in a ball trying to protect her baby from me made me feel like I didn't deserve to live and I didn't deserve the woman waiting for me at home.

"I need to see the pictures and video," I managed to say without falling apart.

"What makes you think I have any of that?" he asked with narrowed eyes.

"A man in your position has to protect yourself. You get a lot of big name people under your care. If you get thrown under a bus, you're not going alone."

His mouth formed a fine line as he walked over to a door in the hall between the living room and kitchen. He opened the door, looked down and listened carefully for a few seconds before quietly closing it again. When he spoke again, it was just above a whisper.

"Why should I do this for you?"

"Because I've never asked you for a damn thing my entire life," I snapped. "Because you used to pat my head after fixing my mother from whatever suicide attempt she chose, but you never stepped in where it counted – for *me*."

I got in his face and grabbed onto the collar of his shirt.

"And because I know enough about you to bring you down wherever you go. There will never be a hiding place for you if you screw me over, Ben."

I released him. He seemed unfazed by what just happened, but I knew I had him. He knew I had him, too.

"I don't keep that kind of information with me. I need a week or so to get it, copy it and get it to you."

"I'm going to send a couple of my friends to help you and to make sure you don't take off before you give me what I need," I said, glaring at him. "You have one week to get this done."

I pulled a business card out of my wallet with my cell phone number written on the back. "Call me when it's ready."

I turned away from him and walked back through the living room to the front door.

"I don't think this is going to be good for you," Larkin

said from the porch as I walked to my car.

"You're not an authority on what's good for me. Our common DNA means nothing."

I got into my car and left my biological father standing on his porch.

~Lily~

Kyle came back from New Jersey a different person. He smiled at me, he kissed me, and he talked as if everything was normal, but it wasn't. There was great sadness behind the smiles, in the kiss, and pulling on the edges of our conversations. I knew something was wrong, but because I didn't even know where to begin and he was trying so hard to keep things level, I didn't mention it.

On the flight to L.A., I popped in headphones, opened my book and left Kyle to his thoughts. Every now and then he would touch me, stroke my cheek, squeeze my hand, caress my thigh, but even those actions seemed...sad.

In L.A. we ate a leisurely late lunch and entertained each other with trivia from a book I picked up in a bookstore. Kyle laughed. Kyle teased me. Kyle turned me on. But Kyle wasn't Kyle, and I couldn't figure out why.

Almost a whole damn day later we finally reached our bungalow over the water in Bora Bora. It was near dark, but I was able to see how beautiful it was. Exhausted, we showered together and fell into our bed that had a clear view of the sparkling sea.

"Thank you for bringing me here," I murmured into his neck as he held me close.

"Like I said before, you deserve it," he said, caressing my arm. He meant what he said, I know, but...he meant it *too* much.

I maneuvered my body onto his and kissed him. It was a good kiss, but it wasn't my Kyle.

I reached under his shirt as I kissed him, feeling his rippled abdomen and smoothed my hands over his muscular chest. I pulled my lips away from his and nipped at his chest before forcing him to pull his shirt off. Repeatedly, I sunk my teeth into his chest and abs and made him hiss slightly with each nibble. When I reached his pelvic bone, I ran my tongue along that V shaped part of his body that seemed to be pointing to heaven under his boxers. My fingers hooked in his boxer briefs and pulled until his erection sprung free.

Unable to wait until I got his briefs off all the way, I took the large bulbous tip of his cock into my mouth and groaned when I tasted the pre-cum there. Kyle groaned and gently raised his hips to press more of his cock into my mouth. I granted his wish and met his gentle thrust.

"Ahh," he breathed as his cock moved past my tonsils and down my throat. "Lily..." he groaned my name after I pulled back and then took him all the way again.

The only way I could think to bring him back to me was to bring him to the brink of losing his sanity while he was inside of me. I held him deep in my throat and sucked as hard as I could, and used all of the muscles in my mouth and throat.

"Baby, stop or I'm going to come," he groaned as he tried to pull out of my mouth. "Lily! No!"

He grabbed the hair at the back of my head and violently pulled me away from his cock.

"What the hell?" he panted, staring down at me.

Ignoring him, I forced him to release my hair when I got on my knees to pull off my shirt. I climbed on top of him and kissed him again, lacing my fingers behind his head to deepen the kiss and hold him where I wanted him. I kissed him with a ferociousness I've never exhibited with him before – biting, sucking, licking, and more biting until –

Kyle pushed me away and said my name with such shock, it was almost funny. Almost, but not really. I had bitten him. Hard. On the tongue. I drew blood.

"What the hell is going on with you?" he asked before hanging off the side of the bed to spit red onto the floor.

"What the hell is going on with *you*?" I asked.

He sat up and looked at me. "What are you talking about?"

He wasn't going to concede that the problem wasn't me biting him, but it was his behavior that sparked the biting. It was our first night in paradise and it was already ruined. Between Kyle not being Kyle and my cannibalism, the whole damn week was well on its way to being ruined.

"I'm sorry," I said, trying to cover the quavering in my voice. "I guess I'm just super excited to be here."

I got out of the bed, rushed into the bathroom and shut and locked the door. I put the lid down on the toilet and sat down.

"Lily, what's going on?" Kyle asked from the other side of the door.

"Nothing. I have to pee," I said and then silently cursed myself for letting my voice crack.

"Baby, open the door," Kyle said softly.

"My god, Kyle!" I shouted. "Can I please pee in peace! I've used public piss rooms all day. I would like to just pee in peace once before I go to sleep for the night!"

There was a moment of silence from the other side, and then finally I heard a loud sigh from him. "Fine. Pee in peace then."

I heard his footsteps retreat and breathed a sigh of relief. After a minute or so, I flushed the toilet and turned the sink on. I stepped back out into the bedroom a few seconds later. I climbed into bed beside Kyle, but I didn't move to him like I normally would.

"Are you going to tell me what's wrong?" he asked.

"I…" I hesitated. He wasn't going to stop asking, but if he did then he'd just be pissed. More pissed. "I just need you here with me," I said softly in the dark.

"What? I *am* here with you. I'm right next to you."

"That's not what I mean and you know it," I snapped. "I need *all* of you here with me. You haven't been yourself since you came back from Jersey. You do all of the things that Kyle does, but you're not him. I'd prefer you to be a dick than to pretend to be here when you're not."

He was very quiet for a long time. I thought he had fallen asleep, so with a sigh, I rolled onto my side to try to force my racing mind to go to sleep. Kyle shifted behind me and then I felt his arm around my waist and his breath on my neck.

"I'm here," he whispered.

"Are you sure?" I asked after a moment.

"I promise."

"What is *wrong*?" My question was a plea.

"Lily, I'm here – with you, so nothing is wrong."

When I didn't respond, he rolled me onto my back. By the light of the moon I could see the sincerity in his eyes as he wrapped my hair around his hand.

"I'm here," he said again before kissing me deeply.

Kyle's hands roamed over my bare skin and dipped into my panties. I moaned into his mouth when his fingers traced over my clit. He pressed down with the palm of his hand. My automatic response was to rock against his skilled hand. The pressure on my clit increased every time I brought my hips up. Soon, I was groaning out my orgasm into his mouth.

He rolled over onto his back, pulling me on top of him. He used one hand to push my panties aside and the other to guide his erection to my entrance. With just the head of his cock inside of me, he placed both hands on my hips and without warning pushed himself inside of me while pushing my hips down to meet his. I cried out as I felt the length of him so deep inside of me I thought it would tear me apart.

Kyle held onto me as he pushed himself up into a sitting position, forcing his cock deeper inside of me. I started to scream, but Kyle cut it off with his mouth.

"Wrap your legs around me," he commanded.

"No," I said, trying to pull away.

"Wrap your legs around me *now*," he grunted as he thrust his cock inside of me harder than before.

I complied, wrapping my legs around his back. If I wasn't already impaled on his manhood, I would have fallen over. The pain was exquisite, as his cock moved unbelievably deeper.

"Do you believe me now?" he panted as he hammered his dick into me. "Do you believe I'm here now, Lily? Can you *feel* me?" he groaned.

In response, my body began to shudder with my next orgasm.

~ 211 ~

"That's it, Lily. Feel me," Kyle moaned. "Feel...unhhh..." he groaned extremely loud. "Feel me inside of you, Lily," he almost shouted just before I felt the first spurt of semen inside of me. "Feel that?" he grunted.

"Kyle!" I screamed his name as I came again. My tight muscles squeezed him even as he continued to pulsate inside of me.

"I love you," he whispered before taking my mouth in a sexy kiss that had my pussy squeezing his cock a little more.

This was my Kyle. My Kyle was back, but the nagging question in the back of my head was...for how long?

~~~

After our long day of traveling, we decided to spend our first full day lounging on the beach. I was wrapped up in Kyle's arms on a lounger built for two. The other Kyle, the man he was being yesterday, was still a no show, but I still couldn't shake the feeling that something was going on and he wasn't telling me.

The day went smoothly. We were in and out of the water, and twice raced back to our bed for orgasmic activity. Later that evening, just after the most beautiful sunset I had ever seen, we went to dinner at a nearby restaurant. There were a lot of people there, mostly couples, but it still had a very pleasant and romantic ambiance.

We were just served our dinner when the man at the table closest to us proposed to his girlfriend. I couldn't hear exactly what he was saying, but I read his lips clearly when he asked "Will you marry me?" With a smile that was just as much of an answer as her words, she nodded and said yes. He wasn't on one knee, and he didn't seem to want to garner the attention of those around him. It was a sweet proposal, low key, but romantic. When they leaned across the table to kiss, I turned away.

I peeked at Kyle while I cut into my fish. His brow was slightly creased, as if he was thinking hard about something. Every now and then his eyes would flicker over to the newly engaged couple, but every time he looked back to his meal, his brow was more creased. I had a sneaky suspicion that other Kyle was back. My Kyle was good at harboring secrets from me and he always wore his game face. This Kyle was wearing his worries on his sleeve, which made me believe that whatever was going on with him was major and I would be just as much affected as him.

"I'm not asking for a proposal or anything," I started slowly, gaging his cautious reaction. "But where do you think we will be five years from now?"

The lines in his head smoothed out. "I don't know," he said.

I stared at him. "You don't have any thoughts on that at all?"

He stared back at me. "I'm not sure if this is the time and place to have this discussion," he said dismissively.

I put my fork down. "We are on one of the most romantic islands in the world. We are surrounded by honeymooners and the recently engaged and you don't think that this is a good time and place for this discussion?"

I wasn't trying to start an argument or be a bitch, I really wasn't. But his answer only confirmed what I had been thinking since yesterday, that something was wrong.

Kyle put his fork down, too, but I saw danger in his eyes. "I just want to enjoy my time here with you, Lily, without the added drama that follows us at home. Can we do that?"

"Talking about our future is considered drama?" I asked, trying to keep my anger under control.

He looked irritated by my words. "As I said a moment ago, it is not the time and place to have this conversation."

I truly believed at that moment that the reason Kyle didn't want to discuss our future was because he didn't see one. It wasn't one of those short sighted things either – I could deal with that. No, this was different. He didn't see us together, probably not even in the near future. I know we never discussed our commitments to each other, but it was much implied. I never questioned whether or not he was in this for the long haul. I knew he was in love with me and that was all I needed to know, but now that wasn't enough.

And why the hell had he brought me to this island if he couldn't see a future? The realization hit me that maybe this was the calm before the breakup, that this trip was being used to soften an impending blow.

Kyle had resumed eating his meal, but my appetite was gone, like my future with Kyle. I caught our waiter's eye, bringing him to our table.

"I'll have a Zombie," I said. "And a shot of Patron."

"Yes, ma'am," the cute Tahitian waiter said with a smile.

Kyle watched me with a guarded expression. Emmy used to drink herself into a stupor when she was with Kyle. Now I understood why.

"Don't do this," Kyle said quietly.

"Don't do what?"

"Don't try to drink away what you're feeling," he said.

I let out a humorous laugh. "I can't talk about it. I can't drink it away. I guess I should be you and let it eat away at me in silence."

The waiter appeared a moment later with my drinks.

"Take them away," Kyle commanded him.

The poor guy looked so startled. He looked at me for confirmation, but I tapped the table indicating I wanted him to put the drinks down.

"If those drinks touch the table I'll kick your ass," Kyle said calmly and quietly, but his eyes were hard and serious. He pulled out his wallet while the waiter stood there, confused and probably a little scared. Kyle threw down a small stack of cash. "We're finished."

He stood up and the waiter hastily retreated. Kyle stood beside me, offering his hand. I didn't take his hand, but I got up and stormed out ahead of him. There were two ways back to our bungalow, a paved path and the beach. Most couples moved to the beach after dinner. It was a romantic way to unwind. Couples walked hand in hand with their shoes in their hands, or sat close on the beach talking or kissing, or other things, but there was no romance for me at the moment. I took the paved path at a record speed. Kyle kept pace behind me.

I wished there was somewhere else for me to go, away from him, so that I wouldn't kill him, but the island would basically be shutting down for the night. Couples were expected to be in their rooms canoodling, focusing on only each other, not dancing or bar hopping. I was stuck here with him until at least the morning. I hoped I wouldn't kill him before then.

When we got into the bungalow, I took my shoes off and threw them against a wall. Kyle was lucky I didn't throw them at his head. As I moved into the bedroom I stripped out of the dress that he had promised to take me out of himself when I first put it on. I threw that, too before rooting through my suitcase for a pair of shorts and a shirt. Kyle stood nearby, watching me with unease. I pulled on the shorts and shirt and moved past him back to the living area. When we arrived, there was a complimentary bottle of champagne in our room. We never opened it. Now was as good a time as any. I opened the bottle, not enjoying the *POP* of the cork dislodging like I usually did.

While Kyle stood in the middle of the living room watching me, I sipped at the bubbles foaming out of the top of the bottle before throwing my head back and guzzling as much of the bubbling liquid as I could.

"I told you not to do that," he said quietly, but made no effort to stop me.

I only looked at him before taking another long sip. He gave me a look that spelled out all kinds of danger, but he walked into the bedroom. I heard him kick his shoes off and a moment later I heard him peeing in the bathroom, which reminded me of how damn quiet this place was. It was too damn quiet. I can hear someone peeing in the next room.

I took his brief absence as an opportunity to get away from him. I slipped out of the door that led to the beach behind us. As soon as my feet hit the sand, I took off at a run. I was not a runner. I tried running with Kyle a couple of times and I always felt like I was dying less than a quarter mile in. Running in the sand wasn't any easier, but my need to put some distance between us pushed me to keep going until I was far enough away from the bungalows that I could not discern which one was even ours. The night was dark, but the moon reflecting off of the water gave me just enough light to see where I was going. My bottle of champagne was pretty shaken up and I probably spilled a good deal of it in my run. As I sat down on a log to catch my breath, I found that I hadn't spilled as much as I thought. I took long sips as I waited for Kyle to come find me, and without a doubt he would.

I knew I couldn't go on like this. I would always feel like the bottom was about to drop out from under me, and that's no way to be in a relationship. Maybe some people liked those kinds of dramatics, but not me. I'd had enough bottoms dropping in my life. Then again, I should have known better. It's Kyle freakin' Sterling, after all. He was moody, hot and cold. Within those first 24 hours that we became intimately familiar with each other, he went from being hostile and insulting to wanting to rip my clothes off and just like that he changed again to indifference. When I first started working for him, he doubted my ability to do anything besides file and mix drinks while he ogled my body. One moment he was personal and the next he was cold. Hell, a classic Kyle moment was when he was telling me how much he wished he didn't care about me while he was trying to fuck me against his front door. I shouldn't have been surprised that he made tender, passionate love to me and then called out Emmy's name as a way to push me away. Classic fucking Kyle.

So, why was I so surprised that he brought me to an island that was set up for couples but then he pushed me off when I wanted to talk about our future relationship?

In the moonlight, I saw someone walking towards me. I knew Kyle would come and find me, but…well this person was a little smaller than Kyle in size.

I started to panic in my mind. Just because this was a couple's retreat didn't mean that I couldn't get raped or murdered. I was suddenly aware of my folly, running out onto a dark beach alone, and far from where anyone could hear me scream.

I was getting ready to get up and run when the guy came to an abrupt halt and cursed.

"Holy shit, you scared me," he said with a faded British accent. "I didn't expect to find anyone else out here."

"Me either, and quite frankly I'm still scared. How do I know you're not going to hit me with that bottle you have there?" I asked, looking at the bottle he was carrying in his right hand.

"And waste good rum? Are you mental?" He moved in closer, revealing his face in the moonlight. He was a good looking guy, I guess. Light hair, slim but had a toned build under a button down white cotton shirt and lounge pants.

"You shouldn't be out here alone at night. Where is your companion?" he asked.

"What makes you think I have a companion?" I took another sip of my champagne.

"This is Bora Bora, my dear. Everyone has a companion."

"Where is yours then?" I challenged.

"Sleeping too damn comfortably after declining my proposal of marriage," he sighed.

"Oh," I softened a bit. "Sorry about that. My 'companion' is probably out looking for me now. I took off while he was taking a piss."

He sat down beside me on the log. "Don't tell me you ran away from a marriage proposal."

He offered me his bottle. I took it and handed him mine. We both took a few good gulps out of the bottles. My throat burned from the rum. Without looking at the bottle I knew it was Jamaican rum. I loved the stuff.

"I didn't run from a marriage proposal," I said after we switched bottles again. "At dinner, a man proposed to his girlfriend. It was quiet and sweet. I specifically said 'I'm not looking for a marriage proposal' before asking him where he saw us in a few years, and I got nothing."

"You're friggen kidding me," he said incredulously.

"No shit. You know what I got? I got 'this isn't the time or place for this discussion, Lily.' Psh." The combination of the champagne and the rum was starting to go to my head. Though I spent most of my life behind a bar, I didn't drink much. Kyle and I had beer a few nights a week after work, and wine with some of our meals, but for the most part we didn't drink often. Now I was feeling that lack of drinking in my low tolerance level.

"Lily," he said, rolling my name off of his tongue. "I'm Michael."

I took his extended hand and gave it a firm shake.

"So, your 'companion' has commitment issues," he said, before taking another swig of his rum.

"Amongst a host of other issues," I mumbled and took a sip of my own drink.

Wordlessly, we switched again.

"Melanie said she isn't ready for marriage," he sighed. "We've been together for three years. At what point is she going to be ready? We've been living together for two of those years."

"At least she told you she wasn't ready. Kyle just keeps pushing the conversation off."

"Yes, but she won't tell me *why* she isn't ready."

"Maybe *they* should get together," I suggested. "She doesn't want marriage and he doesn't want to talk about it. Perfect for each other."

"I thought you weren't expecting a marriage proposal?" he looked at me with a small grin.

"I wasn't!" I said defensively, but then sighed. "I wasn't. Really I wasn't, but his response made me realize that it was something I'd want eventually – with him – and he doesn't want it from me."

"I have to be honest," he said softly, staring out at the sea. "I don't think I can continue to be with Mel if she doesn't want me wholly. I know that some people are just as happy without the marriage aspect, but not me. She's always known that I wanted a wife for life, not a girlfriend, not a fiancé. If I'm asking her, it means it's extremely important to me, right?"

"Right," I nodded.

"I feel that step will make us complete, but if she doesn't want to be...one with me, to be whole with me, then I can't be with her at all. It's been long enough for her to know what she wants by now. Obviously, it isn't me."

We both took long pulls from the bottles before switching again. I actually started feeling a little worse for Michael than I did for myself.

"How long have you been with Kyle?" he asked.

"A few months. I've known him for a few years though."

"Friends first?"

"Not exactly. He's my boss, and before that he dated my previous boss."

"Shit, that sounds awfully complicated," he said.

I shrugged. "You don't know the half."

"Maybe that's why he can't see into the future with you, if it's always complicated," Michael said.

"But it's always been complicated," I said, taking another sip. "That's exactly why I was so reluctant in the beginning, but he's hard to resist."

"Maybe you need to move on," Michael suggested. "I think I need to move on, too. Mel and I are supposed to be here for another couple of days, but I think I'm going to cut out early."

"That sounds like a good idea, actually," I said and we clinked our bottles together.

"Maybe we can meet in Venice or Paris or London and start our own love affair," he grinned at me.

I was drunk, and Michael looked like he might be a good kisser, but even drunk I knew better. As far as I knew, Kyle and I were still a couple – or something like – which didn't put me in a position to kiss other people, regardless of how hurt and angry I was. I bit my bottom lip and turned my attention back to the sea before us.

"I don't know about your Melanie, but Kyle isn't good at letting go."

"Speaking of which," Michael said distractedly. "Someone is coming."

I looked back towards the bungalows. Another figure was marching through the sand. The moon had risen a little higher, lighting more of the beach. I couldn't mistake Kyle for anyone else this time, or the look of rage on his face.

"You should probably go," I said slowly to Michael as I watched Kyle advance.

We both got to our feet. I swayed as the alcohol really hit me. Michael reached out to steady me.

"I'm good," I said after a moment. "Thank you."

The time it took for him to steady me was wasted and Kyle was too close for Michael to effectively walk away. I put the rum in the sand and took a stance in front of him, which made him snicker.

"I don't need your protection, love," he said in a low voice.

I put my hands up to stop Kyle from barreling into Michael. Only my hands on his chest kept him back. He wouldn't risk hurting me to get to him.

"Stop!" I yelled at him as he tried to go around me with rage in his eyes. "Nothing was happening here. We were just talking. Kyle!" I shoved him back.

"He just had his hands on you!" he roared.

"To keep me from falling over, you asshole!" I quickly picked up the bottle of rum and shook it at him. "We were drinking and I got dizzy when I got up."

Kyle started pacing back and forth, like a freakin' lion in a cage desperate to reach the prey on the other side. "I don't know who the hell you are or why the hell you are out here with my girlfriend, but if you don't walk away now I'm going to knock your teeth out of your fucking head."

"Kyle!" I snapped.

"Are you going to be okay?" Michael asked with

genuine concern.

"Yes," I said quickly. "I'll be fine – physically."

"What the hell does that mean?" Kyle raged.

"Shut up, I'm talking to my friend!" I yelled at him. I turned back to Michael and held out his bottle of rum.

"I think you need it more than me," he said, eying Kyle with doubt. "Don't waste it." He gave me a wink. Kyle saw it and started raging again.

"Shut. Up." I said through my teeth before glancing over at Michael. "Good luck with everything, Michael," I said.

"I'll be fine," he said with a shrug. "I hope you will be, too."

I didn't know if I would be fine or not, but I nodded. Michael took his newly acquired bottle of champagne, made a wide berth around Kyle and left us alone on the beach.

"You take off without a word, at *night* in unfamiliar territory with a stranger?" Kyle yelled in my face. "What the *hell* is wrong with you?"

"I didn't take off with him. I took off alone and he just happened to come along."

"That's even *worse*, Lily! He could have raped you or killed you!"

"Well, he didn't, so you can get the hell out of my face now."

I tried to walk around him, but he gripped my arm, almost to the point of pain.

"Stop running away from me!" He spun me around to face him. "What do you want me from me, Lily? I'm giving you every fucking thing I can right now!"

"Except a real commitment," I shouted back at him. "You can't even see past this moment. Do you have any idea how fickle that makes me feel? I don't want to feel fickle, Kyle! I had enough of that in my life."

I tried to break away from him, but he held my shoulders tightly.

"I can't give you more than a day at a time, Lily," he said, shaking me a little as he spoke.

"Because I'm not her? Because I'm not Emmy?" I asked bitterly.

"Because I'm not good for you!" he shouted.

His words felt like a bucket of cold water splashing me in the face. I suddenly felt sober and clear. Kyle still thought he was going to break me. It wasn't about *me* per se, as much as it was about what *he* might *do* to me.

"You *are* good for me," I said softly.

"It's only a matter of time before I completely ruin you," he said bitterly. "I can't look months and years ahead. I have to treat each day with you like it will be my last because I am *not good for you*, Lily."

I dropped the rum in the sand and wrapped my arms around Kyle's neck. His arms circled me and he held me tightly.

"Please," he said softly in my ear. "Let's just get through this week."

"Then what?" I asked, swallowing back my tears. "What happens after this?"

Even though his arms were wrapped around me and I could feel his heart beating in his chest, I felt him withdrawing once again.

"I'm not sure," he said in a harsh whisper.

I held back my sobs and tears, because I knew in the near future Kyle was going to give me plenty of reason to cry.

Chapter Fourteen

~Kyle~

The phone call and obligatory lunch invite from my mother came in on day four in Bora Bora. Lily and I were just about to take a midday nap. She had been sick all morning with nausea and vomiting. I suspected it was the large amounts of seafood she ate last night at dinner. As soon as she was asleep, I was going to go down to the restaurant and give them a hard time for their tainted fish.

"Who is it?" Lily asked, with tired, puffy eyes while I hesitated answering the call.

"My mother."

"You want to answer it," she sighed. "So answer it."

"Hello," I answered just before it went to voicemail.

"Hi, Kyle," my mother said softly. "How are you?"

"I'm okay. How are you?" I asked as I helped Lily into bed. She didn't really need my help, but I felt better helping her. She gave me a soft smile after her head hit the soft pillows. The smile warmed me and wrecked me all at once.

"I'm…I'm fine," she said after hesitation. "He's gone. Again."

"How much money did he take this time, mom?" I asked, holding the bridge of my nose between two fingers.

"I'm not sure how much he spent while he was here," she said with a sigh. "I haven't had the accountant add it up yet, but I gave him four hundred to leave."

I knew she meant four hundred thousand dollars and not four hundred thousand sea shells or cookies or ass holes. Usually, I'm patient with her about this. Kicking Walter out usually meant that she was also on a new set of meds and that she was on the road to recovery. I usually jumped in to help her out any way I could, but now she was taking time away from Lily, and that was all I really cared about at that point.

"How many more times are you going to do this before

you learn your lesson?" I asked her.

She was silent for a long time. "I don't know," she admitted. "I suppose I have to do something differently this time."

"I suppose so," I snapped. "Listen, we'll have to talk later. I'm on vacation with Lily and I just want to focus on us right now."

"Lily? The girl you brought here with you?" she seemed surprised.

"Yes," I said in a tone that dared her to say anything negative about Lily.

"Oh. She isn't..."

"She isn't what?" I snapped.

"Well...she's different."

"So?"

"So nothing," she said impatiently. "I'm not really one to judge who you love, am I?" she asked bitterly.

"No, I don't think that you are."

She sighed and then tried again to be polite. "Why don't we have brunch when you come back? Bring Lily with you."

"Fine," I said, watching Lily. She had already fallen asleep in those few short minutes. "I will call you when I get back. I'll have someone come take care of any security issues in the meantime."

"Thank you," she said. "Enjoy the rest of your trip."

"Thank you," I said and ended the call.

I sat down beside Lily and stroked her cheek. She pressed her cheek into my palm even though she was sound asleep. It was only a matter of days before I got those pictures back from Ben. Moments like this would be gone after that.

I didn't mean to pull her into this relationship only to spit her out. For a little while, I thought we could be happy for a long time, but soon I was thinking about forever and not just a long time. When she asked me where I saw us five years from now, I wanted to tell her where I really wanted to be five years from now – married, with kids, happy, but I couldn't give her that hope. That hope would have just been crushed later.

The fact of the matter was that I was a guy with a history of terrible mistakes. The drugs weren't just an Emmy-time thing. I had been on and off them since high school. I had been violent then and in college, but never towards a woman until Emmy. My obsession for her was a drug in of itself. Mixed with the meth and sometimes pure cocaine and alcohol, I became a lethal weapon towards the person I loved most in the world. Lily could very well be next.

My feelings for her had grown exponentially, almost literally overnight. I felt as if she had crawled into my skin and had become a part of me. I couldn't stand to be away from her. When I went on a business trip to Chicago only a week or so into our official relationship, it physically hurt to be away from her. Even before our relationship began, I couldn't stand the weekends when I couldn't be close to her. I had to watch her from a distance. I didn't recognize the ache for her then, but I couldn't mistake it for anything else now.

Anytime, I could fall off of the wagon and find myself snorting something up my nose. Anytime my obsession with Lily could consume me while I was high. Anytime, while high and consumed with Lily, I could drink the right mix of alcohol, or add in the right amount of other drugs. Anytime, I could break her and walk away without even the memory as a punishment...

I needed to see the pictures and video of Emmy's injuries. I needed to see how big of a monster I really was. The guilt and shame I felt needed to be bigger and run deeper. I lost Emmy for what I did to her beautiful soul, but I was otherwise unpunished. Even a meeting with Luke in Chicago didn't punish me even half as much as I needed to be punished. I needed to feel the pain I inflicted and I don't think I experienced even a fraction of it yet, but I knew I would when the pictures were in my hands, and when I had to leave Lily. Even then I wasn't sure if that would be enough.

I got into bed with Lily and curled my arms around her, sucking up every second I had left.

~~~

"We're going home," I said, as I stuffed Lily's clothes in her suitcase.

"What? Why?" she stared at me from the bathroom doorway.

Her face was red and blotchy from puking and her shorts were noticeably bigger on her because of the few pounds she had lost in only two days.

"We still have three more days," she said, stepping into the room.

"You're not getting any better. You need to see a doctor."

"It's just food poisoning," she argued.

"Food poisoning can be dangerous," I reminded her. "And no one else got sick, just you. Maybe you're having an allergic reaction to something."

"I don't want to leave."

"Lily," I said in warning.

"But..." she said. Her chest began to rise and fall a little faster. "This could be..."

I knew what she was trying to say. This could be it. This could be our last little bit of time together and I was about to take it away by taking her home. Knowing there was a breakup on the horizon was taking a toll on Lily. I didn't tell her a when or a where. Though I knew it was a matter of days, I tried to give her the impression that it could be months, years, or never, but she wasn't stupid. She felt that something was really wrong.

"Listen," I said, holding on to her. "You have to stop worrying about that. I was just trying to deal with my own insecurities, okay? You're very ill and you need medical attention – at home. Okay?"

Reluctantly, she nodded. I kissed her gently. She tasted like toothpaste and mouthwash, which she was getting plenty of over the last couple of days.

At the airport after check-in, I made Lily sit down at our gate while I went to buy her a couple of magazines and some crackers and juice. When I returned, she was standing up (damn it) and talking to a man and a woman. As I got closer, I recognized the man from the beach a few nights ago, the man who I swore was trying to pick up my girl, but now he had his arm around this other woman. Then again, that didn't mean much, after considering my situation with Emmy and Jess.

"Kyle," Lily said excitedly as I approached. "You remember Michael," she said. "This is his *fiancée* Melanie."

"You decided to say yes, then," I said, trying to be cool, trying to really give a fuck about the strangers before me. I put the magazines and food down in a chair.

Melanie looked embarrassed as she looked up at her future husband. "I still can't believe he told a complete stranger, but yes. I said yes. Both of my parents have been married *three* times. Of course I was reluctant to get married."

I nodded as if I understood and cared. Lily laced her fingers with mine as she listened to the couple chatter about what happened after Michael returned to their bungalow. Finally, the couple made a show about not missing their flight to Hawaii. Apparently they extended their vacation so that they could get hitched in Hawaii.

"Good luck with everything," Michael said as he hugged Lily. Of course "everything" meant me.

I shook his hand and then Melody's or Melanie – whatever. They started to walk away, but then Melanie had to turn around and totally rock my whole fucking world.

"I hope you feel better, Lily. You know what?" she said thoughtfully. "It may not be food poisoning at all." With a shrug and then a wink, she said "Maybe you're just pregnant."

I cursed under my breath.

Lily passed out.

~Lily~

Twenty-three hours after we left Tahiti, Kyle and I stumbled into the penthouse exhausted, with our nerves worn thin. We left the luggage by the front door and walked wearily up the stairs. I kicked off my shoes and headed towards the bed, but Kyle started stripping out of his clothes as he headed towards the bathroom.

"I'm going to take a shower," he said. "Do you want to join me?"

I wanted to say yes, but he looked like he was hoping I'd say no.

I shook my head. "No, unless you think I stink."

He walked over to the bed, gloriously naked, and bent over me. His nose nuzzled my neck, making me squirm a little bit.

"Hmm," he murmured. "I'm not sure...I should test taste to be sure..." his tongue eased across my jugular. "Mmm...sweet sweat and day old soap."

I smacked his arm as he pulled away chuckling.

"I don't care," I pouted. "I'm not moving off of this bed."

"Maybe I can have you moving across the bed when I come back," he said wriggling his eyebrows before disappearing into the bathroom.

I pulled my phone out of my pocket to return my mother's ten phone calls. Honestly, I didn't know when she was going to get it - that I would eventually return her call. She didn't have to call me twice an hour for five hours.

My finger was poised to return the call when "Mom" lit up on my phone. Seriously, this was out of hand.

"Mom, you don't have to call me a million times - I was in the air most of the day," I said in lieu of a hello.

"For once, could you think of someone else besides yourself," my sister shouted into the phone.

I was so stunned to hear her voice I couldn't immediately speak.

"Mom had a heart attack, Lily," she said frantically.

~ 228 ~

"She's in the hospital - I can't get to her and they won't tell me anything over the phone. Shawna and Cliff were on vacation in Florida. They're driving back now but it will still be hours before they get here to stay with the kids." Her frantic speech gave way to sobs. "Her heart wasn't beating when they took her out of the house. They were doing CPR."

Sometime after the words heart attack, I had gotten out of bed and slipped on my shoes, though I don't remember doing it.

"I will be there as soon as I can," I said, wiping away tears. "If you hear anything, call me."

"Okay," she sniffed.

I hung up the phone and rushed into the bathroom. I started to call out to Kyle, but then I saw him. He was standing under the water with his hands locked at the back of his neck, making his hard muscles in his chest and arms bulge. His eyes were closed, his forehead was creased with worry, and his mouth was set in a frown. He looked so troubled...haunted...and helpless. I needed him, but he needed...I don't know, but it wasn't me that he needed right then. I wasn't sure if I'd ever be what he needed. If he was sure that he needed me as much as he wanted me, he would have been able to see a future for us. I would have been enough to chase away his insecurities, but I wasn't.

To add to an already complicated matter, I was pregnant. As soon as we landed in L.A., we found a store in the airport that actually sold pregnancy tests. When the pink plus sign appeared on the pee stick, I had sat in the stall crying softly for twenty minutes before Kyle sent a female security guard in to look for me. He had an initial surprised reaction but after that he wore a good poker face, until now, when he thought he was away from my watchful eyes.

I started to back away, but he must have sensed my movement because he suddenly looked up at me. He blinked a couple of times until his eyes focused and then his expression became concerned.

"What's wrong? Are you sick again?" he asked, wiping

water out of his eyes.

"I have to go to Ohio," I said, using my arm to wipe my face clear of tears. "My mom had a heart attack. I don't know how long I'll be gone – I don't even know if she's okay yet."

Kyle immediately shut off the shower and rushed out of the stall to wrap a towel around his waist.

"I'll go downstairs and find us a flight," he said, touching my cheek.

"No," I said before I could think about it.

Kyle looked at me with confusion. "What do you mean no?"

"You stay here," I said as if it wasn't a big deal. "I'll go alone."

"Lily, you've been sick and you're..." His voice trailed off as he let his eyes drop to my abdomen. "I don't want you to go alone."

"I'll be fine," I said. "I'm not feeble. I haven't lost my ability to walk and operate like a normal human being."

Frustrated, he put a hand in his wet hair. "You passed out yesterday. You can't keep anything down and you haven't had any real sleep in over twenty-four hours. I'm not letting you travel alone."

"You need some time alone," I spoke with honesty. "You need to digest...everything...and frankly so do I."

"You think now is a good time to spend some time apart?" he asked dubiously.

I pressed the palms of my hands to my eyes, trying to hold my tears in and trying not to scream. "Please! I don't have a lot of time, Kyle. I don't even know if my mother is dead or alive right now. Please don't make this any harder!"

After a moment, Kyle sighed. "Okay. I'll go book a flight for you." I felt his lips on the top of my head. "Get whatever you need packed into a carryon bag to speed up the process."

I dropped my hands to my sides and nodded. Tears flowed freely from my eyes as I followed him out of the bathroom. I went into my room, which had just become my own personal closet after that first week, and retrieved a bag I could carry on to the plane. I went downstairs to my suitcase and carelessly dug out the things I needed, leaving an ungodly mess of clothes in my wake. As I was zipping up my bag, the front door opened and Corsey walked in.

"Hi, Lily," he said with a short wave.

"Hey," I said, hanging my head so he wouldn't see me crying like a fucking baby.

With a thick manila envelope in his hand, he turned away from me and headed down the hall to Kyle's office. I wondered what was in the envelope, but then figured it was probably more crap on Vic. I wish I was privy to the information; then again I wasn't sure if I really wanted to know how deeply his insanity ran.

Corsey and Kyle stayed in his office for another five minutes. Corsey gave me a short wave before leaving, but thankfully didn't linger. Kyle trailed out a moment later looking grim.

"The flight leaves in three hours," he said distractedly. "I'm going to fly to Columbus with you and make sure you're safely on your way and then I'll fly home."

"I'll be safely on my way once I step on the airplane," I said, watching him carefully.

What the hell bad news had Corsey brought to him?

"I'm not giving you an option, Lily," he said, holding the bridge of his nose between his fingers.

I said nothing as I turned away from him to head back upstairs, but he grabbed my elbow a little rougher than necessary. I looked at his hand on me and then at his angry yet sorrowful eyes.

"Why don't you want me to go? Why do you want to be away from me so badly?"

"You have made it pretty clear that we don't have a future together," I said with my voice trembling. "I'm trying to soften the blow I'm bound to have."

He softened and the grip on my elbow slacked. He cupped my face with his hands and said "That's the last thing

~ 231 ~

you should be worried about right now."

When I should have pulled away, I allowed him to press his lips to mine with a sweet, but sad kiss. He continued to hold my face where he wanted to as the kiss changed from sweet to needy. Kyle's tongue searched for my own and when I gave it to him he sighed and moaned lightly into my mouth as if I had just given him the one thing that he had been desperate for. It made me feel needed, though not in the way I had hoped for, but I took it anyway.

I rested my hands on his hips as Kyle laced his fingers into my hair, angling my head so that he could kiss me deeper. His tongue tasted mine, flicking over my tongue ring, stroking along the sides of the muscle, as his breathing changed, deepened and quickened. Keeping his hands in my hair and his mouth on mine, he walked us over to the couch. His hands released my hair, slid down my back and cupped my ass. He pressed my body to his, allowing me to feel how aroused he was. I wrapped my hands around his neck as he lowered me to the couch, his tongue continuously enjoying my mouth. He settled over me, bracing himself with one arm so that he wouldn't put all of his body weight on me. That was never a problem before. In the past, Kyle would crush me with his weight while we were copulating, and I loved feeling his body on mine, possessing me, but now he was probably just as scared as I was to do that.

Kyle reluctantly detached his mouth from mine and gazed down at me. His lips were just as swollen as mine felt from kissing. I slowly dragged two fingers across his mouth.

"I love you," he said, his voice thick with emotion. "You have revived something in me that I thought was gone and dead. You don't just make me feel alive, but you make me feel like I am *living*."

I gripped his face in my hands and lifted my head to plant kisses on his lips and face.

"Then don't you ever let me go," I said, but I couldn't keep the pleading out of my voice, nor could I keep the tears from falling from my eyes. I felt like multiple worlds were teetering, ready to come crashing down at me at the same time.

"I'll do what I have to do to keep you safe," Kyle said as he struggled to emotionally pull away from me again.

"Damn it, Kyle!" I held his head still, made him look at me. "Safe from whom?"

"Me."

"I'm safe *with* you," I said.

Kyle took a deep breath before he spoke and I felt as if an impending doom was about to drop on me.

"Before we left for Bora Bora, I realized that I could get photographic evidence of what I did to Emmy. I requested it. That's why Corsey was here. He brought it to me."

I froze. I wasn't sure I was really hearing him correctly. I played his words over in my head until there was no way I could misunderstand what he was really saying.

"Did you see them?" I asked hesitantly.

"No. Not yet."

"Don't *ever* look," I pleaded. "You're the only one still suffering for this and it's time to let it go."

"I can't let it go," he snapped at me, but then briefly closed his eyes to regain his composure. "That can be you – today, tomorrow, next year."

"But-"

"Don't be naïve, Lily," he said through gritted teeth. "I'm a fucking meth head. I can relapse *any* time."

"But you haven't!" I shouted. "And you won't."

"How do you know I haven't?" he asked so steadily, that I jolted back away from him and pulled my hands away from his face as if it was too hot to hold.

"When?" I whispered.

"Right before you came to work for the company, right after Emmy left," he said, trying to appear nonchalant, but I could see his shame in his eyes.

"That was several months ago," I said, shaking my head. "You've been clean since then."

"Are you sure about that?" he whispered, but he did it in a way to taunt me.

I hesitated before asking my next question. I wasn't sure if I really wanted to know the answer. "Did you do it again?"

His eyes were pained when he spoke again. "No, but the craving is so damn strong I'm not sure I can resist it."

"Because of those fucking pictures!" I screamed vehemently, surprising even myself. I shoved him hard, but he didn't move off of me. "Why did you have to go *looking* for pain?" I cried. "Why couldn't you just be fucking *happy*?"

"I can't pretend it didn't happen, Lily! History is bound to repeat itself – I *needed* to do this!"

I cried uncontrollably now. This was too much. Kyle was looking for the one thing that could tear us apart. His drug problem was possibly taking over his life. He couldn't stop punishing himself for what he did to Emmy and he was afraid he'd do it to me and *our baby* next. On top of it all, my mother was laid up in some hospital struggling for her life or already dead. I felt completely helpless to help her, completely helpless to convince Kyle that he deserves to be happy, and I was scared shitless that I would lose another baby, except this time I'd be completely alone.

Kyle got up and attempted to scoop me into his arms, but I fought him off of me, punching, slapping, and shrieking at him until he stood back and away from me. I got up off of the couch and moved away from him, trying not to stumble into any furniture as my tears blinded me.

"Lily," I heard him say my name, his voice breaking. "I'm sorry."

I pulled a pair of flip flops out of my suitcase, slipped them on my feet and then picked up my carryon bag.

"What are you doing?" Kyle asked, beside me.

I ignored him as I picked my pocketbook up off of the floor. I checked my pocket to be sure I had my phone and started for the door. Kyle grabbed my elbow, rough and unyielding as he spun me around to face him.

"What the hell are you doing?" he demanded.

"Why delay the inevitable?" I snapped at him. "I'm

going to Ohio – alone, and when I return I am moving the hell out of here. You can sit here in this big house alone with your drugs and your pictures."

I tried to pull away from him, but he held fiercely to my upper arms.

"I'm not trying to hurt you," he said harshly. "I'm trying to protect you and our baby. This is *killing* me."

"It's not killing you enough, or else you'd burn that fucking envelope without ever looking in it."

"I can't do that," he said, grimacing.

"Then let. Me. Go." I said through a clenched jaw.

"I'm going with you to Ohio," he said with finality.

"I can't stop you from getting on the airplane," I said bitterly.

"And I'm staying with you," he said, releasing me.

"I don't want you there." I took a few steps back from him.

"You will," he said grimly and walked away from me.

~~~

Harry, one of Corsey's men was waiting for us in the Escalade when we got downstairs. I climbed in first and slid all the way over to the other side. When Kyle got in and saw how far I had moved over, he gave me a look that said "Really?" but I ignored it.

"Harry, before you go to the airport, drive us by the building site," Kyle said.

"What building site?" I asked with suspicion. Surely it wasn't the one that he supposedly went to before our trip. I was ninety-nine percent positive that he didn't go to a building site, but went to whom ever had access to those photographs. He and Marco had started building at a site in Delaware, but I didn't think we were going there either.

Kyle looked at me with a bland expression but didn't answer. I shook my head in disgust and looked out the window. I was lost in my own thoughts as we jumped onto the Ben Franklin Bridge and rolled into New Jersey. I was thinking less about my own problems and more about my mother, my sister, and the kids. If my mom died or needed care herself, who was going to help Lydia with the kids? I wasn't sure if I was up for the job. Even if mom was okay to care for herself, it wouldn't be fair to put her in that stressful situation again. There were going to have to be changes and I wasn't sure where I would come in, or what I was even willing to do for my estranged sister.

I narrowed my eyes in confusion as we sped by familiar scenery. As far as I knew, as Kyle's personal assistant and office manager, he didn't have any projects going on in this area of South Jersey. Then as the car slowed, I saw it. I couldn't close my mouth if a hundred flies threatened to fly into it. When the Escalade came to a stop, like a little kid I pressed my nose and hand to the window, staring, gawking. I heard Kyle get out, but I didn't pay any attention to it until he was opening my door and catching me before I fell out. I stumbled out of the truck under his strong care and stared at the construction scene in front of me.

The framework was almost complete. It was two stories high, with a decent size balcony on the second floor and spaces that looked like they were for French doors and floor to ceiling windows that made the outside area and inside flow well together. There was also a patio on the first floor and that, too flowed through holes in the wall that looked like they were meant for the double doors and enormous windows.

"What...when..." I couldn't figure out what question to ask as I felt Kyle's arm slip across my shoulders and he pulled me close.

"I bought the lot in December," he said. "In February I bought the house that used to be behind it and had it demolished. We started building as soon as the weather was acceptable. Marco designed it. The designs for the inside are spectacular."

I couldn't stop looking at what was quickly becoming a bar – more than a bar – a destination for watching ball games, drinking, eating, and playing.

"It's all yours, baby," Kyle said softly, watching me for

a reaction.

"What do you mean it's all mine? You barely liked me in December. Why would you do this for me?"

"I *loved* you in December. You deserve this."

"You...saw Emmy in December?" I asked gingerly.

"No," he frowned. "I saw Luke."

"How did that go?"

"He went off," Kyle shrugged. "Ranted and raved and shoved me around, but when it became clear to him he wasn't getting a fight out of me, he calmed down and got down to business."

"Oh...you must be disappointed that he didn't kick your ass."

He frowned. "Yes, but I don't want to discuss that. I want to know how you feel about this."

There were too many conflicting emotions crackling through my chest right then. I was sad, angry, scared shitless, hopeful and hopeless, and grateful. I couldn't cry, smile, laugh, scream, or swoon. I could only stand there, leaning on Kyle, and stare at the building before us. It was all too much – all of it – everything – my mom, my surprise pregnancy, Kyle, the bar.

"Thank you," I managed thickly. "I wish I could say more, but I'm so...overwhelmed right now."

"I know," he said and kissed the top of my head. "I don't have any control over what's happening to your mom, but the rest is my fault. I thought maybe this would make you feel a little better. You're getting your dream."

"I would give this up just to have you," I said, barely audible over the sounds of the workers and their machines.

Before he could answer, a familiar face in a hard hat approached us.

"You weren't supposed to see this until the completion," Marco scowled at Kyle before sweeping me into a hug that lifted me off of the ground.

"You've been keeping secrets," I managed a smile for Marco once he put me down.

~ 237 ~

"Siamo spiacenti, princess," he apologized with a sexy smile. "I'll make it up to you over lunch tomorrow."

"Oh," I said as my smile faded. "I'm sorry. I can't. My mother is ill. We're on our way to the airport now."

Marco frowned, but looked at my sympathetically. "I hope she gets better soon. You look like you could use some rest yourself."

I wished then that I had grabbed my sunglasses to hide my red and puffy eyes. I knew I probably looked like shit since I hadn't slept in twenty-four hours and I had cried all morning.

"We have to go," Kyle said as he started to steer me away from Marco.

"I'm glad you were a part of this," I said to him, finding another smile for him.

He gave a shrug. "I thought it would be great way to sneak into your good graces in the event that Sterling screws up."

His innocent remark was meant as a joke, but he had no idea that it would poke at currently weeping wounds when he said it. Kyle and I both frowned. I looked at the ground and Kyle looked somewhere to the right.

"What the fuck did you do?" Marco said, poking Kyle's chest.

Kyle scowled at him now. "I suggest that you not provoke me right now, Mangini," he said in a tone that meant business. I didn't think Marco was afraid of Kyle, but he backed off after a moment anyway.

"You call me if you need me – for anything," Marco said to me.

I nodded and he leaned and gave me a lingering kiss on the cheek. Kyle ushered me back into the Escalade. Instead of walking back around to the other side, he made me slide over, but when he got in he didn't let me slide away from him. As if I were a child, he buckled me into the middle seat. He was very quiet for the first few minutes back on the road. When he finally spoke, it was in a clipped tone.

"You smiled for Marco," he said, staring out the

window.

"He hasn't given me a reason to do otherwise," I answered in an equally icy tone.

"I understand that you two get along well and that you have met him for a lunch a few times, but is that all?"

"What do you mean is that all?" I asked, irritated by what I recognized as an interrogation. "You would know if that was all – you're the one that assigns me a Lily-sitter every time I step out of your sight."

His dark eyes settled on me. "Do you speak often?"

"What do you think?" I growled.

"I think deciding not to occasionally check your phone was a bad decision on my part," he said sharply.

"And you won't start checking my phone either. Besides, by your estimation, we won't be together very long anyway – if you want to call this being together – and you won't need to check up on me at all."

"Regardless of what happens between us, as long as we are connected..." he placed his hand over my lower belly. "I will always 'checkup' on you, Lily."

I pushed his hand off of me, disgusted. "If you must know, I talk to Marco regularly. We text almost daily and I talk to him on the phone at least once a week. Do you feel better knowing that information now?" I asked roughly.

"No," he growled. "It pisses me off. Neither of you mentioned your secret relationship until now."

"It's no secret, you ass. I don't need to know every time that *you* talk to him."

"I would never cheat on you with him," he said dryly.

"Wow," I said with a cynical laugh. I threw my head back against the headrest and stared at the ceiling. "Wow. Are you high *now*?" I looked at him.

"No!" he barked.

"Are you sure? Because you're being so...crazy. You are *all over* the place today, Kyle. You know, when you finally cut me loose, make sure it's a clean cut because I can't deal with your insane mood swings."

He started to speak, but I cut him off.

"No! Don't speak. Almost everything that has come out of that stupid mouth of yours has somehow conflicted with the previous stupid thing you've said. Just stop talking. I don't want to hear your voice until we land in Ohio. Then I want you to get back on the next flight back to Philly. Look at your pictures, check my phone records, take a hit of meth – do whatever makes you happy and leave me out of it."

"You *are* what makes me hap-"

"I said hush!" I unbuckled my seatbelt and moved over to the other side where I buckled myself in again.

Kyle didn't speak again for the rest of the ride to the airport, but he didn't take his eyes off of me either.

~~~

As soon as we deplaned, I was on my dying phone calling Lydia to let her know I was in Columbus and to see if she had heard anything.

"She's stable," she said and then I heard muffled yelling at a child.

I breathed a sigh of relief and got the necessary information from her so I could go directly to the hospital.

"You sound like shit," she said before I could end the call.

I paused before answering her. This wasn't how I envisioned our first real conversation beginning. "I feel like shit," I assured her.

"I will feel better about myself if you also *look* like shit."

I couldn't stop the small smile from popping up on my face. "I promise you, Lydia, you will feel extremely good about yourself."

There was a few seconds of thoughtful silence. "I hope so. I found a babysitter. I'm going to get a cab and go to the hospital in a little while. I'll see you there."

"Okay," I said and ended the call.

Kyle heard the whole conversation with his super human hearing, and plus he was hovering over me so closely I

~ 240 ~

couldn't exhale without part of my body touching his.

"Why is she taking a cab?"

Annoyed with his presence, I answered quickly as I moved through the airport. "She hasn't driven a car since Gavin died. She couldn't at first – her leg was badly mangled in the accident, but now she's afraid to. She was driving when the accident happened and she blames herself. So, now she doesn't drive."

"You know a lot for a sister you haven't spoken to in years," Kyle said.

"My mother talks about her whether I want to hear about her or not. The ticket counter is *that* way," I pointed without looking at him.

"I'm staying with you, little bully," he grumbled and took my bag away from me.

I didn't feel like arguing with him anymore and allowed him to take my hand. He led me outside to a waiting Escalade.

"You really like your Escalades," I muttered before climbing inside.

We had to stop once on the side of the road when my stomach suddenly flipped. Kyle watched with worried eyes as I puked up yet another snack that I had on the plane.

"You really need to see a doctor," he said. "This can't be normal."

"It's *your* baby," I said icily once we were moving again. "There's nothing normal about it."

When we arrived at the hospital, I practically ran to my mom's room in the Intensive Care Unit.

"I have to die twice to get my first born to visit me," were my mother's first words when I appeared at her side.

"I'm sorry, Mom," I cried as I took hold of her cold hand. "I'm so sorry."

"Don't cry," she said, trying to comfort me by patting my hand. I instantly felt guilty that she was trying to comfort me when she was the one who looked like she was knocking on death's door, and apparently death answered twice.

"How are you feeling?" I asked.

"I feel like I died. Twice," she said as her lip curved to one side in a sarcastic smile.

"That's not funny," I stared at her in disbelief as I wiped at my tears.

"You look so different," she said, touching my face. "You're not hiding behind all of that makeup and hair dye anymore. I can see your beautiful face, but you look so tired." Her eyes widened. "Oh, no did I pull you from your vacation in Tahiti?"

"No, we just got back a few hours ago."

"I thought you were supposed to be there for seven or eight days," she said, wincing with confusion.

"I wasn't feeling well," I said evasively. "We left early. It's a good thing, too. I would have gone out of my mind if I had to wait almost a whole day to get to you." I rubbed her hand lovingly as I tried to blink back more tears.

"Don't start crying again," she warned. "Tell me about your mystery boyfriend and your trip to Bora Bora."

"Tahiti is beautiful," I said, skirting the activities I did not get to enjoy there. "Crystal blue waters, white sandy beaches, hot Tahitian men with bulging muscles…"

She snickered. "You should have brought one of them home for me."

"Next time," I promised.

She sighed as she squeezed my hand. "You're pretending to be happy for my sake, but I know you very well, Lily. Why are you so sad?"

"You're laid up in the hospital after a major heart attack, mom," I said incredulously. "How am I supposed to feel?"

"It's not just me, though is it?" she said knowingly. "What's going on between you and Kyle?"

Under normal circumstances I learned not to unload on my mom about my problems, especially after she moved in with Lydia. She had her own plus three to deal with then. I didn't want to start now after she had 'died twice'. Besides, I wouldn't even know where to begin. "I don't know what's going on between me and Kyle," I admitted. "But he came here with me. He's in the waiting room now."

"I want to meet him before I die a third time," she said. "Don't tell me I'll have to die a third time to meet him."

"You're really not funny," I said, shaking my head as she chuckled.

"I don't understand what's so funny," Lydia's voice admonished from the doorway.

Kyle was standing beside her, supporting her as she struggled to walk without pain. It was the first time I had laid my eyes on her since my suicide attempt many years ago. She was two years younger than me but she looked at least ten years older right now. Her once long, flowing red hair was now chopped into a bob. Her gentle curves were now straight lines and sharp angles, and her gray-blue eyes seemed darker, figuratively and literally. This person in front of me was a shell of what my beautiful younger sister was, and it all changed overnight only about a year ago. I was shocked by how bitterly sad I felt. I was rocked by how much I had missed and all that I lost when I cut her off.

I looked at Kyle, whose eyes were locked on me. Despite the confusion and ridiculousness going on between us, I was glad he was there.

"I found this preppy guy lurking in the hallways and assumed he belonged to you," Lydia said to me as she hobbled to the chair on the other side of my mother, assisted by the "preppy guy".

"Finally," mom said, reaching for Kyle with her IV hand.

I watched with amazement as Kyle squeezed between Lydia and the bed and bent over to hug my mother. If someone would have said seven months ago that Kyle Sterling hugged and kissed the cheek of an older, sickly complete stranger, I would have laughed. Hard.

"My god," mom said when he stepped away. "He's so handsome, Lily. Look at those dark, mysterious eyes and that jawline."

~ 243 ~

"Mom!" Lydia rolled her eyes. "He can hear you, you know."

"You didn't tell me he was an Adonis," mom looked at me with shock.

"I think dying twice sucks a lot of oxygen from your brain," I said worriedly. "But I died twice and I'm fine."

"You don't think I'm an Adonis?" Kyle asked, his tone playful, but his eyes were so very weary.

"I think you're the second hottest man on Earth, but it's creepy that my mom also thinks so," I told him.

"Second hottest?" He crossed his arms. "Who is the first?"

"Shemar Moore," my mother, my sister, and I all said at the same time.

"I can't compete," Kyle held up his hands in defeat.

For the next hour, we all played a good game of make believe. Lydia and I pretended that we had not been estranged for seven years. Kyle and I pretended that the last few days had not happened and we were still a happy couple. Mom pretended that her current health condition wasn't as serious as it really was. We all played a very good game, so well we all almost really believed it all. Mom joked that she wouldn't die a third time before we returned in the morning.

On the way out, Lydia and I stopped in the bathroom. My stomach was pitching, but I managed to not barf. I inwardly cringed to Lydia walking with a terrible limp. She was in pain but she put on a good show of positivity, never once complaining.

"You really do look like shit," she said, looking at me in the mirror as she washed her hands. I had finished first and was waiting, leaning against another sink.

"I probably don't smell too good either," I said, stifling a yawn.

"What's wrong, Lily?" Lydia asked seriously, her voice quiet but demanding.

I tried to play it off with a small smile. "I'm tired as hell, Lydia. I've basically been traveling for almost thirty hours. I'm tired and as you pointed out, I look like shit."

"I know it's been years, but you're still my sister and I still know you better than anyone ever will," she said as she dried her hands on a paper towel. She threw it in the trash behind her and looked at me straight on. "What is *wrong*?"

I had treated Lydia like shit for seven years, refusing to even offer my condolences after Gavin died and refusing to even acknowledge her physical and emotional pain thereafter. Yet, here she was standing before me, just being my sister, the one I used to love and confide in so many years ago.

I dipped my head as the tears hit me full force. My body reacted violently to the emotional torment I was feeling, jerking with my sobs, and my stomach felt like it was going to leap out of my mouth. Lydia lost a husband, a father to her children, a best friend, a sister, her mother twice, and would live in pain for the rest of her life, but she didn't hesitate to wrap her arms around me and hold me tight while I cried.

I couldn't find the words to speak, I could only cry and hold her back. Her words from earlier in the day haunted me though. *For once, could you think of someone else besides yourself?*

I pulled away from her, apologizing as I grabbed wads of rough paper towels to dry my face.

"I'm sorry," I said, trying to stop my crying. "You're right. I'm so selfish, always thinking about myself."

"I didn't mean that," she said softly, rubbing my arm.

"Yes, you did," I laughed through my tears.

"Not in the context you think," she said evasively. "But that's a conversation for another time."

I looked at her. "No, I know what that's about. I thought about it on the flight over. After Anna died Gavin spent all of his time caring for me, but no one took care of Gavin," I said, with new tears spilling over. "He lost a daughter, too and I only focused on myself. You took care of him and it's no wonder he fell in love with you."

Lydia shook her hands and blinked up at the ceiling, her old trick for trying not to cry.

~ 245 ~

"You bitch," I poked her. "I just bawled like a baby. The least you can do is let a tear slip."

She looked at me with watery eyes. "I'll never forget…" she covered her face and let out a couple of gut wrenching sobs. She uncovered her face and tried again. "I'll never forget seeing you bleeding on the bathroom floor, all the blood, the hopelessness on your face and knowing I did that to you."

"I did it to myself, Lydia," I said, holding her hand.

"But I helped. I didn't mean for any of it to happen," she said, wiping away tears. "Gavin was devastated afterward. I think he only married me because I was as close as he could get to you."

"What? No. He married you because you are you."

"You don't understand," she said shaking her head. "He never got over what happened, and he never got over you. When he was dying he kept asking for *you*, Lily. Not me, not the kids, only you."

I was stunned to hear this. I felt like a total ass for not going to Ohio after the accident. So fucking selfish. "I'm sorry," I said, wiping at new tears.

"Don't be," she said with a shrug. "He was still a good husband and father, and I'm sure he really understood how hurt you still were."

"I'm such a bitch," I cried.

"I know, right?" she laughed.

We threw our arms around each other and hugged again. A woman walked in then. She looked at us with leeriness before closing herself into a stall.

"So, tell me," Lydia said after she released me. "What else is going on with you?"

I gave a small shrug. "I'm pregnant by an amazing man who doesn't realize he's amazing. The father of my baby hurt someone else really bad a couple of years ago and though she has moved on, he can't forgive himself and he's headed down a road full of hardships and turmoil. He's trying not to take me with him, but of course I'm going." I didn't know I could cry so fucking much in a single day. I should have been dry and dehydrated by now.

Lydia wiped my tears away with her thumbs. "Do you want me to steal this one, too?" she asked, and we both laughed. It was all I could do to hold on to a small piece of my sanity.

We left the bathroom after drying our faces. Kyle stood nearby, waiting patiently as if we had not just spent forever in there. He didn't comment on the red puffy eyes or the sniffles my sister and I had from crying. After helping Lydia into the Escalade, Kyle stroked a hand down my cheek and gave me a brief but tender kiss before opening my door for me. It seemed like everything would be alright, but I knew better than that.

Chapter Fifteen

~Kyle~

Lily was sound asleep after only five minutes, leaning heavily into me as I held her. Lydia looked at her sister with affection and regrets.

"She puts on a tough act, she always has," she said to me in a soft tone so not to wake Lily. "But she's not as tough as she pretends to be."

"I know," I agreed.

"Do you?" she challenged. "Because whatever it is you're doing, you're tearing her apart. I didn't even think she would ever fall in love with someone after Gavin. She doesn't do anything half way, Kyle. If she loves you, she loves you whole heartedly. I strongly suggest you not fuck it up – don't fuck *her* up."

"I don't want to fuck her up," I argued as softly as I could. "I want to save her from…"

"From yourself?" Lydia questioned knowingly. "What exactly have you done in the past that is so horrible that you would risk losing her to save her?"

I wasn't in the habit of discussing what I did to Emmy with strangers, but Lydia was Lily's sister. Maybe if I told her what I did she would help convince Lily that I wasn't good for her.

"I was in a love triangle – sometimes square – with an incredible woman. To make that disastrous long story short, I mixed meth with alcohol and more meth one New Year's Eve and went berserk on that incredible woman. She was five months pregnant at the time," I sighed heavily. "I don't remember it, but I was able to obtain pictures and video documenting how badly I hurt her. I haven't looked at it yet, but it's sitting on my desk at home, waiting for me."

"And you're going to look?" Lydia asked incredulously.

It was pissing me off that people were so against me looking.

"Of course I'm going to look," I snapped. "I need to."

"What about what Lily needs? She needs you. You know damn well you're going to go off the deep end when you see that shit. I don't even know you and I know you'll go off the deep end. You'll never be able to scrub those images from your mind and you will punish yourself just by closing your eyes."

"I can't *not* see those pictures and video," I said harshly. Lily shifted at the sound of my gruff voice, but she just cuddled closer to me and continued to snore softly.

"When I started falling for Lily, I tried to keep my distance as much as possible," I said to Lydia. "I was mean to her and pretended she didn't mean anything to me. Even after I gave in, I tried to push her away again and we still ended up together. I thought maybe I could do this, be good to her and make her happy for a long time, but when I started thinking in terms of forever, and not just a long time, my outlook changed. I *am* a recovering drug addict and I have done some really cruel shit to people while I was on drugs and in my first stages of recovery. I realized that I couldn't risk doing to her what I did to that other woman. I know I broke her and I don't want to break Lily."

Lydia stared at me for a long time before speaking. "You *are* breaking her," she whispered.

"She's hurt, not broken. I'm going to spend what time I can with her and then…"

"Then you're going to dump the mother of your unborn child so that you don't 'break' her, but you should know something, Kyle," Lydia said with conviction. "She let Gavin go, but I don't see her doing that with you. You're going to drag her down with you."

I knew she was right. I knew it, and I'd have to find a way to keep that from happening.

We arrived at her house a couple of minutes later. I slipped out from under Lily to help Lydia into her house.

~ 249 ~

"Nice house," I said on the foyer, though I could only see the living room and part of the kitchen.

She looked at me with eyes similar to Lily's. "I gave you a hard time, and I will continue to do so, but I do appreciate all you have done for me and my family."

"I don't know what you're talking about," I said, with my hand on the door.

"My mortgage was mysteriously paid off by a private foundation out of Philly. That same private foundation provided my family with thousands of dollars in gift cards for the grocery store and a couple of department stores. My medical bills stopped being medical bills and became receipts for payment in full. My heating bills were paid and before it even started getting warm, the electric company informed me that I have an enormous credit on my account."

"That's...something..." I said, opening the door.

"Oh, you're home," a teenage girl said as she came downstairs. "With a date?" The way the girl stared at me with a small smile made me feel uncomfortable.

"He's not mine," Lydia gave the girl a fake frown. "My sister's. Are you calling your mom to pick you up or are you spending the night?"

"I'll stay," the girl said, walking backward toward the kitchen. "You have enough ice-cream to keep a teenage girl happy for days and there's a *My So Called Life* marathon on tonight. Get to see the Jared Leto of the nineties," she grinned.

She gave me a wave and disappeared into the kitchen.

"I better go," I said, backing out the door. "Lily is exhausted. I need to try and get some food and fluids into her and get her to bed."

Lydia took the few steps between us and kissed my cheek. "Thank you for taking the pressure off of Lily. I wasn't sure how much longer she could take care of us *and* herself. Does she know about your foundation?"

"Yes," I said after a moment of hesitation. "But she doesn't know what I did for you and I'd like to keep it that way. I didn't do it for recognition and I certainly didn't expect a thank you."

"Okay. Just…take care of my sister, Kyle."

"I'll do whatever is best for her and the baby," I said and closed the door before she could say anything more.

Lily was awake when I got back in the Escalade.

"Is Lydia okay?" she yawned. "I should have gone in with her."

"She's good," I said. "You needed to rest. Are you hungry? You haven't eaten all day."

"Umm," she sighed, resting her head on my chest. I draped an arm over her, happy that she didn't move over to the other side of the bench seat again. "I can go for some ice-cream and French fries."

"Together?" I questioned, with my eyebrows raised. I shouldn't have been surprised. Emmy's crazy craving was bacon and cheese curls – together.

"Mmm hmm. Let's find a McDonalds and get somewhere and go to bed."

"Showers first?" I suggested and kissed her forehead.

"Now you're saying I stink," she said.

"You smell pleasant," I lied.

"Liar," she said, punching me in the chest. "Thank you for coming, Kyle," she said quietly.

"You didn't want me to."

"I know, but you paid me no mind and I honestly don't know what I'd do without you here right now. So, let's just…relax. I don't want to argue or talk about the obvious shit while we're here."

"Okay," I agreed easily. I tilted her head up and pressed my lips to hers. "Yum. You don't need to brush your teeth either. Your breath is awesome."

The bully punched me again. "Fuck you."

"Later, I promise," I whispered in her ear and watched her squirm in her seat.

~~~

I watched with fascination as my two fingers, coated with Lily's moisture, slid in and out of her tight channel. She was propped up on her elbows, watching with equal fascination. She moaned with satisfaction every time I pushed in deep, and she rolled her hips, taking advantage of my fingers.

"More?" I asked.

She looked at me with lustful eyes and nodded. She bit down on her bottom lip as I withdrew two fingers and pushed in three. Moaning, she circled those ample hips again. I rewarded her eagerness with my thumb on her swollen clit and pressed. Her pussy squeezed my fingers as she shrieked and grinded against my hand.

"Mmm. I think you can handle one more finger," I said, and added a fourth finger.

Lily's eyes rolled to the back of her head and her mouth formed a great big O as I slid my fingers deep into her.

"Look, Lily," I commanded. "Watch me finger fuck your sweet pussy."

She looked down at my fingers glistening with her sweet cream.

"Harder," she demanded and bit her lip.

I shook my head. I had been going slow and easy with her out of fear. We didn't really know how safe it was for Lily to have sex. The last thing I wanted to do was let lust take over and then suffer terrible consequences. Until she got the okay from a doctor, I wasn't going to fuck her as hard as I normally would, even if it were just my fingers.

"Please," she pleaded.

"No," I said firmly.

I repositioned myself on the bed and between her soft thighs. I kept my fingers inside of her as I flattened my tongue against her clit. Lily cried out and threw her head back again.

"Watch me," I said against her moist flesh.

Her eyes, delirious with heat, fell on mine. I sucked hard on her clit as I flexed my fingers inside of her. Her instant orgasm made my fingers and mouth slick. I groaned deeply as I tasted her juices on my tongue.

"Fuck, baby," I murmured against her clit. "You taste sweeter after every orgasm."

"Make me come again," she begged. "Please, Kyle."

I slowly pulled my fingers out of her. I reached up and coated her lips with her own juices. "Open," I commanded. Obediently, Lily opened her mouth and I slid those four fingers into her mouth.

"Suck my fingers clean," I said huskily. Lily sucked on my fingers as if they were a cock. She took them all the way to the first knuckle and slowly slid her mouth to the tips before inhaling them again.

When I was satisfied she had cleaned my fingers, I made her lie back on the stack of pillows I had placed behind her. I got on my knees and angled her body so that her legs were on my shoulders and her pussy was right where I needed it while I looped my arms under her thighs. Her back was arched off of the bed while her shoulders and head were on the bed. She used her arms at her sides to steady herself. I buried my face between her legs, moaning when I tasted the trickles of her nectar sliding out of her cunt.

Lily thrashed against me, beat the bed with her hands and screamed as I rammed my tongue into her hole over and over, tasting her from the inside out. My tongue slid out of her and through her folds and over her clit. Her thighs attempted to clamp shut when it became too much, but I held them open and licked her harder before punching my tongue inside of her again. I couldn't get enough of tasting her and feeling her squirm and hearing her cries of pleasure.

With a determined grunt, I dislodged myself from between her gorgeous legs and moved to her side. I pushed two fingers back inside of her and pressed on her clit with my thumb as I moved my fingers, beckoning her to come. I used my other hand and pressed down just above her pubic bone, adding to the beautiful pressure I knew she was feeling.

"It's too much!" She screamed. "I can't!"

"You can, and you will, baby," I urged her. "I want to

see your cum gushing out of that pussy, Lily."

"We tried before," she panted, tossing her head back and forth in ecstasy. "We tried. I can't."

"You *will*," I demanded. "I can't wait to see you squirting all over the place, Lily. You're going to soak me with your cum, baby."

Suddenly her body jerked, her pussy went into spasms around my fingers and when I moved my thumb off of her clit, she screamed louder than I've ever heard a woman scream before as stream after stream of her sweet cum burst from her body, hitting me, squirting to the floor, and pooling on the bed beneath her. I groaned uncontrollably as I rubbed the liquid all over her pussy. She sobbed with pleasure as I poised my body over hers, careful not to crush her. I brought my cum-soaked hand to her mouth and spread her cream across her lips, pushed my fingers into her mouth. Before she could lick any away, I planted my mouth on hers, sucking her juices off of her lips and licking the inside of her mouth.

I needed to be inside of her while her pussy was still soaked in her cum. I pressed in slowly, groaning and cursing because the wetness with her tight hole was almost too much to bear.

"You're so wet," I grunted, trying not to pound into her. "So fucking tight."

"Fuck me hard," she pleaded, pulling on my hips with her hands, but I was in complete control, not allowing her to pull me in balls deep.

"Kyle," she whined.

"We have to be careful," I said through a clenched jaw as I pushed ever so slowly into her.

She rocked her hips up, trying to get me deeper and succeeded a little, but only a little. I stopped moving and looked at her disapprovingly.

"Please," she panted, pulling on me as she was pushing her hips up. "Please."

I shook my head as I gave her a little bit more.

"Guess I have to play dirty," she said with a gleam in

her eye. I watched wide eyed as she took one ample breast and pushed it towards her face. With her eyes set on mine, she leaned into it and took a jeweled nipple into her mouth and bit down.

"Fuck..." I moaned. "Stop, Lily. Please." Now I was the one pleading.

She moaned as she sucked on her nipple, never breaking eye contact with me. When I thought I was still in control of myself, she stuck her studded tongue out and giving her nipple a full lick until the metal in her mouth hit the metal on her nipple. She groaned loudly and thrust her hips up as she did it repeatedly, making the hard bud grow impossibly harder. That's when I lost it.

With a feral growl, I buried my cock in her pussy with one hard thrust. Lily cried out, but she didn't stop licking her nipple. It was the hottest thing I had ever seen her do and I couldn't help myself as I pulled out and rammed back into her again. I did it again, but harder. In seconds, I lost my fucking mind as I pounded into her while she screamed around the nipple in her mouth. When she switched to the other one, I wanted a piece of that action, too. I bent my head and my tongue joined hers, licking her hard nipple. I had never experienced anything like it in my life – the taste of her tongue and her nipple in my mouth at the same time.

"Shit!" I yelled as her legs wrapped around me and I fucked her with a maddening frenzy. "I'm going to come so fucking hard, baby!"

Suddenly Lily screamed like she did earlier and I could feel her cum squirting on my pelvis and coating my cock and balls. Her wet orgasm set mine off and I yelled incoherently and ferociously as I violently slammed my cock into her and started spurting semen inside of her. She wrapped her arms around me and kissed me as we soaked each other with our orgasms.

"Shit," I cursed after my head started to clear. I started to scramble off of her, but she held me tightly.

"No, it's okay," she said hurriedly. "I'm okay. We're

okay."

"How do you know?" I questioned, looking into her gray eyes.

"I just know," she gave a small shrug. "Trust me. I want to feel you inside of me a little longer," she whispered as she cupped my face with one hand. "I want to feel the weight of your body on mine for a little while longer."

I gave in. I buried my face in her neck and wrapped my arms around her. Her fingers stroked over the back of my head and down my back soothingly, but she never said anything about the tears that were soaking her neck and hair.

Chapter Sixteen

~Kyle~

I watched as Lily tried to hold back her tears when she met her nieces and nephew for the first time. Six and a half year old Gavin Jr. was talking a mile a minute about his Lego creations. Four year old Cora brushed Lily's hair with a brush met for a small doll, but Lily didn't seem to care. She balanced two year old Amanda on her lap while the girl stared at some kiddy show on the television. Gavin's mother stood off to the side with Lydia, both women wiping away tears as they watched Lily interact with the children who were the children of the deceased love of her life and siblings to her deceased daughter. The children were all she had left of both Gavin and Anna.

Lily glanced up at me with shiny eyes and a big grin that made my heart lurch in my chest. She was very patient as the two older ones tried to talk to her at the same time, and she couldn't stop touching them, putting her hands in their hair, holding their little faces, or planting kisses on their cheeks. I had never seen Lily's face so lit up. She was glowing after the way we closed out our night last night, but this light blasting from within her was blindingly amazing. She dazzled and glimmered, shiny and bright. I had never seen her look as stunning as she did surrounded by those kids.

I pulled my phone out of my pocket and started taking pictures. Some of them they posed for, most they didn't. Even after she followed the kids into the family room to play, I continued taking pictures, wanting to savor these moments, as I was sure she'd want to, too. I couldn't take my eyes off of the mother of my unborn child. She was going to be the mother I never had and I was so grateful for that.

"Can you build a starship with me?" Gavin Jr. asked after getting my attention with a tap to my arm.

Lily looked over nervously. She had never seen me

with children. Hell, I wasn't even sure I knew how to act around kids, but I didn't think about it.

"Sure, buddy," I said and went to sit on the floor with him next to the biggest bucket of Legos I had ever seen in my life.

"This is serious work," Gavin said with the utmost seriousness I thought a child his age could have.

"Right," I nodded, keeping a serious face for his sake.

He scratched his blond head absently as he talked. "Maybe we should build two starships. You have bigger hands. You might be able to build faster than me."

"Possibly."

"If you find some of Cora's Legos in here *toss them out!* I don't build *pink* starships!"

"Gotcha."

I looked over at Lily and winked. She smiled and returned to being pampered by Cora and tickling Amanda.

Gavin talked a lot while building. I went into a zone, building my starship as Gavin and I had serious conversations about school, *ICarly*, Amanda's pooping habits, and more. The kid could talk a hell of a lot, but I hung onto every word and proved I was paying attention by asking questions and sharing my opinions. When he grew quiet after an hour or so, I thought maybe he was getting tired. Our starships were enormous and we were still building.

"My dad used to play Legos with me," he said quietly just as I was considering asking him if he was tired.

I peeled my eyes away from my starship and looked in his little face. I could feel the adults' eyes on us, waiting for my reaction.

"I probably can't build a starship as big as your dad's," I said.

"Yours is okay," he shrugged as he stared at his ship in his hand. "Just miss building stuff with my dad."

Fuck.

"What kind of stuff did you guys used to build?" I asked him.

"Everything," he gestured wildly. "Cities, towns, boats, cars. I use to have a lot more Legos but when he died I got mad and threw them all away. Now I wish I still had them because they were *ours*."

What could I possibly say to make him feel better? I couldn't bring his dad back and replacing the Legos with new ones wouldn't necessarily make him feel any better. Shit, I wasn't good at this kind of thing, obviously. I'm Kyle Sterling, the Dick, not Kyle Sterling the child whisperer.

"You know what?" I started before I could even think about what I was going to say. "My dad didn't build Lego cities, towns, and starships with me. My dad didn't build anything with me. I don't have nice memories like you do. I am so glad for you because you can remember doing fun things with your dad. When you grow up and have a son of your own, you can do the same things with him and you can say 'my dad and I use to do this.' And he'll do the same for his son when he grows up. It's good to have nice memories even if you don't have the person anymore."

He looked like he was thinking about that while he fumbled with his starship. I wasn't sure if I really said the right thing. Maybe I shouldn't have said anything and left it to his mother or grandparents.

"I have pictures of the stuff we built," he said thoughtfully. "My teacher says that pictures are memories frozen in time so that we never forget. That's cool. Why didn't your dad do anything with you?"

I looked down at my pile of Legos. "He was too busy I guess," I said, sparing him the truth, that Walter hated me even when I tried very hard to get him to love me as a child.

"Okay so don't be too busy for your kids," Gavin said with a shrug. "You can give them good memories. *This* is a good memory, too. Our starships are super! Mom take a picture!"

Gavin sat beside me and we held our ships on display as his mother froze this memory.

~~~

~ 259 ~

Four days after we arrived in Ohio, I had to return back to Philly to handle a zoning problem at the bar site. Marco was in California handling his own business, so I had to go to the site myself. I needed to get back to work soon anyway. Then there was the obvious, the manila envelope sitting on my desk.

I hired a full time nanny to help out while Rose, Lily's mother, recovered. Whether or not the family decided to keep the nanny after a few months was entirely up to them, but I let them know I will cover the service as long as they needed it. I also made sure that both women had a way to get around until Rose was able to drive again, and I did end up buying Gavin several more containers of Legos and left them with a note that said "Keep building new memories."

"You're the sweetest dick I know," Lily said, standing on her toes to kiss me.

"That's what all the girls say," I said, wriggling my eyebrows.

She punched me and went back to folding my clothes and putting them in my carryon bag. I was leaving, but I felt Lily needed a little more time with her family. She had years to catch up on with Lydia, and I wanted her to feel comfortable leaving her mother so soon after her heart attack, and she was so in love with the kids. I knew it was going to be hard for her to leave them when she finally did.

"So," she started slowly. "What are you going to do when you get home?"

"After I take care of the zoning shit I'm going to jump on network for a while, see what's been going on. I've never taken such a lengthy vacation before – except when I was in rehab."

"What else?" she asked as I watched her refold the same shirt twice.

"What are you asking me, Lily?"

She hesitated. She absently shook the shirt out and began to fold it a third time. "What am I going to come home to?" she asked softly.

"I don't know," I answered truthfully.

~ 260 ~

"You're selfish," Lily said. Her voice was still soft, but her tone was dripping with anger and pain. "You are so damn selfish. You just couldn't leave me alone." She looked at me, her gray eyes hard and cold. "I would have been fine without you. Anything I felt for you back then was tolerable. I would have been okay! Even though you were still hung up on Emmy, you *had* to have me and you didn't care about the consequences."

I was stunned to hear such similar words from Lily as I heard from Emmy almost a year ago.

"You don't give two shits about the aftermath when you get what you want."

"Don't look so surprised," Lily snorted. She tossed the shirt she was holding into the bag and moved away from me. "You got what you wanted," she shrugged. "Now you can be on your way."

"Lily," I moved towards her, desperate to ease the aching in my chest, but she backed away towards the door with her hands up in a defensive gesture.

"Don't," she said harshly. "I know you want me. I know you love me, but you don't need me. You still need Emmy. That's why you cried last night," She touched her neck with remembrance. "Because as strongly as you feel for me, you don't need me. I'm not enough. I just wish I didn't need you, too."

Before I could make my feet move across the room, Lily was out the door. I raced out after her, but she was already half way down the hallway, running full speed to put some distance between us. I started to run after her, but a whole damn family exited a room in front of me, and as if coordinated, the family across the hall came out, too. They stood in the middle of the hallway chattering, blocking me from Lily. By the time I got through the cluster fuck, Lily was gone and I wasn't sure if she had taken the stairs or the elevator. I ran into the stairwell and could hear faint footsteps racing down the stairs.

"Lily!" I called after her as I raced down the stairs.

"Stop!"

By the time I reached the first floor, she was nowhere in sight. I ran outside, almost crashing into a small crowd of people waiting to board a shuttle bus for some tour. I scanned the parking lot for the rental car I got for her the night before, but it was still there. I turned in a circle.

Where the hell did she go?

I thought maybe she was still inside, hiding out somewhere, but then as the shuttle started to pull away, I saw her. She was in the very back seat, watching me through the dingy window.

"Lily!" I screamed, but the shuttle pulled out into traffic and she was gone.

~~~

I missed my first flight out, trying to track Lily down. Lydia and Rose had not heard from her and I believed them. I stayed at the hotel past check-out, waiting for her to return for the car, but by mid-afternoon, she still hadn't returned. I called her, texted her, emailed her and called some more, but my calls always went straight to voicemail and everything else went unanswered as well.

Her words ripped me apart inside. I would have been extra insecure if I thought that Lily didn't need me. Was that how I made her feel? Insecure? Had she felt like she was in Emmy's shadow the entire time? I couldn't even imagine how that must have felt. The entire time we were together I was hurting her and too damn stupid to see it.

By the time I was on the next flight to Philly, I knew what I had to do. I had to burn the damn pictures of Emmy without looking at them. Lily was right, I hadn't let Em go. I still loved her and my heart still ached when I thought of her, but it was Lily and our baby that I wanted – that I *needed* and I had to prove that. I was such a fucking idiot. Lily was the best thing that ever happened to me, accepting me as I was from the very beginning, from that first night I went into *SHOTZ* looking for Emmy. I couldn't imagine my life without her, and the truth was that she kept me in line, kept me from burying myself in drugs, grief, and self-hate.

I had Corsey and Harry drop off my own car at the airport. I raced across the bridge to take care of the issues on the construction site. It took up more time than I would have liked. I wanted to find Lily and do what I needed to do to get her back, but the bar was for her. It was the only reason I remained patient, but as soon as it was over, I took off at speeds higher than legally allowed to get back to the penthouse. As soon as I got inside, I took my phone out of my pocket to call Lily again, but it was dead.

"Fuck," I muttered, dropping my bag by the door. I went down the hall to my office so I could plug my phone in and maybe jump online to see what was happening at work.

The manila envelope was on the center of my desk, seemingly the biggest thing in the room. I tried my best to ignore it, setting my laptop on top of it as I fired it up and plugged in my phone. I jumped on the Sterling network and started sifting through my emails, a job I would have assigned to Lily. It was tedious and time consuming, something I never had time for, but Lily was MIA and even if she wasn't, I wouldn't have taken any time away from her family to make her work.

I threw myself into the task, responding to emails that needed responding to, flagging others that needed more attention at a later time, and deleting junk. A couple of private instant messages popped up from people in the office. No one sent me messages to ask me how my vacation was or to chit chat – I wasn't that kind of guy at work, but there were things that needed my immediate attention. I talked to Brian, my newest employee who works directly under me, for a long time about some important matters. I got a new email from Warrick and sighed loudly when I read it. Traveling is part of my job, but now they wanted me to go help build my same department in the U.K. headquarters. I knew from experience that it wasn't a request, but a command.

I couldn't go to the U.K. until Lily and I were where we needed to be. I needed her with me, at least figuratively if not physically across the pond with me. I picked up my phone to call her again and saw that I had a message from her. I scrambled to unlock the phone so I could listen to it.

"Kyle, listen closely," she said, her voice strong and confident. "I'm not doing this. I *can't* do this. I love you, but you've already made your decision. I am scared stupid about losing another baby and I just want to focus on taking care of myself during this pregnancy. I can't have all of this angst and stress, and…" she paused and took a deep breath. "And maybe I don't want to worry about when you're going to take another hit of meth – during or after the pregnancy. I'm not enough to anchor you, clearly, or we wouldn't even be in this situation. I don't know when I will get my things out of the penthouse. I guess…I guess I don't need any of it." She paused again. I could hear cars in the background, as if she were walking down a city street. "I guess I'll work on not needing you, too. Please stop calling. Just…just leave me alone."

The message ended. I listened to it twice more, trying to calm my rippling emotions.

"Fuck that," I growled as I returned her call. I fully expected it to go to voicemail, but to my surprise she answered.

"What?" she snapped. "I told you not to call me."

"You're just going to leave?" I yelled into the phone, surprising even myself by my burst of anger. "You're going to try to keep the baby away from me?"

"What? No. I didn't say that."

"It damn well sounded that way, Lily," I shouted. "That's *my* baby and you won't keep it away from me, Lily!"

"I'm not!" she yelled back. "You ass, I still have to come back to work eventually!"

I closed my eyes, squeezed the bridge of my nose. I needed a hit so badly, the urge swarmed over me suddenly.

"You'll be back in the area then," I said, trying to control my anger.

"Yes, I'll be back in the damn area, and I'll be back at work soon, too. I just need a little time to get my head straight."

"When?"

"I don't know when," she sighed wearily.

"I have to go to London very soon and for a long time. I need to see you again before I go."

There was a moment of silence from her end. "Okay," she finally said in a quiet voice. "I have a doctor's appointment Friday morning. You can meet me there. At least maybe there you won't cause a scene."

"Lily," I said, my emotions swinging from anger to despondency. "Please don't do this. I love you and you are more to me than you know, and I'm so sorry I haven't -"

"No," she said with strong, painful emotion. "Don't say this shit now because I'm gone. Don't do it. You don't mean it, you're just upset. I'll text you the details for the appointment. I'm hanging up. Don't call me. Don't text me. Just *leave me alone*. And don't you *dare* stalk me. If I find out you have anyone following me around, you'll lose your chance to be in your baby's life."

With that, she ended the call. I stared at the phone for a long minute in disbelief.

"Fuck!" I yelled and hurled the phone across the room. It smashed against a bookcase and fell to the floor in pieces.

I slammed the laptop close and tossed it to the side. The manila envelope sat there, equally enticing to me as a few hits of meth or cocaine. I didn't have any drugs in my possession, but I had the envelope and its contents.

I was going to burn the whole thing without looking, but that was when I thought I could get Lily back. It was possible I could still win her back, but most likely not with the way I just behaved on the phone with her. Chances were high that she would resist me at every turn and I'd never have her again. I took Emmy back over and over before I beat the shit out of her, but Lily's resolve was higher. She didn't do anything she didn't want to do. If she folded for me, it was because she chose to, not because I made her.

I picked up the envelope and weighed it in my hands. My fingers itched to tear it open. My heart pounded with anxiety. I carefully released the golden clasp on the back. With a deep breath I shook the envelope, releasing proof of my fury onto my desk. I picked up the pictures with shaky hands. It only took three out of forty photos to make me come undone.

Chapter Seventeen

~Lily~

Vomiting sucks. I had puked my face off into my barf bag when I got a whiff of someone's Greek yogurt on the flight back to Philly. I apologized to the flight attendants and those around me profusely.

My stomach was still feeling queasy as I caught a cab from the airport to the OB's office in Center City. I checked my phone again on the way to see if Kyle had answered my text. I texted him twice, telling him the name and address of the doctor and he never responded. I was tempted to call the office, but I wasn't ready to hear his voice. It took a pep talk from Lydia for me to even get on the plane to meet him for the appointment.

Well, you told him not to call or text, I told myself as I handed the cabby money for the fare. I definitely fully expected to see him inside when I arrived, but even after I checked in and filled out paperwork, there was no Kyle. I texted him once more to let him know I was going into the back, but I got nothing.

I went through the appointment, expecting Kyle to show up apologizing for being late, but he never came. By the time I left the doctor's office, I was anxious and worried. What if he gave up altogether? What if he wanted nothing to do with the baby? It was so difficult to tell him the things I told him on the phone, but I knew I had to do it. I wasn't sure that I wanted to be without him forever, but I needed that space. What if I pushed him away forever? The thought made me queasy again.

After a few minutes of indecision, I caught another cab to the penthouse. I was actually surprised that he had not sent Corsey to pick me up from the airport, but then again I had warned him about having someone follow me and I definitely would have assumed just that if I saw Corsey waiting for me.

"Miss Whitman," the concierge nodded to me as I

walked to the elevator a little while later.

I acknowledged him with a nod, but I didn't trust myself to speak. It seemed like the elevator ride to the top floor took twice as long as usual. When it finally stopped, I bolted out before the doors could even open halfway. I used my key to let myself in and immediately knew something was wrong. The house was a mess. I don't mean dirty dishes and empty pizza boxes. I mean it looked as if King Kong had walked through, destroying everything in his path. The furniture in the living room was askew, the couch was turned at a funny angle, and the coffee table was across the room, upside down and broken. The other little pieces of furniture in the living room were broken or way out of place. The glass dining room table was shattered and the chairs were everywhere.

Afraid to call out Kyle's name, as quietly as I could I made my way down the hallway to his office. The first thing I noticed was his phone, shattered on the floor by the bookcase, which explained why he wasn't answering me. His work laptop was in pieces on the floor by the desk – everything that was once on the desk was on the floor in various parts of the room. The window behind Kyle's chair was broken and anything breakable was definitely broken. What stood out the most though were the pictures on the floor. I picked up the one closest to me and choked to keep down the bile that had risen from my gut. Emmy's back was bright red all over, the beginning stages of bruising. There was an actual partial shoe print on her back. I picked up another photo and this one showed her face – another shoe print there. He had kicked her in her face, I just couldn't fathom it. I picked up more photos, each one seemingly worse than the one before. The one that made me stop looking for more to look at was the one of Emmy's pregnant belly, bright red in spots from getting hit or kicked.

I lost whatever was left in my stomach then, right there on the littered carpet. After dry heaving for five minutes after that, with the pictures gripped in my hand, I stumbled out of the office and back down the hall. Judging by the way the house looked Kyle had been on a rampage after seeing what he did to Emmy. The question in my mind was whether or not he was grounded when he did it.

I should have just left and called Corsey on my way out, but needing to know if Kyle was okay outweighed my need to leave. I put the pictures in my bag and jogged up the stairs. I paused in front of my bedroom door. My belongings were strewn across the room. Anything that wasn't too heavy was broken, smashed against a wall. I moved onto Kyle's room and found the same type of disarray. It became obvious that he wasn't home, but I was no less worried. What if he was out buying drugs? What if he hurt himself?

I jogged down the stairs and was almost to the foyer when the front door opened, stopping me in my tracks. Kyle stopped for only a moment to stare at me before continuing through the door. He went to throw his keys on the table that was usually by the door, but that table was lying on its side on the floor. Pinching the bridge of his nose with one hand, he slipped the keys into his pocket. He looked terribly reminiscent of how he looked that night he came into *SHOTZ*. He hadn't shaved, his eyes were red rimmed and bloodshot, and his hair looked like he had been running his hand through it an awful lot.

"I'm sorry I missed the appointment," he said. I could hear how weary and tired he was in his voice.

"It's okay. Nothing important happened. You look like shit."

His hand went through his hair as he sighed. "Yeah."

He walked past me and started up the stairs. Unsure of what the hell just happened, I followed him. He went into his room, stopped a few steps in and looked around as if he was searching for something. When he moved again, he went to his suitcase, which still had clothes from Tahiti in it. He picked it up and dumped out the rest of the clothes and put the empty suitcase on the bed.

"What are you doing?" I asked from the doorway.

"I'm leaving. Someone will be here this afternoon to

start cleaning up the mess and fix anything major, like the office window."

"Okay…" I said slowly.

"I opened an account for you a long time ago," he said as he pulled clothes from his chest of drawers and put them in the suitcase. "A bank card and checkbooks are in my desk, bottom drawer. It's locked but the key is in the book *The Time Machine* on the bookshelf in the office."

"What…why…" I didn't know what to say. I was so confused, and scared. Why the hell did he open an account for me and why the hell is he talking as if I would never see him again? Why wouldn't he *look* at me?

"Look at me!" I yelled.

He froze with his back to me. After a few seconds he turned around and looked at me.

"What the hell is going on?" I demanded. "Were you high when you went all Hulk on the house? Are you high now?"

"I wasn't high," he said quietly. "I was drunk, and angry. As much as I want to push something up my nose, I'm not."

I felt an overwhelming sense of relief at hearing that from him. My whole body seemed to relax some, not completely, but some.

"Where are you going and why are you talking to me as if you're never going to see me again?" I asked, my trembling voice betraying me.

"I have to go to London to get them up and running," he said, still using that quiet voice.

"For how long?"

He shrugged. "A few months. A year. I'm not sure."

"I'll go with you," I said, totally forgetting that I broke up with him a few days ago.

"I don't want you to go with me, Lily," he said. "I want you to stay here in the penthouse and take care of yourself and the baby. Just live your life. You don't have to work if you don't want to; I'll always take care of you – both of you."

My head was spinning. I covered my eyes with my hands, trying to comprehend what was happening.

"I don't understand what's happening here," I said, frustrated and scared.

"I'm giving you what you want. I'm leaving you alone."

"I don't want that anymore," I said, feeling tears threatening to squeeze out of my eyes. "I don't want that."

"*I want it*," he said with such conviction it took my breath away.

"I love you, Kyle. I don't care what happened in the past. Stay here or I'll come with you – don't cut me off."

He looked at me for a long moment and I could not doubt the sadness that he felt. "I will call you once in a while to see how things are going with the pregnancy, see if you need anything," he said as he turned away.

I stood there crying as he continued talking.

"You don't have to send money to your family anymore. They are taken care of. There's more than enough money in your account or theirs to take the kids to Disney. Gavin will really like the Lego store."

I moved across the trashed floor to Kyle's side. I squeezed myself between him and the bed, forcing him to drop the clothes he had in his hands. His eyes were glazed with unshed tears as he looked down at me. He put his hand in my hair with one hand and stroked my cheek with the other. He tilted my head and ran his nose down the side of my face and down my ear until his lips reached the stars under my neck. I sighed when he tasted me there. When his lips finally met mine, I wrapped my arms around him and kissed him back, hard. Kyle groaned as I repeatedly flicked my tongue with his and his hand tightened into a fist in my hair. He kissed me as if he wanted to climb into my mouth. I certainly wanted to climb into his.

I put my hands under his shirt and touched the bare skin of his back before slipping my hands into the waistband of his jeans and squeezing his bare ass. Kyle grunted and moved his hands down to my ass and squeezed while pulling me against him. When he pulled away, I started to object, but he grabbed the hem of my shirt and pulled my shirt over my head before taking his off. He reached behind me, grabbed the suitcase and threw it on the floor, uncaring that all of the things he had just carefully put in there were now on the floor.

When he kissed me again, his hands got to work unbuttoning the jean shorts I was wearing. He pulled them off with my panties at the same time. He quickly got out of his own pants without taking his lips off of mine before pushing me back on the bed.

No words were said when he broke the kiss to kiss down my throat and across my chest. When I felt his tongue on a nipple, I groaned and gripped at his hair. His tongue swirled around the hard bud before he sipped it into his mouth. He moved to the other one after a minute, giving it equal attention before kissing his way down my belly, scooping his tongue into my navel and continuing down to my hot and waiting sex. He pressed my legs open as he settled between them. He nipped at one inner thigh and then the other, making me jump but anticipate what was coming next.

Kyle carefully spread me open, exposing me to his hot breath and warm tongue, and then I felt his tongue flick across my clit. I cried out as he repeatedly flicked my clit with his tongue. When he pushed two fingers inside of me and started that "come hither" motion, I knew what he was attempting to do. He attacked my clit with his mouth, sucking and nibbling and licking as his fingers were busy inside of me. One of his hands was pressing down just above my pubic bone, applying pressure to the pressure he was already applying from the inside. It was too fucking much. The bottom half of my body bucked against him as I felt my body reacting to his ministrations.

"Suck your nipples," Kyle commanded against my sex.

I complied, immediately, though I knew it would throw me over the top. The second my mouth closed over my nipple I started to fall to pieces. My body jerked as I came all over my lover's face. I screamed incoherent words and tore at the sheets beneath me. Kyle groaned as he tasted me and continued licking my wet cunt. Before I could begin to recover from the explosive orgasm, he was on top of me, kissing me as he pushed his hard cock inside of my sensitive sex.

"Lily," he breathed my name as he held his dick deep inside of me.

I gripped his face in my hands and kissed him deeply, passionately, trying to give him all of my love in this one kiss. Kyle's hands moved under my ass and pulled me up to meet his slow deep thrusts. We were hot and sweaty as our bodies slapped against each other. I could hear how wet I was as he drove into me.

"I love you," he panted before his mouth found the sensitive flesh on my shoulder. He kissed and then bit down, making me cry out as his thrusts became deeper and harder. After the bite, he kissed me there to soothe the little pain he had given.

"Kyle," I groaned. "I love you so much," I cried out as my orgasm hit me.

Grunting incoherent words, Kyle started to come, pumping me hard as he shot rope after rope of cum inside of me. As his orgasm subsided, he lazily continued to stroke himself inside of me while he kissed me. He was still hard and I still wanted him.

"Again?" I whispered, stroking his hair.

In response, he dipped his head to suck a nipple into his mouth. I took that as a yes.

~~~

I woke up alone in Kyle's bed. It was the sound of someone knocking on his bedroom door that startled me awake. Kyle wouldn't knock on the door...would he? I pulled the sheets up to my chin and told whoever was on the other side to come in.

A woman wearing a uniform for a cleaning service poked her head in.

"I'm sorry, Miss," she said. "I'll come back later."

"Wait," I said, stopping her. "What are you doing?"

"We're cleaning the house?" she answered in a question. She looked a little uncomfortable to be standing there with the door open while I was naked under the sheets. It was only then that I heard several vacuums running throughout the house and what sounded like a lot of chattering. I had forgotten about the cleaning service coming in to clean.

"Umm, give me a couple of minutes to get dressed," I told her. Before she could close the door, I stopped her again. "Where is Mr. Sterling?"

"Who?"

"Mr. Sterling? The man who called your company?"

"Oh. He left right after we got here. He gave us some directions and left."

"Thank you," I said, swallowing hard. I had a very bad feeling in the pit of my stomach.

As soon as the woman closed the door, I jumped out of bed and went into the bottom drawer of Kyle's bureau where I kept some of my own clothes. It used to be a pain in the ass to have to go all the way back to my room for clothes. I kept just basic things in there – bras, underwear, a couple of pairs of pants and a couple of shirts. I grabbed what I needed and hurried into the bathroom to take an amazingly fast shower. I dressed just as quickly before stepping back into the bedroom. I looked around, but the suitcase Kyle had been packing earlier was gone.

I threw open the door and almost crashed into the same woman.

"Did Mr. Sterling leave with a suitcase?" I asked.

She looked reluctant to answer, but slowly nodded yes. She immediately scurried away into the bedroom with her cleaning stuff. With a heavy heart, I went downstairs and zigzagged through the team of cleaners and went into the office. The office was already cleaned up. I didn't think Kyle would let strangers into his office. I imagined he cleaned it himself.

I sat down in the chair and stared at an envelope with

my name on it. It took me a few minutes to get the nerve to pick it up and open it. A micro SD card fell onto the desk. I looked at it quizzically. It looked like it came out of a phone. I put that down and pulled out the handwritten, one page letter.

> *Lily,*
>
> *By the time you read this, I should be on my way to London. I'll forward you an address and phone number where I can be reached as soon as I can, but I* do not *want you to make a trip out there.*
>
> *I know life will be hard for a little while. I know you are scared and you never intended to be in this position alone. I apologize from the bottom of my heart, but I can't be the one there with you. As I said before, I will always take care of you and the baby, and I'll check up on you from time to time, but you deserve a stable man without a tainted past, someone who needs you as much as he loves you, someone who will bend over backward to keep you happy, as well as safe, and secure. You deserve someone who isn't selfish, who puts your needs and desires above his own.*
>
> *Please take full advantage of everything I leave to you: my cars, the penthouse, the money, and whatever else you have access to. I know you won't like it, but Corsey will be keeping an eye on you. Enjoy your bar when it opens. You will be a great success.*
>
> *I'll Love You Always,*
> *Kyle*

I was *so* over crying. Now I was angry. He fucked me to knock me out and then escaped while I was snoozing, *and* had the nerve to leave me a Dear Lily letter!

I balled up the piece of paper and threw it across the room. I slammed my hand on the desk and noticed the little black card jump. I had forgotten about it that quickly. I would have loved to plug it into my laptop, but it was busted on the floor in my bedroom. I went upstairs to Kyle's room where three girls were busy cleaning. I moved around them and grabbed my purse. I took my phone out, careful not to knock out any of the pictures of Emmy. I carried my purse and the phone back down to the office and sat down as I dialed.

"Corsey," Corsey said when he answered his phone.

"Corsey, are you around?"

"Yes, what's up?" he asked.

"Can you come by with your laptop?"

"Be there in five."

"So, that's what it's like to have someone at my disposal," I murmured to myself as I looked at the card in my hand.

True to his word, Corsey appeared in the doorway of the office five minutes later, carrying his laptop.

"I have this card and nothing to plug it into," I said, holding it up.

"Yeah," he grimaced as he put the laptop down in front of me. "I'm really sorry about that."

"You were here?" I looked up at him in surprise.

He shrugged. "I was around. Had to keep him from going off the deep end."

I gestured wildly towards the living room and other rooms. "That's not going off the deep end?"

He looked grim. "Lily, you know how much worse that could have been..."

Of course he was talking about the drugs. Kyle had only been drunk and angry. It could have been far worse, and if I showed up while he was still binging, it could have been a whole lot of physical pain to go with my emotional pain.

"You're right," I nodded, firing up the laptop.

I plugged the SD card into the slot and chose the option of looking at pictures. The program that opened the file automatically set the photos on a slide show. The first picture to pop up on the screen was a picture of me sleeping. Half a dozen more were of me sleeping. I was pretty sure they were taken in the hotel room we stayed at in Ohio. Then there were pictures of me smiling at the camera, pictures of the two of us smiling at the camera. There were at least two dozen pictures of me with my nieces and nephew. I couldn't help but to smile as I looked at how happy I was to be with them. I was *glowing* and not anything like I glow after Kyle and I have a wild night. When a picture popped up of Kyle and Gavin rough housing in Lydia's backyard, it made my heart ache. He had no idea how happy he had made that kid over those few days. He had no idea that he was more than capable of making someone happy or that he could be a good dad. What he said to Gavin that first day was probably the best set of words I ever heard come out of his mouth. He had no idea how happy it made me and how much more I fell in love with him at that moment, and he'd never know because he chose to walk away.

I guess I wasn't over the crying after all.

Corsey discretely stepped out of the room while I sat in front of the laptop crying over the man that was and could have been.

Chapter Eighteen

~Lily~

I sat down at the small table across from a smiling Felicia Sterling. I couldn't deny her beauty and where Kyle got his good looks. Her dark hair was no longer strung with gray, her figure had improved, and her eyes were lively and no longer dead looking. She had called me at work a couple of days before to ask me to lunch. I guess she had some apologizing to do for what happened months ago. I took the day off for my mid-morning doctor's appointment. I didn't really need the whole day for that, but the last thing I felt like doing was sitting at work after being violated at the OB/GYN.

"Thank you for meeting me, Lily," she said with a big smile. "You are looking well. How are you feeling?"

"Fine," I said, not returning her smile.

"I thought we could meet to discuss the baby," she grinned.

"How long have you known?" I asked suspiciously.

"I spoke to Kyle last weekend. He sounds terrible."

A waiter appeared just then to take our orders. I ordered a glass of water and a bowl of soup while Felicia ordered salad, no dressing, and a cup of hot tea with lemon.

"Is that all you're eating?" she asked me with disapproval. "You should eat more; it will be good for the baby."

"Let's cut to the chase, Felicia," I said, putting my palms flat on the table. "We're not friends and I'm not sure if I really want you to be a part of my baby's life."

Her face fell. She took a moment to answer me. "Are you still angry about what you witnessed all of those months ago?"

"Am I still angry that you and your asshole ex-husband have been verbally and physically abusing Kyle his entire life? You bet your sweet, rich ass I am angry. Am I still angry that the only way you know how to apologize to your son is by taking him to brunch? Fuck yeah, I'm angry. You have *no* idea the damage you have done."

Her eyes flitted around the restaurant, worried that someone overheard me, but I really didn't care if anyone had overheard me. I had been without Kyle for over two months. He only called me once a week if I was lucky and never spoke for more than five minutes. He sounded as terrible as I felt, but he was adamant that we couldn't be together, that he was not good for me. If he didn't feel good enough, it wasn't by my doing, but it started at home when he was a child. Having the opportunity to finally lay it out for his mother was one I was going to use well and to hell with anyone who overheard.

"You don't understand," she started in a soft voice.

"I know you have psychiatric issues, Felicia, I'm not faulting you on that, but you treat your son like shit. You keep abusing him and he keeps coming back for more, desperate for you to show him even a little bit of love, but you keep kicking him down. You blame him for Walt's death -"

"I don't blame him," she interjected, looking at me as if I were crazy.

"You do, too! Do you not remember the things you say to him when you're off your meds?"

She blinked hard as she sat there staring at me, now oblivious to anyone who may be watching or listening. "He knows I don't mean it," she whispered.

"Does he? Are you sure about that? Because he feels pretty damn guilty and I'm pretty damn sure it's coming from you and Walter. You *never* actually say 'I'm sorry, Kyle' and you *never* actually tell him that you don't blame him and when has he *ever* heard you tell him you love him?

"My baby's father hates himself. He doesn't think he's good enough for *me* of all people and he doesn't think he's good enough to be a dad. He's had some real problems along the way, but it started with you and that asshat ex of yours. I watched him take a beating from Walter once, so that Walter wouldn't go home and beat *you*. How many times did that

~ 279 ~

happen? How many times did that happen and you not appreciate it?"

I let out a sound of exasperation and stood up. I was getting so stressed out telling her what a bitch she was and it probably wouldn't matter in the long run. I walked away from her without another word. I got outside to the sidewalk where Corsey was waiting for me at the Escalade.

"Everything cool?" he asked, looking at my flushed face.

"Nothing's cool!" I snapped as I started to get into the car.

"Lily, wait," Felicia called behind me. She looked up at Corsey. "Corsey, can you drive me home? It will give me a chance to talk privately with Lily."

"Yes, ma'am, if it's okay with Lily," he said. I was thankful that he took my side.

I nodded my assent and climbed in and moved over to the other side.

"What about your car, Mrs. Sterling?" Corsey asked as she slid in.

"I rode into the city with a friend," she smiled up at him. He closed the door, leaving us in the backseat to have it out.

"I wasn't sure if I would like you," she said after a couple of minutes of silence. "As soon as I saw you walk into my house with my son, I thought 'what the hell is this?' I wasn't sure if it was something serious or if he was just experimenting. Like so many in my position do, I judged a book by its cover."

"So, what now? You want to get together and drink lattes and paint each other's nails and braid each other's hair?" I asked dryly.

She grinned at me. "You're so straight forward and...rough around the edges. I like that you're not phony, even if it is at my own expense."

"I don't know what you want from me," I said, frustrated by her stupid grinning.

~ 280 ~

Her grin faded though and her eyes got misty very quickly. "You're right. I have said horrible things to Kyle and I've done horrible things to him and I don't know how to make up for any of it. How do I make up for the time he had to staunch the flow of blood from my wrists after I tried to take my own life? He was only eleven years old then." Tears flowed freely down her cheeks now. "How do I make up for the times that I was out of my mind and beating him for reasons I can't even remember? I don't mean spanking. *Beating*. I don't know how to thank him for always trying to take care of me and look out for me and protect me from Walter. I don't know how to apologize for blaming him for his brother's death. I've become accustomed to just taking him out for lunch and sweeping it all under the rug, but that hasn't been good for him has it?"

She reached into her pocketbook for tissues. It wasn't until she handed me one that I realized I was crying, too. Damn hormones.

"I didn't protect him when he was a child and I didn't stand up for him when I *knew* he loved that Grayne woman and despised being with Jessyca. I didn't call him or visit him during any of his stays in rehab or help him stay clean when he came out. I just…let it all go and pretended all was well in the world," she sobbed. "I've totally let my daughter go – how can anyone do that, Lily? How can someone give birth to a beautiful little girl and then just…let her go? I practically wrote her off by the time she was twelve years old. I feel like I've lost three children."

I wiped at my eyes and took a couple of minutes to stop crying so hard. "Now you know," I said and then shrugged. "You suck."

She laughed through her tears. "I know."

"So what are you going to do about it?" I asked. "Your son needs you – *now*. He doesn't need me, but he needs *you*."

She looked at me though she was lost in her own thoughts. After a moment, she said "I'll go to London then. I have some things to settle here first, but maybe in a couple of weeks."

~ 281 ~

"Good," I smiled. "It makes me feel better to know he won't be alone."

"Don't give up on him," she said to me, looking at me fiercely. "He's never run away like this. He must feel pretty strongly about you if he has to run away to keep himself from coming to you."

"It's not me," I shrugged. "It's Emmy. He feels bad for what he did to Emmy and he can't let it go."

"He could have brooded about that anywhere, Lily, not half way across the world. Think about that."

My stomach chose that moment to growl. Felicia looked at me with one eyebrow raised. She leaned forward and said "Corsey, we need to stop somewhere to actually eat lunch now. What would you like, Lily?" she asked, looking back at me.

"Ice-cream and French fries," I said longingly.

"Together?" Felicia asked, making the same face Kyle had made when I first said it to him.

It made me smile, but I felt sad at the same time and missed him more than ever.

"How are you holding up emotionally with the baby?" Felicia asked me over our lunch a little while later. "Kyle mentioned that you have lost a baby before."

I was surprised to hear that Kyle had told his mother something so deeply personal about me. If she was a normal mother, that would be different, but she wasn't. Though we seemed to be building a relationship even after all of the bullshit, I never knew when Felicia may hurl Anna's death at me like a weapon. However, knowing that he shared that with her gave me a little more insight into how he feels about his mom.

"I'm nervous," I admitted. I didn't want to tell her that I was scared to death and that I was having nightmares a couple of nights a week about losing the baby. Just last night I woke up in the middle of the night convinced that he or she was gone. I jolted up gripping at my womb, crying hysterically. I needed comfort but there was no one there to comfort me. It took me hours to fall back to sleep.

"I'm sure everything will work out just fine," she said.

I couldn't share in her enthusiasm or optimism. I needed a change of topic.

"You aren't at all the hoity toity up tight spoiled rotten socialite heiress bitch I thought you would be while you're medicated," I said to her.

I thought I heard Corsey chuckle from the front seat. Felicia looked taken aback by my words, but then offered a small smile.

"I can be a hoity toity up tight spoiled rotten socialite heiress bitch as well as the rest of them, Lily," she said.

Felicia proceeded to tell me about some of the major cat fights that had gone on in high society over the years. I learned that she could get very catty herself, and though I would think I would be disgusted, I was very much impressed. Maybe just maybe I would be able to work things out with her and have a relationship for the baby's sake, but I knew I would always have to be on my guard.

~~~

When I got back to the penthouse later that afternoon, I threw my purse onto the couch and rushed down the hall to the powder room to pee. My bladder was really feeling the effects of having someone sitting on it. I rushed in and almost peed myself because I had to put the toilet seat down. I was thinking about how I'd have to yell at Corsey for leaving the seat up when another thought occurred to me. Corsey had not been in the penthouse all day. He was with *me* all day. I usually don't utilize him as a chauffeur, but I was exhausted from the lack of sleep and my feet were slightly swollen. I didn't feel up to driving myself around and Corse would have given me a speech about taking public transportation when I could use him or Harry. I hate speeches.

Kyle was good for leaving the seat up if he was in a hurry, but Kyle was in London, right? As I flushed and then washed my hands, I began to panic a little. What if there was some stranger sneaking around in the penthouse, waiting to jump out and murder me? Hell, what if it was Vic? I stood in the doorway of the bathroom, trying to decide if I should call Corsey, but then I would feel silly calling him over a raised toilet seat. Besides, I was more than capable of defending myself.

I cracked my knuckles and neck and pushed my fears aside as I stepped into the hall. I decided to check the office first. Nothing seemed askew or missing at first look. When I got closer to the desk, however, I discovered the book *The Time Machine* was on the desk. I froze. I had not left it there. In fact I had not touched it even once after Kyle told me about it. I had been using the money in my own account that I'd had for years. Just to be spiteful I chose not to touch the money Kyle had set aside for me. I couldn't be bought. *Asshole.*

I picked up the book and weighed it in my hand for a moment before gingerly flipping it open. The key Kyle mentioned was taped inside on the cover. I ran my fingers over it but didn't dislodge it. I put the book back down on the desk as my brain tried to register how and why it was there. I glanced around but didn't see anything else out of place. I left the office, my mind trying to fathom why the book was there. Did Kyle have someone put it there? I didn't get it.

I went into the kitchen to get a bottle of water. I opened the fridge and stared.

Since Kyle left, I had no desire to go food shopping. I had been eating a lot of take-out and just using up whatever we already head. Before I left for the doctor's appointment, the fridge was almost empty. It was like a bachelor's refrigerator: some souring milk, a few eggs, water, the beer that Kyle never finished and a few other odds and ends – some edible and some not. Now, it was stocked full with fruits, vegetables, fresh milk and eggs, juice, cheese, and yogurt. I left the door hanging wide open and went to the cabinets. They were stocked full with the cereals I liked, pasta, peanut butter, rice, sauces, soups, and a few treats I liked to enjoy. Out of curiosity, I opened the freezer and found plenty of vanilla ice-cream and a big ass bag of frozen French fries along with some packages of chicken, boneless pork chops, and lean ground beef.

In a bit of a daze I found myself traveling upstairs to Kyle's room – my room, too – and slowly opened the door. I had to flip on a light because the day had turned cloudy and rainy and the room was cast in shadow. When the light came on, I found that there were two pregnancy pillows on the bed and a few extra regular pillows. On the centermost pillow was a single flower, a Lily.

I sat down on the bed and picked up the flower. I held it to my nose, inhaling the scent for a minute before I was up and moving again. I went downstairs into the kitchen and poured myself a glass of 100 percent pure apple juice. I leaned against the island and wondered what else Kyle had brought into the house while I was out with his mother. I wondered if it was all a ploy to keep me out so that he can come in without running into me. I was unsure if Felicia knew that her son was in town, but I'm sure Corsey had to know. I had no doubts that it was definitely Kyle and not one of his cronies. If it was one of his people, it wouldn't have been a big clandestine operation.

As I drank my juice, I didn't know how to feel about the situation. I should have felt grateful that he went through so much trouble and showed he obviously still cared. Then again it should have made me cry to know that he didn't want to see me.

I hurled the glass of juice across the kitchen. Juice was flung in every direction and the glass shattered against a cabinet door, sending glass flying all over the counters, stove, and floor.

It was decided. I was pissed off.

I stormed back into the living room and pulled my phone out of my purse. I learned to stop calling Kyle long ago. He never answered and he only ever responded in text messages. He only spoke to me on the phone on his terms, when *he* wanted to, which wasn't very often. No matter how deeply I felt for him, I wasn't going to play the desperate girl, calling him repeatedly and begging. I had begged enough.

I was surprised when he picked up on the third ring. At

least I wouldn't have been yelling at a voicemail.

"You fucking pansy!" I shouted. "You didn't have the balls to face me!"

"You're welcome," he said coolly. In the background I heard what sounded like city noise. Knowing he was on this side of the pond, he was probably on the streets of Philly. "Judging by the stack of take-out menus on the coffee table and the bare cabinets and fridge, you haven't been eating well. You have to eat better than that. You should be well stocked for a while and I've set you up with a grocery delivery service so you will always have the basics."

Again, I should have been thrilled that he thought of me, but I wasn't.

"If you ever do anything like this again, I will leave this place. I will drop off the face of the map, do you understand? I let you keep tabs on me, but I can go away. The next time you set foot in this house you better make damn sure that I am here and that you are looking me in the eyes."

I ended the call before he could speak again. Seconds later my phone was ringing. Kyle was calling, but I wasn't going to answer. I was going to play his game. As I searched for my now missing takeout menus, Kyle called five more times. I came to the conclusion that he had thrown them away, but luckily for me, I had a few of the places on speed dial and I almost always ordered the same thing, but before I dialed, I came up with a better idea.

I slid my swollen feet back into my flip-flops, picked up my purse, and grabbed the keys to the Cadillac XTS. In minutes I was in the garage, pulling out of one of the parking spots reserved for us. I drove a few miles down the road to the casino and paid for valet parking. I went to the back of the casino, put my preggo ass on a barstool and ordered yummy, fattening, salty, unhealthy Chinese food and a big glass of soda. I pulled some cash out of my purse and leisurely played the video Black Jack game built into the bar. While I waited for the food and played the game while sipping on my soda, I checked my phone. Kyle had called twice more, but the calls ended and he sent no texts. It was just as well, because for the first time since he left, I didn't want to be bothered with him.

~~~

At exactly the eighteenth week mark of my pregnancy, I felt a fluttering in my womb that made my heart stop. I was sitting in my office at Sterling Corp when I felt it. I leaned back in my chair and put my hand over my belly. I couldn't feel it from the outside, but I was definitely feeling the quickening from the inside.

There was only one person worth telling, but he wasn't around to tell. Kyle called me a couple of days after the grocery incident. This time he left a message and just asked about the doctor's appointment since we didn't get to discuss it a few days before. That only set me off again because he had been in the city and didn't make an effort to show up for the appointment. I didn't return his call. I pulled *his* usual and simply sent a text in response. I only said "It was fine." He called me again the following week, but I sent that call to voicemail, too. He wanted to know, as always, how I was feeling and if I needed anything. I replied with two words in text: "Fine. No."

Why should I have continued to put in so much effort to hang on to him when his efforts were so little?

I could have called him or texted him to tell him about the baby's movement, but since he chose not to be with me, I decided he had no right to know.

Chapter Nineteen

~Lily~

I wanted the bar open by the time Football season kicked off. I was there every day after working in the office, helping to get it set up. Even though Marco's part in building the bar was long over, he stepped in after Kyle left to help me hire a staff, plan menus and events and other necessities. We were just about finished with the set up process, only needing some basic items a couple of weeks before Labor Day.

It was pretty late one night. Marco and I were the only two left. I was sitting sideways in a booth and he was sitting in a chair that he had pulled up, and he was rubbing my feet.

"You really need to keep a pair of sneakers here in the office," he admonished. "Running around in those hooker heels is not good for your feet."

"They aren't hooker heels," I argued.

He stopped rubbing my foot and picked up one of my four inch heels off of the floor. He raised an eyebrow at me.

"Okay, so they're a little hookerish, but damn I look good in those heels, and they make me feel tall."

"You look good in anything you wear," Marco said absently as he went back to rubbing my feet.

I couldn't explain how good it felt to have this hot guy rubbing my feet. Not just a hot guy, but a hot billionaire guy who almost a year ago thought he was too good for people like me. I tilted my head back, closed my eyes, and sighed.

"When are you going to quit Sterling?" Marco asked. "You're going to wear yourself out running back and forth between here and there. You're already wearing out."

"I promised Mayson I'd work at least a year, but I won't just up and leave. I need to actually make money here first. Ohhh that's perfect," I whispered as he rubbed my foot in just the right spot. I had heard that there were erogenous zones on the feet, and I believed Marco was hitting them. As terrible as it seems, I didn't stop him. Would you have stopped him?

"Doesn't Kyle take care of you financially?" he asked.

"Ummm…wow…" I groaned. "In a way yes. I stay at the penthouse and he keeps paying for things and buying things on the sly, but I want to try to take care of myself. I don't want to rely on him anymore." I frowned. "In fact, I want to pay him back for the cost of building and opening the bar. Anything I make here for at least a year or more will be to repay him."

"He will not take that money," Marco warned.

"I can damn well try to give it to him," I said before groaning again.

"Kyle is a good friend," he started slowly. "But I am struggling with the fact that he left you like this."

I opened my eyes and looked into Marco's eyes. "Me, too," I whispered.

The way he stared back at me made me feel…uncomfortable. Not in a creepy way, but in a way that made my heart flutter in my chest and funny tickling sensations travel up my spine. I pulled my feet off of his lap and turned around in the booth, touching the cool tile with my toes as I looked down at my hands on the table. Marco slid into the booth next to me and put his hand under my chin to make me look into his steel blue eyes.

"Kyle is a fool," he said in a soft tone that made me shiver. His face inched closer to mine. I think I stopped breathing. I think my heart stopped beating. I think the whole world stopped spinning as Marco Mangini's lips skimmed over mine.

"I am only going to do this once," he whispered, his lips moving against mine. "Just this once. I may never have the opportunity to do so again. Hold still and don't fight it."

Then his lips were on me, moving gently but with erotic intention against my lips. His tongue gently slid across my bottom lip and like magic, my mouth opened slightly to let him in. His tongue slipped between my lips until it met my own. I couldn't help but to moan as he very slowly and very gently tasted my mouth. He didn't increase the depth or speed of his tongue, but his lips and tongue moved with clear intent, and it was working. It was probably one of the most hedonistic kisses

I had ever had in my life. His mouth was giving me a preview of what he could do to other parts of my body, and my body was *aware* of it.

When Marco finally pulled away, I sat there frozen as I stared at his mouth. It was an incredible kiss but my mind and my heart were crying out for Kyle. I blinked and looked away from him as I felt the beginning waves of guilt.

"Don't feel bad, okay?" Marco whispered next to me. "I kissed you, not vice versa, and you're technically single. He left you."

I nodded, unable to trust myself to speak. Marco was right, but it didn't necessarily make me feel any better. I didn't feel like I cheated, but I felt as if I betrayed Kyle nonetheless. He made it clear in his Dear Lily letter that he wanted me to find someone else, but I was sure he didn't mean his good friend and really I was pretty sure he had not meant it at all.

Marco slid out of the booth and returned the chair to its proper place. He came back a moment later and offered his hand to help me up. I silently accepted it and got out of the booth. He held my hands and helped me step back into my heels and then took my hand in his. Holding my hand was something he had always done, but it felt differently now. Together we walked throughout the bar, turning off the lights. With his own key, he locked the door and then walked me to the Cadillac. I used the key fob to unlock the doors, but Marco opened my door for me and held it until I slid in behind the wheel. Leaning on the open door, he looked down at me as I started the car.

"I'm not sorry I did it, though it was impulsive," he said quietly. "But if it will make you feel better, you can tell him what happened. I'll suffer the ass beating that will follow."

"He may not care enough to beat your ass," I said. I crossed my arms over the steering wheel and rested my cheek there as I looked up at him.

"Trust me, princess, he still cares. I'll tell him myself. Did you at least enjoy it?"

"Immensely," I admitted.

Marco grinned for a moment before his face grew serious again. "You are a good friend, Lily. Don't let this come between us."

"It won't," I promised.

"Drive safely, okay?" he closed the door and took a few steps back. I put my seatbelt on and waved to him. Just before I pulled away I saw him pull his phone out of his pocket. I had a feeling he was texting Kyle.

By the time I fell asleep that night, Kyle had not texted or called. Either Marco didn't tell him or Kyle just didn't care. The latter weighed me down with sadness.

~~~

More than a week later, in my dream Kyle was straddling me, careful not to put his body weight on me as he kissed the stars under my ear. His tongue was warm and moist and his breath was hot on my skin. His strong hands sought out a nipple through my t-shirt and we both groaned when we were awarded by it hardening under his skilled fingers. I ran my hands over his hard body, feeling the muscles under his soft skin.

His lips met mine in a fury of passionate kissing that made my heart race. He possessed me through this kiss. His lips were demanding and hungry for mine. He sucked on my tongue, nipped at it and nipped at my lips.

He pulled back and looked into my eyes. His features were illuminated by the moonlight streaming through the windows. "Can you still feel his kiss on your lips, Lily?" he asked thickly. The sharp pain that was needling him was obvious in his voice and his gaze, and it also made one thing clear: I wasn't dreaming. It was really his skin I was feeling under my hands, and his body pressed lightly against mine, and it was really his mouth that had just owned mine.

"He said he didn't take you to bed, but I need to know the truth," Kyle said, his forehead resting on mine. "I know I don't deserve to know and I probably deserve every bit of pain I get, but…did you let Marco make love to you?"

I was stunned that he would think so. "No," I said firmly. I held his face in my hands. "I did not sleep with him, Kyle. He kissed me and that's it, and I'm very sorry that it happened."

He pulled back and looked at me. "Did you kiss back?" he whispered.

I covered my face with my hands as I tried not to cry. I felt like such a betraying scum bag. I didn't start the kiss, but I didn't finish it either. I didn't make him stop kissing me and I did kiss him back.

"Baby," Kyle sighed, pulling my hands away from my face. "I wanted you to move on and you did. It's not your fault."

"I didn't move on!" I cried. "It was just a kiss, but I didn't move on. How can I move on with your baby moving around inside of me?"

He was silent for a moment. "You...you felt it moving?"

"Yes."

He looked at me for a moment longer before moving down my body. Resting between my legs, he slowly pushed my t-shirt up and put his warm hands on my skin over my little baby bump. He rested his head on my thigh and caressed me. It wasn't the most comfortable position for me, but having Kyle's body touching mine and feeling his hands caressing our shared child was worth the discomfort. It was worth more than anything in the world at that moment.

~~~

When I woke up the next morning, I was alone in the bed. I knew in my heart that Kyle wasn't in the shower or downstairs in his office or anywhere in the penthouse. I felt his absence, the dark hole it left in me, and I knew he was already flying across the sea back to London.

I angrily wiped away my tears after checking the entire house, even though I *knew*. I didn't get a letter, a note, a fuck you or anything this time. I couldn't keep doing this. I couldn't keep up with the vague voicemails and text messages and the random surprises and appearances. What was it going to be like when the baby was born? Would our child even know him as a father or just the guy that randomly shows up from time to time? I wouldn't want that for my baby anyway. He would have to be there all the way or not at all, and that went for me, too. I loved Kyle more than anyone, but I was tired of feeling this way. I was tired of his shit.

I took a quick shower and packed an overnight bag as I called out of work. A little while later I was in the Cadillac with the GPS set and ready to go. I stopped at a super Wawa to fill up on gas and get some cash and snacks for the road and then I was off. I took note of the Escalade several cars back, but when it became obvious I wasn't out for a joyride, my cell rang with Corsey's ringtone – *Cryn' Like A Bitch* by *Godsmack*. I assigned him the tone after the first time I kicked his ass and he kept whining about not being able to hit a girl.

I pressed a button on the dashboard, answering the call. Corsey's voice boomed throughout the speakers in the car.

"What the hell are you doing?" he asked.

"Driving," I said, chewing on a Twizzler. "What are you doing?"

"Trying to figure out what the hell *you* are doing. Listen, I'm low on gas. Pull over at the next rest stop so we can discuss this."

"No can do, my friend."

"I'm really being rather kind right now, Lily. I'm giving you the option of having a discussion opposed to me tracking you down, which I will do."

"If you lost Vic, you can lose me," I pointed out.

"Oh, Lily, silly girl," Corsey said with a sigh. "I can track you through your cell phone and there is a tracker in the car. I'm going to pull off to get gas, but when I catch up to you I won't be a happy man."

I looked down at my cell phone. "Thanks for the info," I said. I opened my window, picked up my phone, and chucked it out. When the car behind me ran the phone over, the phone call dropped.

I rolled past the next rest stop and noted that Corsey did indeed pull off for gas. I knew he would still catch up to me as long as I was in the Cadillac. I punched the gas as I tapped the GPS, searching for what I needed. When I found it, I punched the gas a little more, flying down the highway entirely too fast. I made a phone call through the car's phone service and a half hour later I was standing at the counter of a rental car place. I was able to get in and out fairly quickly. I deposited my bag into the passenger's seat of the rental car and jumped back on the highway. Before leaving the Cadillac in the lot, I deleted the course I had set in. Chances were that Corsey knew how to find the deleted routes, but it would take him a little bit of time, which was what I needed to get ahead.

After an hour or so, I started to relax, confident that Corsey wasn't on my tail. I was finally able to focus on what I was going to do. I ripped open a bag of beef jerky, found a good radio station, and settled in for my drive to Chicago.

Chapter Twenty

~Emmy~

"I just want one drink!" I cried out, holding on fiercely to the bottle of tequila.

"If you don't let go of this bottle, I will smack the shit out of you," my mother said in a tone that had me letting go of the bottle *and* taking a step back.

"It's not fair," I sulked, crossing my arms like an angry teenager. "It's not right that I have to be sober when you're here."

My mother, the beauty queen, rolled her eyes at me and put the bottle of alcohol back in the cabinet. "You'll harm your baby drinking that shit."

"No I won't. She can drink formula," I argued.

"Stop being melodramatic," she said, returning to her cooking.

"Wonder where I got that?" I murmured and walked over to my three month old daughter sitting in a baby seat on the table. "Hey, precious," I cooed in my baby voice.

She gave me a toothless grin that made me forget about the tequila. I was about to take her out of her seat to spoil her with hugs and kisses when Luke walked into the room and literally swept her off of her diaper.

"Hey!" I said, putting a hand on my hip. "That's mine!"

In response, Luke leaned in and gave me a ridiculously sexy kiss, way too indecent with a baby between us and my mother in the room, but it left me grinning.

"Hi, baby," he said, smiling at me before turning to Kaitlyn. "Hey, Kay Kay!" he said in a tone he used just for our daughter.

He didn't even stop to take his tie off or change his clothes before escorting the lovely young lady into the living room to watch the news. I went over to the stove to check on the progress of the dinner my mom was making. No matter how much she drove me to want to drink, she still cooked one hell of a meal and if that meant I had to soberly tolerate her a couple of days a month, so be it. Though I wasn't eating too much these days, at least I was guaranteed that every bite would be deliciousness.

"How are things between you two?" she asked quietly.

I shrugged as I stuck a finger into her homemade mashed potatoes. She swatted my ass and shooed me away.

"What does that mean?" she asked. "The shrug. What does that mean?"

"It means things are fine," I shrugged again. Now I was sticking a finger in the chocolate cake she had made earlier in the day.

"Stop touching everything!" she yelled. "You're worse than Lucas."

I looked out of the window at my two year old rambunctious blond haired little boy. My father had managed to find odd things to do in the yard to keep him busy and Lucas was out there following him around and keeping him company.

"So?" mom pressed.

"So what?" I sighed.

"Are you and Luke okay?"

"We're more than okay," I said, trying to convince her as well as myself. "But I don't want to talk about that anymore. I just want to move forward."

"Well...maybe you can move forward with a nice new haircut, and a gym membership," she suggested.

"There isn't anything wrong with my hair and I just had a baby, mom," I said, backing away from the sharp objects on the counter so I wouldn't be tempted to pick one up and hurl it at her head.

"He almost cheated on you," she whispered harshly. "There had to be a reason. I'm just sayin' maybe you should start *some*where. Why not start with a little after baby makeover?"

"Oh my god, don't start!"

"I'm just sayin'! A little bit of a makeover never hurt

nobody."

"I'm going upstairs," I said and started up the kitchen stairs to the second floor.

"Supper is almost ready. Why are you going up there?" she whined in her southern twang.

"Because if I don't, I might drown you in the mashed potatoes!" I yelled over my shoulder as I stomped up the stairs.

I didn't want to talk to her about Luke's almost infidelity. I was trying to forget about it, or at least put it behind me, but now thanks to my mother it was at the forefront of my mind.

I collapsed onto the bed. My eyes fell on the framed picture of Luke and me at our wedding. I reached over to the table and picked it up. The glass was still missing from the frame from when I hurled it across the room last week. It had only been two weeks since it *almost* happened, and since the woman's bookstore was right next to the law firm, the chances of him seeing her on a daily basis were extremely high.

Her name was Iris. She was forty-something, sophisticated, wicked smart, charming, and beautiful. She had long, wavy blonde hair, big golden eyes, and curves that Jessica Rabbit would envy. I had really liked her myself. When she first opened the little coffee shop bookstore, I was still pregnant with Kaitlyn. A couple of mornings a week, if I had a sitter, I would meet Luke there for a mini date. He would have coffee and I would have tea. Iris would serve me a freshly made muffin of my choice and Luke always got an enormous cinnamon bun with frosting. We would only be able to hang out for sometimes only a few minutes at a time, but I enjoyed it and I believe he did, too. I thought it was sweet moments like this that would fortify what I already considered to be a strong relationship.

I often would stay there after Luke went back to work and read a book over another cup of tea. Sometimes if business wasn't out of control busy, Iris would sit across from me and we would chit chat. I talked to her about Lucas and our impending Kaitlyn at length. She had met Lucas on several occasions on those mornings when I really wanted to spend a few minutes with my husband but didn't have a sitter. She would always give him an enormous cookie, on the house. We discussed our families – she quickly became aware of my love/hate relationship with my mother, my close relationship with Luke's sisters Lena and Loraine, and she knew how much I adored my mother-in-law Grace. We shared recipes, funny stories, and had deep discussions about Jane Austen's novels. I *liked* Iris, and I didn't mind at all that Luke often wandered over during the day to get out of the office for a few minutes and to clear his head. I was *glad* that the little shop was there for him to do that.

After Kaitlyn was born, Iris had even sent me a muffin basket, and I had taken Kay Kay in there several times, especially when she was still new to the world. I started leaving her with the sitter, too after six weeks or so. I loved my kids but I felt my occasional mornings with Luke were good for both of us and good for our family overall.

A little more than two weeks ago, I had told Luke early that morning that I wasn't going to make it to the shop. Lucas and Kaitlyn both had doctor's appointments early in the day and then I had grocery shopping to do and other random errands that would take me nowhere near the city. The doctor's office called early and asked me to reschedule the kids' appointments, as the doctor had a family emergency. I decided to get my errands out of the way, but I really didn't feel like packing the kids in and out of the car all morning. It was looking cloudy outside anyway, and I didn't want to have to deal with getting them in and out of the car in the rain. I called Luke's young cousin Diana, my favorite sitter. Now that she was out of school for the semester, she was always ready and willing to make a few bucks babysitting. I left right after she arrived, heading towards the city first. Even if Luke couldn't meet with me for a few minutes, I could eat an incredible muffin while chatting with Iris or one of the other regulars for a few minutes. If Luke wasn't in court or a meeting, I'd stop by for a little bit.

Instead of driving in, I took the L so that I didn't have to worry about traffic and parking. With my umbrella in hand, I walked the few blocks to where the firm and shop were. The sky looked like it was about to let loose the hounds of hell and I was beginning to regret my decision, but it was too late. I was there now.

I walked into Iris's shop and the first thing I noticed was that she wasn't at the counter and there were only a few other customers in there and they were engrossed in their books or laptops. I thought about hitting the little bell on the counter, but just as my hand was poised to smack it, I heard her voice. I started to open my mouth to call to her, but then I heard Luke's voice. I froze, knowing I had not heard wrong. I *know* my husband's voice. Why the hell was he in the back room with her? As I moved quietly around the counter, I still didn't think anything of it. We were all pretty chummy with each other, maybe him more than me since he worked right near her.

I stepped into the little hallway that led to her office. The door was slightly ajar. Again I almost announced my presence when I heard distress in Luke's voice. I stood a foot away, listening more closely to their words.

"I can't," I heard Luke say. "You're...you're a great woman, beautiful and intelligent...and sexy, but...I have my wife and two kids."

"I know," I heard her say, but I couldn't miss the desperation in her voice. "I love Emmy and the kids but I can't...I can't help the way I feel about you. I'm not asking you to leave them – just give me one night. One night, Luke. Or one day. I'll even close the shop for a day and we can go somewhere and just be together for one day."

"One day will turn into one more day and one more day will turn into another day after that until it is out of control, Iris," Luke said. "And this...this is madness. I would never do that to Emmy."

What struck me was that he didn't say that he didn't *want* to.

"I know you feel something for me, Luke," she said.

~ 299 ~

"Don't you think about what we could be like together?"

"No, Iris, I don't think about it," he said, sounding a bit disgusted.

"The fact that you are still standing here and having this conversation tells me that you aren't as satisfied with your life at home as you pretend to be," Iris said.

"I love my wife," Luke said.

"I don't doubt that you do, but if life with Emmy is so perfect, you wouldn't still be standing here considering this."

"I'm not..."

"But you are," she said in a silky voice. "I have my hands on you and you're not pushing me away. I made a proposal and you didn't scurry away back to your wife. You're still here. We've been flirting with this for months, Luke. I'm tired of flirting. I'm forty-three years old and I'm over the flirting game. I know what I want and I don't want to play games to get it. I don't know...maybe one day will lead to another day and another day after that, but if you think that will happen then it means something. It means that maybe...maybe there's a chance for us. Don't you want to find out? Do you really want to be left wondering 'what if' when we can find out?"

I heard an exasperated sigh from Luke. Was he considering her offer? Why hadn't he walked away yet? Then I heard it. The distinct sound of lips on lips and clothing rubbing together, and I knew without looking that he was kissing her, or she was kissing him. It didn't matter who initiated it, the other person didn't back away. I had to hold my breath to keep from gagging on the half a banana I had eaten before leaving the house. I felt like my whole world was collapsing around me.

Suddenly I heard Luke's haggard breathing. "No. I can't do this with you. Oh my god," I heard him say, near panic. "I can't. I *won't*."

"Luke," I heard her plead.

"No, Iris! Fuck..." I knew my husband well. I knew he had his hands in his hair and I could hear him pacing back and forth. "Fuck fuck fuck. I can't believe I just did that. I can't believe I just did that."

"I know you're torn but -"

He cut her off. "I'm *not* fucking torn. I'm a fucking idiot. I'm not coming back here – don't come to my office again, don't call me, and stay away from my family. If Emmy comes in here, you give her a fucking muffin or whatever it is she wants and stay away from her. I had to fight so hard to get her; I'm not going to throw my life with her away for you or anyone else."

I was frozen in place, unsure if I should burst in or run away. No matter what he had just said, I was still burning with hurt. They had obviously been building towards this moment and I wasn't even sure if this was their first kiss.

Before I could decide what to do, someone hit the bell a few times from the counter. I heard low murmurs from the office door as the bell was hit again and then the door swung open. Iris looked at me with wide, teary eyes. Luke stepped behind her, looking like he had just been through hell. When Iris still didn't move, Luke looked up and met my eyes.

"Emmy," he said, but I had already turned and dashed out of the hallway. "Emmy!" he yelled my name as I ran out of the shop. The clouds chose that moment to dump the hounds of hell, but I wasn't thinking about the umbrella in my hand as I ran away from my husband screaming my name.

The L wasn't far, but if I had to wait for a train back to my car, Luke would definitely catch up to me. He was practically on my heels now. I ran into the street at the first sight of a cab. I didn't know if anyone was in it or not, I didn't care. I almost got hit by one car as I darted across the street and actually got tapped by one as it came to a halt, honking its horn. I stumbled and my left side ached, but I kept running, waving frantically at the oncoming cab with Luke screaming my name behind me. I was jumping into the cab before it could come to a complete stop.

"Just go!" I yelled to the cabby as Luke closed in.

I watched as his hands landed on the back of the cab,

but then we were moving away, leaving him standing in the middle of the street in the pouring rain yelling for me.

I told the driver where to take me so I could get my car. By my estimate, I could beat Luke home by ten minutes. I had no doubts that he would skip court, meetings, or whatever he had to do to race home. I had to think about what I was going to do. Was I going to take the kids and leave? I couldn't just skip out myself, I had my babies at home, and I couldn't lock Luke out of his own house. Well, I could, but since he had a key and I had no time for a locksmith, that wasn't really an option.

The aching in my hip and thigh made itself known as we drove through the city. The car had barely touched me I thought, but it was possible it hit me pretty damn hard and I just didn't feel it because of my emotional pain. I couldn't worry about it though. I had to figure out what I was going to do when I got home. Luke was calling my phone repeatedly. When there was a pause between his calls, I got text messages begging me to answer the phone.

When the cab stopped at the park and ride lot where my car was parked, I threw some money at him and hurried out into the torrential downpour. My leg and side was definitely more than achy now, but again I couldn't worry about it. I pushed the pain aside and climbed into my car. I got Diana on the phone between Luke's calls as I pulled out of the parking spot. In the most controlled voice I could muster, I instructed Diana to pack overnight bags for the kids and reminded her not to forget Kaitlyn's bottles and such.

"Is everything okay?" she asked, clearly alarmed.

"Yes. I'll be home in about fifteen minutes at the most, but I need them ready to go by then. I know that's asking a lot, but I would really appreciate it."

"You got it."

I ended the call and continued to ignore Luke's frantic phone calls. I couldn't speak to him yet. No matter what, the fact still remained that for some time he had been attracted to Iris and had even acted on it on some level. After all of the shit we had been through, I couldn't believe he had done this, and so soon after we got married.

When I got to the house, I dashed inside and found the kids not only packed, but Lucas was dressed in his raincoat and boots and Kaitlyn had on a jacket and was buckled into her seat.

"I fed her so you wouldn't have to worry about it for a little while," Di said, pulling on her own coat. She looked at me with a grim expression. "Luke has been calling the house like crazy. I didn't tell him that you had me get the kids ready. I don't know what's going on or what he did, but I imagine you want to get the hell out of here before he gets here. I'll get the kids into the car while you go grab whatever you need."

I didn't trust myself to speak. I handed her the keys and nodded my gratitude before running upstairs. Di was practically still a kid herself, not even old enough to drink, but she was very mature in some ways. I appreciated that she got it without asking a lot of dumb questions.

I threw a couple of pair of jeans and a couple of shirts into a bag, along with some underwear and the cosmetic bag I use for traveling. It already contained everything I needed from a toothbrush and toothpaste to deodorant, brushes, and makeup. I stuffed my laptop and chargers into the bag and took off down the stairs. Di already had the kids in the car. She was sitting in the passenger's seat to keep an eye on them, but as soon as I got in, she opened her door to get out.

"Good luck and be safe," she said and leaned across the seat to give me a quick hug. She jumped out and ran to her own little car.

I backed out of the driveway and took off in the opposite direction in which Luke would come from on his way home. I still wasn't sure where I was going to go, but I couldn't drive around all day in the rain with my kids in the back of the car. I couldn't drive all the way to Louisiana by myself with two small children and I didn't think the trip to Jersey would have been wise either. Flying with the kids would have been difficult and really, I didn't want to take the kids away from

Luke. Finally, I decided to just go to the Fairmont.

By the time I checked in and got to the room, my mother, Donya, and Mayson were also calling me. What the fuck – did he have to alert everyone I knew? I didn't know which one I wanted to talk to. My mother – well I didn't like to talk to her on any ordinary day, let alone on one as emotionally burdening as this one. Mayson would listen but play devil's advocate, and I didn't want a devil's advocate. Donya would give it to me straight, whether I was wrong or right. I answered her call while the kids were quiet.

Diana had a mind to pack Lucas a lunch and put it in the little *Toy Story* backpack he apparently had on when I stopped home to get him. It was a little early for lunch, but he was sitting in front of the television eating quietly so I let him have at it. Kaitlyn was sound asleep in her car seat.

"Why is Luke calling me as if he is on fire and I am the only one who can put him out?" she asked when I answered. "Then again, he *is* hot. If it weren't for my own hot husband, I would put him out."

"Someone already beat you to it," I said.

"I'm sorry. What?"

"Remember Iris?" I asked as I started pacing the room.

"The book muffin lady?"

"That's the one."

"What about her?" Donya asked, but her voice was suspicious.

I told her what I had walked in on, what I had heard and about running away from Luke.

"First thing is first," she said, and I could tell she was about to let loose. "You got hit by a damn car and kept on running?"

"Yeah," I said, rubbing my aching side.

"That's some top rate action movie shit right there, but that's beside the point. Did you get hurt?"

I pulled on my jeans to look at my hip. It was already turning black and blue. "I'm bruised, but I think I'm okay."

"Okay, now that is out of the way," she said and took a

deep breath. "What in the hell is wrong with him!"

I shrugged. "Wish I knew," I said, wiping away at the tears that finally hit me. "I don't know."

"If he was any other man, I would tell you to give him a chance because he *did* tell the woman where she could go, but this is Luke. The same man who told you he hoped Kyle Sterling would break your heart and make you choke on it. This is the same man who treated you like shit for *months* after you reconnected with him. In addition, he *knows* what it is like to be hurt like that and back then you guys weren't *married* with *children*. He should have known better!"

"I don't know what to do," I said through my tears. I turned my head so that Lucas wouldn't see me crying. "What do I do?"

"Frankly, Emmy, I'm baffled on this one. He's the last person I would have thought to worry about under these circumstances. I feel like you should hear him out, but at the same time I feel like he should suffer."

"I feel like...I feel like I'm being punished for all of the stuff I did in the past, all of the stuff with Kyle."

"Em, you *more* than paid your dues for that. You punished yourself and he punished you on top of that, and it's something you'll have to live with for the rest of your life. No, this isn't punishment. It's idiocy on his part, and carelessness."

"So...what do I *do*?" I asked pathetically.

"You're thirty-three years old, Emmy. You can't run away from home when things go awry. I know this is pretty intense, but that's your home and your kids need to be there, not holed up in some hotel room; and I hate to say it, but they need their dad and he needs them. You go home and you make your stand there."

I knew she was right. I didn't see any point in arguing, but... "Should I make him sweat a little?" I asked her, feeling hopeful for a positive answer.

"You don't think watching you get hit by a car made him sweat enough?"

I was silent for a moment. "Not really."

"Then yeah. Make him sweat a little."

The kids and I went home later that evening. When we walked through the door, Luke was standing in the foyer with surprise, hope and relief spread across his handsome face. He looked terrible with his red, puffy, teary eyes and he still had on his work clothes. His tie was gone and his clothes were wrinkled and disheveled. He kneeled down to hug Lucas.

"I missed you today, buddy," he had said, his voice cracking. Lucas was tired and whiny. Luke picked him up and looked at me, his eyes wide with hope. "I'll put him to bed and then we can talk?"

I looked away from him and carried Kaitlyn in her car seat into the living room. I wasn't sure if I wanted to talk. Donya had told me to make my stand, but I didn't know what that stand was. The emotions rolling through my veins varied and I couldn't really get a hold on how I was really feeling besides hurt and betrayed.

"Emmy?" Luke called my name and though my back was turned, I knew he was on the verge of breaking down.

"Just put Lucas to bed," I sighed as I started to take Kaitlyn out of her seat.

I sensed his hesitance, but then I heard him start up the stairs, murmuring softly to Lucas. I had already changed Kay Kay into her pajamas before I left the hotel. I carried her upstairs to her pink and periwinkle room and sat down in the gliding chair to feed her. Luke came in a little while later as I was pulling my shirt down.

"Can I put her to bed?" he asked with outstretched arms.

I handed him his smiling daughter and stood up. "Make sure she burps," I said in a dead tone I didn't recognize as I left the room.

"Em, I'll be out in a little while and we'll talk, okay?" he called after me, but I didn't answer.

I went into our bedroom and into our master bath. I stripped out of my clothes and turned on the shower. I stood in front of the mirror and looked at the bruising along my left side. It was ugly looking. It looked like I had been hit by a damn car.

While I was there I checked out the rest of my body and for the first time since before I got pregnant, I was unhappy with what I saw. I had put on more weight during my pregnancy with Kaitlyn than I did when I was pregnant with Lucas, and I hadn't even lost all of that weight before I was knocked up again. My boobs were sagging from being used as feeding bags. Though I had lost a good amount of weight since I had Kay, I was still flabby in the belly area and my thighs looked pretty disgusting, too. My once pleasantly plump ass was just…plump, without the pleasantly part. My hair was a mess in its ponytail and my skin just didn't look as vibrant as it once did, what with the lack of sleep with a new baby, and being a housewife was no joke. My kids, husband, and normal everyday life ran me ragged. It was no wonder Luke was attracted to Iris, who seemed to have her shit very much together.

I got into the shower and turned it up as hot as I could stand it. A few minutes later I heard the door open and half a minute later, Luke was stepping in behind me.

"Shit," he whispered as he gingerly touched the bruising on my side. "Shit," he said again and this time I could tell he was crying. He carefully made me turn so that he could get a better look at the bruising. "Shit," he said once again.

I couldn't stand to hear him crying. I knew how he must have been feeling – beating himself up on the inside, unable to turn back time but wishing and praying that he could. It was probably ten times worse than what I felt three years ago, because now we had children, and the potential emotional damage to them could be staggering.

I turned around and wrapped my arms around my husband and let him cry.

~~~

"Hey," Luke said now, entering the room. He looked at the picture frame in my hands and his eyes immediately looked pained.

The day I threw it across the room was like a normal pre-Iris day, but something snapped in me halfway through the day. I thought about her kissing *my* husband and *his* hands on her and I hurled the picture across the room. Luke had looked at me, startled and weary, but he said nothing as he walked across the room, cleaned up the glass and then set the picture back where it belonged.

"Hey," I responded and then tossed the frame onto the bed next to me instead of putting it back.

"You okay?" he asked, biting his lip, looking incredibly sexy and sad at the same time.

"Great."

"Dinner is ready. Do you want me to bring it up to you so you don't have to deal with Sam?"

"No," I said and offered a small smile. "I'm not very hungry."

He frowned. "Em, you've been skipping meals like crazy lately. Are you sick?"

"No," I shook my head. "Just trying to lose a few pounds and I haven't had much of an appetite."

He stood there looking unsure. "You know I think you're beautiful no matter how many pounds you are, right?"

"Sure," I said in a noncommittal tone.

"Em," he said tiredly before sitting on the bed beside me. "Just…just say what's on your mind."

"I have nothing to say. I said all I have to say. I'm not hungry and I'm trying to lose a few pounds."

"And you went to see a plastic surgeon," he said darkly.

I had not told him about my consultation. I used my own money for it. Luke was against me using my own money for just about anything, but I specifically wanted to use my own money for this, especially since I didn't want him to know, but he had found out.

"How do you know about that?" I asked quietly.

"They called your phone while you were in the shower the other day. I answered. Why the hell are you seeing a plastic surgeon?"

"I need some work done. It's no big deal."

"You don't need any work done and you were never into being plastic before. Why now?"

I stared up at the ceiling. "Just because. It's my decision, right?" I asked, trying to keep it light.

"It is your decision," he agreed softly. "But it's not like you."

"I guess we're all being someone we're not lately," I said before I could stop myself.

Out of the corner of my eye I saw Luke hang his head. I hurt him, but I guess I was still hurting, too.

"Em, I wouldn't change anything about you. I think every part of you is perfect."

I palmed my chest. It ached. A lot.

"Will you please come downstairs and eat something? You love Sam's cooking."

"Maybe later," I lied.

He sat there quietly, deep in his own thoughts. Finally, he asked a question I wasn't expecting. "Do you want to…separate? Do you want to leave me?"

I looked at him, stunned. "I never said that."

"You act like it. You're acting happy when you're not and I've tried everything to try to prove to you how sorry I am how much I want *you*. What I did has not only devastated you but it's devastated *me*. I don't know what else to do."

"Luke, it's been two weeks," I spat out. "I would think that you would give me a little more time. It took you nearly two years for you to stop being angry about what I did to you."

He ran his hands through his hair. "Emmy, I just don't want to find out six months from now that you can't get over it."

"I don't know what you want from me," I said. "I'm handling it the best way I know how."

"I just…I just want to know what you're thinking," he said, looking desperate.

"You don't want to know what I'm thinking," I snickered without humor.

"Damn it! Emmy, I just told you that's what I want from you!"

I looked at him again. I sat up and turned around to face him, crossing my legs.

"Okay. Here it is," I said. "Every morning that you have to go into the office, I feel like I can't breathe. I put on a good show when you're leaving, but once you're out the door, I have to struggle to *breathe*, Luke, because I don't know – will today be the day you run into Iris? What will you say? What will she say? What will you *do*? Will today be the day that she walks into the office despite what you told her? And will you let her in and close the door? What will happen behind that closed door? Will today be a day when you say you're working late but you're really with her?"

Luke's eyes were huge and his mouth was slightly ajar. He started to speak, but I held my hand up. "Oh, I'm not finished yet," I snapped. "I wonder how long you guys have been talking as more than friends. I wonder at what point you knew you were out of line and what did you think that made you continue. I think about how you told her she was beautiful and sexy while I'm walking around with baby vomit in my hair and my fat flabby ass. I wonder how many times you've kissed her before, if you've touched her, if you've made her come. I wonder what you think is wrong with *me* – what am I lacking that would make you even turn your head to look at someone else. I wonder how you could do this after all the hell we had gone through to get to the happy place we were in – at least I thought it as a happy place. And..."

I stopped. I had said enough. He didn't need to know the rest of it. His eyes were already tearing up. I hated how I could bring this big, strong, sexy man to tears with my words and actions. I didn't think any less of him for crying, but I thought less of myself for making him do so.

"And what?" he swallowed. "Finish."

"I've said enough," I said softly and looked down at my hands.

"But you haven't said everything you're thinking. Say

it all," he snapped.

I swallowed hard and couldn't meet his eyes.

"Just fucking say it!" he yelled.

Instead of telling him the rest of my thoughts, I shifted onto my knees and wrapped my arms around him. He held me close and buried his face in my hair.

"I never touched her before that day, I swear," he said, his voice weak. "I liked her but I didn't think anything of it until she said something on *that* day. There is nothing that you are lacking, Emmy. You're perfect."

"My mom thinks I have unattractive hair and need to join a gym," I said.

"Your mom is a crackpot," Luke said and I laughed. He pulled back a little to look at my face. "Please don't get plastic surgery. When I say you're perfect, I mean it."

"Luke...did you kiss her or did she kiss you?" I asked the question that had been on my mind ever since it happened.

"No, Em, she kissed me."

"But you kissed her back," I said, frowning.

"No, baby, I did not. I was so shocked I just stood there," he sighed and shook his head. "I can't believe I just stood there like that."

"But she said she was touching you. Was she?"

"A little bit," he admitted, looking at me with apprehension. "Mostly she kept touching my arms."

I ran my hands over his perfect biceps. "Well...you do have yummy looking arms."

"But they're yours, not hers," he said sadly.

"I think she gets that now," I said. I climbed onto his lap and rested my head on his shoulder.

"Have I told you I loved you lately?" Luke softly said as he stroked my hair.

"No," I smiled. "You should sing it to me."

In a sexy, sweet, singing voice of a hot, hot angel, Luke began to sing *Lately* by Tyrese. By the time he reached the end of the song, I had turned and straddled him.

"I love you, too," I said and brought my mouth to his.

Luke put his hands under my shirt and caressed my back. My hands were roving over his strong shoulders and arms but I wanted to feel his skin on mine. I pulled back from the kiss and quickly started to unbutton his shirt. I got frustrated and tore it open and helped him shrug out of it.

"Someone is a little eager," he grinned as his hands tugged at the hem of my shirt.

"Just take my damn shirt off," I commanded and kissed his lips.

With a chuckle, he pulled my shirt off and threw it to the floor. My bra landed on top of that seconds later.

"Did you lock the door when you came in?" I asked him as I kissed along his jawline.

"Nope. Hopefully your mom will have enough sense to know what's going on up here."

"She probably knew it was going to happen before us," I said rolling my eyes.

"Mmm," he murmured as I nipped at his neck. "You're probably right. She's the one that sent me up here. I started to just text you, but she gave me a hard time."

"Well, let's not disappoint her," I said, pressing my breasts against his bare chest.

"I can't wait for these to stop being a source of food," Luke frowned as he massaged one breast.

"If you don't want a source of food all over you, I suggest you make your hand migrate south."

Luke flipped me onto my back on the bed, making me squeal. He kissed me as one hand unbuttoned my jeans and pulled down the zipper. His hand slid under my panties. I moaned and squirmed as he palmed my clit before slipping a finger inside of me. He sat up suddenly and started to pull my jeans and panties off.

"Someone is a little eager," I repeated his words.

"Very," he agreed as he pulled off his own pants and boxers.

He crawled back on top of me and kissed me again. His monstrous penis rubbed against my clit. I moaned into Luke's mouth and pushed my hips up to increase the friction. He pumped his hips, making the whole length of his cock slide across my clit.

"Shall I make you come like this?" Luke asked, propping himself up on his arms.

"Yes," I moaned. "Please."

"You don't have to beg me, baby," he panted as he increased the friction and speed. He groaned and said "You're so moist, Em."

I could feel how wet I was as his cock spread my moisture over my clit. I could feel my first orgasm building. Luke leaned down and kissed me again. My moans grew louder as I climbed towards my climax. Just as I began to come, Luke slammed his cock inside of me, sending my orgasm into hyper-drive. He covered my mouth with his hand as I screamed. It was so painfully exquisite, being stretched and violated by his massive erection. After almost a year and a half of having it on a fairly regular basis, I was still surprised by his length and girth once it was inside of me.

Luke held still until my orgasm began to subside. He took his hand off of my mouth and pulled one leg up under his arm, making him go impossibly deeper. I tensed up and put my hands on his abs as an attempt to keep him from going in any further.

"I'm yours and you are mine," he said firmly. "I'm going to have you *all the way* and you are going to have me *all the way.*"

"Too much," I grunted as I felt him press a little deeper.

"I need to feel you, Emmy," Luke said and with one quick thrust, he was nearly balls deep. I had to cover my own mouth to keep from crying out.

"Mmm," Luke moaned as he swirled his hips. "You feel me?"

"How can I not?" I bit out.

He grinned as he reached for my other leg. I didn't fight him on it this time. I knew he was going to be so deep inside of me that I was going to feel like his dick was coming out of my mouth, but he wanted me and I wanted him – all the way. He pulled out until just the head of his cock was inside of me as he held both of my legs.

"Ready?" he asked, smiling down at me.

"How can I possibly prepare to be invaded by your obscene freak of nature?" I asked, bracing myself.

Without any further preamble, Luke drove his cock inside of me until he was balls deep. He groaned very loud and there was no hand to muffle the yelp that escaped my lips. If there was any question as to what we were doing up here, it was answered.

"You feel so fucking good," Luke said, pulling out. He thrust into me again and I cried out again. "You're so fucking perfect, Em," he growled as he began to ride me hard and fast.

I felt like I was being torn apart, but it felt so damn good at the same time. I couldn't be quiet if I tried. Luke suddenly rolled over, holding on to me, so that when I was upright I was impaled on his beautiful cock.

"Oh my god!" I screamed. It was deeper than before and I wasn't sure if I could take it.

Luke grabbed my hips, holding me in place as he moved his hips in a slow, agonizing circle.

"You're so beautiful, Emmy, so perfect," Luke groaned as he started to pump his cock into me. "Come on my cock, baby! Shit, I'm going to come! You feel too damn...fucking...PERFECT!" he yelled as he began to spurt inside of me.

I was sobbing through my own orgasm as I felt his cream filling me. My whole body was suddenly weak. I collapsed onto Luke's chest, still impaled on his erection.

"I love you so much," Luke whispered in my ear.

I had only shed tears when I spoke to Donya on that crazy day. I didn't cry again after that, but it suddenly hit me how much I could have lost that day. With my head resting on Luke's chest, a deluge of tears forced its way out of my eyes. He wrapped his arms tightly around me and whispered loving words in my ear while I allowed myself to fall to pieces.

Early the following morning, Luke drove my parents to the airport for their return trip home. My father never gave any indication that he had heard anything the night before, but as my mother was walking out the door, I heard her tell Luke that maybe I needed to wear a muzzle in the bedroom. I didn't say anything to her, because she was walking in the right direction – *away from me.*

Diana arrived moments later, a plan perfectly executed by yours truly. Luke would be gone for about two hours, because the trip to O'Hare wasn't fun, but it gave me just enough time to go do what I needed to do.

On a Saturday, it took me about half the usual weekday time to get into the city. I drove all the way because parking would also be a cinch. I popped some change in the meter a little ways down the street and walked into the store. There were about a dozen people in there enjoying fresh pastries and coffee, chatting, or reading, or tapping on tablets, completely oblivious to what was about to go down. Iris stood behind the counter watching me warily.

"Can I have a blueberry muffin please?" I asked kindly.

She looked confused, but she got the muffin. "Coffee today?" she asked.

"No, the muffin is fine," I said, throwing two dollars on the counter. "I have a few questions for you, Iris," I said as I peeled the paper off of my muffin.

"Okay…" she gave me a sideways look.

"How long were you lusting after my husband? Don't be afraid. I'm not going to hit you or anything. I'm just trying to get answers. I deserve answers, don't you think?" I kept my voice low, but conversational so that I wouldn't cause a scene. "Just be honest," I encouraged.

She stood up a little straighter. "I don't know. Months."

I nodded as I took a bite of the muffin. "This is good," I said through a stuffed mouth. I swallowed a few bites before speaking again. "Did he show any interest in you before a couple of weeks ago?"

"He was…very kind and seemed interested in actually getting to know me."

I believed her, because that's how Luke was, but she didn't know that. She took something innocent about him and warped it.

"Did you try to throw yourself at him at all before that day?"

She pursed her lips at my choice of words, but after a moment answered "No."

"How did you get him into the back? Did you hold his hand? Did you tell him you'd pull up your skirt?"

She rolled her eyes and made an exasperated sound. "I told him I needed to speak to him privately."

"Did you kiss him or did he kiss you?" I asked as I took another bite of the muffin. "Damn, this is really good."

She eyed me with speculation. "I kissed him, Emmy. I think you already know the answers to these questions."

I shrugged. "I do. I believe my husband, but I want to hear you admit to what you did."

"I think I just did, didn't I?" she snapped.

I nodded slowly. "Pretty much. Just one last question," I said and stuffed the rest of the muffin in my mouth. I waited a few swallows again before speaking. "Would you say that this whole fiasco is your fault entirely?"

"Absolutely not!" she almost shouted. Well, *now* there was a scene. "Luke was always in here. Sometimes he wouldn't even buy anything, but he'd just stand right where you are and talk to me. If I was here late, he'd walk me to my car and talk to me some more. I didn't miss how he couldn't keep his eyes off of my body either. He didn't say it, Emmy, but he wanted what I wanted."

I gave her a patronizing smile. "Iris, Luke is naturally a good natured, nice man. He loves shooting the shit and getting to know some people, and he's such a gentleman that he will even walk you to your car at night. That's just the way he is. The only people who think it is more than it is are the pathetic people like you, desperate and lonely for someone to care. As for looking at your body – who wouldn't? I'm a heterosexual female and I would say that you have an incredible body, but it doesn't mean that I want to slide between your legs, know what I mean?" I reached into my bag and pulled out a thick manila envelope.

"Thank you for answering my questions, Iris. I really appreciate it. Luke and I already made up, by the way. Last night he apologized without his words, if you know what I mean," I smiled knowingly at her. "He's very well endowed – I'm so sore. I guess you'll never know what it feels like to have my husband sliding between your old thighs. Ah well. You tried, right?"

I threw the envelope down on the counter.

"What's this?" she asked tightly.

"Your eviction notice!" I grinned. I leaned forward as if I were going to speak confidentially to her, as if everyone in the shop wasn't witnessing this. "Luke makes pretty good money, but the truth is that I'm a trust fund baby. Luke doesn't like for me to use my money for much – it's important to him that he knows that he is supporting his family and I understand that. But every now and then if there is something I really want, I buy it with my money. I really, really wanted this building. The owner wasn't interested in selling at first, but you see, I have plenty of money stowed away. I made him an offer he couldn't refuse. This building is mine now. You only have a month to month lease, so at the end of this month, I'm not renewing your lease."

I watched as her mouth fell open in shock. Her eyes grew wide with panic. "You can't do that!"

"I can, and I have," I said. "I'm not usually vindictive like this, Iris, so please don't think poorly of me, but Luke and I have been through hell already. I will obliterate anyone who tries to take us back there. Now, I'm not completely heartless. I have a buddy across town that is willing to rent a space to you. His number is on a card in the envelope. I don't see any point in destroying your dreams just because you tried to destroy mine, but I have no problem moving your ass out of here."

I stood up straight and patted the envelope. "Thanks in advance for cleaning up the space when you're finished with it."

I walked out of the store without looking back. I felt bad for Iris, but not that bad. She tried to take Luke away from me and the kids and that was just unacceptable.

When I pulled into the driveway, Luke was already back. I cursed under my breath. I wasn't ready to tell him what I had done yet, though I was sure he would find out soon enough.

I walked into the house, expecting to find Luke waiting for me, I stopped dead in my tracks when I saw her wild red hair, troubled gray eyes and...*Oh*...My eyes fell on the swell in her midsection.

Lily Whitman stood in my kitchen looking hurt and pissed off at the same time, and she was pregnant.

Chapter Twenty-One

~Lily~

"Can I get you anything?" Emmy asked after her initial shock and then excitable greeting. "Water? Juice? Milk? Tea?"

"Umm," I said, a little overwhelmed by her happy housewife hospitality.

"What about something to eat?" Luke asked as he cradled their pretty little girl in his arms. It warmed my heart to see a dad being so involved and loving, but it also made me feel bad, because I wasn't sure if I'd get that from Kyle.

Little Lucas appeared at my side. He looked very much like Luke. He was a cute kid, but in the five minutes that I had been there, he had made me fear the impending toddler years.

"Five!" he yelled, his hand held up. I gently slapped him five and he took off laughing like he was on something. *OOOkay.....*

I looked up and both Emmy and Luke were looking at me expectantly.

"Umm," I said again. "Water will be fine and I'm not really hungry. Thank you."

She pulled two bottles of water out of the fridge and handed me one before sitting down across from me.

"So, what brings you to Chi-town?" Emmy asked, sitting back in her seat.

"Umm," I glanced at Luke. "I actually...I need to talk to you in private, Emmy," I said.

Luke gave me a long look. I had a feeling he knew why I was there, and I also had a feeling he wasn't happy about it.

"Oh," Emmy said, looking at me, then Luke and back to me. "We can talk upstairs?"

"No," Luke said with a sigh. "I'll take the kids to Lena's for a while."

"Don't leave your house on my account," I said to him.

"It's fine," he said before turning to Emmy. "Baby, can you run upstairs and get Kaitlyn's diaper bag? And make sure

Lucas goes to the bathroom. Once he starts playing over Lena's he doesn't stop, not even to pee."

Emmy nodded, but she looked at both of us curiously before disappearing into the family room. I heard her scold Lucas for something and his squeals of objection and moments later the ruckus started up the stairs.

Luke looked at me as he adjusted Kaitlyn in his arms. "Is the baby his?" he asked. "Is it Kyle's?"

"Yes," I said, absently running a hand over my belly.

"Where is he? He did something didn't he?" Luke looked angry, but I guess I couldn't blame him. My guess is that he didn't have a very high opinion of Kyle.

"He's in London," I said softly.

"What are you about to drag my wife into, Lily?" his eyes narrowed on me.

"I'm not *dragging* her into anything," I said defensively. "I have no one else to talk to about this, no one who understands him like Emmy does."

I couldn't miss the anger that filled his facial features, though he tried to pull it back some.

"If he's gone, then maybe he actually did something right for a change. What happened to my wife could easily happen to you and your baby."

"I'm not going to argue with you about that, Luke," I said firmly. "I don't believe that he ever meant to hurt Emmy and I sure as hell know that he won't hurt me that way, but you have a right to feel how you want about it. I may even feel the same if I was in your shoes, but I don't want to *hear* it, do you understand? This is his child I am carrying," I said, gesturing towards my belly. "Not someone else's. I can't just walk away. I *need* to know what Emmy thinks, what she would do if she had all of the facts that I have."

"That's what I'm worried about, Lily," he said darkly as we heard Emmy and Lucas descending the kitchen stairs. "What will she do when she has all of the facts?"

Emmy appeared then, toting a diaper bag and holding Lucas's hand. Luke forced a smile for his family.

"Thanks, baby," he said and gave Em a quick kiss on the lips.

She looked at him with suspicion. "What's wrong?"

"Nothing," he said quickly and took Lucas's hand. "Let's get Kay Kay in her seat, buddy."

"I'll help you get them in the car," Emmy said.

"I got it, honey. Relax." He gave her a reassuring smile and walked the kids out of the room.

Emmy looked off in that direction with some concern for a moment before settling down in the chair across from mine.

"He looked pissed off – he didn't get any phone calls while I was upstairs, did he?" she asked, her eyes suddenly wide.

"No," I said, eyeing her questioningly.

"Okay, good. He's gonna be mad when he finds out. Maybe. Maybe not." Her brow furrowed.

"You realize I have no idea what the hell you are talking about, right?"

She leaned forward and started whispering. "There was a woman trying to get Luke. She pretended to be my friend and she was nice to my kids but she really wanted my husband. She owns a little muffin shop next to the firm. Anyway, things kind of came to a head and it could have really fucked us up, you know? So..." she motioned for me to lean forward also. "I bought the building and served her with eviction papers this morning."

She smiled smugly. "Never thought I could be so vindictive, but this is my family we're talking about here."

"Well, that definitely trumps what I would have done," I said admiringly.

"Yeah, you would have just kicked her ass, right?" Emmy laughed.

"You do know me, after all," I grinned.

"I think I do know you fairly well," she said, as her face grew serious. "So, I know you're here to talk to me about the father of your baby."

"That's an easy guess," I said, looking at the water bottle in front of me.

We heard the front door close, indicating that Luke had finally left with the kids.

"Shit," Emmy said. I looked up and her eyes were closed. When she opened them again, they seemed a little moist. "I never thought that could hurt as badly as it does," she whispered, rubbing her chest.

"I didn't come here to rub it in your face," I said quietly.

"I know, but why are you here, Lily?" she asked, sitting back in her chair.

I reached into my purse and closed my fingers over the photos I had of Emmy. I looked at her with reluctance before finally placing the photos on the table in front of her.

"What...what is this..." she asked in a whisper. She didn't move to reach for them. She just sat there, staring at the top picture.

"You know what it is," I said softly, and waited.

"But...how?" she asked, as she gingerly touched the first picture.

"Larkin apparently records every visit, just in case," I said. "There is video, too, but I haven't seen it."

"Why did you get these?" she asked, finally looking through the pictures with wide and teary eyes. "Why would you do this? Please tell me you didn't show Kyle these pictures."

"Actually, Kyle is the one that obtained them. I begged him not to," I bit my lip to hold back the hard emotions I felt. "I begged him, Emmy, but he felt like he needed to know."

"He had asked me and I refused to tell him how bad it was," she said, shaking her head. A big tear drop fell onto one of the pictures. More followed that one. "Even if I had *told* him, it wouldn't have compared to *seeing*. Why would he do this to himself?"

"He's still punishing himself for it," I said.

"Stupid idiot," she said, wiping away her tears.

~ 322 ~

"He already had a lot of burdens to carry," I said, wiping away my own tears. "He blames himself for his brother's death, he blames himself when his mom isn't well, he feels deserted by his sister and he's still living with the fact that Walter and his real father both didn't give a shit about him."

Emmy's eyes widened. "Real father? Walter isn't Kyle's father?"

"You didn't know?"

"No," she shook her head. "And I don't know how his brother died, nor did I know he felt anything about his sister. I know he had some issues with his mom, but I guess I never knew how badly."

She looked at me with both bewilderment and amazement. "Start from the beginning. Start with Miranda."

I told her everything Kyle had told me about his sister. She kept a straight face through most of the story until I told her how Kyle was afraid of being rejected by Miranda. Emmy's face crumpled and more tears slipped from her eyes.

"And what about his brother?" she asked. "He never talked about it."

I remembered when Kyle told me about his brother. It was the same night he told me about Miranda. He was reluctant at first, but I pushed him. He had trembled slightly as he told me and I had immediately felt guilty for pushing him. I tried to make him stop, but he just held my hand and told me anyway.

"Walter..." I started, but didn't know how to say it without crying again. It was so hard to say, but it was harder for Kyle to say. "Walter beat the shit out of him one day, more than the usual. His mom was spaced out on some kind of anti-psychotic drug, but even if she wasn't I don't believe she would have cared. Kyle went outside and climbed this tree that used to be near the pool. He said he climbed and climbed until he felt safe. Walt Junior tried to get him to come down, but he could still hear Walter ranting and raving in the house. He didn't want to get hit again. So, Walt climbed the tree.

"Apparently he was always trying to look after Kyle. His father rarely hit him, so he would often step in to protect

~ 323 ~

Kyle, and he always tried to make him feel better if he couldn't protect him. Walt got pretty high in the tree that day, but not as high as Kyle. Kyle was smaller and able to fit through some of the smaller spaces. He sat in the tree for a long time, trying to get Kyle to come down, trying to comfort him even though he couldn't reach him. The branch Walter had been sitting on started to crack and break away. He managed to hang on to another branch, but he didn't have a very good grip. Kyle tried to climb down to help him, and Walt screamed for help. One of the grounds keepers saw the whole thing unfolding, but he was too far away. All of the shouting finally drew out Kyle's parents, but it was too late for anyone to do anything. Walt lost his grip and fell. He fell into the pool, but not before his head slammed against the cement around the pool."

Emmy covered her mouth as tears streamed out of her eyes. I knew how she felt, because I did the same thing when I first heard the story.

"Kyle was petrified. He hugged the tree trunk where he was as the horror unfolded below him. His parents were distraught and couldn't focus on him, not that they would have been much comfort. In the end it was a fire fighter that coaxed Kyle out of the tree, but that was more than an hour later. Walter always blamed him and when Felicia is going through her shit, she tends to blame him, too."

"Those fuckers!" Emmy yelled. "I didn't even know that he was...he was abused as a kid! I didn't know any of this shit!"

She got up from the table and threw open a cabinet door. She reached for a bottle of tequila and poured some in a glass. This was up a step for her. Usually she'd drink it right from the bottle.

"That's not even the half of it," I sighed.

"Tell me *everything*," she said darkly, and sat down again. She purposely didn't look down at the photos.

I started from the beginning, that night so long ago when Kyle walked into *SHOTZ* looking disheveled and heart broken. I told her every detail I could recall, including my feelings for him before he knew I existed and what had happened that night and the following morning. When I told her about my employment at Sterling Corp, her eyes grew wide and then she frowned.

"Why didn't anyone tell me? Why so secretive?"

"Mayson thought it would be awkward for you," I said. "It wasn't my place to argue with her – I really didn't know in depth at the time what was happening between you and Kyle or you and Luke."

"So…but…Luke said that you and Kyle had run into each other and after a few conversations you decided to build a bar together. Either Kyle lied or Luke lied," she frowned.

"Maybe they both lied," I shrugged. "I didn't even know about the bar until a few months ago."

"Huh," she said, looking thoughtful. "But you two were already together when he bought it?"

"Basically," I said. "I know you and I have been texting off and on since you last left New Jersey, and I don't want you to think I was…I don't know hiding from you to protect myself or anything, but no one wanted you to know what was going on and I felt weird talking to you about the bar once I found out about it."

She sighed. "I get it, I guess."

I continued with my story, starting with that weekend that I got mugged. Whenever I talked about the more intimate and quirky sides of Kyle, Emmy's eyes lit up and looked sad at the same time. When I told her about the day he kissed me in the grocery store and the fight he put up to not hide our relationship she looked down at her hands. I felt bad for her because she never got to have a public relationship with Kyle, and he had fought to keep it secret. I told her about the fracas at the Sterling estate and the nasty things Faux Dad and Felicia said to Kyle. When I told her about the party at the museum and my run in with Jess her face lit up.

"I've always wanted to punch her square in her stupid, snotty face," Emmy said with vehemence. "I'm glad you put the fear of God in her sorry ass."

I told her about Kyle's strange behavior before our trip to Bora Bora, and I told her about my trip home to Ohio. Emmy seemed genuinely happy that I had reconnected with my sister. When I told her about how well Kyle handled my nieces and nephew, her eyes glistened and she seemed proud.

As my story wound down to the present, her face became more and more serious.

"So, here I am," I said with a sigh. "And I don't know exactly what I was hoping to accomplish when I got here," I said thoughtfully. "I guess...I guess I wanted to know your thoughts. You're the only person who can kind of understand how I'm feeling right now. If you knew then what you now know, would you have left or would you have fought for him?"

"Do you want to fight for him?" she asked quietly.

"I don't know," I said, fidgeting with my second bottle of water. "I'm not a quitter, you know that, but...this is so damn draining. If I'm putting all of my energy into Kyle, I'm not going to have anything left to give to my baby." I blinked up at the ceiling to keep my tears from slipping again.

Emmy was quiet for a moment. When she finally spoke, her voice was soft and full of emotion.

"I would not have fought for him," she said.

I blinked at her. Honestly, that wasn't the answer I was expecting to hear at all.

"Don't misunderstand me," she continued when she saw my face. "I *love* Kyle Sterling and I *always* will. I miss him, *all of the time*. I love my family, I love and adore my husband and I wouldn't trade him in for anything or anyone, but I still love and miss Kyle. You have to understand how it was between us. It was like we got off on being fucked up together – I mean there was never a time in our relationship where things were as they should be. Instead of falling away from each other, the screwed up core of our relationship seemed to make us gravitate towards each other. It didn't even make sense."

She looked down at the pictures. She traced a finger over the bruises that had been on her face, put there by the man

~ 326 ~

she loved and missed.

"He was my drug, and I was his," she said so softly I almost didn't hear it. "Our love was one of addiction and instability. Kyle broke me," she said and then paused for a moment. Then she looked at my face with a hard expression. "But I broke him first."

I stared at her, stunned by her words. I knew that Kyle was a broken man, but I never placed any of that blame on Emmy. She didn't force him into their relationship and she didn't beat him to end it.

"I don't understand," I finally said.

"I knew things were hard for him. I didn't know all that you know, but I knew life was hard, and I knew that he had no one. I allowed him to believe that he could rely on me, that I could soothe his aching soul, but when it got too rough I pushed him too hard. If it wasn't for me, he would have never fallen back into drugs. I was the straw that broke the camel's back for Kyle.

"What he did to me was terrible and he has every right to take some of that blame, but I can't blame him entirely. He was pushed – from all directions, and my push is what pushed him over."

Emmy got up from the table and poured herself another glass of tequila. "Thank goodness I froze some breast milk, just in case I needed a drink." She took a sip of the liquid and it seemed to soothe her. She rejoined me at the table and looked at me.

"As I said, I will always love Kyle, but I was never meant for him and he was never meant for me. *You* were meant for him and he was meant for you."

"But...he doesn't need me," I said, feeling a little embarrassed by the truth of my words. "He doesn't need me and he's sure as hell not addicted to me."

"Lily," she said, reaching across the table to take my hand. "Hasn't anyone ever told you addiction is really bad for you? Nothing good can come from any kind of addiction, especially an addiction to a person. Kyle only wanted me because he was addicted to me and vice versa. Look where we are now. He *wants* you. He *loves* you and I think he really does need you. Just because it isn't carnal doesn't mean that it's not real. Kyle had every opportunity to tell me the things he's told you and he didn't. On some level he didn't...trust me. On some level he knew that I couldn't heal him, but already I can tell that you have already started to do that. So, I really mean this when I say it, so listen hard, Lily."

She leaned forward. With tears in her eyes and a firm voice, Emmy said "Fight for him and don't ever let him go."

~Emmy~

I was pacing back and forth in the bedroom when Luke came in carrying Kaitlyn. I had heard him come into the house with her some time ago, but I didn't go to them. He looked at me with a grim expression.

"You got into the tequila," he said flatly.

"Yeah, but there's milk in the fridge and freezer," I said, not even pausing in my pacing.

"Why don't we just get this conversation done and over with," he said darkly and sat down on the bed.

"Where's Lucas?" I paused then.

"We stopped at Emmet's and he wanted to stay there. They were okay with it. They'll bring him home in a couple of hours."

"Okay," I said, and resumed pacing.

"Emmy," Luke said with exasperation.

I stopped in the middle of the room and looked at my husband. The pressure in my chest was threatening to explode all over the damn place.

"I have to help them," I said, just barely fighting back my tears.

"Help who?" Luke asked me incredulously. "Kyle and Lily? No the fuck way, Emmy!"

Kaitlyn started at the sound of her father's booming voice. I didn't blame her. I jumped a little, too.

In a more controlled voice, he said "Let them take care of their own problems. You don't need to be dragged into that shit."

"I told her to fight for him," I said more to myself. "But he should fight for her, too."

"Well, I'm fighting for you, and I want you to stay out of it," Luke said pushing off of the bed.

"You don't have to fight for me, you already have me," I said, sighing in frustration.

"If you wanted to help, you should have told Lily to stay the hell away from that bastard. She could get the shit beaten out of her, too."

"He won't do that to her," I said, waving him off.

"The hell he won't!"

"He won't do that to her," I said more firmly, looking at Luke resolutely.

"How the hell do you know, Emmy?" he demanded.

I balled up my fists and squeezed my eyes shut. "I know you can't understand this, I know you can't, Luke, but I know he will not hurt her like that."

"Even if you're right, it's none of your business," Luke said in a tone that indicated that the conversation was over, but it wasn't. Not for me.

"It is my business," I said to his back just before he walked out the door.

He stopped and turned around slowly to face me. "Why, Em? Why is it *your* business what happens between Lily and Kyle?"

"Until he knows that I have forgiven him, truly forgiven him, he will never forgive himself and he will never go back to her."

Luke's blue eyes narrowed and he took a few more steps toward me. "You *forgive* him? You forgive that asshole for what he did to you and Lucas? For what he *could* have done?"

I closed my eyes for a beat. "Yes, I do, and I know you can't understand that either."

His eyes flashed hot with anger. He shifted Kaitlyn from one arm to the other as he glared at me.

"Are you trying to just get back at me for what happened with Iris?" he asked in a hushed tone.

"I'm not trying to get back at you for what happened with Iris, I promise," I said pleadingly. "But I can't pretend that Lily didn't come here today."

"I can," he snarled.

I pointed at him. "You're not that heartless, Luke! You're not. You can't pretend you didn't see her round belly and you can't pretend that everything is going to be okay for her without Kyle. You don't know the things she's been through in the past. She needs him."

Now Luke closed his eyes for a moment. When he opened them again, he just stared at me for a long time before speaking again, through gritted teeth. "What can you possibly do to help them?"

I stared at him and he stared at me. My heart thudded hard in my chest. The last thing we needed was another rift between us, but I would not feel right, nor would I forgive myself if I didn't do this.

I told Luke what I needed to do and watched his face fall. My decision could possibly change at least four lives, and not necessarily for the better.

Chapter Twenty-Two

~Lily~

Emmy's words had hit me hard. After all of the bullshit she had been through with Kyle, and after admitting to me that she still loved him and missed him, she still encouraged me to fight for him. I knew it probably hurt her to say that to me, but she seemed to really mean it. However, despite what she said, I wasn't sure if I really felt like fighting for Kyle. Maybe it was pride, but I felt like *he* should have been fighting for *me*.

After leaving Emmy's, I was on the road for only a few minutes before I noticed Corsey in my rearview mirror. This pissed me off. Why was Kyle sending someone after me if he didn't fucking want me? He sure as hell didn't need me. Emmy said that Kyle does want and need me in his own way, but I was having a very hard time believing that. Sending Corsey or one of his minions after me was more about control than love or wanting. He looked at me as a possession, especially since I was carrying his child, and having the minions follow me around was more about asset protection.

I drove into a parking lot at a strip mall and parked in the furthest corner away from the stores and customers. Corsey parked right behind me and in the rearview mirror I could see his eyes trying to discern what the hell I was doing.

It took a run-in with an armed mugger and a crazy ride in Vic's truck for me to get smart and carry some sort of protection. I had the usual pepper spray, but I also carried a small switchblade. I touched my back pocket as I got out of the car to make sure the blade was in place. I walked up to the driver's side window and waited for Corsey to put the window down. He looked so pissed off. I had never seen him looking so angry before. I knew it was my fault and Kyle was probably giving him hell. I felt bad that he was away from his wife and child, but maybe he should have chosen a different line of work.

When the window was all the way down, he extended his arm out of the car, trying to hand me his cell phone. I looked at it as if it was alien.

"Kyle is on the phone," he said through a clenched jaw.

I sighed noisily and snatched the phone from him.

"What do you want," I snapped.

"What the hell are you doing in Chicago?" Kyle growled into the phone. "Moreover, why the hell did you ditch Corsey?"

"I don't have to answer your questions anymore because we're not together anymore, asshole! You can't tell me you don't want to be with me and then have your goons following me around."

"I'm trying to keep you safe!" Kyle yelled back at me.

"I don't need or want your fucking protection, Kyle!"

Up until that very moment, I had not been sure what I wanted to do about him, but my decision flew out of my lips before I could really consider it.

"I'm done with this," I said and then swallowed back a sob. "I'm done with *you* and being in second place to Emmy. I'm over this. Take your bar, your penthouse, and your hired stalkers and shove it all up your ass."

I threw the phone at Corsey and he just barely caught it before it could hit his face. He looked at me with a surprised expression on his face. He put the phone to his ear, and I had no doubts that Kyle was giving him some kind of instruction. I walked to the back of the truck as I pulled my knife out of my pocket. Quickly I opened it and stabbed the back tire. I went to the next back tire even as Corsey was stumbling out of the truck shouting at me. I put the blade into that tire, too. Corsey caught up to me with the phone still in his hand and to his ear.

"What the hell is wrong with you?" he shouted at me.

I reached up and snatched the phone from his ear and hurled it as far as I could across the lot.

"Fuck you!" I yelled at him and marched back to my rental car.

Corsey followed after me and tried to stop me from

closing my door. I know this was wrong…so very wrong, but I was so very angry and so very over this shit. I reached into my purse with one hand and brought the pepper spray up to his face. He froze instantaneously.

"I promise I will spray so much of this shit in your eyes that your future children will feel it," I growled.

"I can't believe that you'd do that to me," he said in disbelief. "We're *friends*, Lily," he said, looking hurt.

"If I am your friend you will go back to your truck and wait for triple A to fix your tires and you will let me go. You know this is bullshit, Corsey. You know it!"

He leaned in close to me. His dark eyes were weary, but hard. "If you were the mother of *my* unborn child, I would do *anything* to keep you safe, and if you cared anything about your baby, you would allow me to do my damn job."

I stared at him with an open mouth. He just insinuated that I didn't care about my baby. I wanted to spray him just for saying that.

"The person you need to keep me safe from is your boss," I answered. "He's the only one hurting me, and if *he* cared about this baby, he wouldn't have run away like a little bitch. Step. Away. From. The. Car." I held the spray with my finger on the trigger.

Corsey stared me down for a half a minute more before stepping back. He must have really known I wasn't bluffing. I closed my door and drove away.

~~~

I drove through the evening and night. I stopped at the rental car place and discovered the XTS was where I left it. After some thought, I parked the rental and dropped the keys in a mail slot. I got into Kyle's Cadillac and continued the next couple of hours towards…what I didn't know.

I had told Kyle that I was going to move out, and I really felt that I should, but even after all of my hours of nothing but time to think, I couldn't decide definitively what I was going to do. Moving back in with my friend in Camden was out of the question with a baby on the way. Since Kyle had apparently set Lydia, Mom, and the kids up so that they wouldn't have to worry about anything, I now had more money. I could afford to live on my own while working at Sterling Corp. As for that, I decided that staying there would be okay while Kyle was in London. Maybe by the time he'd come back I would be on maternity leave and I wouldn't have to deal with him. Taking the position that was meant for me at the bar was out of the question. I didn't want anything else from Kyle, and if that meant having to throw my dream away in the process, I was prideful and stubborn enough to do just that.

I just wanted one more look at it before I threw it away.

The sun was just beginning to rise when I pulled into the newly paved lot at *Lily's*. Marco had come up with the name, but maybe he should change it to *Marco's*, because Lily wasn't going to be there.

I got out of the car and used my key to let myself into the bar. I walked around, zigzagging through the tables, running my hands along the mahogany bar and straightening the bottles of alcohol. It was like Marco had been in my brain when he designed the place. It was exactly how I wanted it, and it made me sad that I was going to give it up, but I had to break away from Kyle before my broken heart killed me.

A slight sound in the kitchen made me pause in my wanderings.

"Hello?" I called out, expecting Marco or one of the managers to shout hello back, but all I got was silence.

Okay, stop spooking yourself out, Lily.

I waved it off. My nerves were a little shot.

I knew that the moment I started the Caddy up that the chance of Kyle's goons tracking me again was high. I was surprised no one had showed up at the diner yet. I pushed the door open to the kitchen so I could get one last good look at it. I made it half way down the long isle between the prep table and the stoves when I realized I wasn't in the place alone. Someone stood off to my left, in the doorway that led to the walk in refrigerator.

The alarm system was supposed to be installed later that day. It was almost overlooked completely, until Marco asked me if I wanted all of my liquor stolen. *SHOTZ* had not had an alarm system, but I was willing to do it anyway for my place. The problem was that it simply wasn't installed in time.

"You can try to run, but you won't get very far before I catch you, and then I'll be angry that I had to chase you," he said, stepping into the light.

Suddenly I understood why Kyle was so protective of me. I understood why I always had to have someone nearby incase trouble sparked up, because trouble was right in front of me and I was completely alone. Instinctively, I put my hands to my belly to protect my baby. I had left my pocketbook with my pepper spray and pocket knife on the bar, which was of no freakin' use to me now.

"Where have you been?" I asked in a rush of breath.

"Under the radar," he grinned. "Those assholes that were following me thought they were smarter than me, but they weren't. It's really just luck we're here together today, but I'm not going to waste my opportunity."

"To do what?" I choked out.

"To make you mine once and for all," Vic said.

I would like to say that I fought him and won, but when he held up the enormous gleaming kitchen knife, I knew it was a fight I would lose. To make matters worse, a pain tore through my abdomen and back that nearly brought me to my knees. I let out a terrified cry as Vic grabbed me. I was less worried about what he would do to me and more worried about the fact that I just went into preterm labor, just like I had with Anna.

Chapter Twenty-Three

~Kyle~

The penthouse felt dead without Lily there. I missed the sound of her little feet padding down the hall to my office, or her talking to the chefs on The Food Network while she watched the little television in the kitchen when she was cooking. I hated the silence that followed when I would close the door, so unlike the sound of her voice greeting me or cursing me - depending on what I did or didn't do that day. Her intoxicating scent that hung lightly in every room was now stale. The bed was especially empty and cold without her body in it. When I was startled awake in the middle of the night by a nightmare, Lily wasn't there to convince me that I had been dreaming, that I had not hurt her or hurt Emmy again.

I felt as if I was in a tomb, and that was only two days without Lily in the house. It made me sick to believe that she had been enduring similar feelings for well over two months, and I was the one making her suffer. I compounded things however by popping into her life, giving her hope only to rip it away. The fact that she was pregnant and most likely terrified probably made her feel ten times worse.

After leaving Lily naked and hopeful in bed again, I went to Marco's place. He took the beating I gave to him and then offered me a beer. We drank in silence for a long time before he finally said "Get your shit together. Next time I won't just kiss her, I'll take her heart."

Even though I had wanted her to move on, the thought of Marco or anyone else winning her heart was almost too much to imagine. The idea of someone raising my child pissed me off. I couldn't imagine Lily with anyone else but me, but I was fucked up and didn't believe I'd be any good for her. I still didn't know my next step whenever she walked her little bullying ass back through the door.

When Corsey told me what she had done to his tires

and how she had bullied him into letting her go, I couldn't even blame him. Lily was a bully sometimes, and Corsey adored her. He would never do anything that may hurt her. I paced the penthouse, waiting to hear something – anything. I blamed myself for pushing her to this point, and if anything happened to her or the baby, I would hold myself responsible and no one else.

Corsey had informed me a couple of hours ago that the GPS had kicked back on in the Cadillac and it appeared that Lily was headed back to Philly. I knew when she finally walked through the door I'd have a fight on my hands, and I'd be lucky if she only ripped my balls off. I had to make sure she took steps to keep her and the baby safe, without me, because the more I thought about it the more I knew I couldn't stay.

The images of Emmy's injuries plagued my mind and haunted my dreams. The video of her walking into Larkin's office looking every type of broken played in a loop in my mind. Sometimes in my nightmares I saw Lily's face instead of Emmy's. What was going to push me over the edge next time? How much would it take before I beat her and possibly injure or kill our baby? It wasn't a risk I was willing to take.

As I was considering this, the doorbell rang, which pissed me off. The concierge should have called me to let me know someone was stopping by, especially so early in the morning. I couldn't even imagine who it could be. I didn't exactly attract many visitors, and I couldn't imagine Lily ringing the doorbell.

I threw the door open, prepared to scare away the person on the other side, but instead I just stood there, staring. I blinked a few times, rubbed my eyes. Were my nightmares now haunting me as I was awake? Was I losing my fucking mind?

"Are you going to let me in or are we going to stand here and have a staring contest? Because technically, I've already won. You blinked like half a dozen times."

Emmy didn't wait for me to invite her in. She pushed past me, leaving the scent of her hair that I once loved so much in her wake.

~~~

I stood in the kitchen at a suitable distance watching her with apprehension. Emmy stood at the stove, apparently very much at home, barefoot, making pancakes. She had exclaimed that she was starving as she made a beeline for my kitchen.

"I love this kitchen," she said for the fourth time. "I love this whole place!" She looked at me with a big smile that made my heart skip a beat. Actually, my heart had not beaten correctly since it stopped at the sight of her at my door.

"Emmy, why are you here?" I finally asked her.

"Aren't you glad to see me?" she frowned now and stared at me with the spatula in her hand.

"Do you really even need to ask me that?" I asked tiredly.

She looked at me thoughtfully for a moment before turning back to the stove.

"You look terrible," she said. "Have you been sleeping?"

"No, not really," I sighed and rubbed my forehead wearily. "My girlfriend happens to be MIA. You wouldn't know anything about that, would you?"

She turned her brownish green eyes on me. "You mean the mother of your unborn child that you deserted because of your sudden case of Mangina? How does it feel to have a vagina of your very own?"

I gave her a warning look and asked again "Why are you here, Em?"

She had turned back to the stove, but her shoulders slumped. "I need you to be happy, Kyle," she said softly.

I stared at her back, surprised. I wanted to see her face, to see what she was feeling. Three years ago I would have walked up behind her and wrapped my arms around her waist and nuzzled her neck before making her turn to face me. I could practically still taste her skin on my tongue.

"You came all the way from Chicago to tell me you need me to be happy?" I asked sourly. "You couldn't write that

~ 339 ~

in a Hallmark card and mail it?"

"Hallmark doesn't sell 'Sorry the Second Most Important Man in Your Life Is a Dumbass' cards," she snapped.

"Finally, we know where I rank," I retorted.

She looked over her shoulder at me, and I saw how hurt her eyes were. "Don't do that," she whispered. "You know what you meant to me, and if my presence is any indication of what you still mean to me..."

"You wouldn't even give me an opportunity to explain anything to you," I yelled, surprising even myself. "You heard what you wanted to hear, gave me back the damn bracelet and left."

"You had a whole year to explain," she yelled back and then she closed her eyes for a moment and took a deep breath. "I didn't come here to argue about us – or what used to be us. We weren't meant to be, but you and Lily..."

"What do you know?" I snapped. "Lily spends a few hours with you and now you're an authority on our relationship? You think you can just walk in here and say 'Kyle, I want you to be happy' and that fixes everything? It doesn't fix everything!"

She looked at me patiently. "No, saying that doesn't fix everything, but it can be a start."

"Go home. Go back to your *husband*," I spat and turned to walk away from her. I made it only a few steps before I felt the spatula smack me on the back of the head. I spun around. Emmy stood at the stove, looking angry as hell, the green in her eyes flashing.

I stormed over to her. Ignoring her squeals of protest, I picked her up and threw her over my shoulder. I carried her across the living room to the foyer. I opened the door and dropped her on her ass in the hallway.

"Hey!" she yelled, but I had slammed the door before she could finish the word.

I started back towards the kitchen to turn off her burning pancakes, but I forgot to lock the door. Emmy was through the door and literally on my back in a matter of seconds. I flipped her off of me and onto the couch and kept moving to the kitchen. I turned off the burner, but when I turned around Emmy was standing in the middle of the kitchen, ready to pounce. Her hair was a little wild and her shirt was hiked up over her belly button. When she advanced, I moved away from the stove to avoid burns, but otherwise held my ground.

When she wrapped her arms around my waist and fiercely hugged me, I was too stunned to move at first. I was even further stunned to feel her crying against my chest.

"I forgive you, Kyle," she said through her tears. "Now you need to forgive yourself."

Before I understood what I was doing, I wrapped my arms around her and held her tightly. I couldn't help the few tears that squeezed out of my eyes.

Kyle sat on the couch with his legs stretched out and his feet on the coffee table. I sat beside him, facing him with my legs drawn up in front of me. His arm was across the back of the couch and his fingers absently wove through my hair and his free hand was linked with one of mine.

"Why did you make Larkin give you the pictures?" I asked him quietly.

"I couldn't just go on with my happy ending as if I had not done something terribly wrong," he said, watching his fingers in my hair. "I couldn't pretend that I had not become a monster on more than one occasion and physically hurt you on more than one occasion."

"I never meant for you to know exactly what you did that night, Kyle," I said sadly. "I didn't want you to live with that."

"You had to live with it," he said, looking me in the eyes. "Probably still live with it on some level."

I looked away. "Sometimes I dream about it," I admitted. "But I can't help that no more than you can help your dreams. Why did you keep me in the dark about Sterling Corp and the jobs you were trying to save?" I asked, changing the topic. "You led me to believe that you really wanted Jess on some level, and you were trying to cover your dad's ass. Why didn't you tell me you were on a mission to save thousands of employees' jobs?"

"That part of my life was complicated and stressful, especially with Walter and Jess thrown into the middle of it all. When I was with you, I didn't want to live in that part of my life. I wanted to keep that part of my life away from us as much as possible. I just wanted my time with you to be my time with you, and not all of the other bullshit that went on in my life at that time. Em, when I was with you, I was able to forget about all of that. I felt at peace when I was with you. I felt like a different man – a better man. I felt like I could be something more than I was, something more than I was set up to be. I didn't want to tarnish our time together with my reality."

I looked away from him and looked at our interlaced hands. I felt extremely bad that I had been that place of peace for him, but all of my whining and complaining aided in its ruin. The fact of the matter was that it was impossible to keep Kyle's 'reality' out of our little bubble for very long, but before the bubble burst, I could have made him happier.

"It's not your fault," Kyle said softly, sensing how I was feeling. "I should have told you all of that and more. I should have told you about my brother, my sister, and all of the bullshit I endured growing up in that house, but I just wanted to pretend none of it happened. I just wanted to focus on us and our future once everything was settled, but I fucked that up. I fucked everything up, Em. You deserved better than what I gave you."

I still could not meet his eyes. I continued to stare at our hands, a sight I'd never thought I'd see again.

"I wasn't enough for you," I whispered.

Kyle started to object, but I finally looked into his startled face and repeated my words.

"I wasn't enough for you. If anything, I made matters worse, gave you something else to worry about. If I was enough to keep you grounded and somewhat happy, you wouldn't have felt the need for the drugs."

"I turned to the drugs because I'm a drug addict, Emmy," Kyle said firmly. His hand that was in my hair was now on my cheek. "Don't blame yourself for my stupid actions."

"I pushed you too hard," I said. "I made things harder than they needed to be. I knew you were struggling with some things, I wasn't sure about everything at the time, but I knew that you were having a hard time and I pushed anyway."

Kyle turned around to face me. He released my hand and put both hands on my face, forcing me to look into his sad, chocolate eyes.

"None of that shit was your fault, Emmy," he said firmly. "None of it. I found *you* in the bar that night. I pushed *you* into our fucked up relationship. *I* held you prisoner there.

You weren't the cause of my problems and *I* should have been straight with you from the beginning. *I* chose to take drugs. *I* broke your wrist and *I broke you*. I am a terrible, dark, fucked up person. You are and always have been perfect to me, Emmy. Please don't blame yourself."

His thumbs caressed away my tears. Through Kyle's eyes and his fingers and his words, I felt an overwhelming sense of love…and regret. I wrapped my arms around his neck and he pulled me into a tight embrace. It was a few minutes later before we released one another and settled back down on the couch. Kyle's eyes were pink and his cheeks were just as tear stained as mine.

"Kyle," I started and then paused for a moment, unsure how to proceed. "You're going to break Lily if you leave her again."

"I'll break her if I stay," he said flatly, his brow furrowed. "I don't trust myself not to hurt her like I did you."

"Kyle, those were different circumstances. You were under a great deal of stress."

"Who is to say I won't find myself under a great deal of stress again? What will stop me from calling up my supplier?"

"You've been clean since September, and before that you were clean for almost two years. I have no doubt in my mind that you can stay clean. You're not using now and you're under a great deal of stress."

"Yes, and the craving is strong, Emmy," he sighed. "After I saw those pictures and the video of you…I still don't know how I managed to stop myself from getting high."

"It's Lily," I said, squeezing his hand. "I was just…I just made you feel better while we were in our bubble, but Lily isn't in a bubble, is she?"

He hesitated a moment before answering. "No, she isn't."

"Lily *is* your reality," I said softly. "She has encompassed all aspects of your life."

Unlike me, I thought sadly.

"I don't want to hurt her or the baby," he whispered,

looking terrified.

"You won't," I promised. "You have to forgive yourself for what you did to me."

"I could have killed you or Lucas," he said.

"But you didn't. Kyle, Lucas is a semi-normal two year old. He's hyper and he drives me up a wall, but he's not emotionally or physically damaged from anything that you did."

"I've scarred you," he said in a choked voice that made my heart clench. He reached up and ran a finger over the little scar in my hairline, a scar that was a reminder of that New Year's morning when Kyle lost his mind.

"I'm not going to bullshit you and tell you that I don't have physical and emotional scars, Kyle," I said and then took his hand into mine. "They are a part of me and who I am today, but I'm not broken, okay? I'm happy with my life and I'm able to live with what happened in my past. I made my own mistakes, too. As much as you want to take the full blame for everything that happened between us, you just can't. No matter what you say, I will always know that some of that was my fault, and I will always have to live with what I did to Luke. But that's just life, Kyle. I keep on moving forward and I don't let the past drag me down. You're letting the past drag you down, except you're taking Lily and your baby with you."

He stared at me wide eyed. "I love her so much it fucking hurts," he said, his voice raspy. "I never thought I could love anyone again after you, but I do, and I love her more than…" He closed his mouth and looked away from me.

"You love her more than you've ever loved me," I confirmed.

He put his head in his other hand.

"It's alright," I said softly and rubbed his hand.

"She's the complete opposite of anyone I've ever wanted before," he said, staring at the floor now. "It doesn't even make sense."

"It doesn't have to make sense."

"I keep trying to let her go and can't."

"Then you shouldn't," I said. "She really loves you, Kyle, and she's really hurting now."

"I don't know why I'm surprised that she came to you," he smiled faintly. "She thinks she's living in your shadow. I haven't done a good job convincing her that you and she are on different planes. No offense."

"No offense taken," I smiled. "She asked me if I knew all of the facts back then if I would have taken you back."

He looked at me curiously. "What did you say?"

"I said no."

He looked a little taken aback my answer.

"The fact is if I was right for you, there wouldn't have been any secrets between us," I said quietly. "If I was the one you were meant to be with...well...things would have been different, but I'm *not* the one you were meant to be with. Lily is. She's healed you in ways I was never able to. In fact, I never healed you. I simply drugged you."

Kyle looked away for a moment with a loud sigh. When he looked back at me, his eyes were again teary.

"I will always love you, Emmy," he said gently. "I will always feel a connection with you that I will never have with anyone else. You will always be a part of me. No one will ever overshadow the strong emotions I have for you."

I leaned forward and gently and chastely pressed my lips against his.

"Thank you," I murmured against his lips. "I will always love you, too."

~Kyle~

"She should have been here by now," I said, pacing the living room.

Emmy looked at her watch and frowned. "I agree."

I had wanted to give Lily the time she needed to think without having any of my 'goons' on her, but it had been too long now. I pulled my phone out and dialed Harry.

"Harry, where is the Cadillac? She should have been back here by now."

"It's parked at the bar. She's been there for about three hours now. I figured she's probably working, like she usually does."

"Thanks," I said and ended the call. Before I could do anything else, my phone rang.

"Dude," Mayson said when I answered. "I know you're across the pond, but I have to tell ya…I'm going to fire your girlfriend. She did a no call no show. Can you please remind her who got her this job and who stuck up for her when you guys wanted to publicize your love? She's not answering her phone."

"I'm actually at home. Lily doesn't have her phone," I said patiently. "But it's not like her to not even call you. She's at the bar; she could have called you from there."

"You sound uneasy, Sterling, which is making me uneasy. Is everything okay?"

"I don't know," I admitted, running a hand through my hair. "Mayson, I have to go."

I ended the call. Emmy looked at me with a quirked eyebrow. "You and Mayson are chummy now?"

"A little bit," I admitted. "Something doesn't feel right."

I punched in another number and waited as the phone rang and rang. If Lily was at the bar, she wasn't picking up. I tried twice more before calling Marco.

"Have you seen Lily?" I asked him.

"No," he said carefully. "Why?"

"Are you at the bar?"

"No, I'm at my real job, Sterling," he snapped. "In fact I'm in the middle of a meeting. What the hell is going on?"

"Lily's been at the bar for a few hours but she isn't answering the phone there and she doesn't have her own phone."

"Shit," he muttered and I heard a muffled brief conversation and a door close. "I've told her repeatedly not to go there alone. There's been some douche bag driving by and even standing in the parking lot a couple of times."

Alarms went off in my head. I stopped pacing and just stared straight ahead at nothing. Emmy sensed that something was very wrong and rushed over to me and put her hand on my back as she watched my face.

"What does this douche bag look like?" I asked Marco.

"Looks like an asshole pumped up on steroids. He always drives away before I can get out there. One of the girls that used to work at the other bar said that it's some guy that used to work there. She didn't seem too concerned about it, but now I feel like I should have done something more."

"Did you tell Lily about him?"

"I told her there's been a man hanging around. Lily said maybe he wants a job. She didn't seem too concerned and I didn't want to worry her. I just warned her not to go alone. I'm in New York or else I'd drive over there, but maybe I should come down?"

"No," I said. "I gotta go. Thanks, Marco." I ended the call and immediately made another phone call as I rushed towards the door with Emmy on my heels.

"Tagher," Harry said in greeting.

"Harry, meet me at the bar. Vic has been seen hanging around there." I punched the button for the elevator.

"Shit. Okay."

I called Corsey next.

"Corsey," he answered tiredly.

"Corsey, where are you?" I asked, as I hit the button for the elevator again.

"Just outside of Norristown. What's up?"

"We should have been keeping an eye on the fucking bar," I growled. "Marco said a man fitting Vic's description has been hanging around, and the Caddy has been parked there for three hours now, but Lily isn't answering the phone and she hasn't contacted anyone."

"I'll be there as soon as I can," he said in a rush and ended the call.

The elevator doors slid open and I waited for Emmy to step on first.

"What's going on, Kyle?" she asked. "Are you talking about Vic Rickers?"

I grimaced. "Didn't Lily tell you what happened?"

"No," she said shaking her head. "She did tell me that some guy had hurt her and you kicked his ass, but she didn't say it was Vic. He gives me the creeps."

"He is obsessed with her," I told her with an exasperated sigh. "I kept most of what I knew away from her. I didn't want her to worry, but I should have told her. He could have her right now."

I felt like their rocks in the pit of my stomach and my chest was so tight with anxiety, I wasn't sure how I was still breathing. My hands trembled with fear.

"Kyle, what do you mean?" Emmy asked gently as the elevator doors slid open.

"When I was...stalking Lily, I realized that Vic was stalking her, too. I wanted to know why. I meant her no harm, but I didn't trust him. With some digging, my guys found out some very disturbing facts about Vic."

I opened the passenger side door to my Audi and let Emmy in. When I got behind the wheel, I continued.

"Vic burned down your bar, Emmy," I said, looking at her for a reaction.

Her face scrunched up in confusion. "The fire marshal said it was an electrical problem."

"Vic did it, Emmy. We found all kinds of shit in his house pointing at him. He had thoroughly studied how to start the fire without laying any suspicion on him. I tried to alert one of my contacts on the police force, but because I technically shouldn't have been in Vic's house and they had no reason to go in either, he was going to get away with it."

"Why did he burn down my bar?" she asked, rightfully confused.

"Lily was going through some hard times. He thought he could push her to need him. He thought if he took away the last thing she had, she would accept not only his help, but him. It was all a ploy to get her where he wanted her, but he had not realized that Lily was, above all things, resilient, and he had not expected her to choose to sleep in the worst part of Camden rather than sleep in his spare room in a nice middle class neighborhood."

"Oh my god," she said, staring at me, her eyes wide.

"That's not even the half of it," I said sourly as I went too fast down the city streets.

"He helped her get a part time job at another bar even after she started working at Sterling. She was still unreceptive to him, though. He got impatient and decided to try something else."

"What?" Emmy breathed.

"He attacked her one night on the street. I knew he was up to something, but I wasn't sure what until it was happening. He went at her with a knife, robbed her of a bag he knew had some sentimental value to her and even stabbed her hand. Even though he had on a hoodie and was partially concealing his face, I knew it was him. I had watched him long enough to know how he moves, how he walks, and how he runs. I think he was going to run around the corner and come back as Vic the super hero that happened to catch the bad guy and rescue her, but Vic wasn't counting on me being there."

"That bastard is the one that stabbed her?" Em yelled. "He could have killed her! What the fuck is wrong with him?"

"A lot, apparently," I said. "I found out that he has some deep psychological issues, going as far back as eleven years old. The records are sealed, but I was able to find bits and pieces of information about a violent childhood, and now he's

~ 350 ~

on steroids and that's fucking with his mind, too."

"What else have you found?"

"In his house, in one room in the basement, there were a plethora of pictures of Lily. In some of them, she was undressed or in the state of undressing. There were even pictures of her sleeping," I ground out, knowing that he had to be up close to her while she was unconscious. "There were chains cemented into the wall, meant to cuff and restrain someone. Handcuffs, rope, duct tape, pepper spray, a taser, knives, chloroform, Rohypnol and detailed notes about Lily's schedule."

"He was going to kidnap her?" Emmy asked with her voice high and disbelieving.

"I don't have any other explanation for it all," I said through a clenched jaw.

Just thinking about his hands on her and the shit that he was capable of had my hands gripping the steering wheel in a death grip.

We were silent for the rest of the trip to the bar. I parked next to the Cadillac and jumped out of the car. Emmy got out, too and met me at the front of the car.

"You should wait in the car," I told her.

"No, I'm not waiting in the car," she said firmly and followed me to the door. I didn't have time to argue.

I used my key to unlock the door. We quietly entered and I stopped to listen for a moment and heard nothing. I moved on towards the office, expecting to find her there, but it was empty. When I came back out, I noticed Lily's keys and purse sitting on the bar. A deep foreboding came over me. Barely able to breathe, I walked into the kitchen. Everything looked normal until I got closer to the back door. There were a few items on the floor and the door was wide open.

"Lily!" I yelled as I darted for the door. I ran outside and found nothing and no one.

I dropped to my knees. I couldn't breathe. That fucker had taken her and the last words we exchanged were unkind and unloving and I hadn't even had the chance to talk to her about the ultra sound she had the week before, because I was being such an asshole. I didn't realize I was crying until I felt Emmy's arms around me and her hand on my head as I leaned on her.

"It's okay," she whispered. "It's okay."

A car screeched to a halt behind us and heavy footsteps raced over to us.

"She's not here," Emmy said to someone. "He must have taken her."

"Fuck," I heard Harry mutter. I heard his phone dialing as he walked away. "Chuck, have you been by Ricker's place? We think he has Lily. Take someone with you, go over there and check it out and get back to me."

I released Emmy and got to my feet.

"Sorry," I apologized to her in a weak voice. "I'm being a pussy."

"You're not being a pussy," she admonished and then rubbed my back.

"Chuck and a few others are going over to his house," Harry said. "Corsey is stopping to check out a few other areas, but Rickers knows we would look there." He paused before he continued and shook his head. "I don't think we are going to find him in any of the places we expect."

"Where the hell has he been these past few months?" I yelled at no one in particular.

"Did you check his aunt's house in the Poconos?" Emmy asked.

Harry and I both stared at her.

"What aunt?" I demanded.

"She's not really his aunt – she used to date his uncle when Vic was a kid. He kept in touch with her…I was kind of under the impression that they were…you know…fuck buddies or something. Anyway, she has a house in the Poconos that they used to meet at on occasion. He told me all about it one day, trying to lure me up there." She shuddered. "He gave me the address and everything."

"That must have been a long time ago," Harry frowned.

"You couldn't possibly remember that address now."

"How do you know how long ago it's been?" she frowned up at him and before I could say anything it dawned at her. She looked at me disapprovingly. "Stalking your exes is not cool," she muttered. "But for the record, I don't remember the address, you are right, Harry. However, I remember the aunt's name. Maybe you can use your stalking expertise to look her up."

Emmy gave Harry the name and he immediately got on the phone as he walked towards his truck. Emmy and I went back inside to lock up, and she grabbed Lily's purse and keys before we left.

"Now, I insist you stay behind this time," I told her. "Use the Cadillac."

"No fucking way," she growled and then opened the passenger's door and got inside.

I sighed heavily and got in behind the wheel.

"When this is all over, Kyle, when you have your happy ending, I'm going to rip you a new one for stalking me."

I didn't doubt that she would, but I was having serious doubts about my happy ending.

~Emmy~

Kyle drove with one hand, while the other hand alternated between an open hand and a tight fist on the console between us. He was quiet, focused not on the road ahead, but the woman he loved more than anything at the end of the road. That was once me. I would be lying if I said that it made me a little sad to know that was gone, for both of us. Lily was the center of his universe now, and Luke and the kids were mine.

I put my hand over his, hoping to alleviate even a fraction of the fear he was feeling. He froze for a moment and then relaxed under me. I turned his hand so that it was palm up and gave him mine to hold. As if our hands had a memory of their own, our fingers laced together without any fumbling around. His thumb dragged across my skin with familiarity. I stared at our interwoven hands with a tight chest.

I felt as if I were holding a part of myself that was left behind with Kyle, forever his willing captive. There was a piece of me within his hands that I will never regain. My life with Luke and our children was everything to me. I would never trade it for anything in the world, but Kyle will always have this small part of me and I will never try to reclaim it. It was his to have forever, just as I was well aware that I had a piece of him with me forever, too. I would never let it go. It was just as much a part of me as my skin, my blood, and my flesh and bones.

~Lily~

I fully expected Vic to violate me in the worse ways, but other than trying to kiss me, he didn't try to touch me intimately. He had me tied to a bed, giving me enough rope to move around and get comfortable, like that was possible.

"All I've ever wanted was to take care of you, Lily," he said as he slowly paced the room. "I wanted you to appreciate me and to care for me like I care for you."

"I'll never care about you," I whispered, flinching at another contraction.

"You will," he said, stopping in front of me. "I'm going to take care of you and that baby, even though it's not mine. It might take some time, but in time you will appreciate everything I will do for you. You will care about me, and you will love me as I love you. I only have to make you recognize feelings for me you already have deep inside of you."

I looked up at him with pleading eyes. "Vic, I need a doctor. I *will* appreciate you if you get me to the hospital and save my baby."

"I think I can deliver your baby here, Lily," he said and touched my face, repulsing me.

"It's too soon for her to be born," I sobbed. "I need medicine to keep her inside of me until she has a better chance. Vic, please," I cried.

"If she comes now and she doesn't survive, we can try again later," he said calmly.

I turned my face into the pillow under me and sobbed harder than I could recall sobbing in my life. My baby was going to be born, under *his* 'care' and there was nothing I could do about it. She would be born and die without a fighting chance. Even though Vic was the asshole that kidnapped me, I blamed only myself for not being more vigilant and for not listening to Kyle and Corsey. They repeatedly told me that Vic was a dangerous person and I repeatedly scoffed at them, even after he had hurt me. Now I was stuck here without anyone knowing where I was or how to find me, and I was going to lose another baby.

Vic touched my hair as I cried. I looked up at him and screamed "Get the fuck away from me!"

His eyes grew dark. "Don't talk to me like that," he said carefully. "I am trying to fucking take care of you."

I screamed as he grabbed a handful of my hair and brought my face up to his. "Show some fucking appreciation!"

He shoved me back down and stormed out of the room.

My cries echoed off of the walls of the bedroom. I found myself calling for Kyle, even though I knew he couldn't hear me. Next to the imminent loss of our baby girl, I was devastated knowing I may never see him again. I had not even told him that he was fathering a girl. I was so angry with him and so hurt; I wanted to withhold that key information from him. I didn't think he had a right to know, but as I lay tied up in Vic's mystery house, I cried for many reasons, but also because I didn't know if Kyle would ever know about his daughter.

Another contraction squeezed me and my panic continued.

~~~

I had fallen asleep at some point. I woke up after every contraction, but instantly fell back to sleep, crying even as I slept. I started waking up sooner and realized my contractions were getting closer together. I just lay there, awake now, and resigned to the fact that there was nothing I could do about it. Not a damn thing.

I also realized the only way I was going to get out of there, if I didn't die giving birth, was if I gave Vic what he wanted. He wasn't a complete idiot, however. He wouldn't believe or trust me at first, but after some time, he would, and then maybe he'd give me enough trust so that I could stab him in the back and run away.

I was contemplating this when I heard the doorbell ring, followed by banging on the door. My instincts told me to scream, and so I did. I screamed for help, louder than I ever thought I could scream in my life. As loud as I was screaming, I was worried that I would still be unheard, or worse yet that whoever was at the door was an accomplice of Vic's, but I screamed anyway.

I felt like I had been screaming for hours, when in reality it was only moments before more than one person burst into the room. I couldn't stop screaming even after I saw their black uniforms and badges pinned to their shirts. I couldn't stop screaming even after they cut me out of the ropes, freeing my hands.

"Ma'am, it's okay," the officer said, sweeping me into his arms. "Are the paramedics here?" he managed to ask the other officer over my screams.

"On the way," he said, looking at me with pity.

My screams died down to loud sobbing as he carried me down the stairs. We walked through a living room where Vic was on the floor, cuffed and fighting and swearing. Several officers were holding him down. When he saw me being carried away from him, he screamed my name like a mad man. I covered my ears even as the officer carried me outside.

"Lily!" I heard someone screaming my name again, but I didn't want to hear Vic screaming my name. I closed my eyes against the bright late afternoon sun and tried squeeze away the pain and fear I felt.

The officer handed me to someone else.

"Lily," he said, and I slowly opened my eyes. I was in Kyle's arms and even through my tears I could see that he was crying.

I wrapped my arms around his neck and sobbed into his shoulder. I wanted to tell him how sorry I was. I wanted him to give me another chance to make it right, but another contraction hit me right then and I cried out.

"I'm in labor," I cried, staring up at Kyle with fear. "She's going to die."

Chapter Twenty-Four

~Kyle~

"How did you find me?" Lily asked me, hours after an officer carried her out of the Poconos house Vic had hidden her in.

She was lying in a hospital bed, hooked up to an IV and a machine to monitor the baby's heartbeats and movements. The doctors had stopped her preterm labor, but warned that Lily needed to be on complete bed rest until the end of her pregnancy, and chances are she may need the drugs again.

The waiting room was full of people: my mother, Emmy, Mayson, Corsey, and Harry. Lily's mom was on her way and Lydia and the kids were to meet us in Philadelphia in a couple of days.

I sat in a chair pulled up to the side of her bed, holding her hand in mine. I could have lost her and our baby girl and there aren't enough words to explain how that felt.

"Emmy," I said simply. "If she had not come to the east coast to kick my ass, I may have never known. She remembered Vic telling her about that place. We were leaving the parking lot to drive up here, but Marco called me. He told me that even though the security system wasn't in place yet, the cameras were fully operational. I had one of Corsey's guys take the tape to my contact on the force. It took some time and strings being pulled but the police up here finally agreed to at least go check out the situation."

I sighed heavily at the memory of that period of time. It was the longest wait of my life as two officers walked up to the door while another four wandered around the perimeter of the house. As soon as they rang the bell and banged on the door, things got crazy. Very faintly I could hear Lily screaming, but the officers close to the house also heard her. They forced their way in as they called for more backup. I tried to run in after them, but Harry and Emmy restrained me until a few minutes later one of the officers carried Lily out.

"Lily, I'm so sorry," I whispered to her. "If I would have been home with you from the beginning, none of this would have happened."

"You should have been home with me," she agreed weakly and then squeezed my hand. "But it's not your fault that Vic is psychotic."

"I should have told you everything so that you could protect yourself."

"I would have lived my life in fear," she said. "You did the right thing. I should have listened to you and Corsey, but I was being so pig headed. I'm sorry I put you through this."

I stood up and kissed her head. "Don't apologize to me. This isn't your fault."

"Kiss me," she whispered her hands in my hair.

I obliged and pressed my mouth against hers. I moaned lightly when my tongue tasted her mouth. I wanted to climb into bed with her and kiss her for a very long time, but the hospital staff probably wouldn't have liked that very much.

"Ahem," a familiar voice said.

Reluctantly, I stopped kissing Lily and we both looked up to see Emmy standing there, smiling at us.

"Sorry to interrupt this love fest," she said, stepping further into the room. "But I must anyway. Kaitlyn is running out of milk apparently. The cow must go home." She sighed.

Lily stretched out her arms. I stepped out of the way so that she and Emmy could embrace.

"Thank you so much for saving me," Lily said to Emmy.

"Thank you so much for saving Kyle," Emmy said just above a whisper.

"Apologize to Luke for me, will you?" Lily said when Emmy pulled away. "He didn't like me showing up and getting you involved in my issues. He's really going to hate what you've been through."

"He's just glad that you're okay and that I'm coming home," she said. "I'm glad I was here to help."

"I'll walk you out," I said. I kissed Lily quickly on the lips. "I'll be right back."

"Take your time," she said softly.

"Corsey is going to drive me to the airport if you don't mind," Emmy said as stepped into the hallway. "I was going to ask Mayson but she's in the waiting room forming some kind of really weird bond with your mom."

"That *is* weird," I agreed as we passed by the waiting room where my mother and Mayson were involved in what looked like a very serious conversation.

"Your mom was really teary when she got here."

I rubbed the back of my head. "I'm still trying to get used to this new 'caring mom' thing. I always knew she cared deep down, but Lily lit a fire under her ass I guess."

"Well, maybe this will be it. Maybe this time the meds will work and she can find some happiness and peace."

"I hope so," I said with a nod.

Emmy punched the button for the elevator. "You don't have to walk me all the way down. I think I can find the front entrance by myself."

"I want to walk you down," I said, looking into her eyes.

"Okay then," she smiled and then stepped onto the elevator.

"I'll never be able to fully thank you for all that you've done today," I said to her.

"Just take care of Lily and the baby and stay on track," she said softly, touching my cheek. "That's the best way to thank me."

I took her hand off of my cheek and left a lingering kiss on it. Her eyes glazed over for a moment before I simply held her hand in mine and led her off of the elevator. We walked outside in silence. Corsey was already waiting at the curb.

"Take care," Emmy said with a sad smile and started to pull away from me to get into the Escalade.

I pulled her to me and wrapped my arms around her. She didn't hesitate to reciprocate as she rested her cheek on my chest.

"Your hair still drives me a little crazy, I have to admit," I whispered to her.

She giggled. "Would you like me to give you a lock of it?"

"I'm so tempted, but I don't think it will be the same as it is attached to your head."

"No, I suppose not," she said softly.

"I never deserved you," I said, my lips moving on her hair.

"No," she agreed. "You deserved better, and you got her."

She pulled away from me then. She wouldn't look at me as I opened the door for her, nor as she climbed into the truck. I needed to see her face and I needed to tell her she was wrong, but I couldn't tell her that. Lily was perfect for me, the one I was supposed to be with. Before I could close the door, however, Emmy looked at me with misty eyes.

"Maybe there will be a place for us in another lifetime," she said softly.

"I have no doubt about it," I told her.

I closed the door and watched as part of me was once again whisked away. This time I was okay, and I knew she was, too. Emmy was going home to her happily ever after, and I was going back to mine.

EPILOGUE

~Lily~

Amara Sterling has lung power, my goodness can the girl scream.

"I'm telling you, she doesn't like your driving," I said to my husband.

"She *loves* my driving. Maybe she doesn't like this stupid music you have on the radio," Kyle said. "What the hell is this? Radio Disney? Put on some Boys II Men or something."

I pursed my lips and turned the radio off altogether. Amara continued to cry.

"Definitely your driving," I said.

"Maybe she just wants her grandma," he said. In an adorable voice used only for his daughter, Kyle asked "Do you want your grandma, sweetie? Is that what you want?"

I reached back into her car seat, blindly searching for her binky.

"Gotcha," I said as my hand closed over it. I stuck it in Amara's mouth and the crying subsided.

"Binky addict," Kyle murmured and took my hand into his. He brought it to his lips and kissed it.

Life has changed for us since the day Vic took me, aka V-DAY. Two mornings afterward as the nursing staff prepared me for discharge, Kyle was on the phone with the big guys at Sterling. They wanted him back to London ASAP. They didn't seem to care about what was going on in his personal life. When they finally did yield, they gave him a whole week of personal time but insisted that he must be back in London by the following Tuesday. Without any hesitation or looks of regret, Kyle quit.

"My unborn baby and her mother need me full-time. This job isn't even secondary in my life. I quit." He ended the phone call and went back to talking to my mom as if he had not just made a life altering decision.

Days later while we relaxed at home, the Sterling men called back and offered Kyle his job back. He could work remotely from home as long as necessary with some light traveling if absolutely necessary. It was the least that they could do. Kyle had saved their asses' big time and they never properly thanked him. In addition, he had been a large part in rebuilding the business and they were only just beginning to appreciate his hard work. Kyle said he wouldn't work more than eight hours a day, and when the baby was born he wanted six weeks off and thereafter he wasn't willing to travel for at least six months. They called back the following day and agreed to his terms.

Corsey took a vacation. A long vacation. I had run him ragged with the whole Chicago debacle, and the kidnapping thereafter. After he dropped Emmy off at the airport, he called Kyle and told him not to call him. He was going home to his wife and kid and he didn't want to be disturbed. Forever. He really said 'forever' as if that was going to stop me from calling him and harassing him for letting me push him around in Chicago.

Marco came to see me two days after we got back to the penthouse. He apologized profusely for not doing anything about Vic. Then he apologized profusely that Kyle wasn't leaving again.

"I was hell bent on seducing you, Lily," he had said in his fading Italian accent. Lydia had been in the room with me at the time. She snorted and rolled her eyes. Marco had glanced at her and then whispered in my ear. "Well...I'll settle for your sister."

I laughed at his joke. In fact I was still giggling about it a few weeks later when I called my sister just for a chat. I wasn't expecting Marco to answer the phone.

"Why are you always taking my sloppy seconds?" I teased Lydia once I got her on the phone.

"Trust me. There's nothing sloppy about him," she had said.

Supposedly, their relationship isn't that serious, but my mother will have you believing they were about to run away to Vegas and elope. Either way I was happy for Lydia and I was touched that Marco wasn't as shallow as I had once believed when I first met him. He overlooked my sister's limp and most likely stepped up to help her deal with her pain.

Felicia was doing very well, better than either Kyle or I could have ever expected. She took her medication religiously and if she didn't feel right she immediately called her psychiatrist for an adjustment. She started going to therapy twice a week the week after I told her off. Kyle started attending some sessions with her so that they could work on their relationship and deal with their past. It is working, for both of them.

When Walter tried to force his way back into Felicia's life, she put her foot down and stood her ground until he finally slunk away back into the recesses of hell. She started reforming friendships and even went out on a few dates, much to Kyle's agitation. If she had a bad day, she no longer apologized with lunches and brunches. She apologized in person by saying "I'm sorry". All of the new changes couldn't have been easy for her, but she really felt she needed to try. She didn't want to lose Kyle the way she had lost Miranda, and she didn't want to miss out on Amara's life.

I couldn't go to the grand opening of *Lily's*, but Mayson told me that a lot of the old crowd from *SHOTZ* was there and more. It was a big hit and stayed busy. Marco and Kyle helped run the business end while I was stuck in bed and continued to do so for a few weeks after I had Amara. When I finally made it in there, I was greeted by a lot of familiar faces and cheers for my return. I only worked a few hours a week because I wanted to spend as much time with my baby and Kyle as possible. When she is older, I will spend more time there, but in the meantime, it is running well and is everything I hoped it would be.

All of Vic's secrets came out in the weeks following his arrest. Since the police now had every reason to search his home in New Jersey, they did so and thoroughly. They found everything they needed to find regarding premeditating my kidnapping and even proving that he had burned down *SHOTZ*. There were other things that they found that also connected him to a couple of other sexual assaults, in addition to some robberies and other things. There was no getting out of it this time. He was going to be in prison for a fairly long time.

Two weeks after V-Day Kyle proposed to me. It wasn't quite the proposal a girl would expect, laid up in bed with a bowl of ice-cream resting on my belly, but I was genuinely surprised when he got down on one knee. We got hitched two weeks after Amara was born, at the Sterling estate. My family came in from Ohio, Marco came, Mayson, and a few other people from work. It was quaint and sweet, but how it was done didn't matter to me. The fact that I married this beautiful person is what mattered most to me.

Kyle is still a dick sometimes, and sometimes his insecurities will trip him up, but he's always trying to be better. He is always trying to do the right thing and to make me happy. He is the most amazing father I have ever seen, tender and loving to our daughter. Every Sunday he sits on the couch with Amara in his arms and they watch football. He talks to her as if she understands what's going on. He changes diapers, feeds her, burps her, bathes her, and spends hours a week just watching her facial expressions or watching her sleep.

Anna and Gavin are never far from my mind. I feel sad that they are gone, but I look at Gavin's kids and feel fortunate to have a piece of both him and Anna living on – three adorable pieces. Kyle didn't forget about Little Gavin either. He called him weekly, even when we weren't together apparently. He didn't want Gavin to feel like another man had deserted him. Could I possibly love this man anymore?

"It looks like mom has some company," Kyle said absently as we pulled into the driveway at the big house.

My stomach knotted up. I wasn't nervous before now. I just nodded, acknowledging him before getting out of the car. My hands were shaking as I picked up the diaper bag. Kyle picked up Amara in her car seat and we walked towards the door. I took a very deep breath as I unlocked the door and pushed it open. I could hear voices drifting in from the kitchen at the back of the house. I let Kyle walk ahead of me and I watched as he came to a sudden stop at the threshold to the kitchen. I stepped up beside him to see her with my own eyes.

Miranda, Kyle's long gone sister stood a few feet away from him with her hands folded in front of her. Hell, she was gorgeous and she and Kyle have similar facial features. Three children, two of them identical, stood off to the side between their grandmother and a man I guessed was Chad, Miranda's husband.

Miranda smiled as tears filled her eyes.

"Hey," she said softly.

"Randi..." Kyle choked out and then looked at me with wide eyes. "You knew about this?"

I nodded slowly. Know about it? I contacted her and talked to her for weeks before I convinced her to visit her mother and subsequently Kyle.

Kyle handed me the car seat and meet his sister halfway for the most emotional, heartfelt embrace I had ever seen or experienced in my life. I wiped away my own tears as the pair murmured and cried. After a couple of minutes Kyle was introduced to his twin nieces, thirteen year old nephew and his brother in-law. I hugged Miranda and each of the children and shook her husband's hand. She cried again when she got to hold Amara, and I couldn't blame her. Our baby was beautiful with her dark hair and gray eyes.

Felicia had made a big dinner. We sat down and ate and talked and laughed. It felt like a real family, something Kyle had been lacking most of his life. It made my heart ache with joy to see his face light up and to see how happy he was. I was so happy for him, I had to excuse myself half way through dessert so that I could go be a girl and cry in solitude.

I shut myself into the bathroom and cried. I was so happy for him, for me...for us. I felt like a pussy sitting on the tub, crying – like a pussy – but I couldn't help it. My life was so different from a year ago, so perfect.

"Lily?" Kyle's voice came through the door after a light knock.

"Yeah?" I said, standing up and rushing over to the mirror to wipe my face.

"Are you okay?"

"I'm great," I said honestly.

"Wanna unlock the door?"

"No," I said with a small laugh and unlocked it anyway.

"Hey," he said, coming inside and closing the door behind him.

"Hey," I said.

"Why are you crying?" He frowned as he wiped my eyes with a towel.

"Because I'm a little bitch," I laughed. "I'm just so happy for us, but especially for you."

He smiled and kissed me on the lips. "You did this for us," he said. "You've done so much for me over the past year and a half. You've made me so happy even when I didn't think I deserved it."

"You don't deserve it," I teased, poking him in the chest.

He put his arms around me and slipped his hands down to my ass. "There must be a way to thank you, Mrs. Sterling," he said in a voice that made my toes curl in my boots.

"I'm sure we can work something out, Mr. Sterling," I said, wrapping my arms around his neck.

"I'm so glad you wore a skirt," he said as he lifted me onto the vanity.

"Mr. Sterling, are you going to take advantage of me in this bathroom in your mother's home?" I asked, appalled.

"Absofuckinglutely," he growled before taking my mouth with his.

While he kissed me, his hands moved under my skirt and slowly tore my panties away. I growled my approval in his mouth as my fingers worked to unbutton his jeans and push them down to spring his erection free. His hands were back under my ass, pulling me to the very edge of the vanity before sinking into me. My moan was swallowed into his mouth as he thrust slowly inside of me.

Kyle broke the kiss and stared down into my eyes as he moved painfully slow, stroking my walls with his cock.

"Thank you," he whispered, running a thumb along my jaw.

"For what?"

"For believing I was worthy of redemption," he said seriously.

"Do you believe you are worthy of redemption?" I asked, running my fingers through his hair.

"I do now," he whispered.

"Then that's all that matters," I said and kissed him again.

Kyle was a new man, mixed with a lot of the old Kyle. He was perfect. He was mine, and he was redeemed.

~*~ The End ~*~

Acknowledgements

Evelyn Erndt, thank you, thank you, thank you for odd hours of brainstorming, reading every little change – as annoying and frustrating as that must have been – and of course for your fine editing skills (and yes, I still say that 'question' deserves an exclamation point). Thank you most of all for your blunt honesty and friendship.

Lorien Vanover, thank you for not bitch slapping me when I yelled at you. Thank you for spending crazy hours reading and editing when you so have a wedding to get ready for! Thanks for the ridiculous text messages that made no sense but cracked me up. Also, I thank you most of all for your friendship.

R.L. Mathewson, thank you so, very much for your attempted sabotage of my diet, turning my scary children against me, luring me to Hershey Park to make me fatter, and for watching in amusement as I struggled with my enormous, heavy bag at the front desk in Virginia. Most of all, thank you for your guidance, for listening to my rants and raves, for putting up with my long list of stupid questions, for giving birth to my two blonde cuties, for finding everything bacon, for wearing the Goonies shirt and most of all for your valued friendship.

Karleigh Lewis-Brewster, where do I begin? Thank you for your patience and all of the HUGE, HUGE help you have given to me on many occasions. Thank loads for your loyalty and I hope the "meth head" has found redemption in your 'side eye'! If not...psh...

Marta Vilaca, thank you for your last minute editing and for sweet talking me into marrying you.

Yes, you may have my babies. If our husbands don't mind...

Now, I must thank a long list of people. Many of you don't even like to read and/or have not even read my books yet, but you have given me tremendous support that cannot be replaced. My career started with *you* when you chose to believe in me and not knock me down. Thank you, thank you, thank you!

Jen (Wifey) Ripa * Tracy Demiani * Debbie Yeager * Sue Reed Pica * Douglas Wade * Steph Kirk *Keiko Harvin * Kathy Kimmerly *my fake oldest, favorite child John Ware * Nancy Warsewicz * Tiffany Marie Elizabeth Bermudez * Teresa Cunningham * Jason Miller * Shaniqua Robinson * Dean Schmidt * Candice Midgley * Jenn P.G. * Carin Batcho * Janell Wilson * And the countless folks at 5476 that hugged me because you loved my book*

If I have forgotten anyone, I'm sorry. Gotcha next book!

And a very special Thank You to the members of the
South Jersey Writers Group
& the talented people within.

About the Author

L.D. Davis lives on the East Coast of the United States with her children, husband, cat, and one fish. In her spare time she enjoys reading, time with her family, and great food and drinks with friends. Mrs. Davis has a bit of an addiction to *Downton Abbey* and similar shows and movies and a secret love for the various versions of *Star Trek*. While L.D. lives a relatively uneventful life, there is always a party in her head. Look for more of her work later this year.

3427498R00200

Made in the USA
San Bernardino, CA
31 July 2013